KITTY QUEST

MONSTER HUNTERS

ASK ABOUT OUR SPECIAL OFFERS

WRITTEN & ILLUSTRATED BY PHIL CORBETT

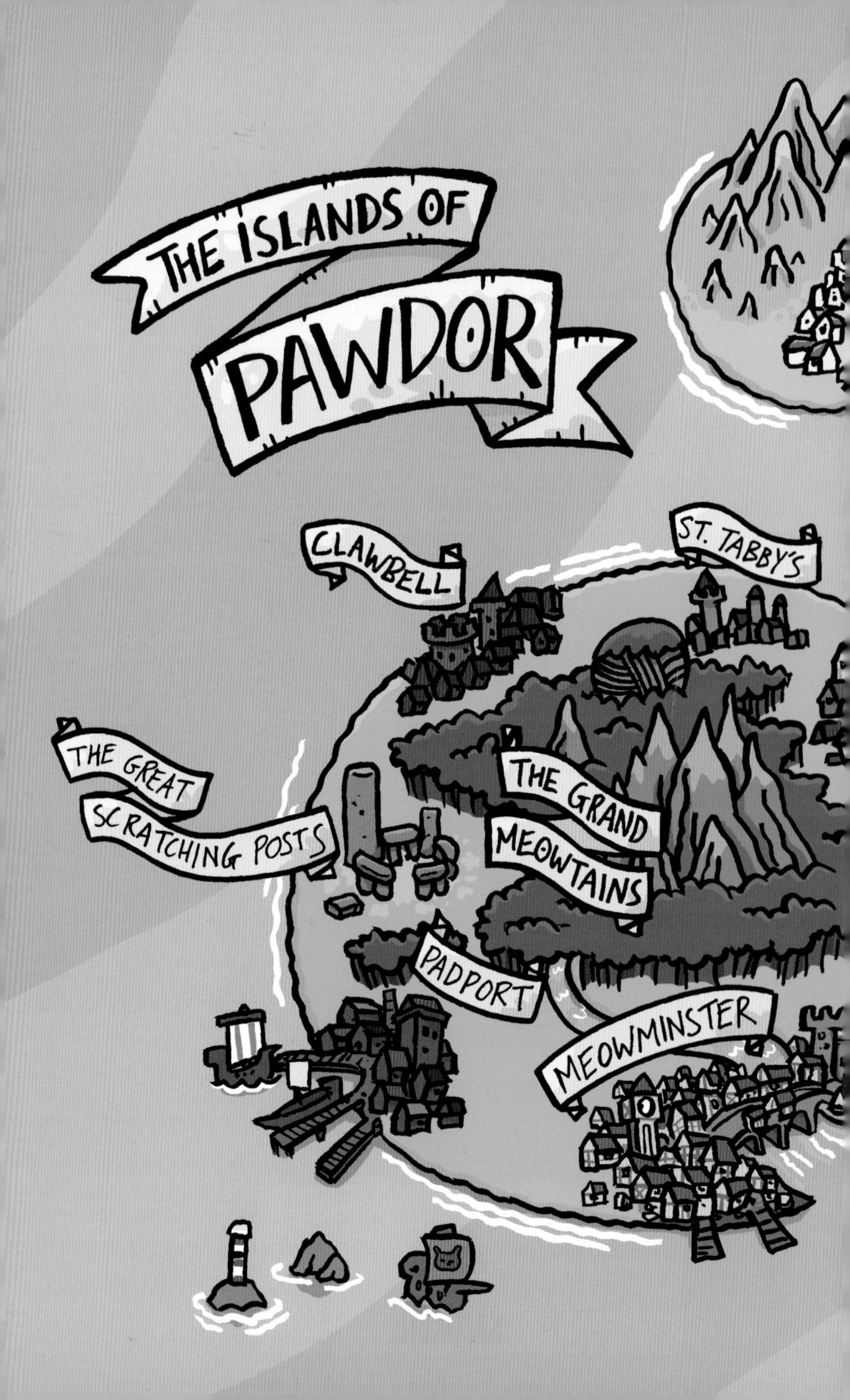
THE ISLANDS OF
PAWDOR
CLAWBELL
ST. TABBY'S
THE GREAT
SCRATCHING POSTS
THE GRAND
MEOWTAINS
PADPORT
MEOWMINSTER

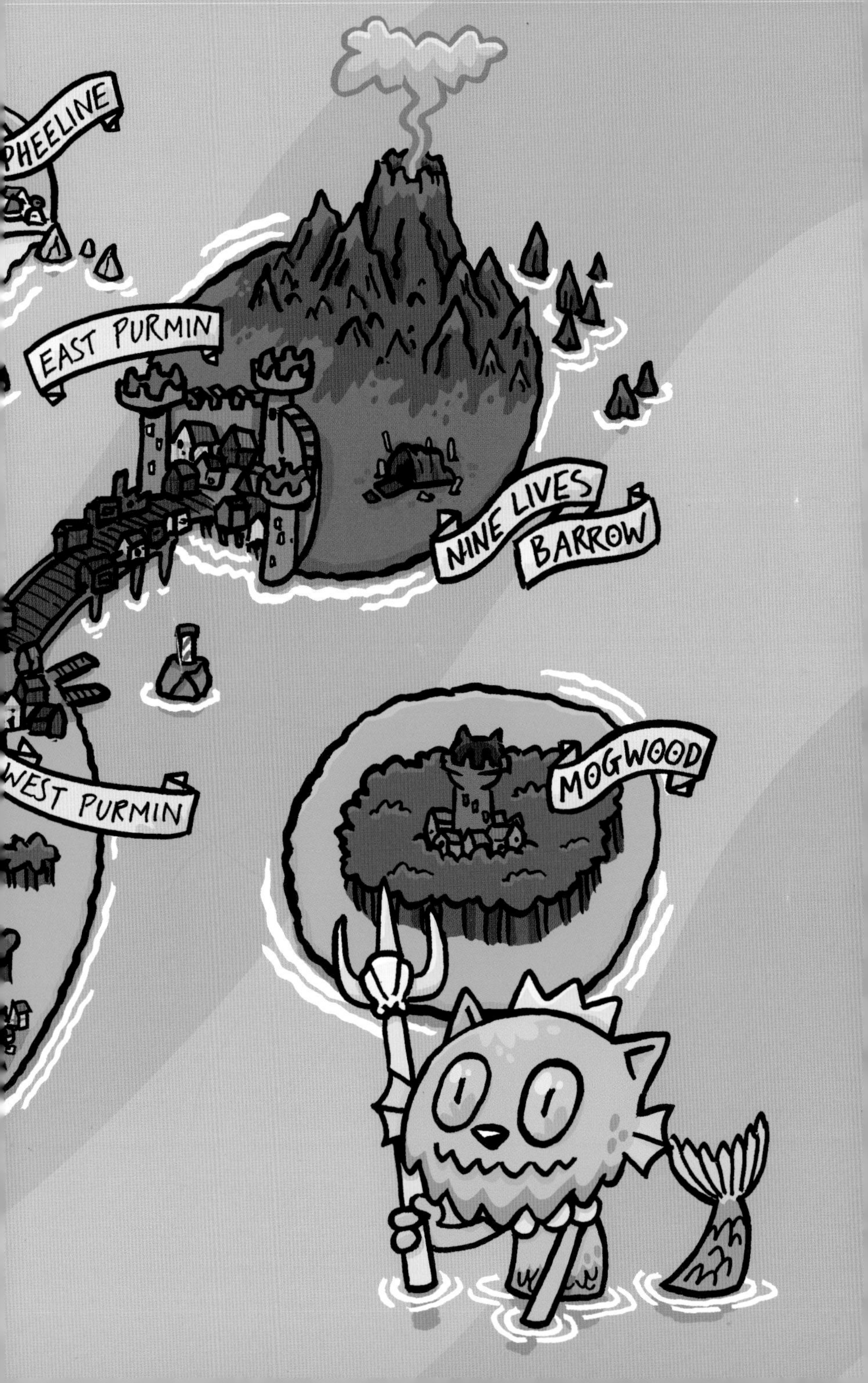
PHEELINE
EAST PURMIN
NINE LIVES BARROW
MOGWOOD
WEST PURMIN

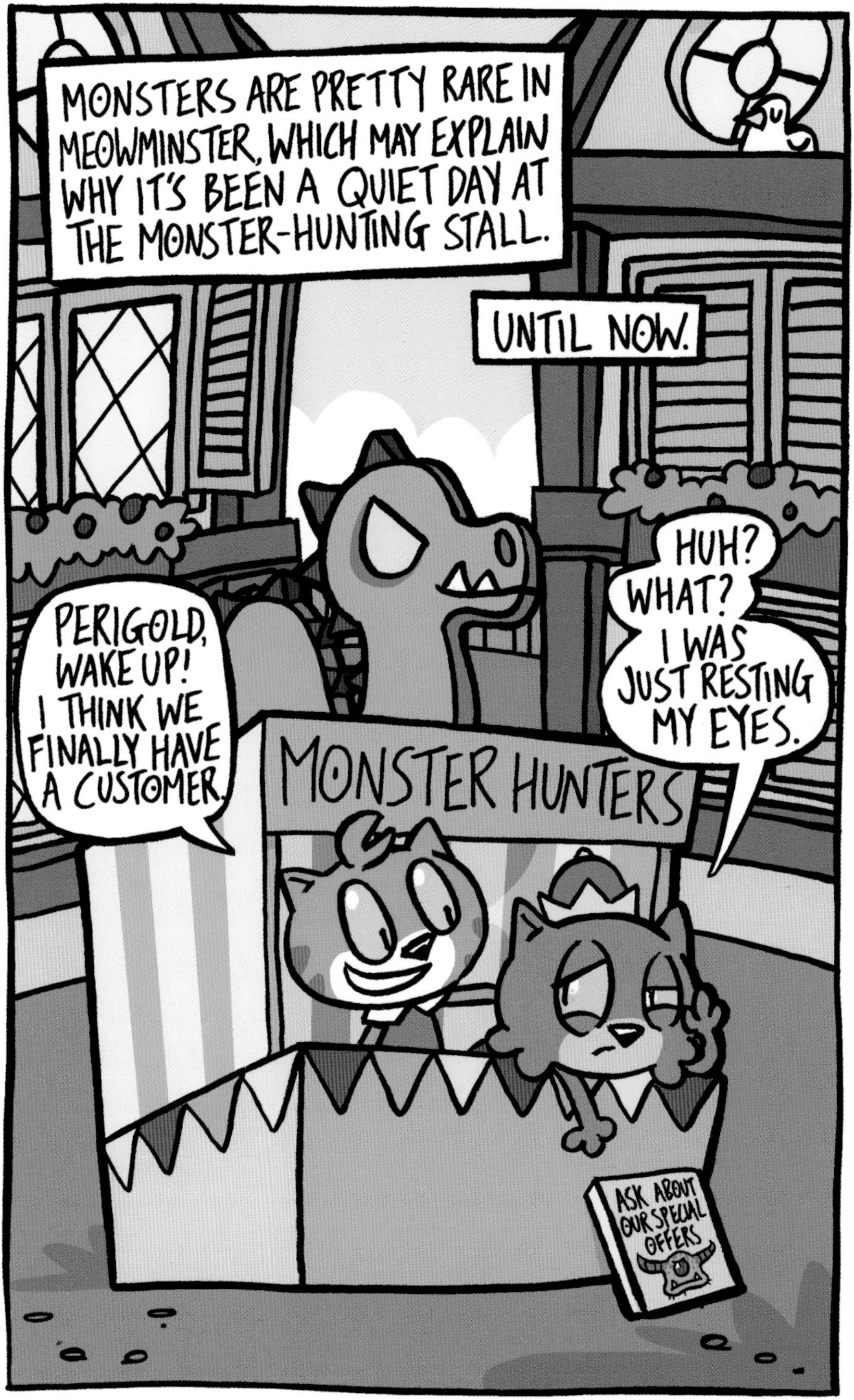
MONSTERS ARE PRETTY RARE IN MEOWMINSTER, WHICH MAY EXPLAIN WHY IT'S BEEN A QUIET DAY AT THE MONSTER-HUNTING STALL.
UNTIL NOW.
PERIGOLD, WAKE UP! I THINK WE FINALLY HAVE A CUSTOMER.
HUH? WHAT? I WAS JUST RESTING MY EYES.
MONSTER HUNTERS
ASK ABOUT OUR SPECIAL OFFERS

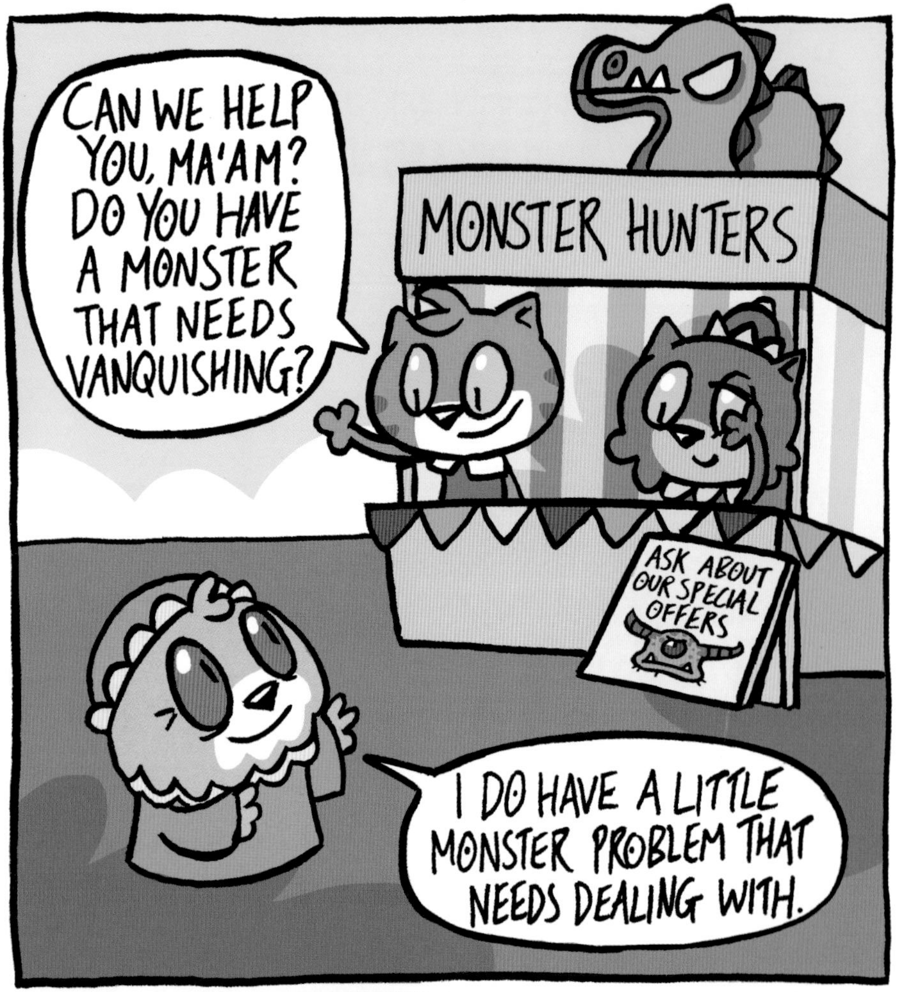
MONSTER HUNTERS
CAN WE HELP YOU, MA'AM? DO YOU HAVE A MONSTER THAT NEEDS VANQUISHING?
ASK ABOUT OUR SPECIAL OFFERS
I DO HAVE A LITTLE MONSTER PROBLEM THAT NEEDS DEALING WITH.

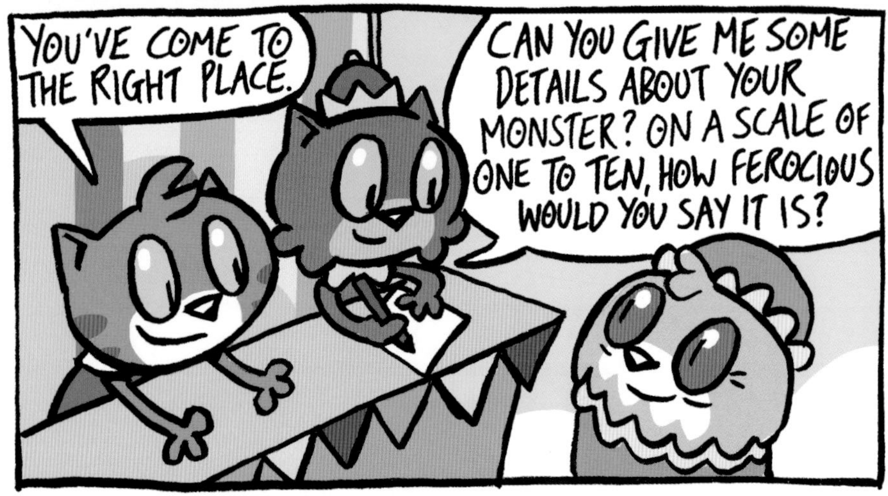
YOU'VE COME TO THE RIGHT PLACE.
CAN YOU GIVE ME SOME DETAILS ABOUT YOUR MONSTER? ON A SCALE OF ONE TO TEN, HOW FEROCIOUS WOULD YOU SAY IT IS?

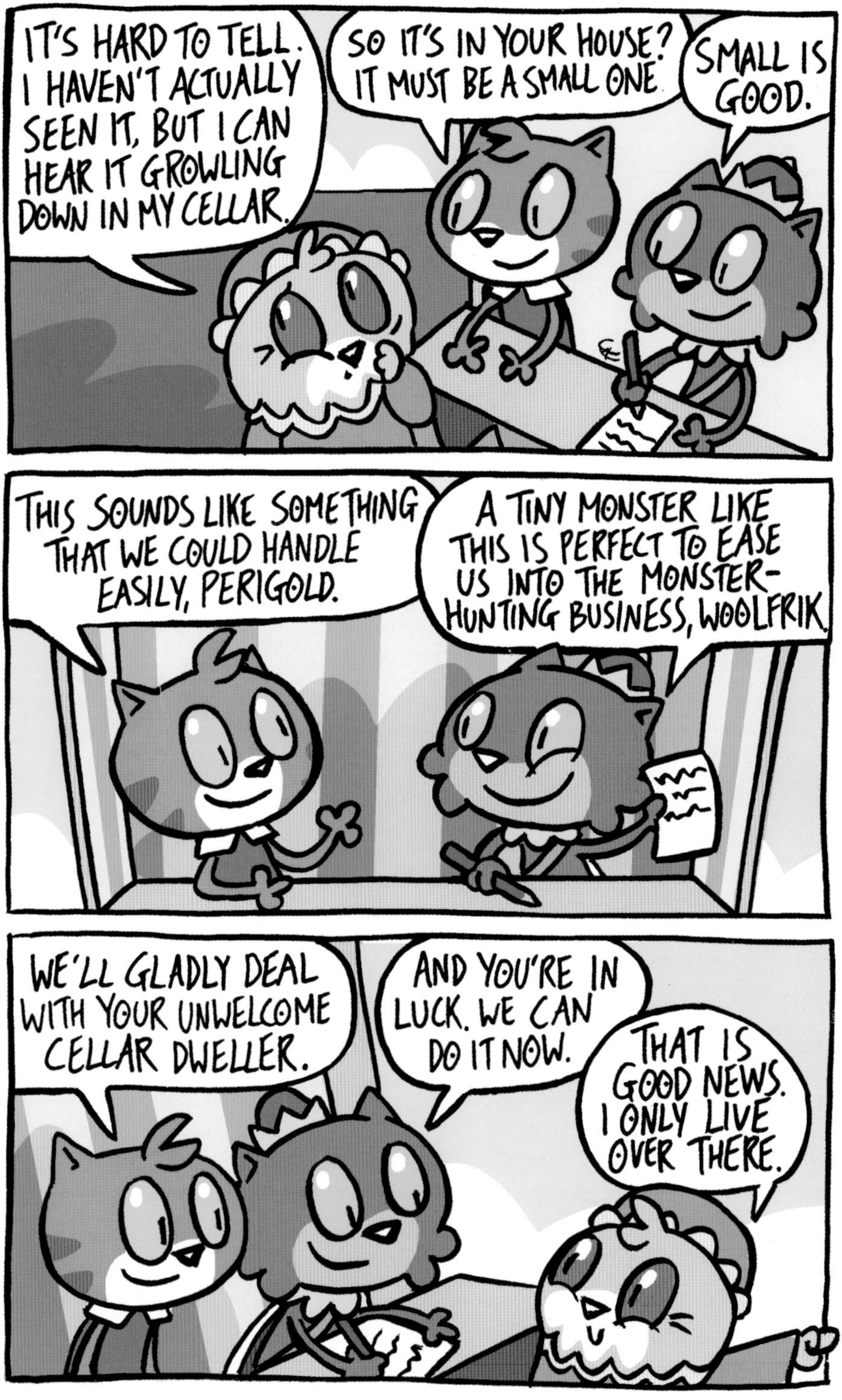
IT'S HARD TO TELL. I HAVEN'T ACTUALLY SEEN IT, BUT I CAN HEAR IT GROWLING DOWN IN MY CELLAR.
SO IT'S IN YOUR HOUSE? IT MUST BE A SMALL ONE.
SMALL IS GOOD.
THIS SOUNDS LIKE SOMETHING THAT WE COULD HANDLE EASILY, PERIGOLD.
A TINY MONSTER LIKE THIS IS PERFECT TO EASE US INTO THE MONSTER-HUNTING BUSINESS, WOOLFRIK.
WE'LL GLADLY DEAL WITH YOUR UNWELCOME CELLAR DWELLER.
AND YOU'RE IN LUCK. WE CAN DO IT NOW.
THAT IS GOOD NEWS. I ONLY LIVE OVER THERE.

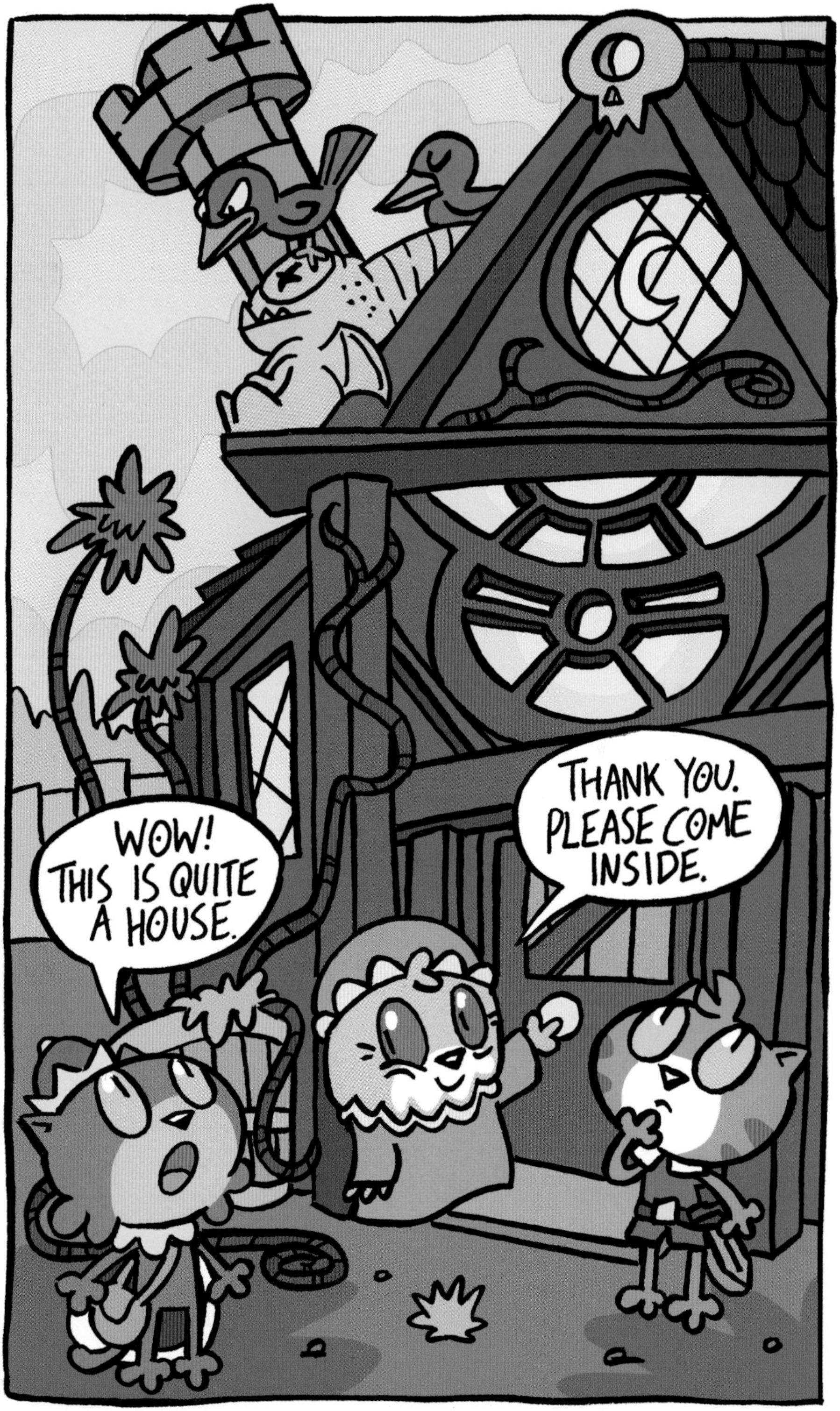
WOW! THIS IS QUITE A HOUSE.
THANK YOU. PLEASE COME INSIDE.

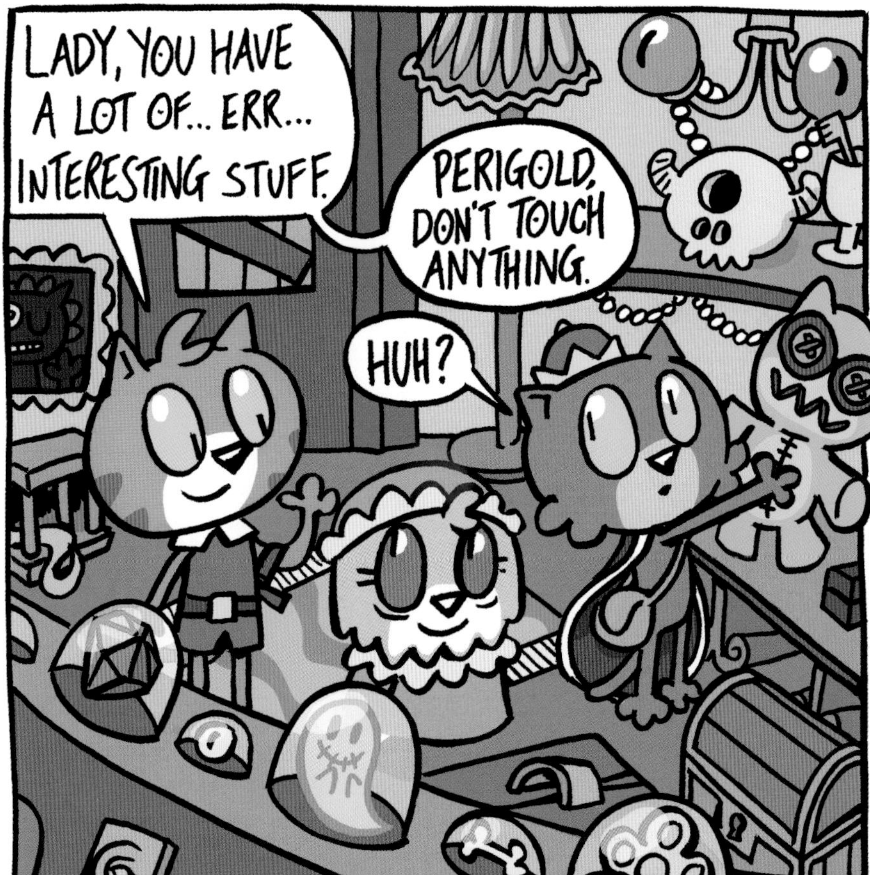
LADY, YOU HAVE A LOT OF... ERR... INTERESTING STUFF.
PERIGOLD, DON'T TOUCH ANYTHING.
HUH?

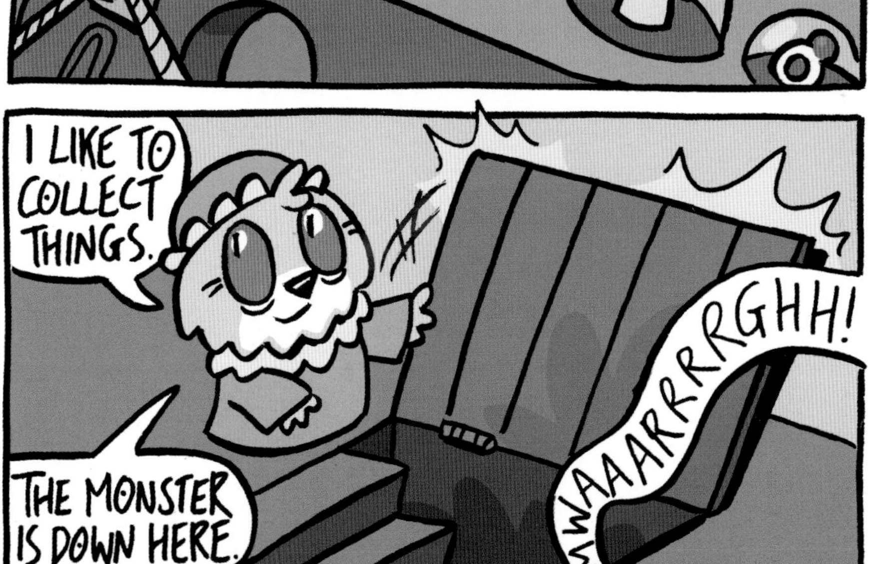
I LIKE TO COLLECT THINGS.
THE MONSTER IS DOWN HERE.
MWAAARRRRGHH!

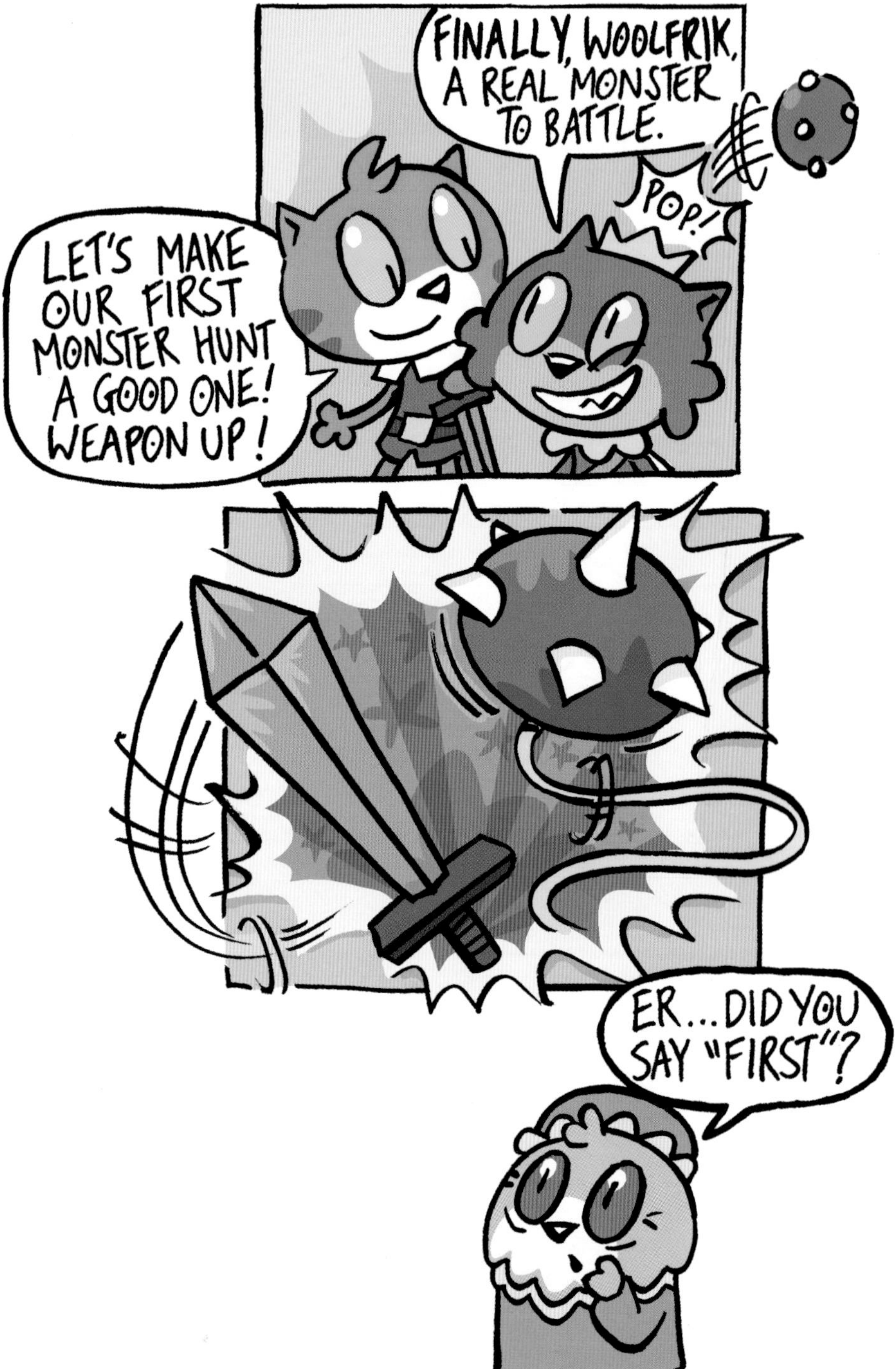
FINALLY, WOOLFRIK, A REAL MONSTER TO BATTLE.
LET'S MAKE OUR FIRST MONSTER HUNT A GOOD ONE! WEAPON UP!
POP!
ER...DID YOU SAY "FIRST"?

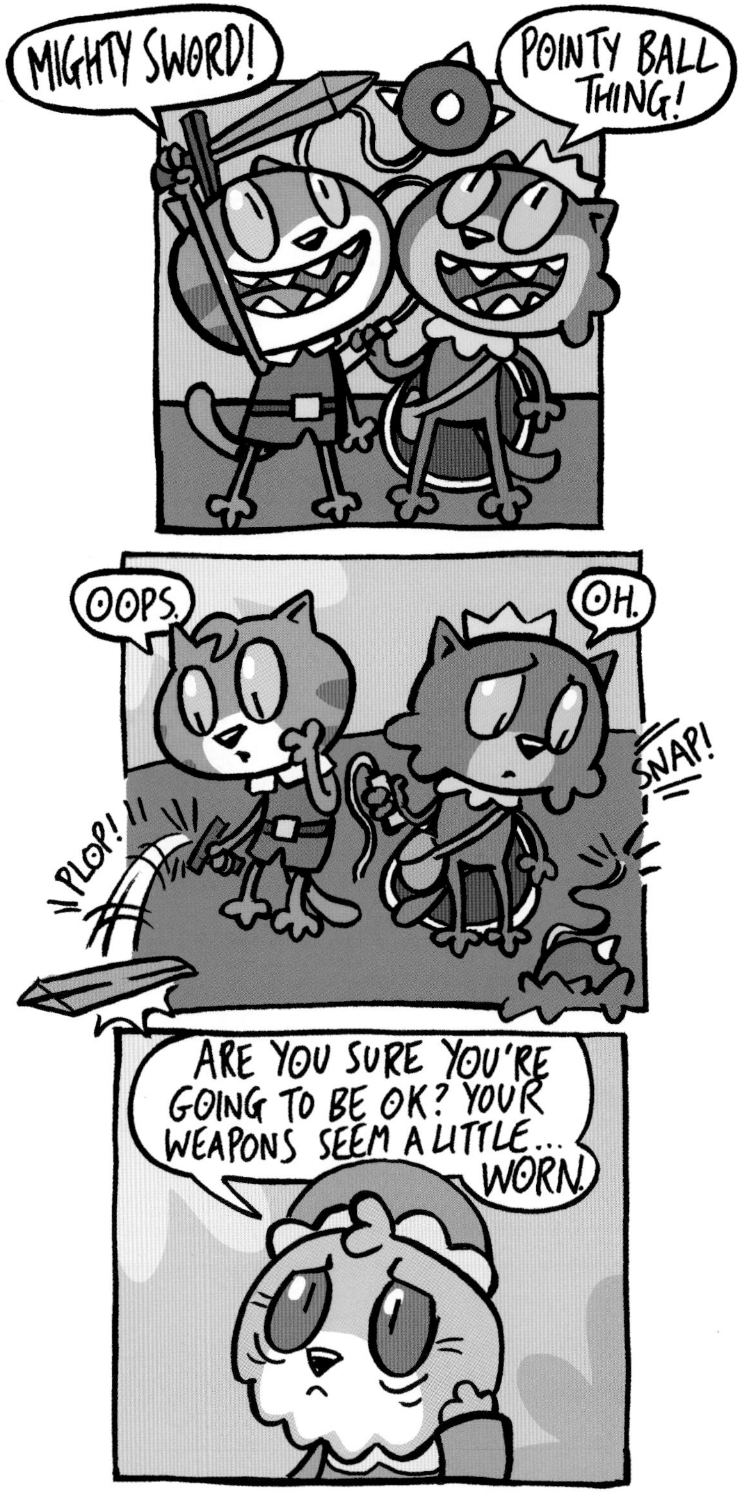
MIGHTY SWORD!
POINTY BALL THING!
OOPS.
OH.
SNAP!
PLOP!
ARE YOU SURE YOU'RE GOING TO BE OK? YOUR WEAPONS SEEM A LITTLE... WORN.

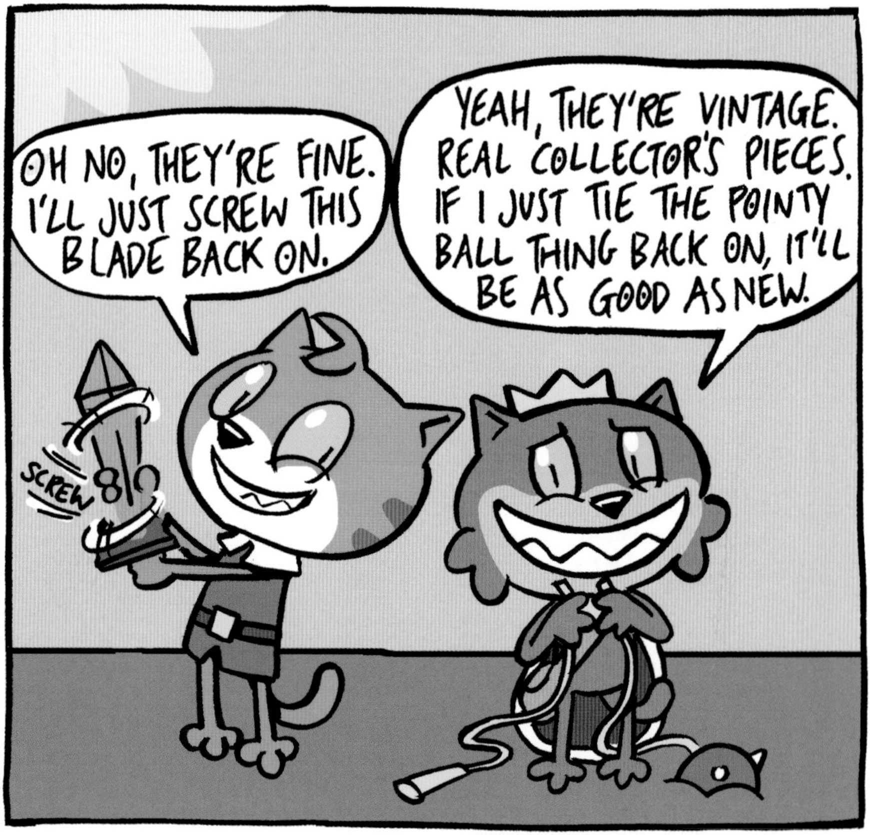
OH NO, THEY'RE FINE. I'LL JUST SCREW THIS BLADE BACK ON.
YEAH, THEY'RE VINTAGE. REAL COLLECTOR'S PIECES. IF I JUST TIE THE POINTY BALL THING BACK ON, IT'LL BE AS GOOD AS NEW.
SCREW

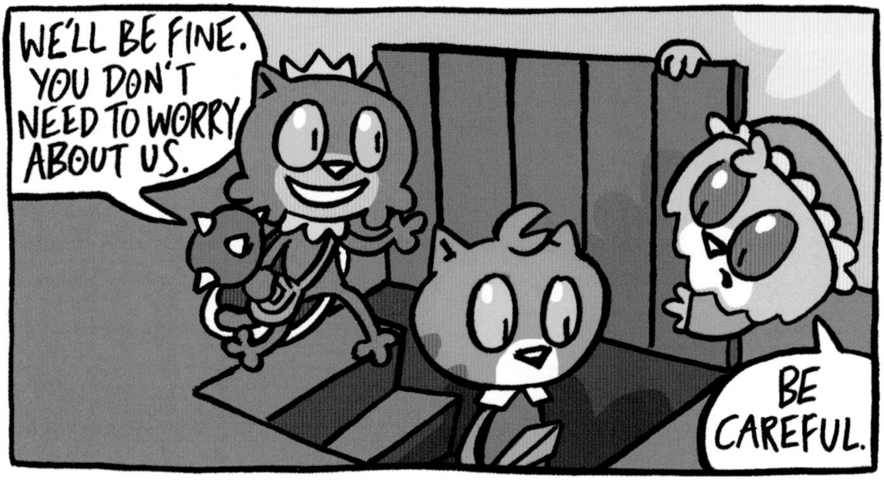
WE'LL BE FINE. YOU DON'T NEED TO WORRY ABOUT US.
BE CAREFUL.

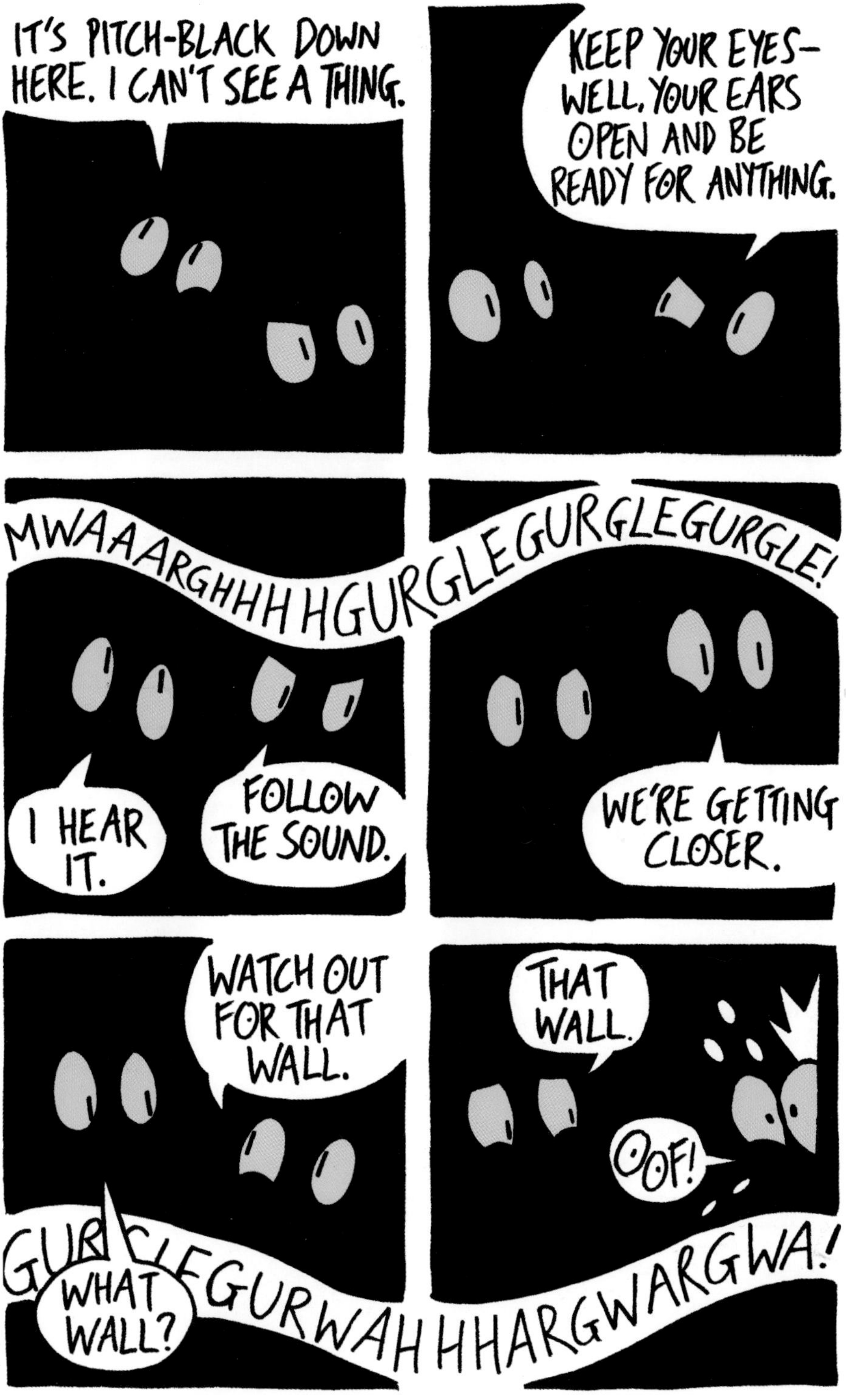
IT'S PITCH-BLACK DOWN HERE. I CAN'T SEE A THING.
KEEP YOUR EYES— WELL, YOUR EARS OPEN AND BE READY FOR ANYTHING.
MWAAARGHHHHGURGLEGURGLEGURGLE!
I HEAR IT.
FOLLOW THE SOUND.
WE'RE GETTING CLOSER.
WATCH OUT FOR THAT WALL.
WHAT WALL?
THAT WALL.
OOF!
GURGLEGURWAHHHARGWARGWA!

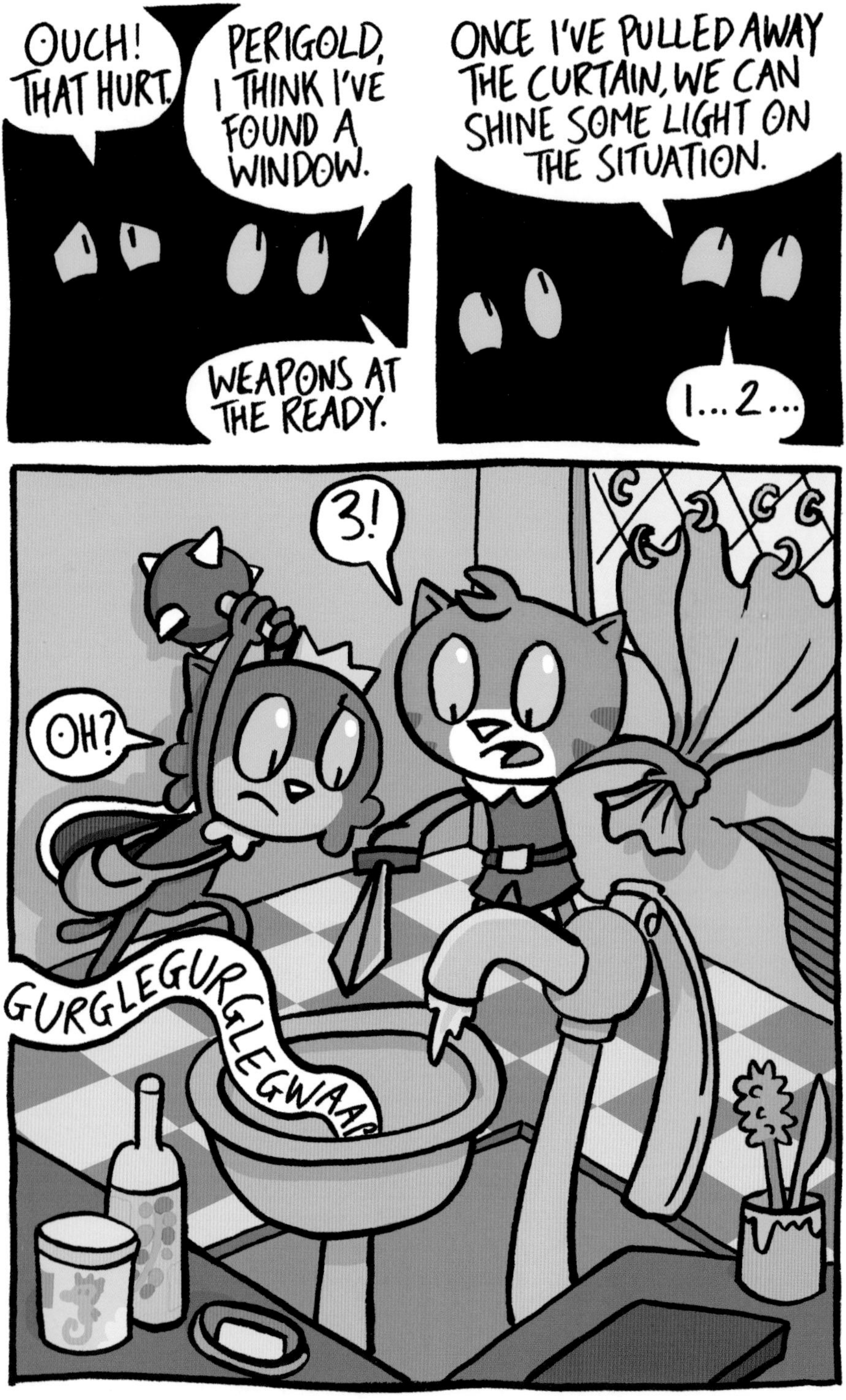
OUCH! THAT HURT.
PERIGOLD, I THINK I'VE FOUND A WINDOW.
WEAPONS AT THE READY.
ONCE I'VE PULLED AWAY THE CURTAIN, WE CAN SHINE SOME LIGHT ON THE SITUATION.
1...2...
3!
OH?
GURGLEGURGLEGWAA

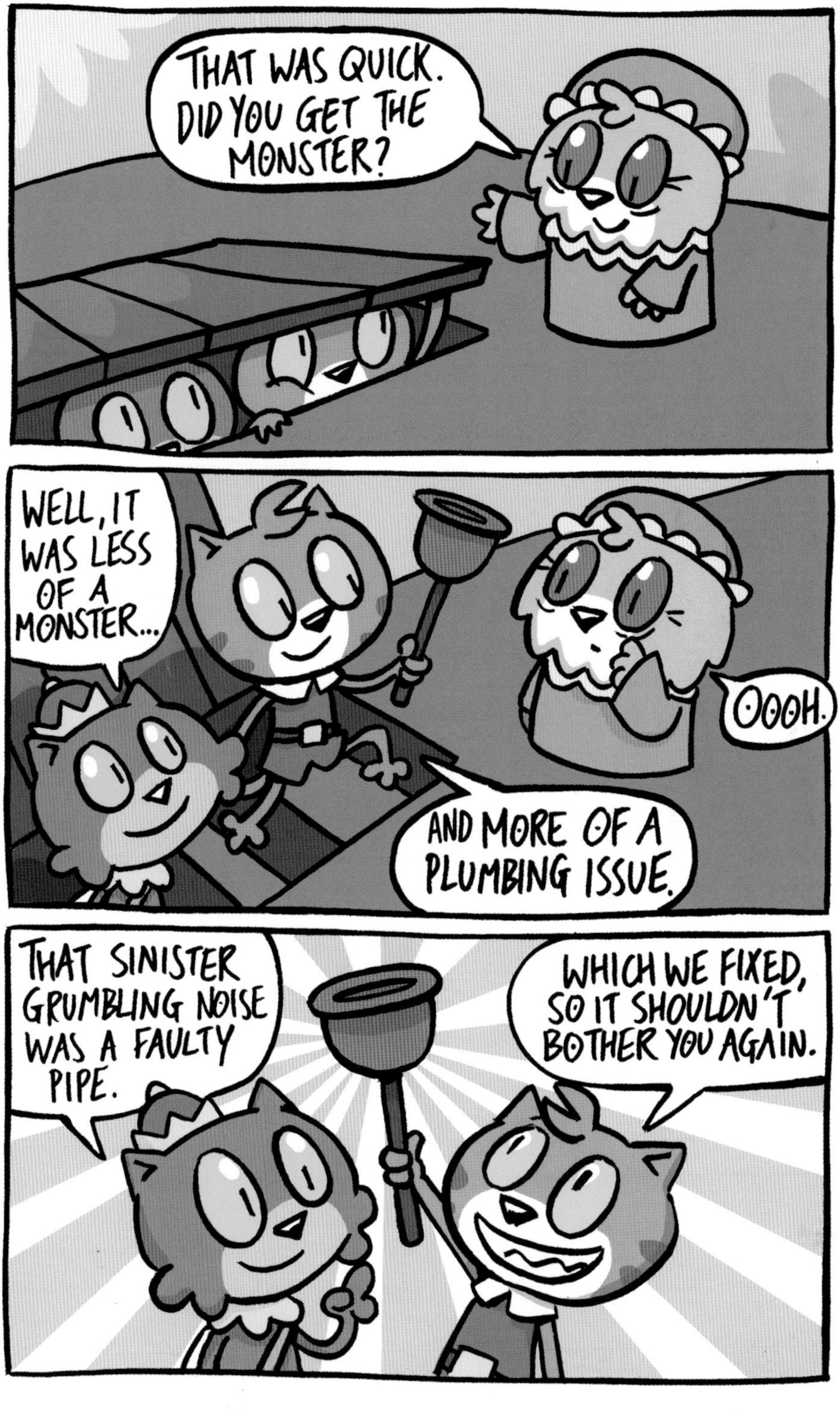
THAT WAS QUICK. DID YOU GET THE MONSTER?
WELL, IT WAS LESS OF A MONSTER...
AND MORE OF A PLUMBING ISSUE.
OOOH.
THAT SINISTER GRUMBLING NOISE WAS A FAULTY PIPE.
WHICH WE FIXED, SO IT SHOULDN'T BOTHER YOU AGAIN.

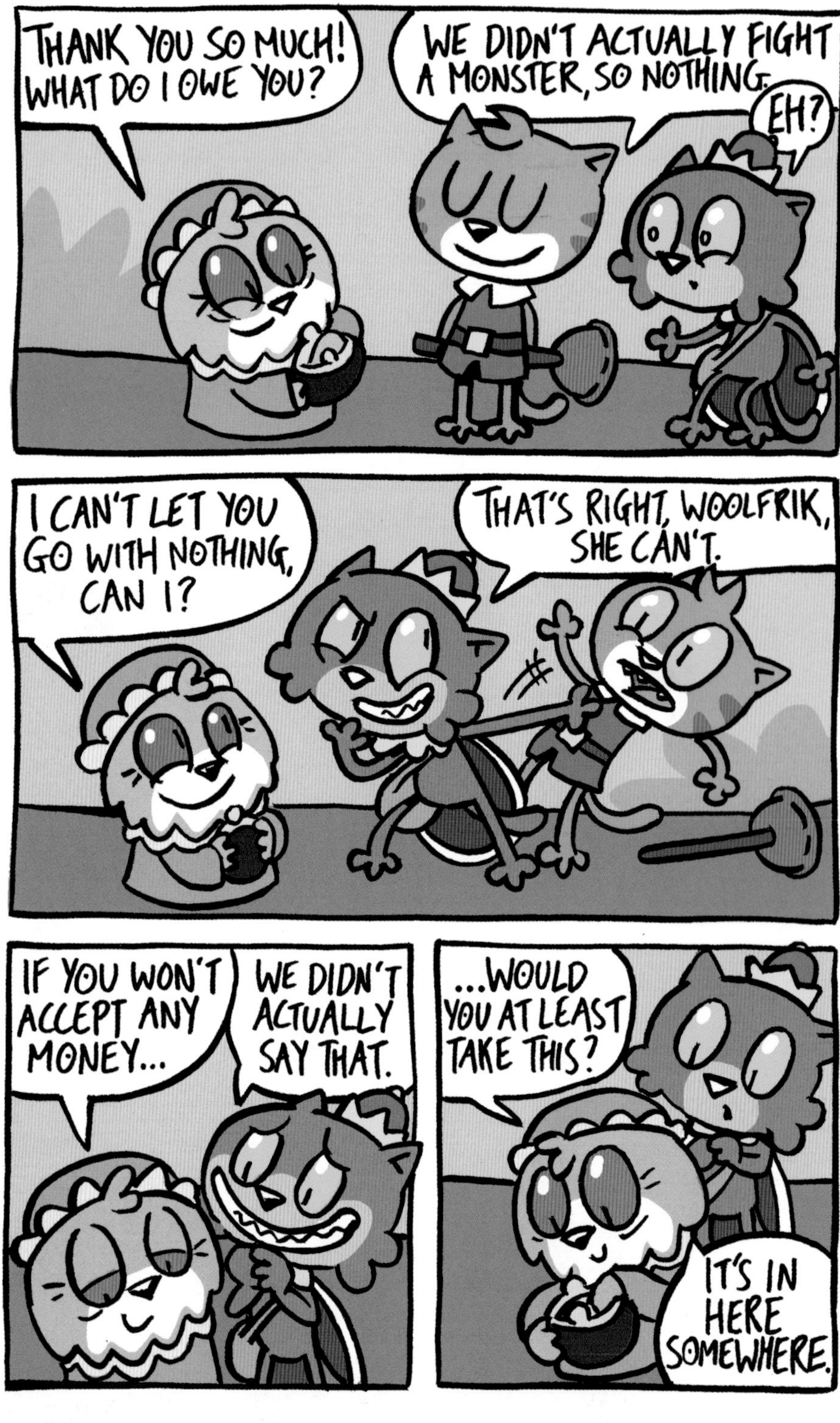
THANK YOU SO MUCH! WHAT DO I OWE YOU?
WE DIDN'T ACTUALLY FIGHT A MONSTER, SO NOTHING.
EH?
I CAN'T LET YOU GO WITH NOTHING, CAN I?
THAT'S RIGHT, WOOLFRIK, SHE CAN'T.
IF YOU WON'T ACCEPT ANY MONEY...
WE DIDN'T ACTUALLY SAY THAT.
...WOULD YOU AT LEAST TAKE THIS?
IT'S IN HERE SOMEWHERE.

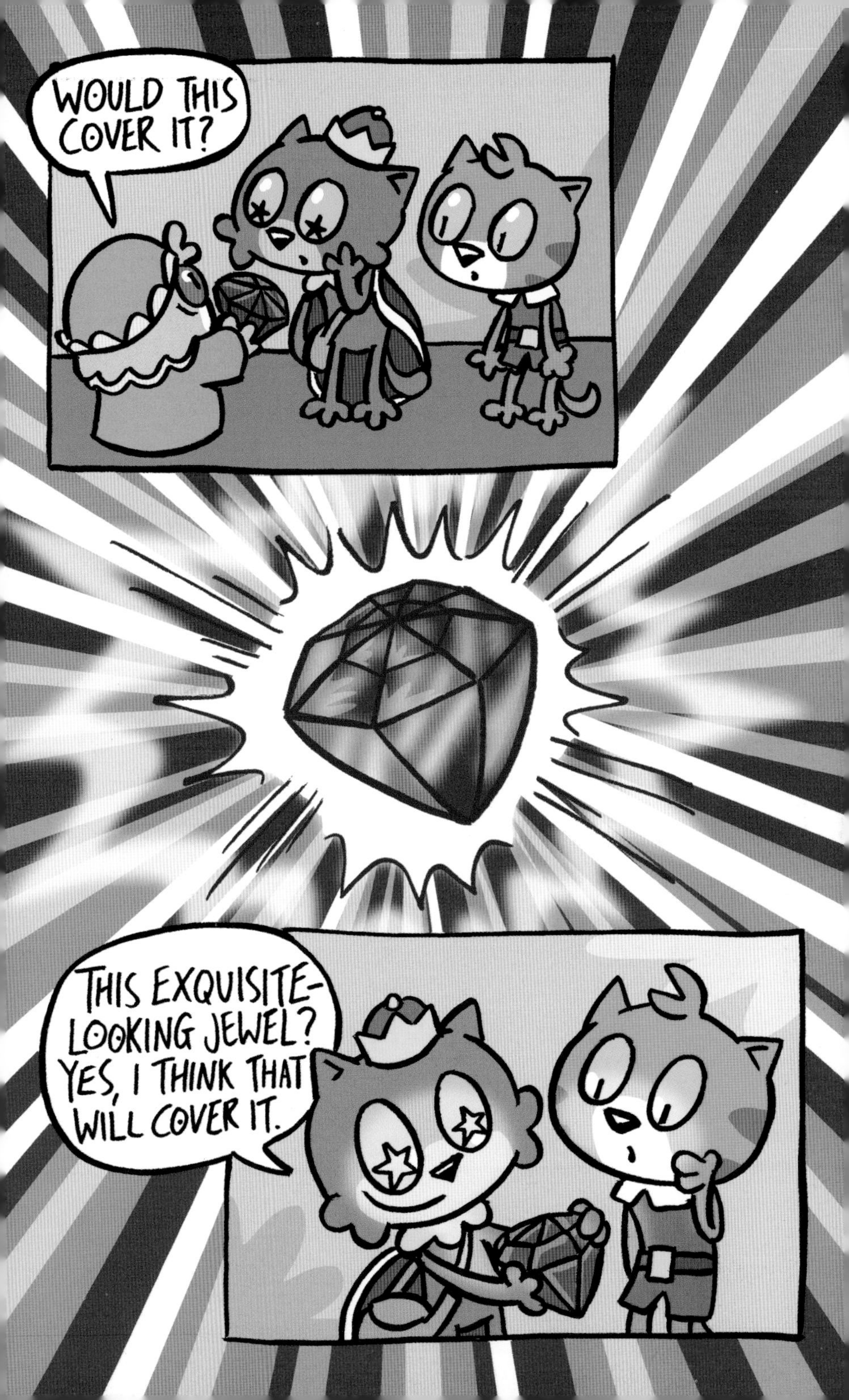
WOULD THIS COVER IT?
THIS EXQUISITE-LOOKING JEWEL? YES, I THINK THAT WILL COVER IT.

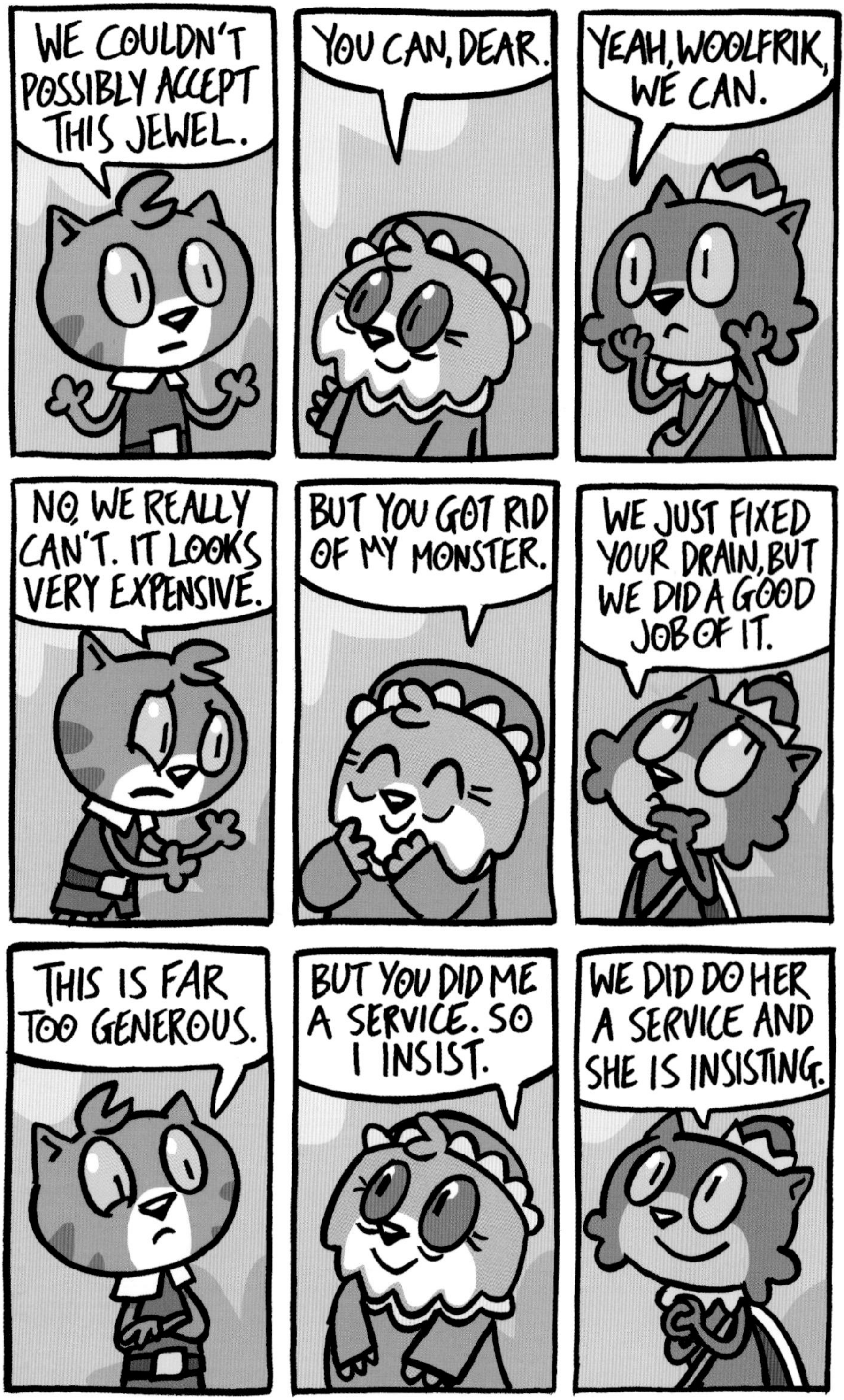
WE COULDN'T POSSIBLY ACCEPT THIS JEWEL.
YOU CAN, DEAR.
YEAH, WOOLFRIK, WE CAN.
NO, WE REALLY CAN'T. IT LOOKS VERY EXPENSIVE.
BUT YOU GOT RID OF MY MONSTER.
WE JUST FIXED YOUR DRAIN, BUT WE DID A GOOD JOB OF IT.
THIS IS FAR TOO GENEROUS.
BUT YOU DID ME A SERVICE. SO I INSIST.
WE DID DO HER A SERVICE AND SHE IS INSISTING.

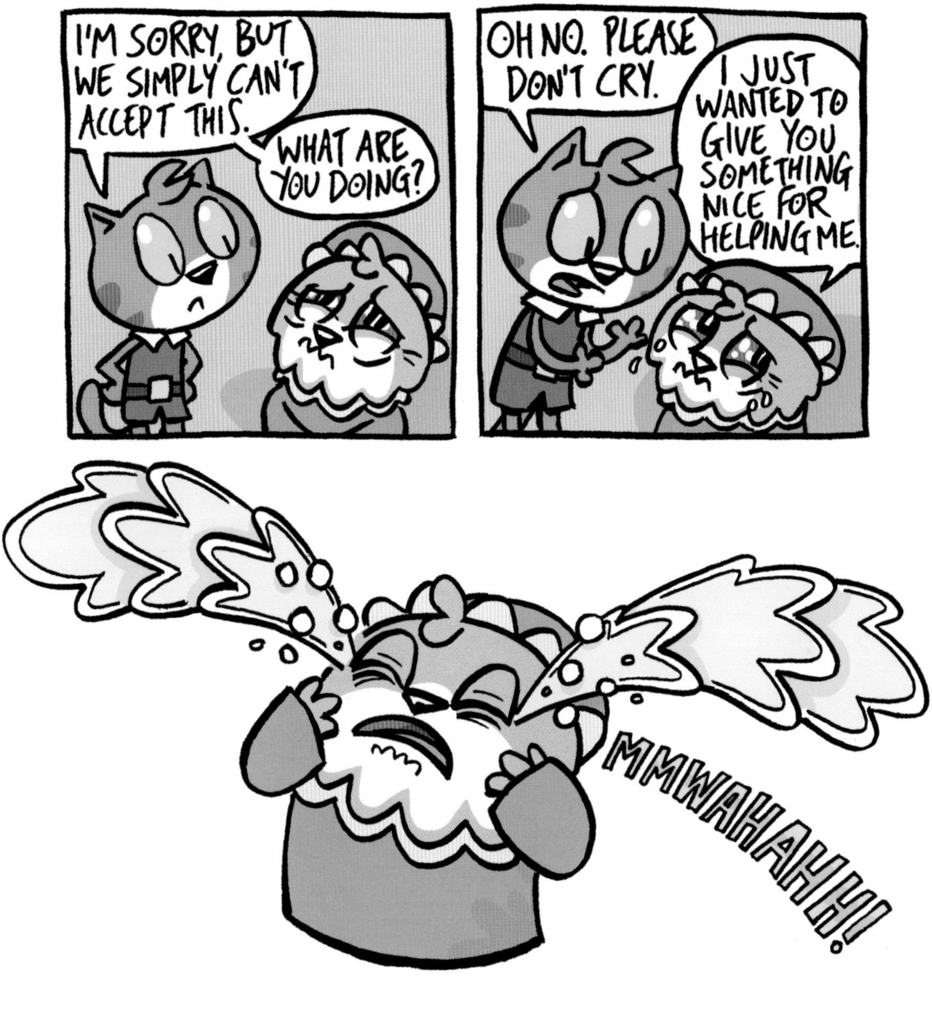
I'M SORRY, BUT WE SIMPLY CAN'T ACCEPT THIS.
WHAT ARE YOU DOING?
OH NO. PLEASE DON'T CRY.
I JUST WANTED TO GIVE YOU SOMETHING NICE FOR HELPING ME.
MMWAHAHHH!

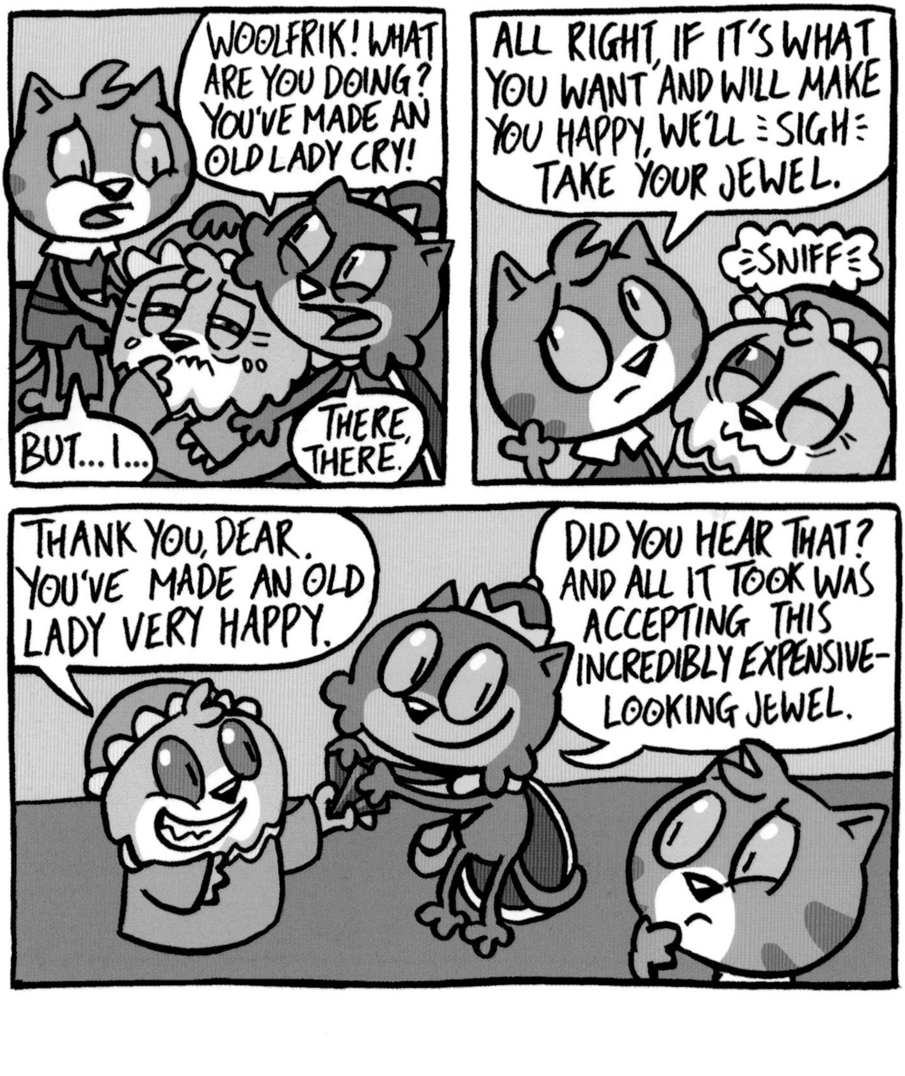
WOOLFRIK! WHAT ARE YOU DOING? YOU'VE MADE AN OLD LADY CRY!
BUT... I...
THERE, THERE.
ALL RIGHT, IF IT'S WHAT YOU WANT AND WILL MAKE YOU HAPPY, WE'LL SIGH TAKE YOUR JEWEL.
SNIFF
THANK YOU, DEAR. YOU'VE MADE AN OLD LADY VERY HAPPY.
DID YOU HEAR THAT? AND ALL IT TOOK WAS ACCEPTING THIS INCREDIBLY EXPENSIVE-LOOKING JEWEL.

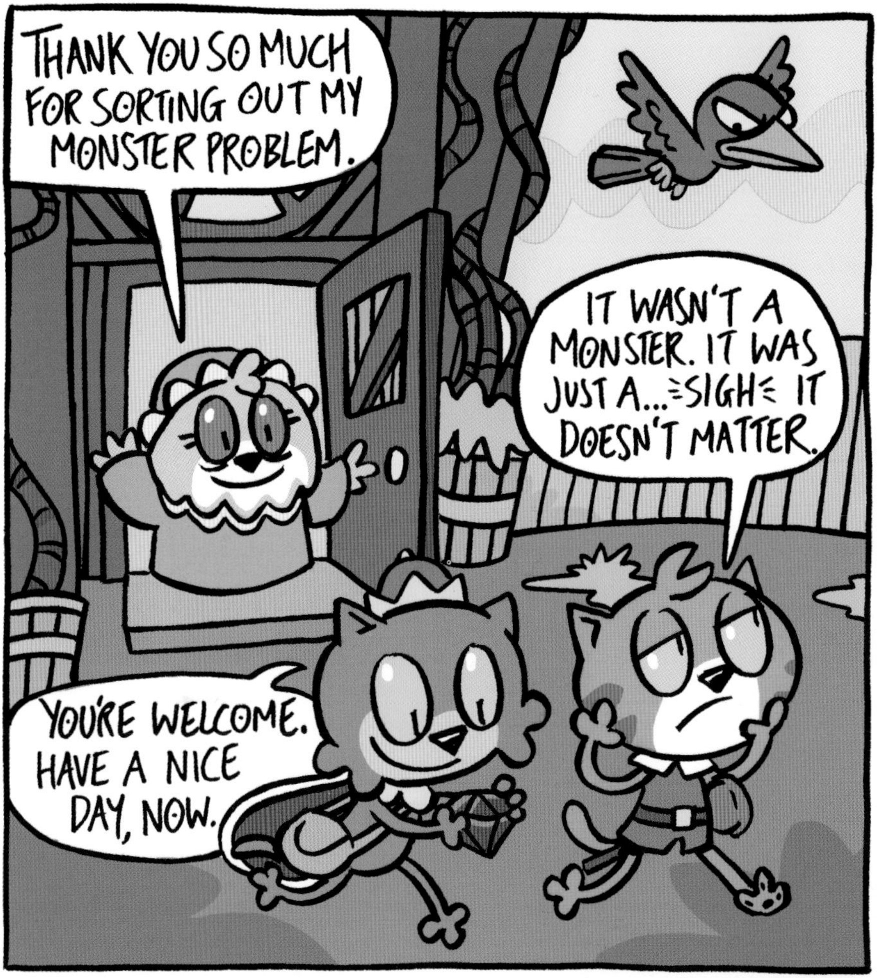
THANK YOU SO MUCH FOR SORTING OUT MY MONSTER PROBLEM.
IT WASN'T A MONSTER. IT WAS JUST A... ≡SIGH≡ IT DOESN'T MATTER.
YOU'RE WELCOME. HAVE A NICE DAY, NOW.

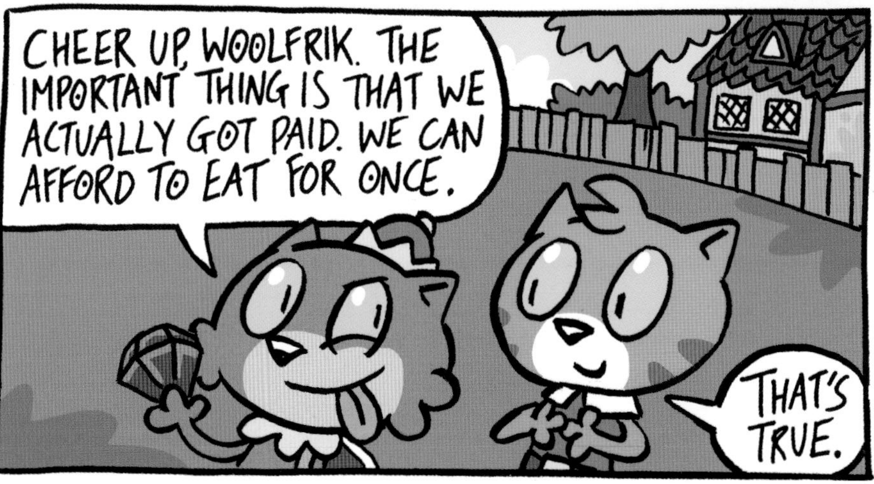
CHEER UP, WOOLFRIK. THE IMPORTANT THING IS THAT WE ACTUALLY GOT PAID. WE CAN AFFORD TO EAT FOR ONCE.
THAT'S TRUE.

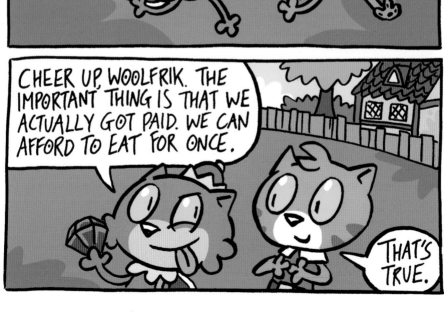

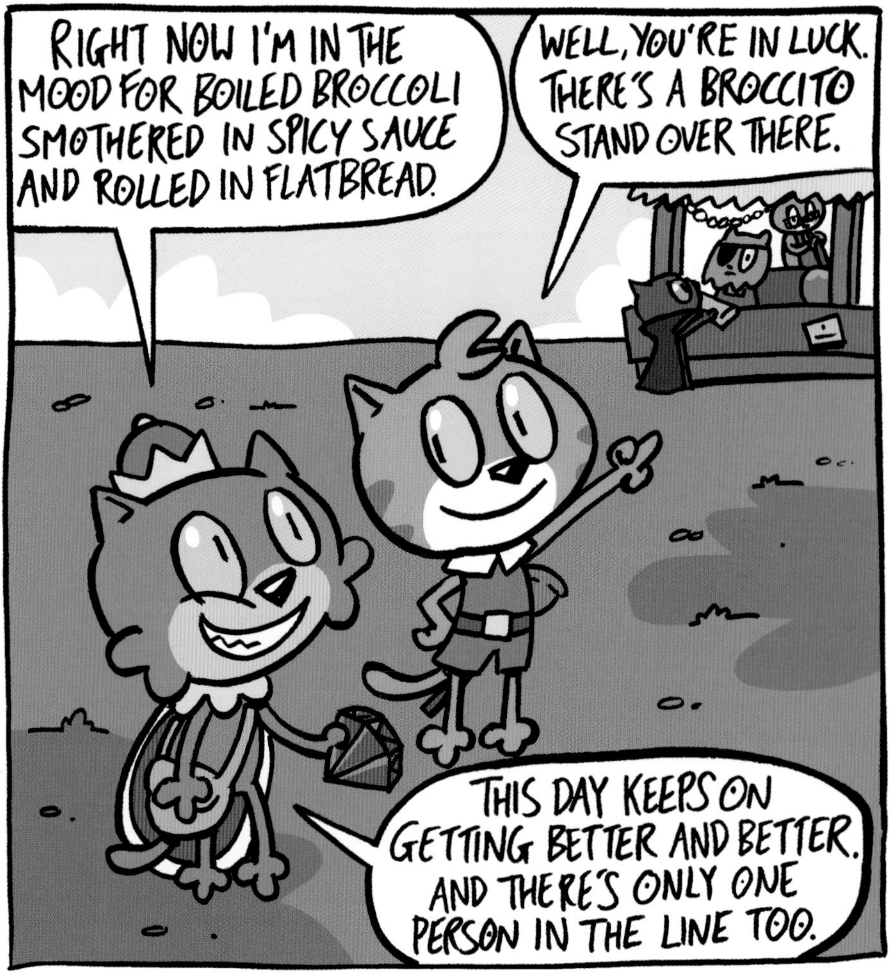
RIGHT NOW I'M IN THE MOOD FOR BOILED BROCCOLI SMOTHERED IN SPICY SAUCE AND ROLLED IN FLATBREAD.
WELL, YOU'RE IN LUCK. THERE'S A BROCCITO STAND OVER THERE.
THIS DAY KEEPS ON GETTING BETTER AND BETTER. AND THERE'S ONLY ONE PERSON IN THE LINE TOO.

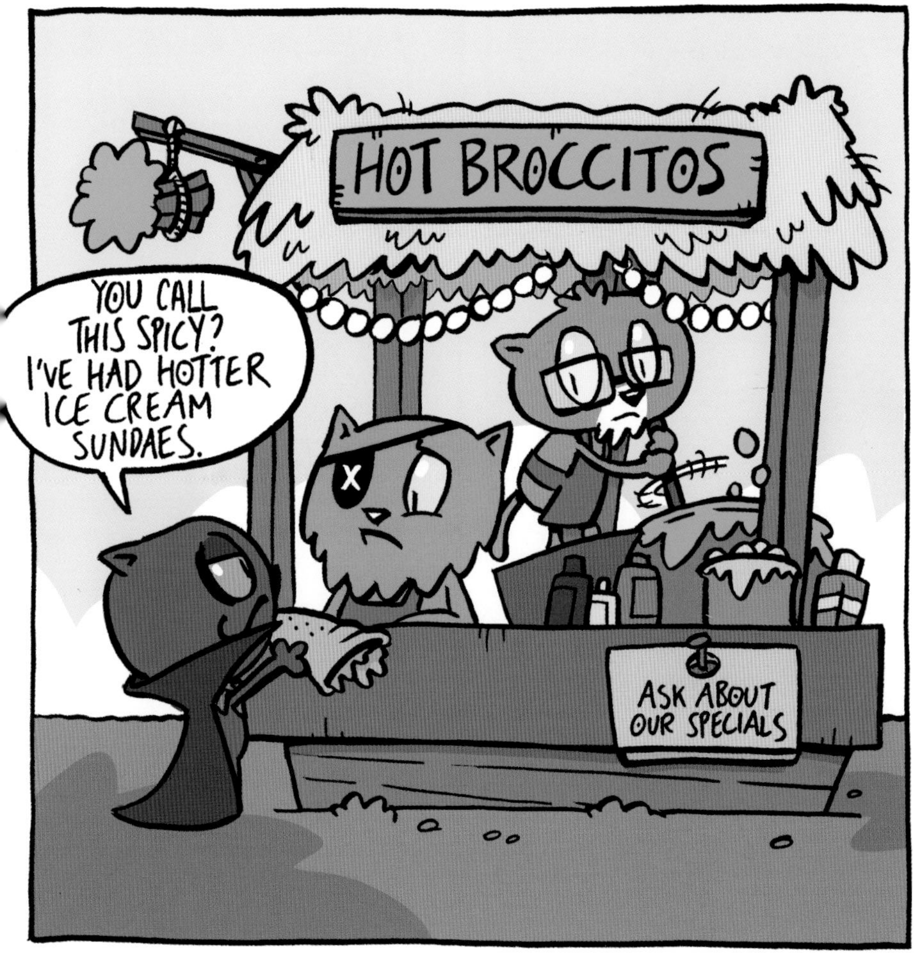
HOT BROCCITOS
YOU CALL THIS SPICY? I'VE HAD HOTTER ICE CREAM SUNDAES.
ASK ABOUT OUR SPECIALS

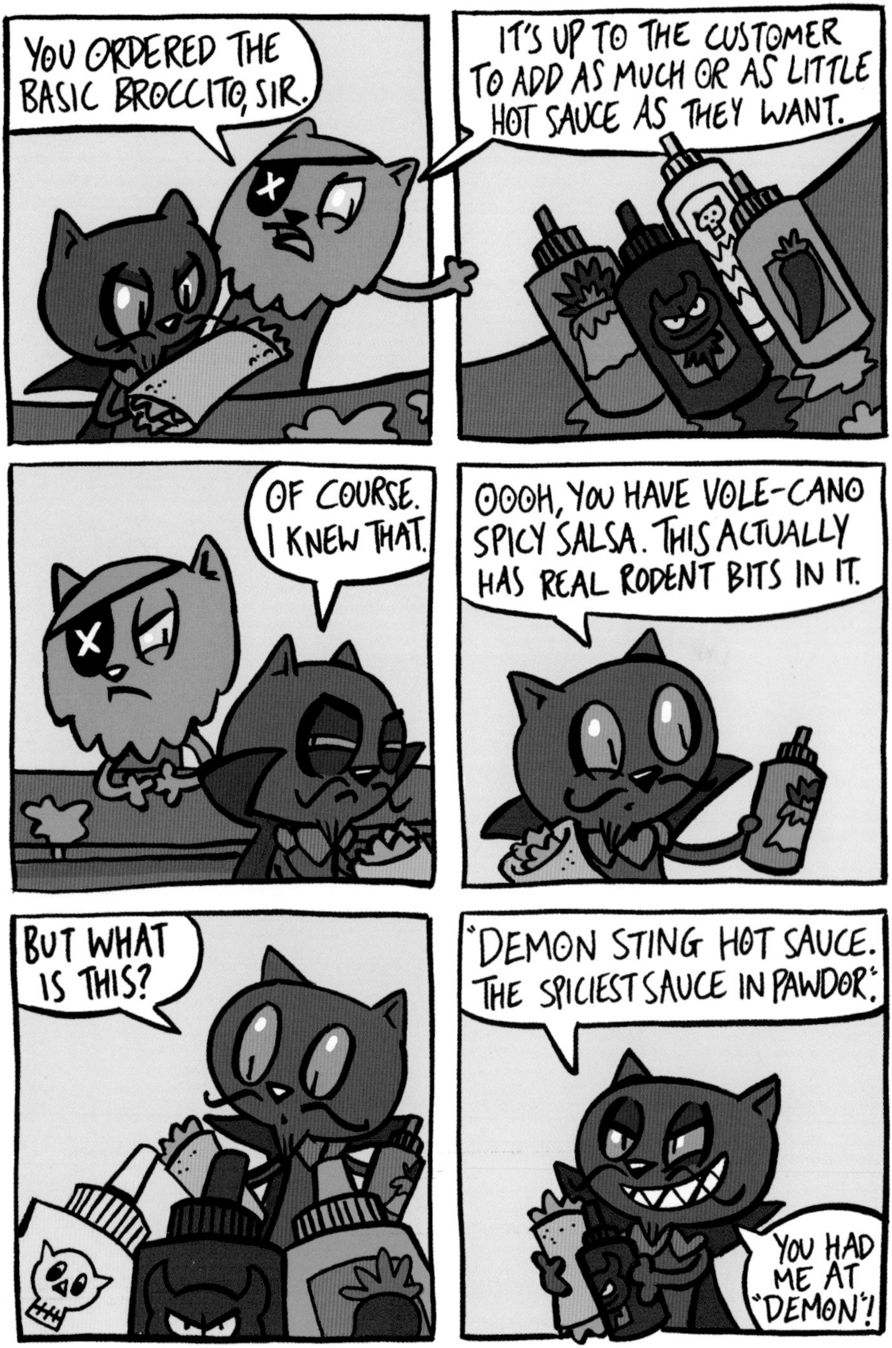
YOU ORDERED THE BASIC BROCCITO, SIR.
IT'S UP TO THE CUSTOMER TO ADD AS MUCH OR AS LITTLE HOT SAUCE AS THEY WANT.
OF COURSE. I KNEW THAT.
OOOH, YOU HAVE VOLE-CANO SPICY SALSA. THIS ACTUALLY HAS REAL RODENT BITS IN IT.
BUT WHAT IS THIS?
"DEMON STING HOT SAUCE. THE SPICIEST SAUCE IN PAWDOR."
YOU HAD ME AT "DEMON"!

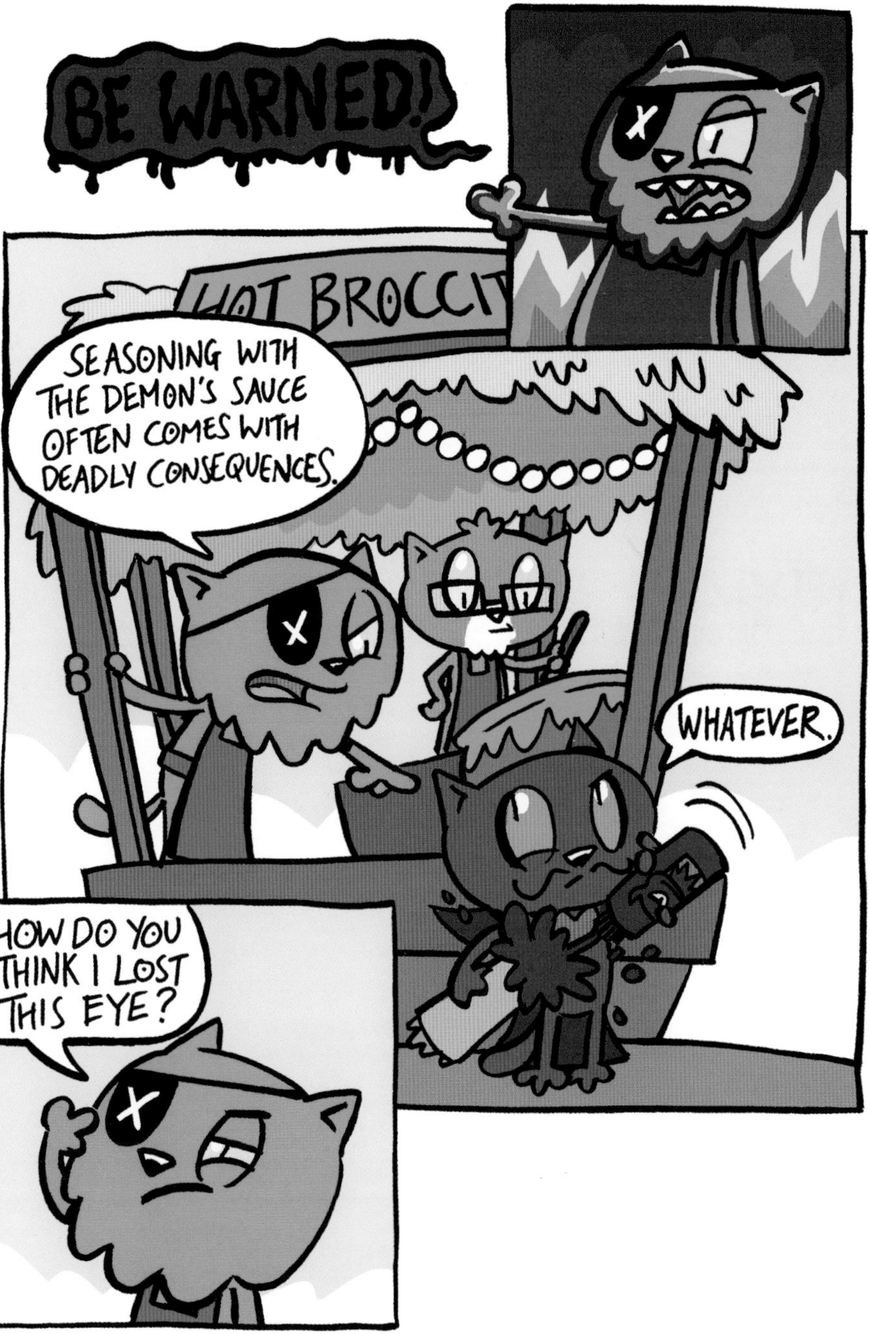
BE WARNED!
HOT BROCC
SEASONING WITH THE DEMON'S SAUCE OFTEN COMES WITH DEADLY CONSEQUENCES.
WHATEVER.
HOW DO YOU THINK I LOST THIS EYE?

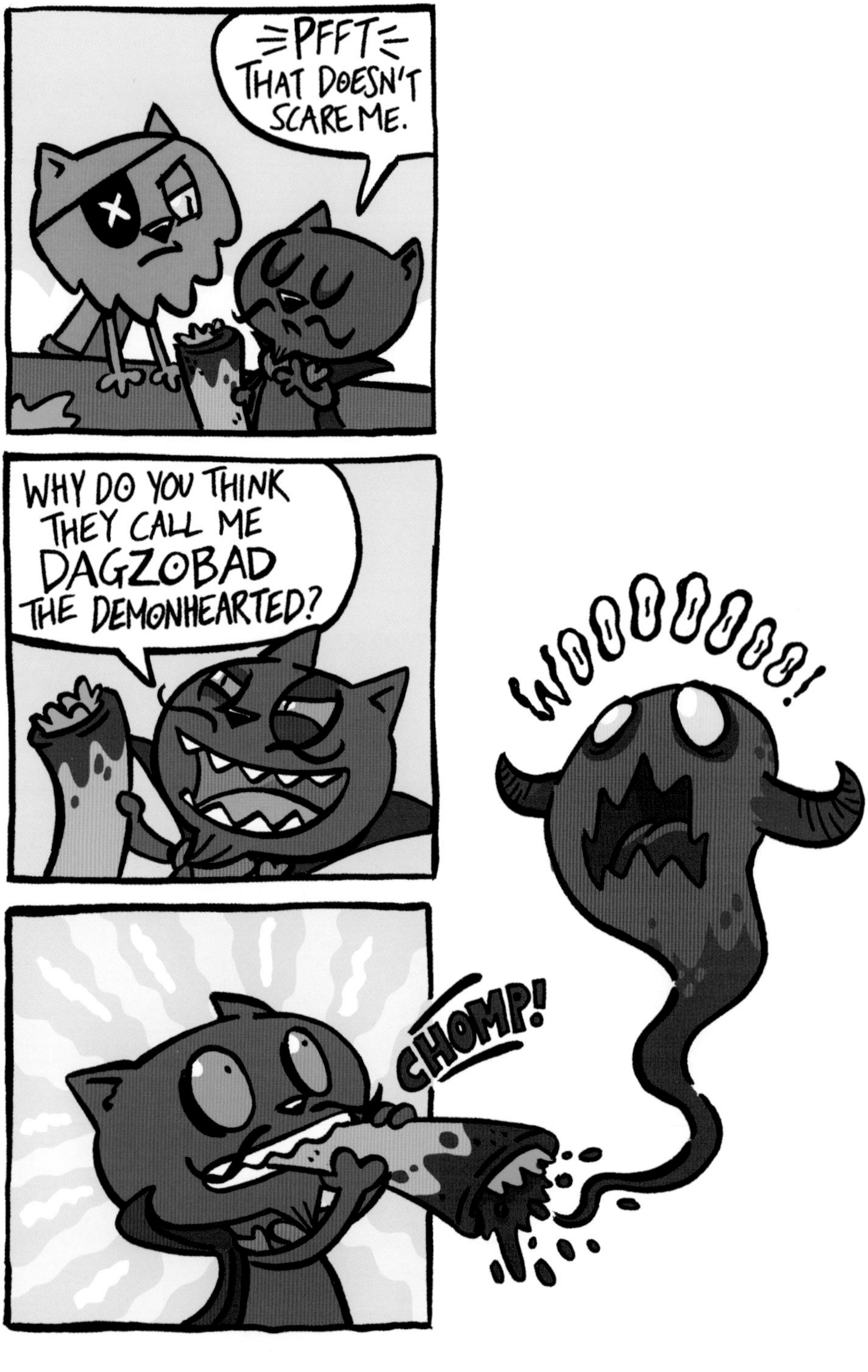

PFFT
THAT DOESN'T SCARE ME.
WHY DO YOU THINK THEY CALL ME DAGZOBAD THE DEMONHEARTED?
WOOOOOOO!
CHOMP!

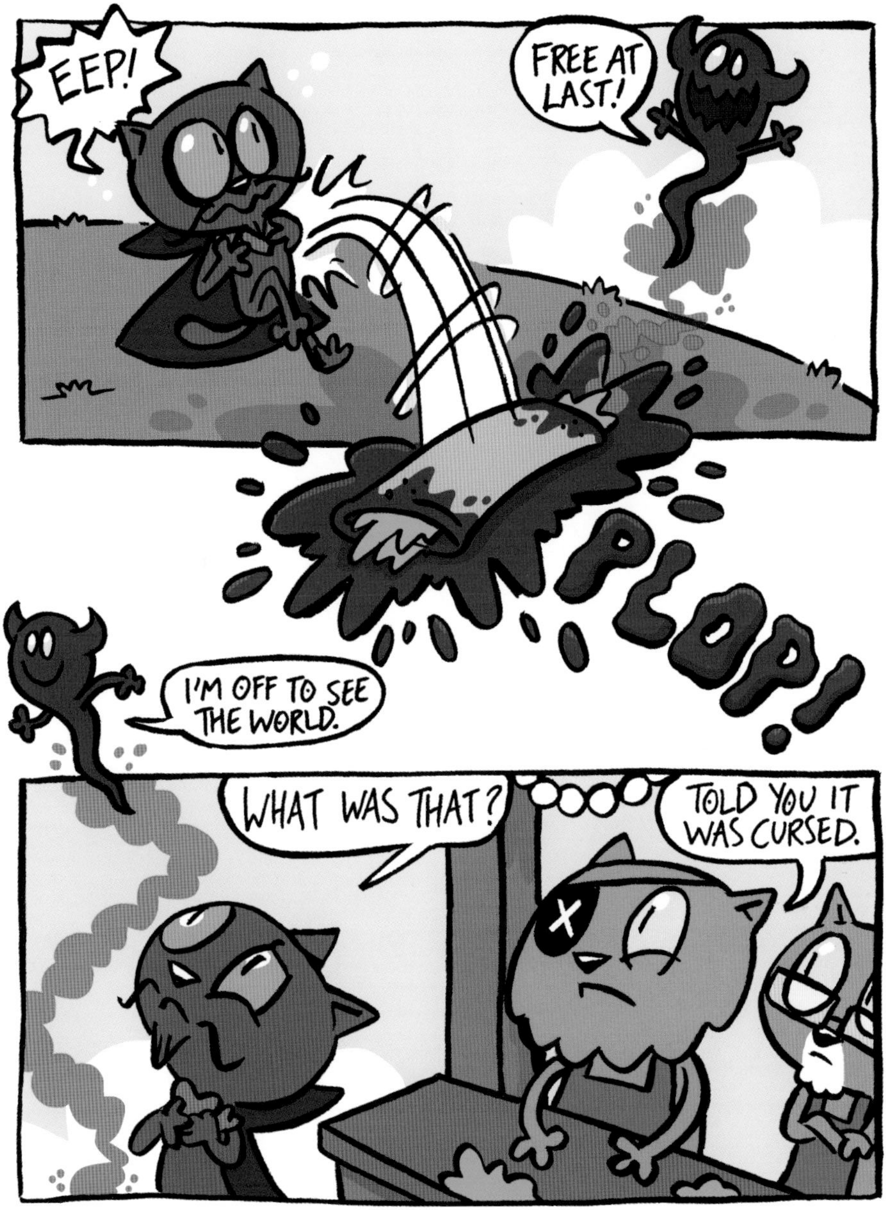
EEP!
FREE AT LAST!
PLOP!
I'M OFF TO SEE THE WORLD.
WHAT WAS THAT?
TOLD YOU IT WAS CURSED.

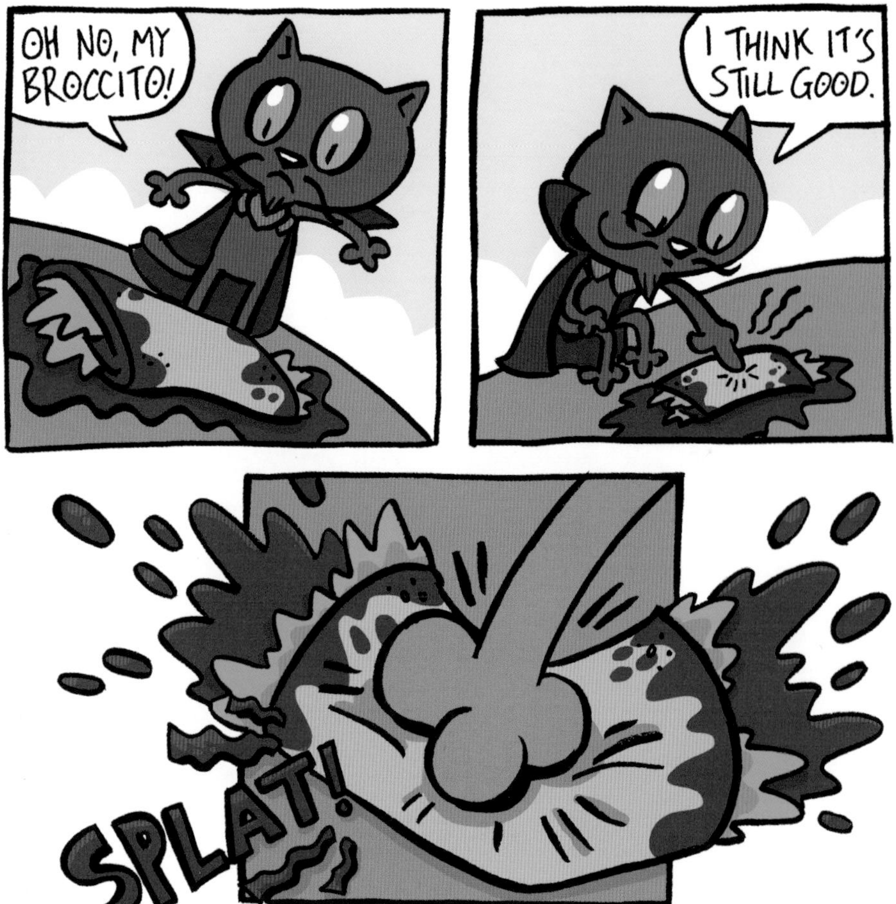
OH NO, MY BROCCITO!
I THINK IT'S STILL GOOD.
SPLAT!

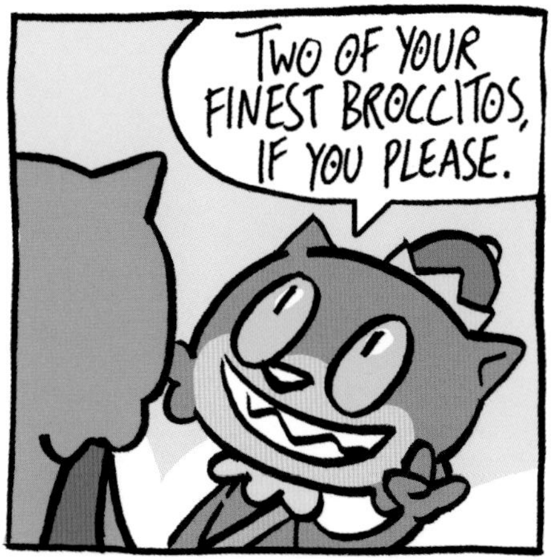
TWO OF YOUR FINEST BROCCITOS, IF YOU PLEASE.

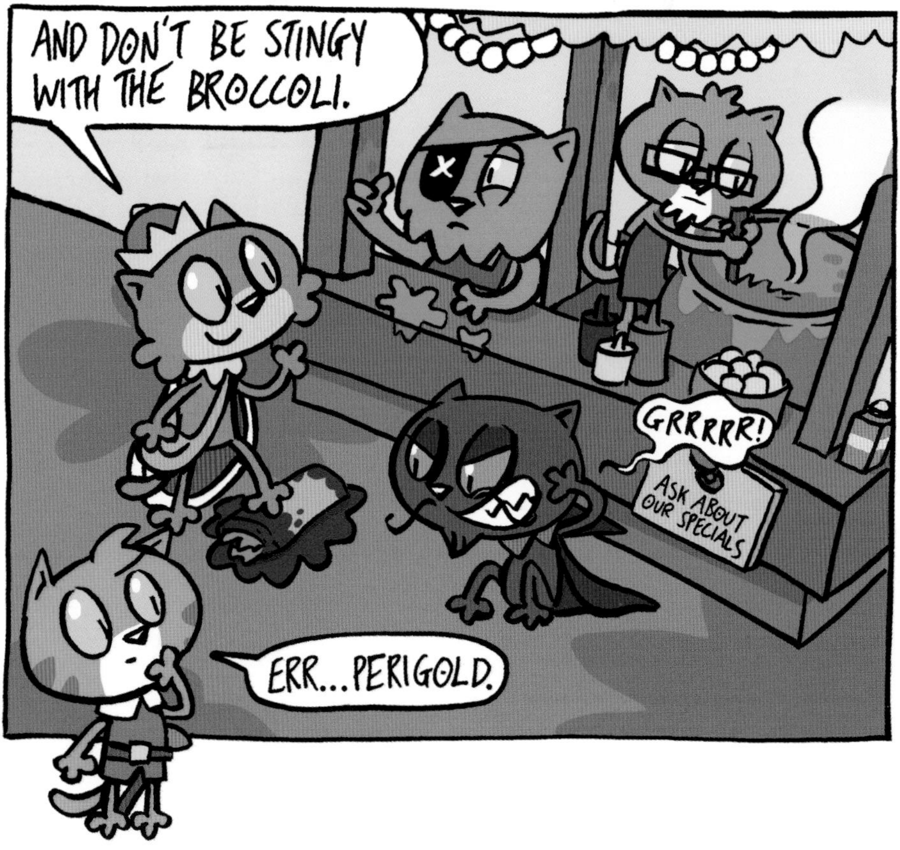
AND DON'T BE STINGY WITH THE BROCCOLI.
GRRRRR!
ASK ABOUT OUR SPECIALS
ERR...PERIGOLD.

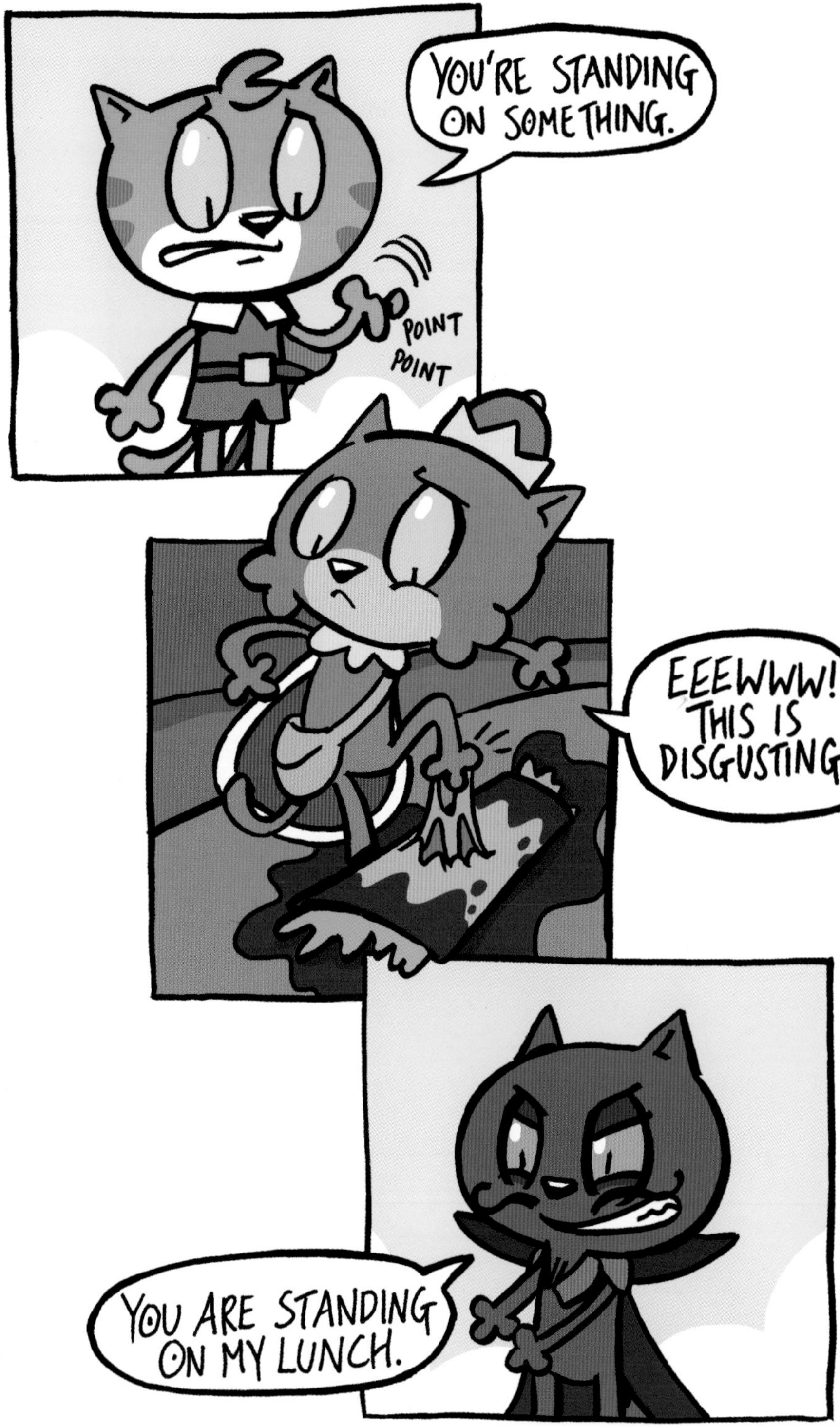
YOU'RE STANDING ON SOMETHING.
POINT POINT
EEEWWW! THIS IS DISGUSTING.
YOU ARE STANDING ON MY LUNCH.

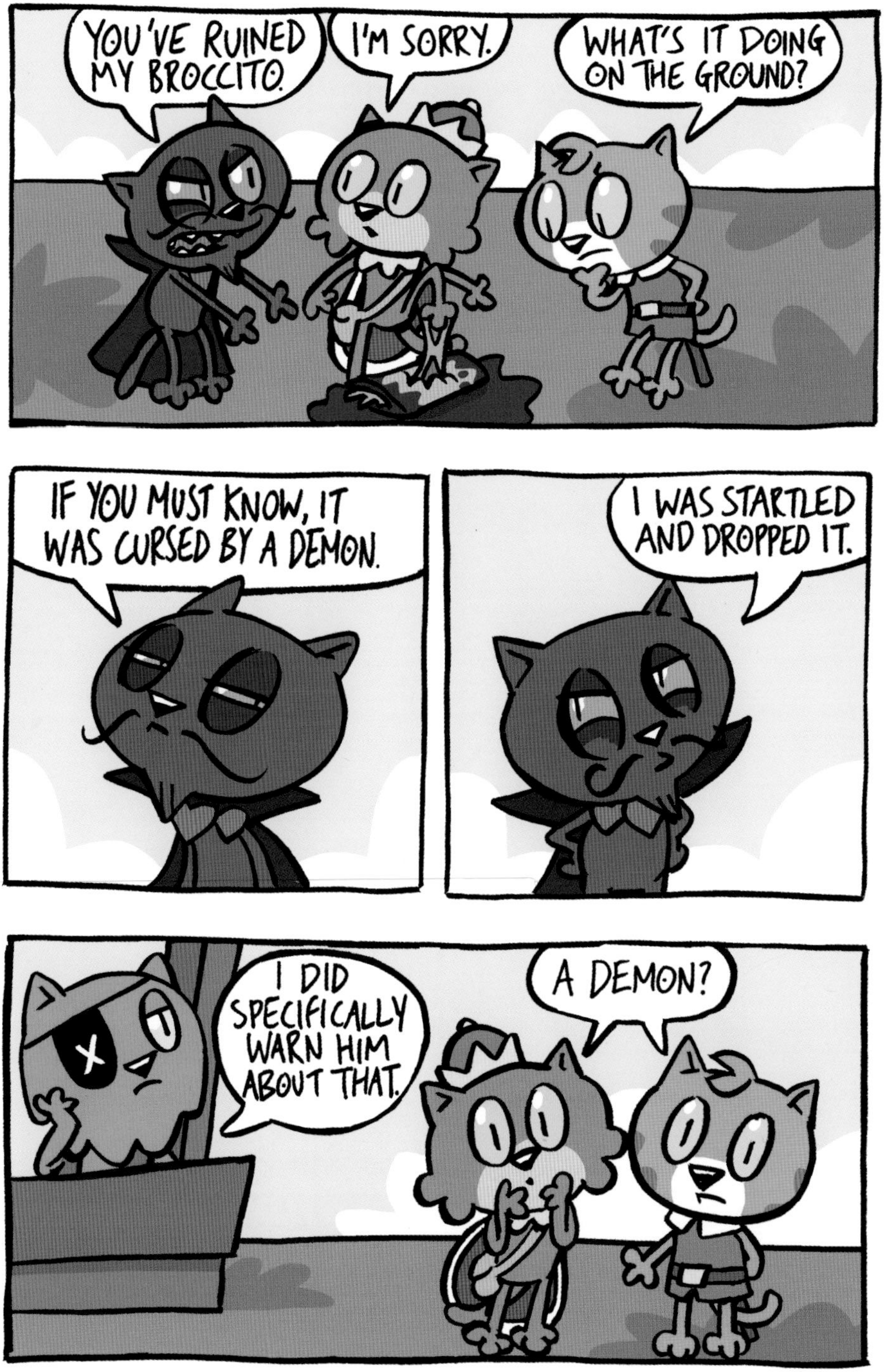

YOU'VE RUINED MY BROCCITO.
I'M SORRY.
WHAT'S IT DOING ON THE GROUND?
IF YOU MUST KNOW, IT WAS CURSED BY A DEMON.
I WAS STARTLED AND DROPPED IT.
I DID SPECIFICALLY WARN HIM ABOUT THAT.
A DEMON?

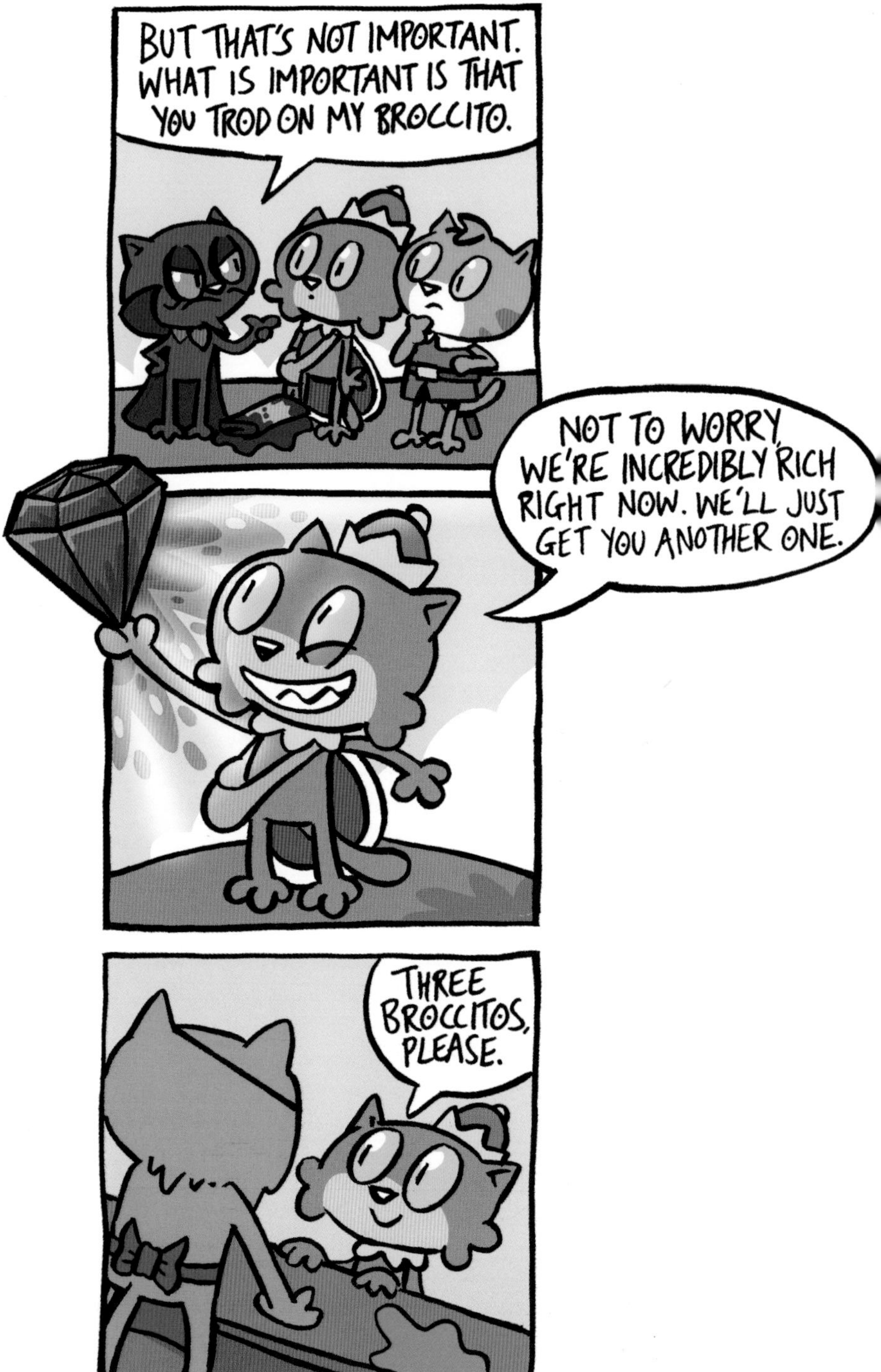
BUT THAT'S NOT IMPORTANT. WHAT IS IMPORTANT IS THAT YOU TROD ON MY BROCCITO.
NOT TO WORRY, WE'RE INCREDIBLY RICH RIGHT NOW. WE'LL JUST GET YOU ANOTHER ONE.
THREE BROCCITOS, PLEASE.

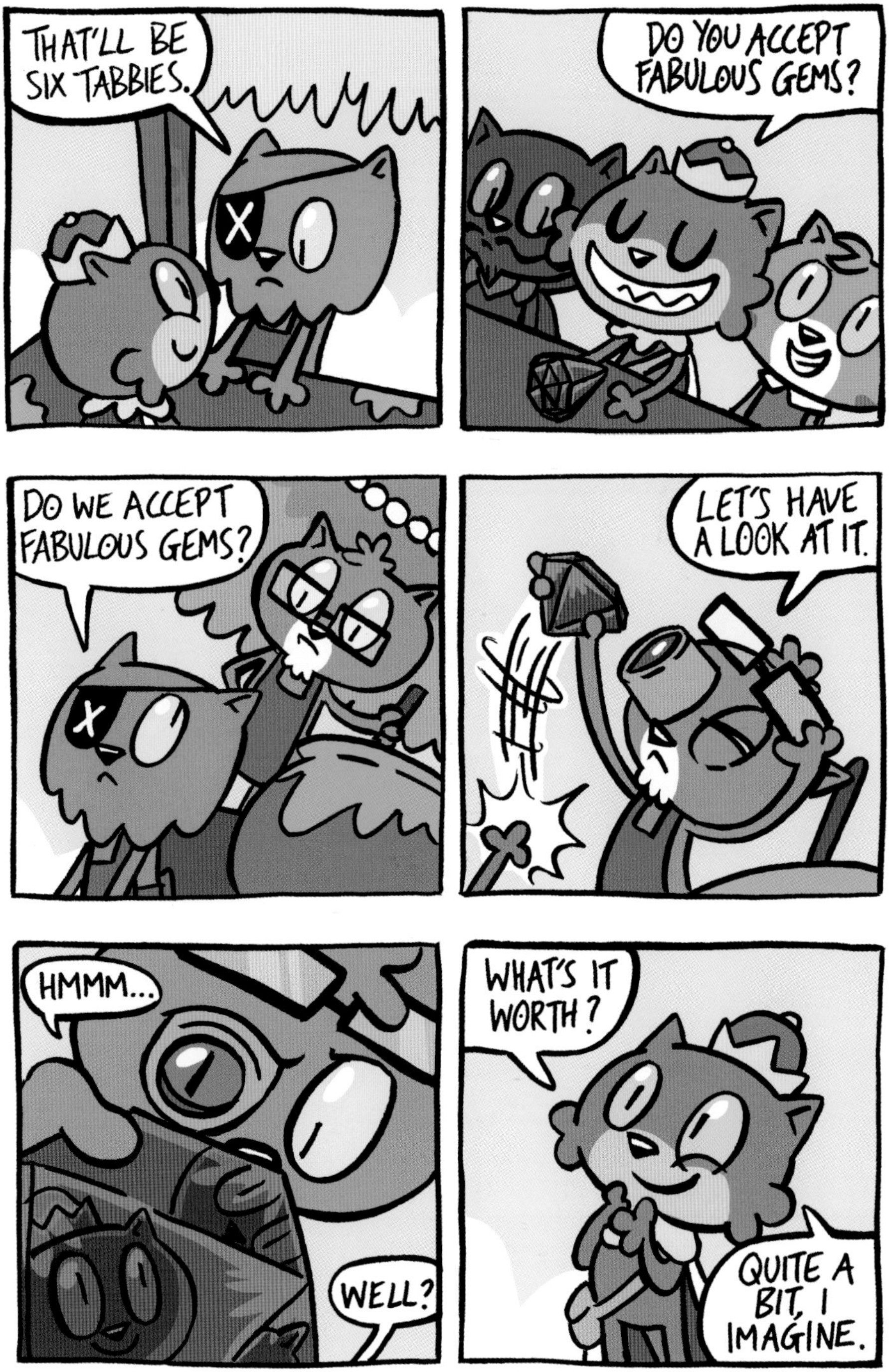
THAT'LL BE SIX TABBIES.
DO YOU ACCEPT FABULOUS GEMS?
DO WE ACCEPT FABULOUS GEMS?
LET'S HAVE A LOOK AT IT.
HMMM...
WELL?
WHAT'S IT WORTH?
QUITE A BIT, I IMAGINE.

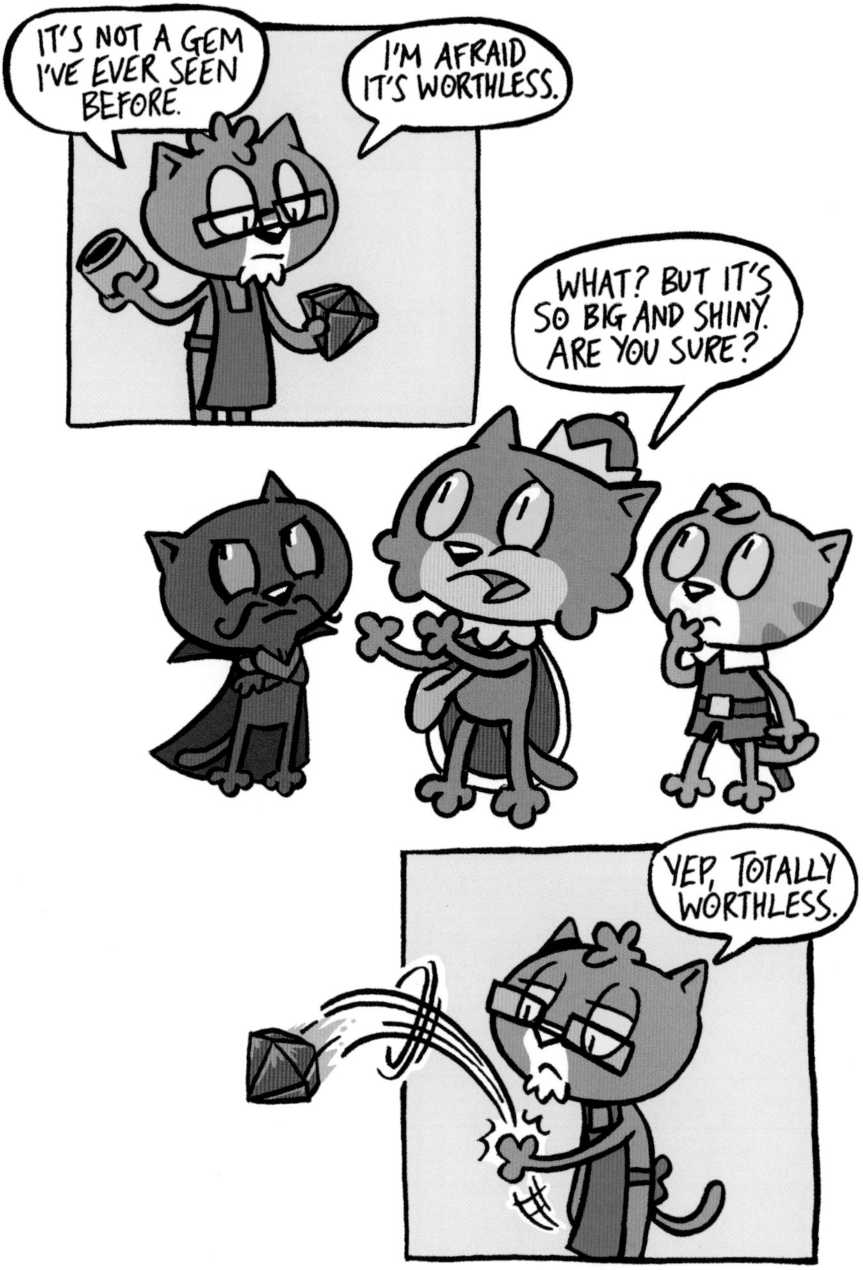
IT'S NOT A GEM I'VE EVER SEEN BEFORE.
I'M AFRAID IT'S WORTHLESS.
WHAT? BUT IT'S SO BIG AND SHINY. ARE YOU SURE?
YEP, TOTALLY WORTHLESS.

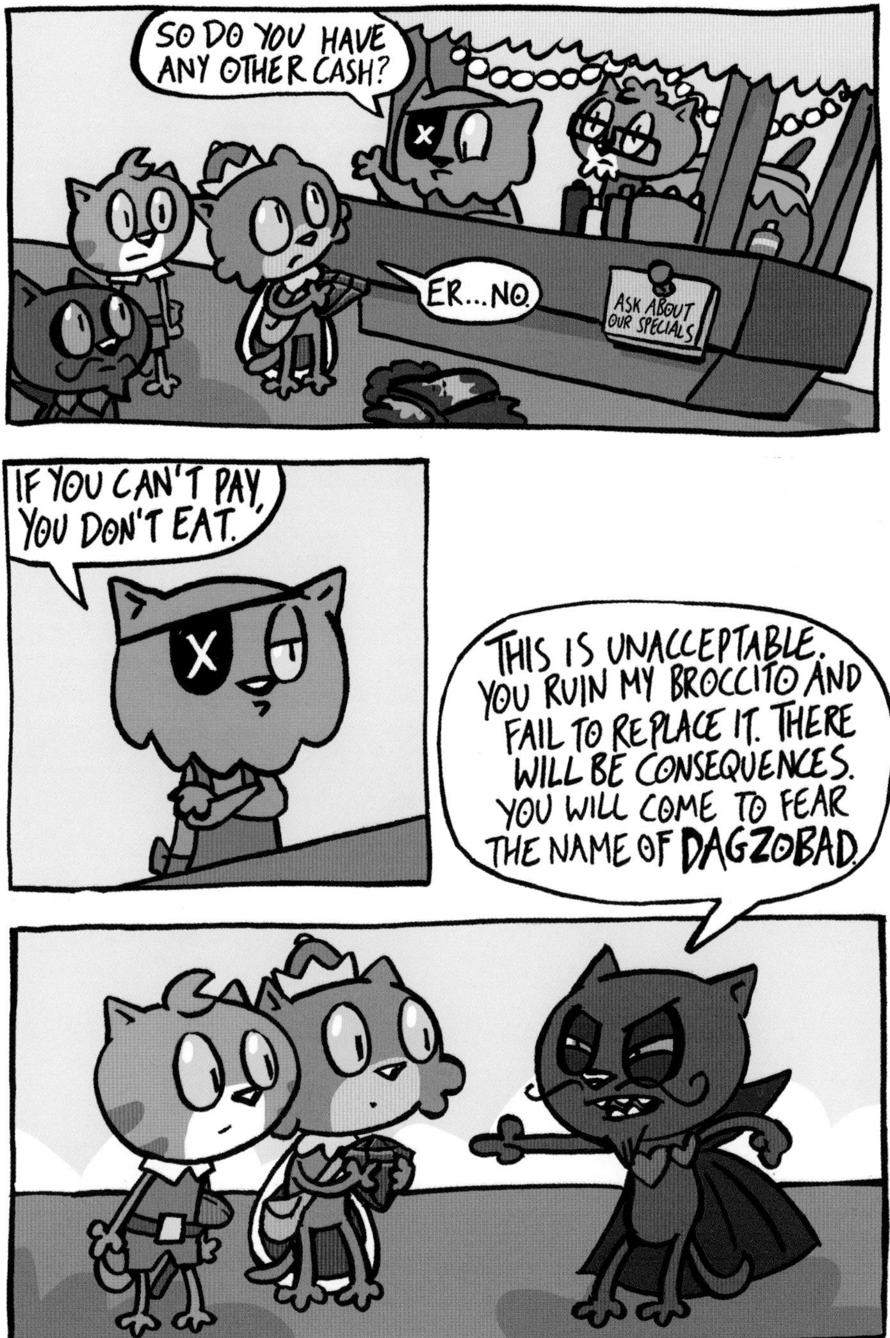
SO DO YOU HAVE ANY OTHER CASH?
ER...NO.
ASK ABOUT OUR SPECIALS
IF YOU CAN'T PAY, YOU DON'T EAT.
THIS IS UNACCEPTABLE. YOU RUIN MY BROCCITO AND FAIL TO REPLACE IT. THERE WILL BE CONSEQUENCES. YOU WILL COME TO FEAR THE NAME OF DAGZOBAD.

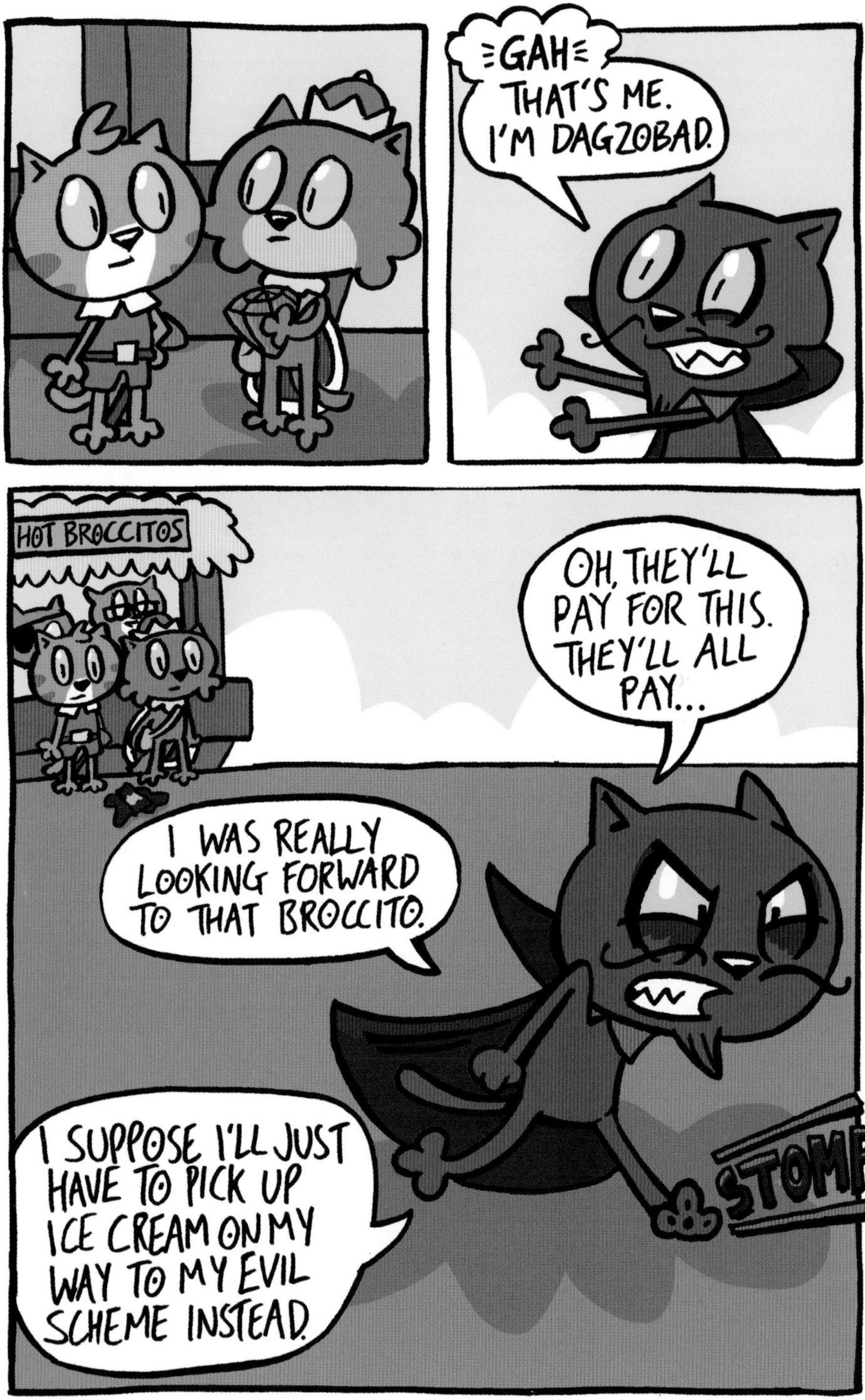
GAH
THAT'S ME. I'M DAGZOBAD.
HOT BROCCITOS
OH, THEY'LL PAY FOR THIS. THEY'LL ALL PAY...
I WAS REALLY LOOKING FORWARD TO THAT BROCCITO.
STOMP
I SUPPOSE I'LL JUST HAVE TO PICK UP ICE CREAM ON MY WAY TO MY EVIL SCHEME INSTEAD.

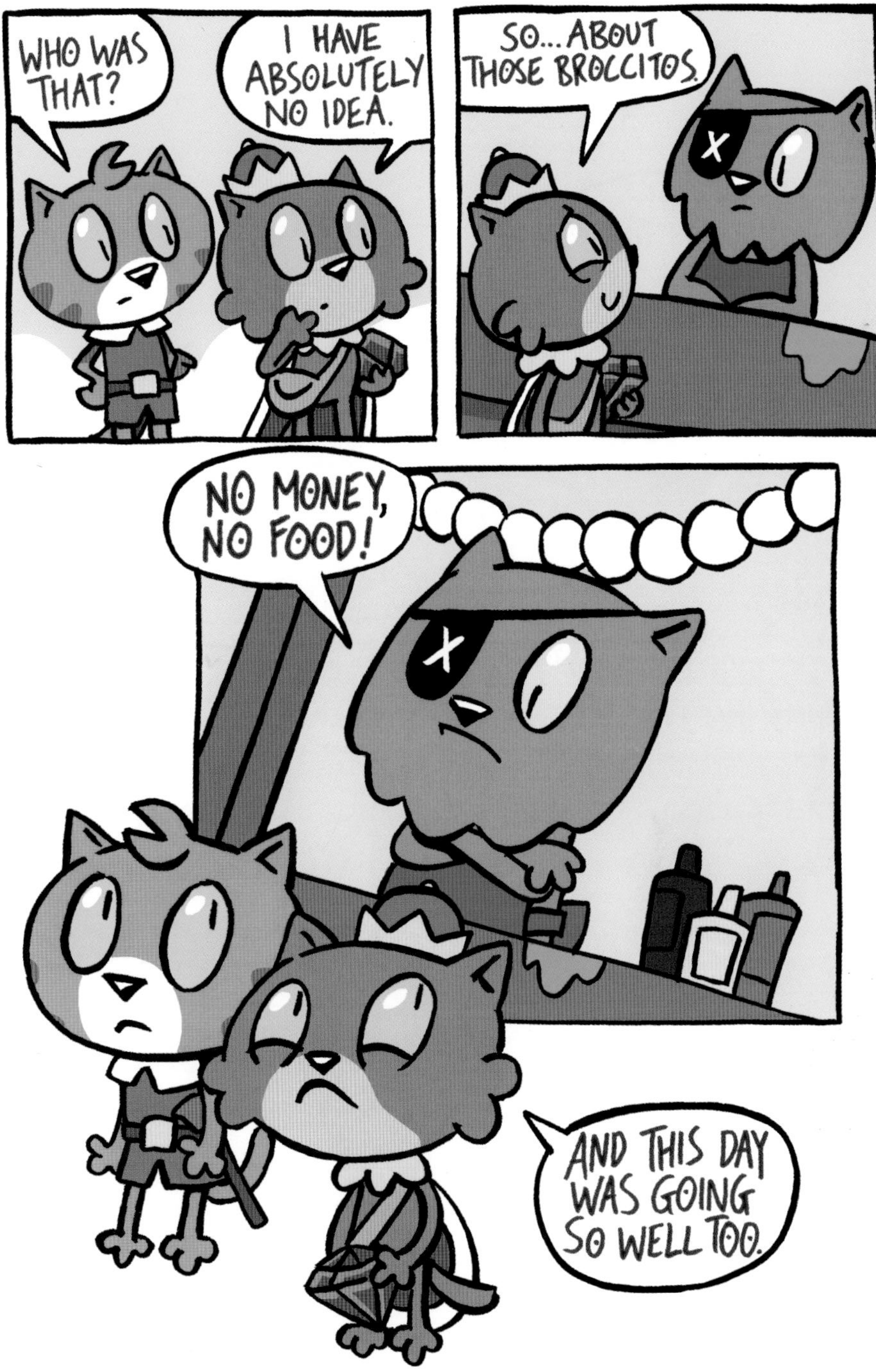
WHO WAS THAT?
I HAVE ABSOLUTELY NO IDEA.
SO... ABOUT THOSE BROCCITOS.
NO MONEY, NO FOOD!
AND THIS DAY WAS GOING SO WELL TOO.

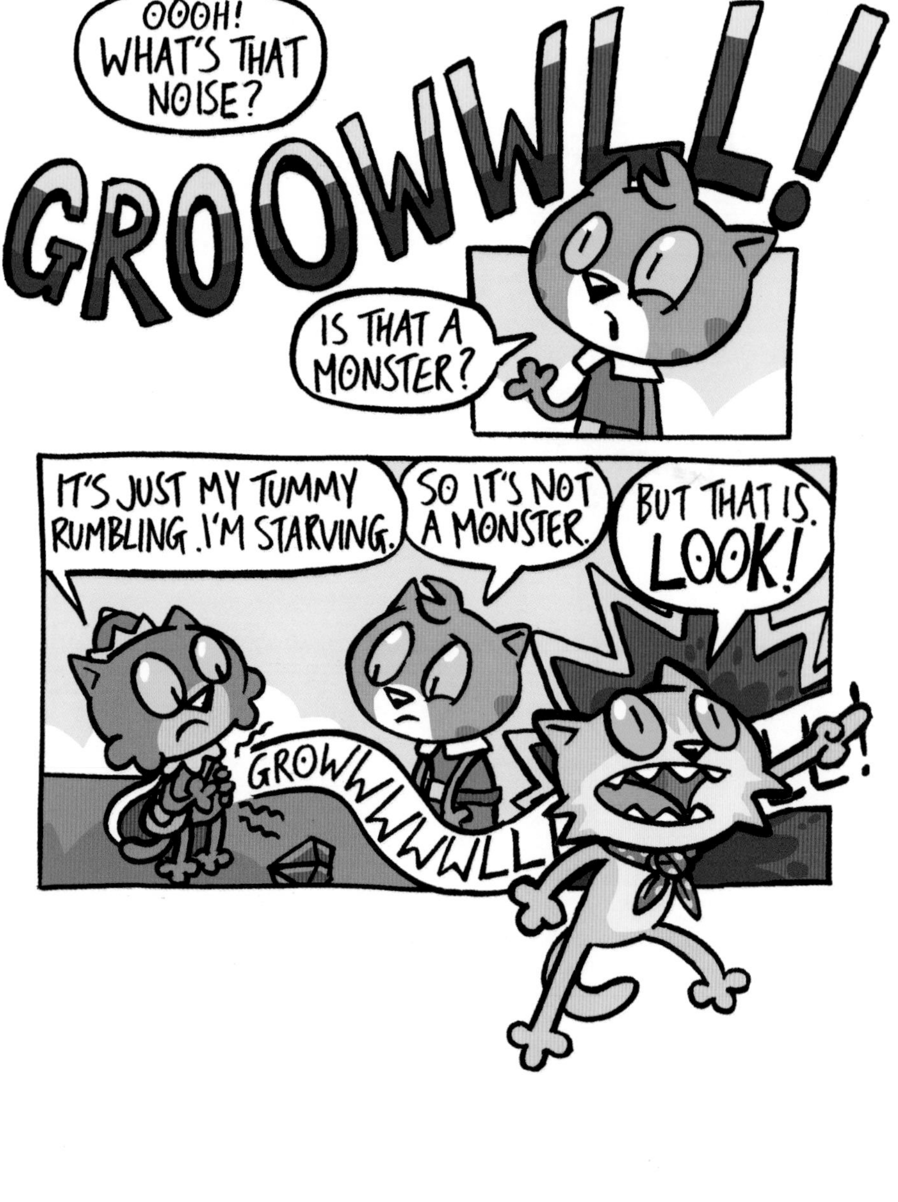
OOOH! WHAT'S THAT NOISE?
GROOWLL!
IS THAT A MONSTER?
IT'S JUST MY TUMMY RUMBLING. I'M STARVING.
GROWWWWWWLL
SO IT'S NOT A MONSTER.
BUT THAT IS. LOOK!

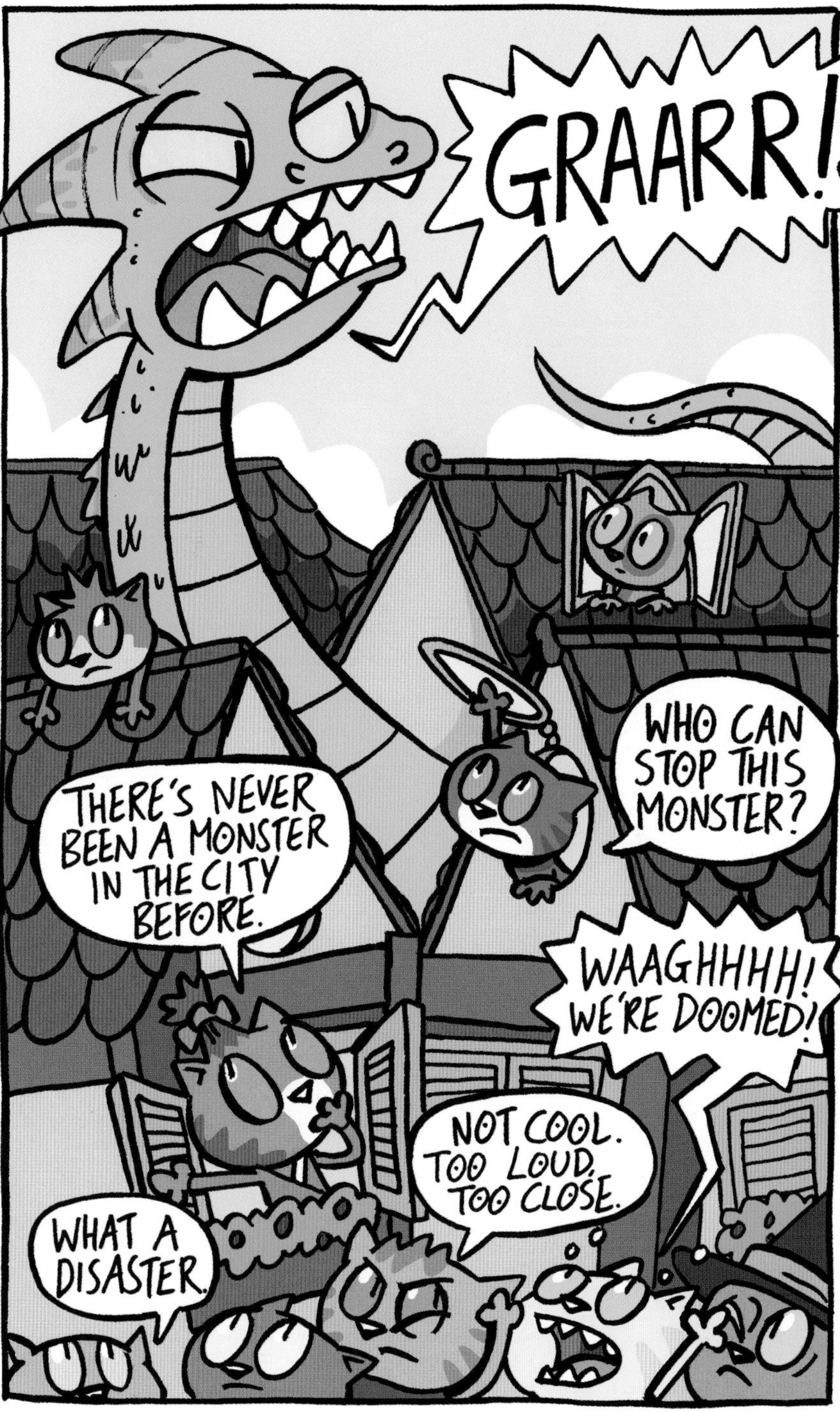
GRAARR!
WHO CAN STOP THIS MONSTER?
THERE'S NEVER BEEN A MONSTER IN THE CITY BEFORE.
WAAGHHHH! WE'RE DOOMED!
NOT COOL. TOO LOUD. TOO CLOSE.
WHAT A DISASTER.

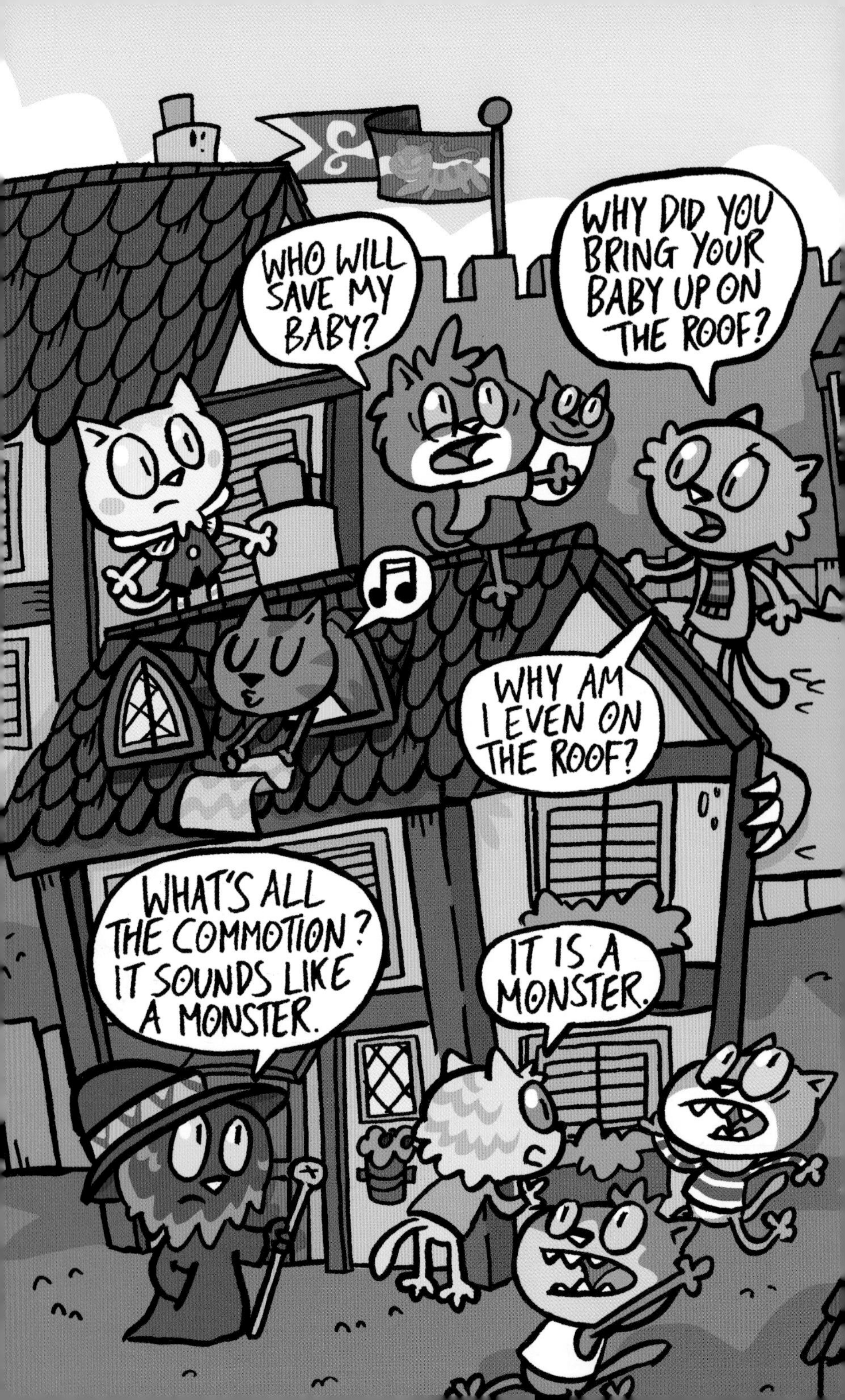
WHO WILL SAVE MY BABY?
WHY DID YOU BRING YOUR BABY UP ON THE ROOF?
WHY AM I EVEN ON THE ROOF?
WHAT'S ALL THE COMMOTION? IT SOUNDS LIKE A MONSTER.
IT IS A MONSTER.

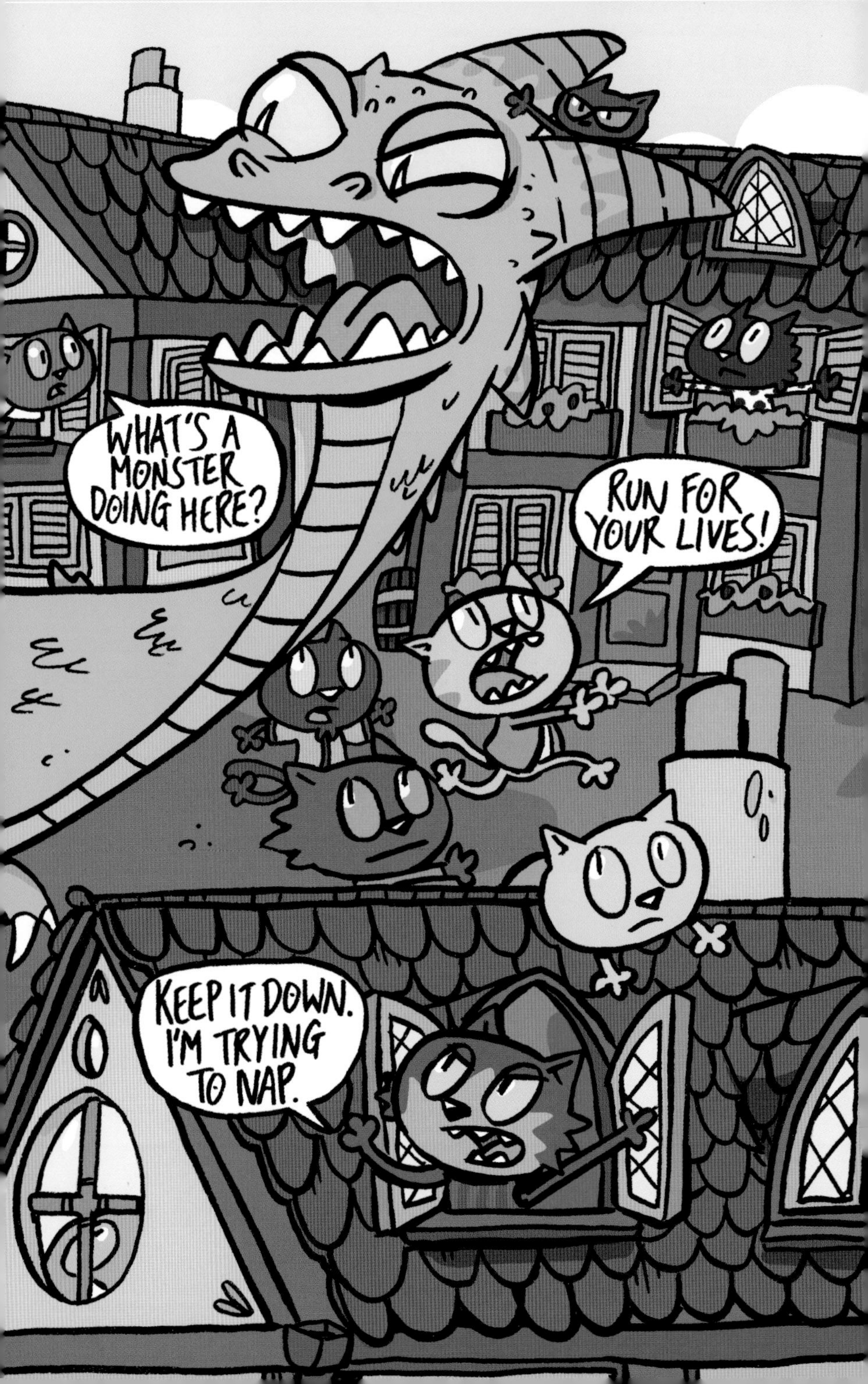
WHAT'S A MONSTER DOING HERE?
RUN FOR YOUR LIVES!
KEEP IT DOWN. I'M TRYING TO NAP.

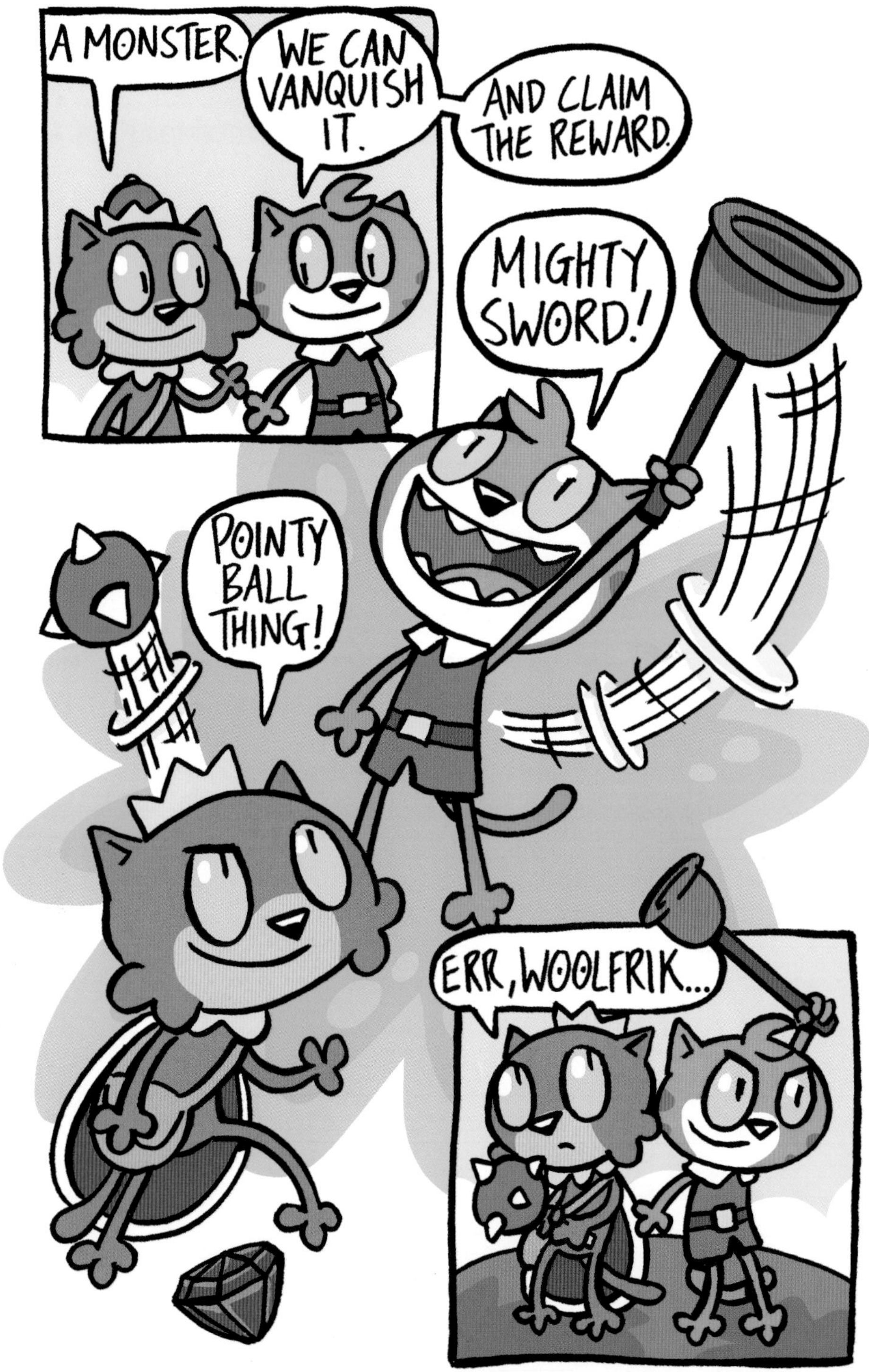
A MONSTER.
WE CAN VANQUISH IT.
AND CLAIM THE REWARD.
MIGHTY SWORD!
POINTY BALL THING!
ERR, WOOLFRIK...

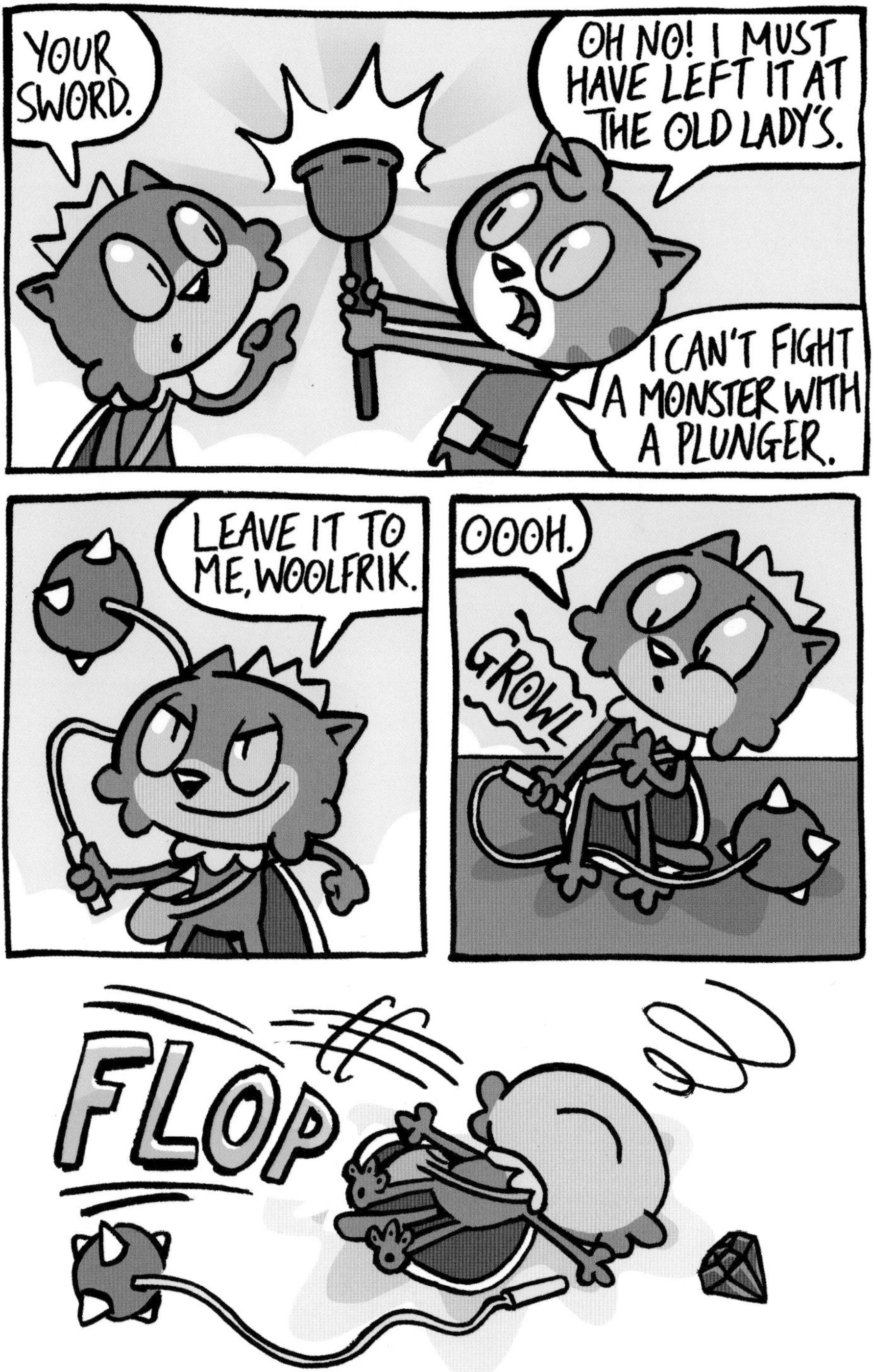
YOUR SWORD.
OH NO! I MUST HAVE LEFT IT AT THE OLD LADY'S.
I CAN'T FIGHT A MONSTER WITH A PLUNGER.
LEAVE IT TO ME, WOOLFRIK.
OOOH.
GROWL
FLOP

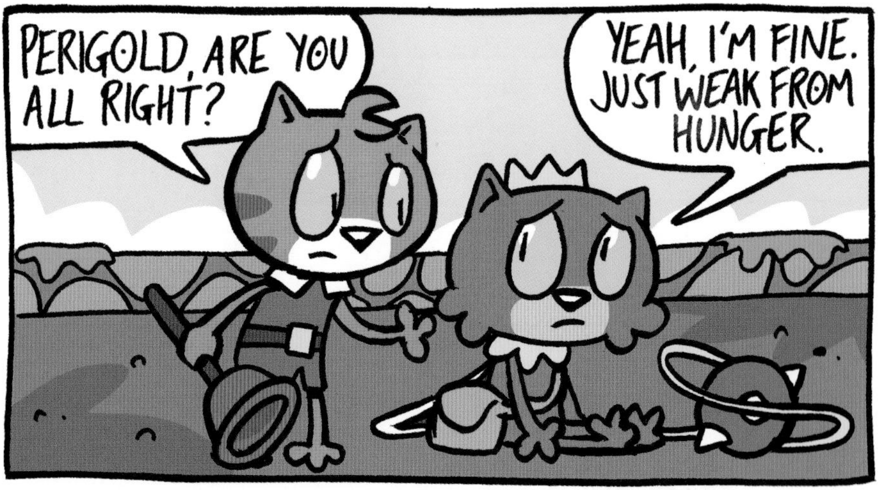
PERIGOLD, ARE YOU ALL RIGHT?
YEAH, I'M FINE. JUST WEAK FROM HUNGER.

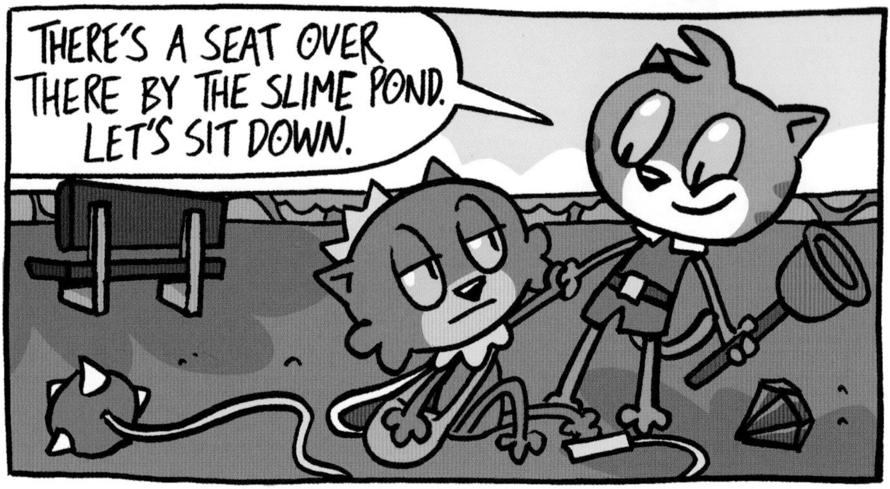
THERE'S A SEAT OVER THERE BY THE SLIME POND. LET'S SIT DOWN.

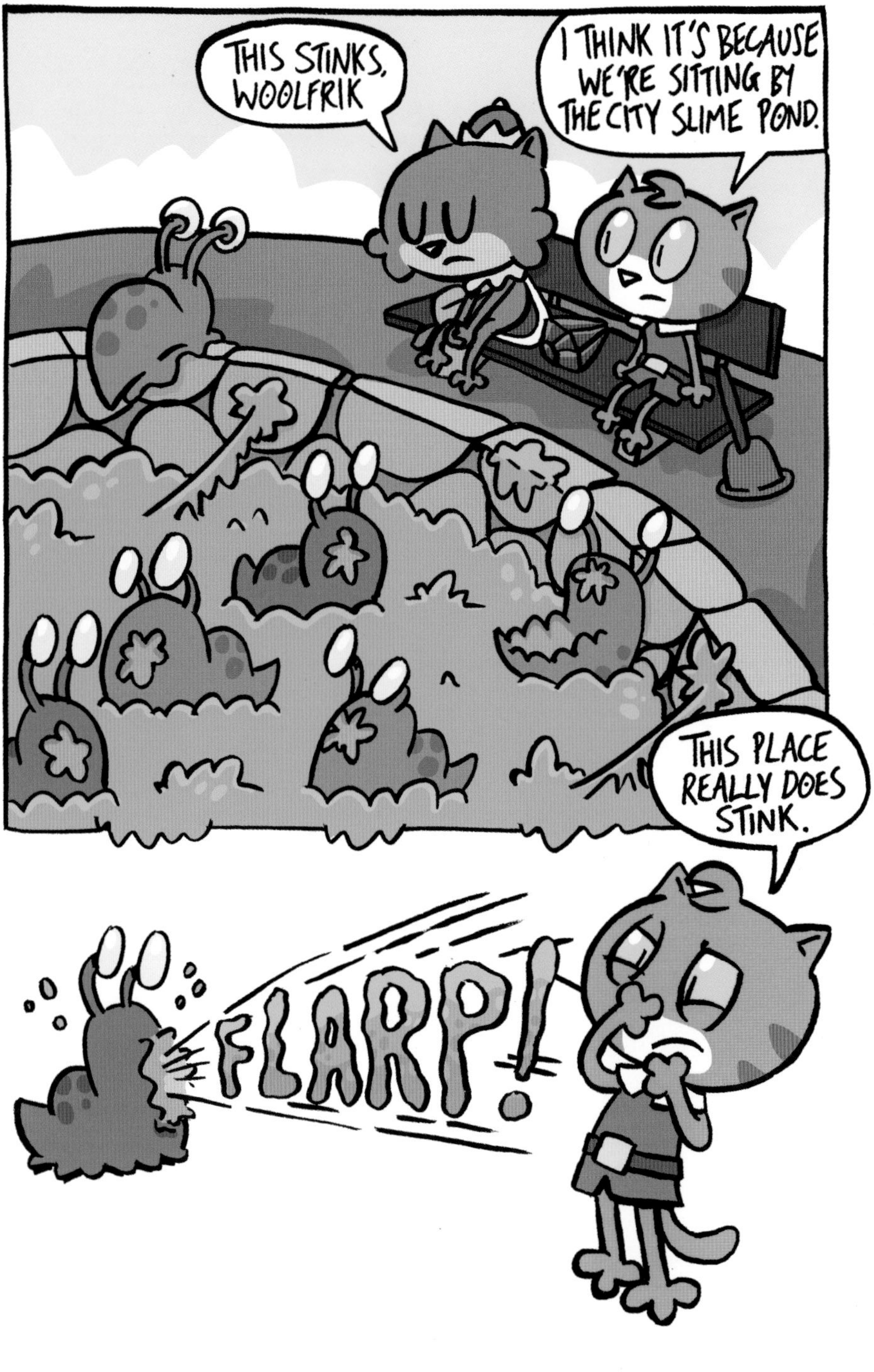
THIS STINKS, WOOLFRIK
I THINK IT'S BECAUSE WE'RE SITTING BY THE CITY SLIME POND.
THIS PLACE REALLY DOES STINK.
FLARP!

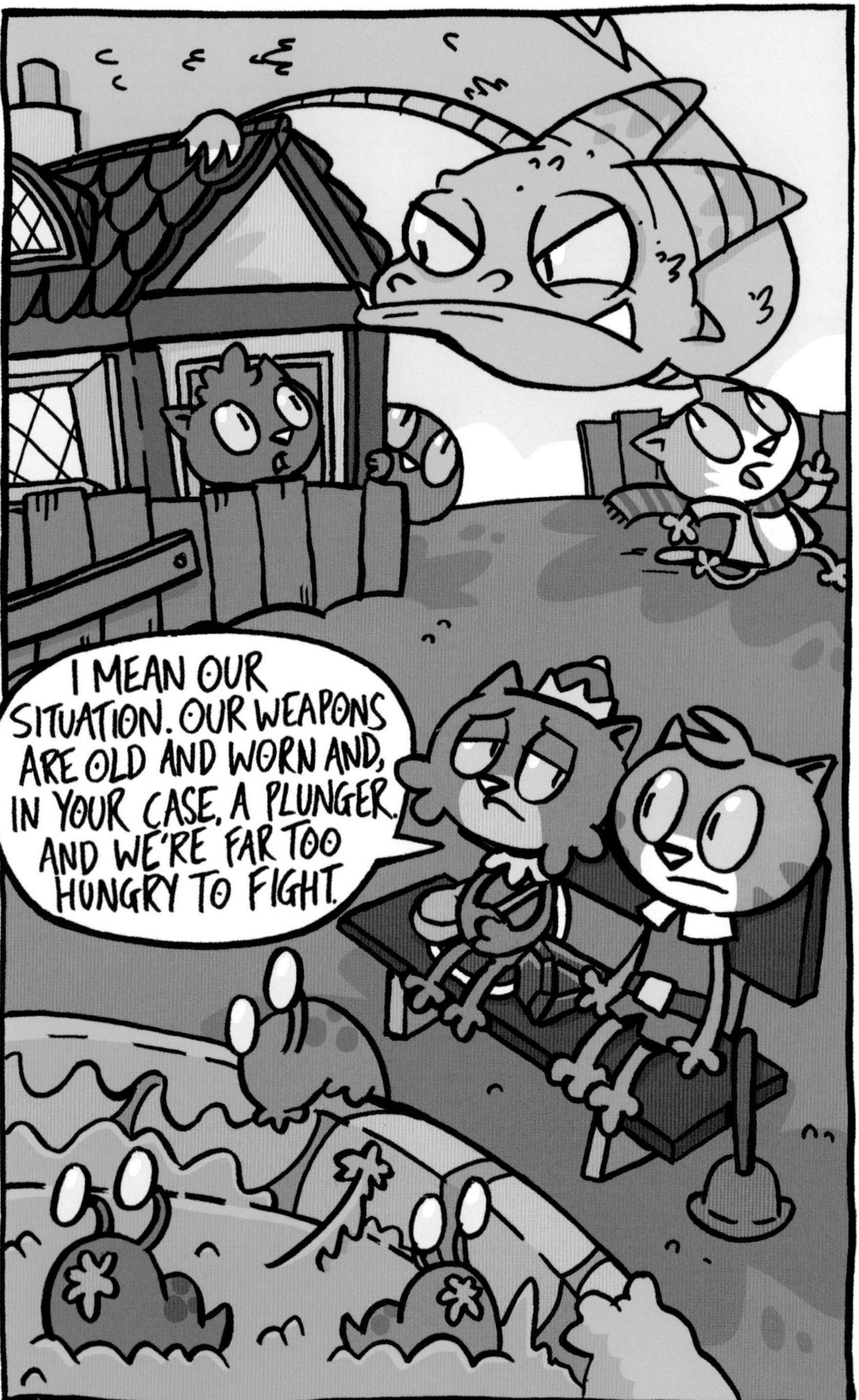
I MEAN OUR SITUATION. OUR WEAPONS ARE OLD AND WORN AND, IN YOUR CASE, A PLUNGER. AND WE'RE FAR TOO HUNGRY TO FIGHT.

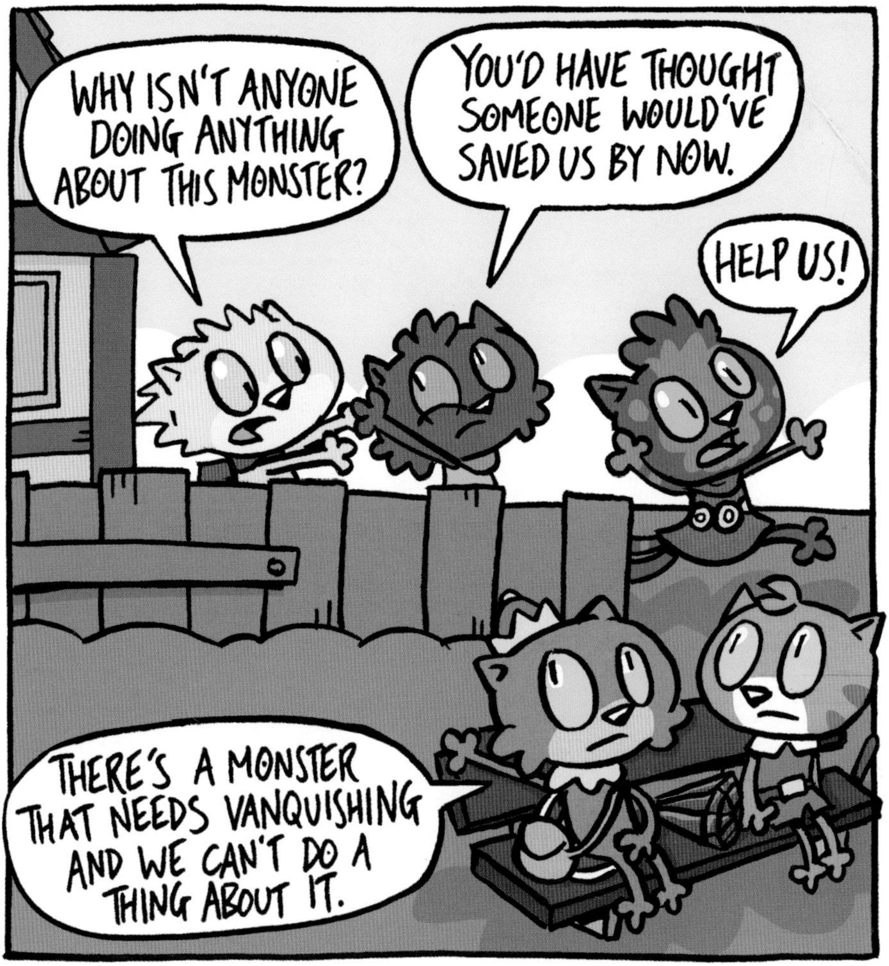
WHY ISN'T ANYONE DOING ANYTHING ABOUT THIS MONSTER?
YOU'D HAVE THOUGHT SOMEONE WOULD'VE SAVED US BY NOW.
HELP US!
THERE'S A MONSTER THAT NEEDS VANQUISHING AND WE CAN'T DO A THING ABOUT IT.

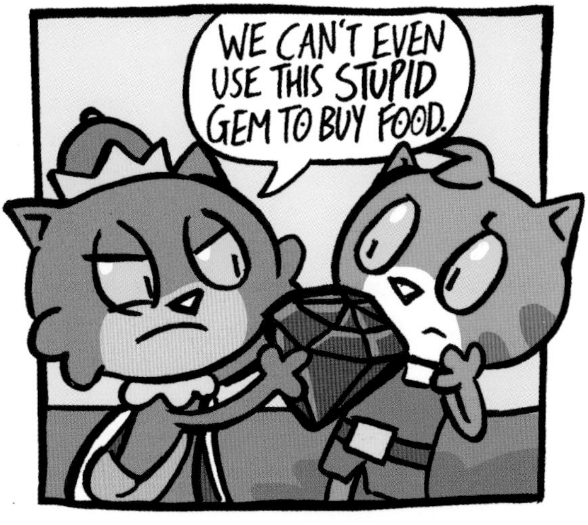
WE CAN'T EVEN USE THIS STUPID GEM TO BUY FOOD.

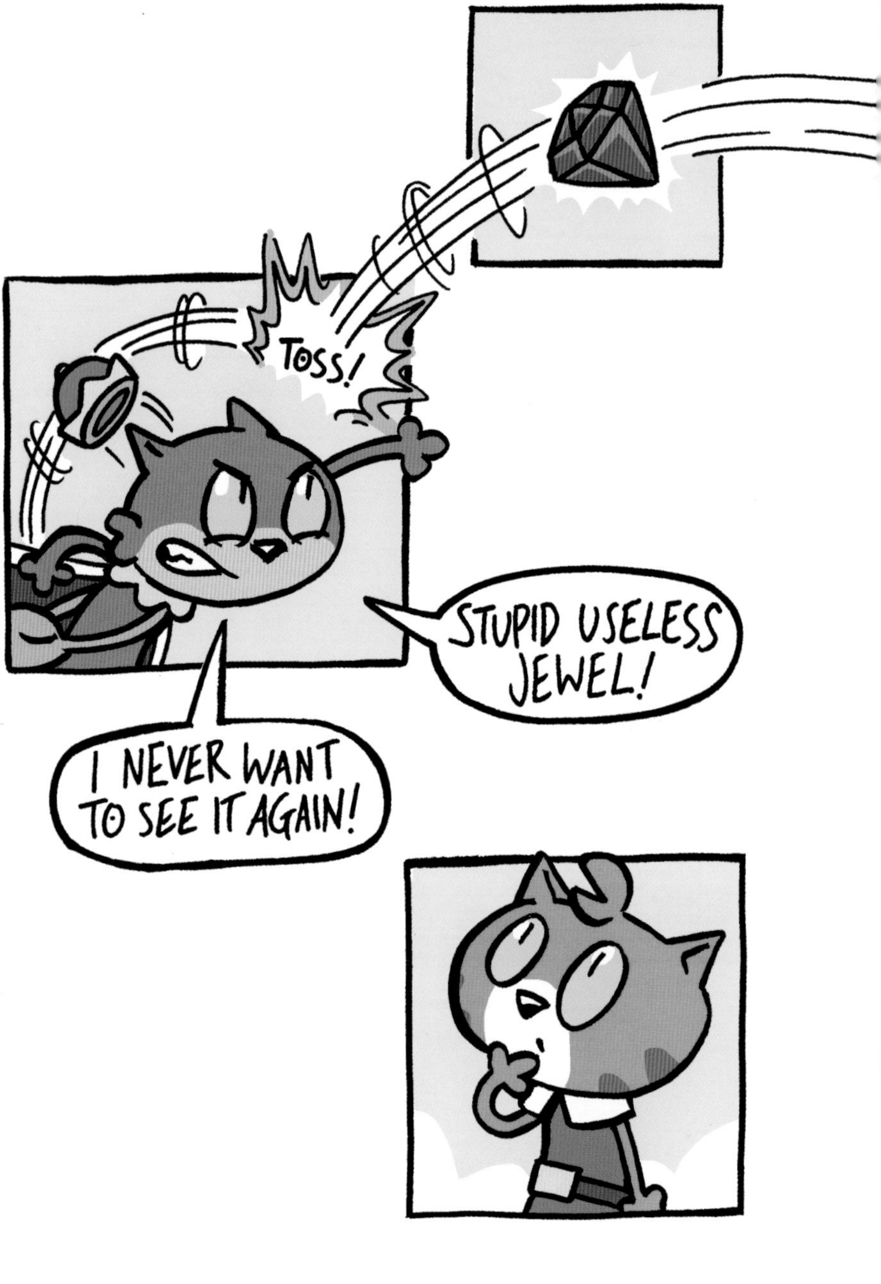
TOSS!
STUPID USELESS JEWEL!
I NEVER WANT TO SEE IT AGAIN!

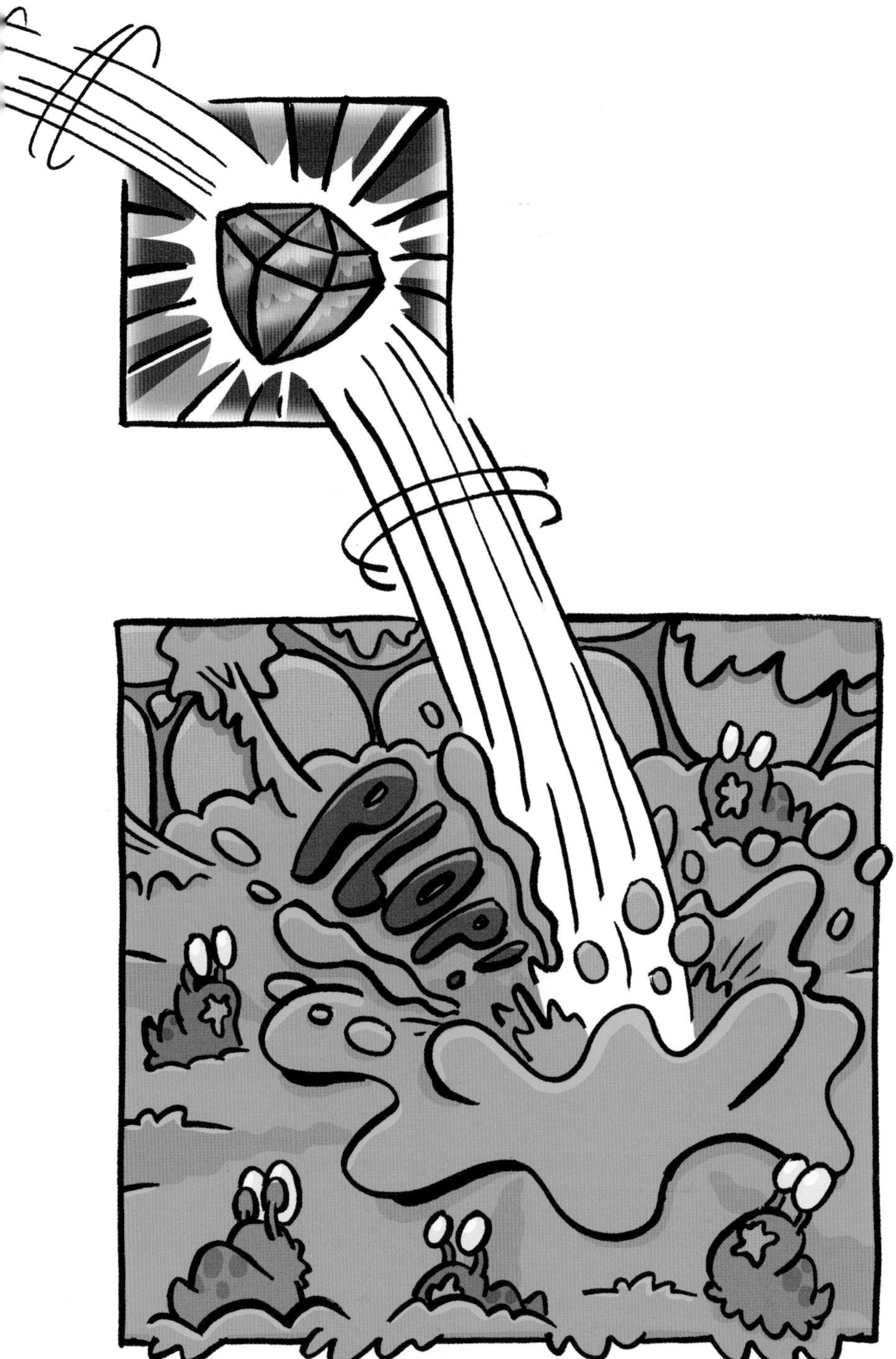
PLOP!

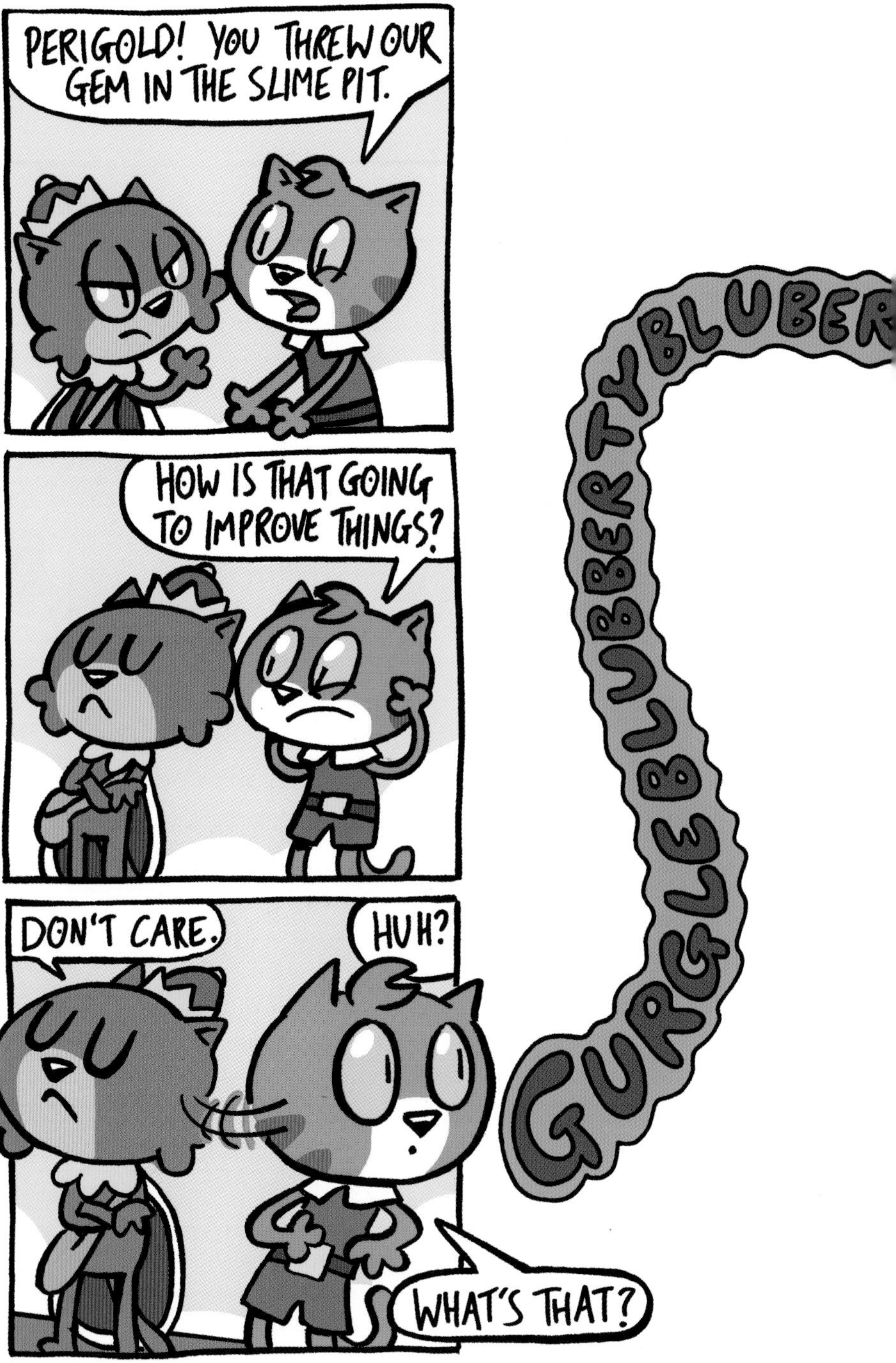
PERIGOLD! YOU THREW OUR GEM IN THE SLIME PIT.
HOW IS THAT GOING TO IMPROVE THINGS?
DON'T CARE.
HUH?
GURGLEBLUBLUBBERBERTYBLUBER
WHAT'S THAT?

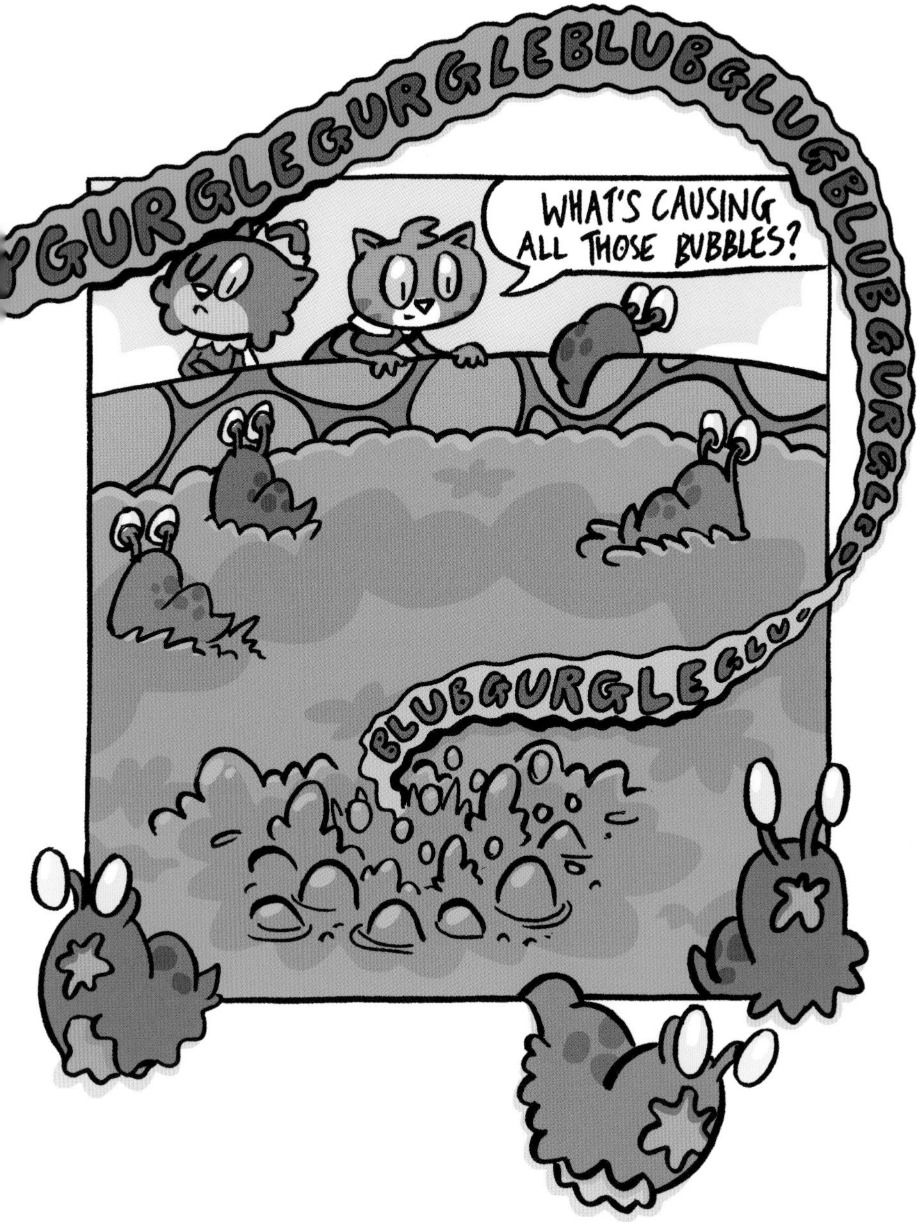

YGURGLEGURGLEBLUBGLUGBLUBGURGL
WHAT'S CAUSING ALL THOSE BUBBLES?
BLUBGURGLEGLU

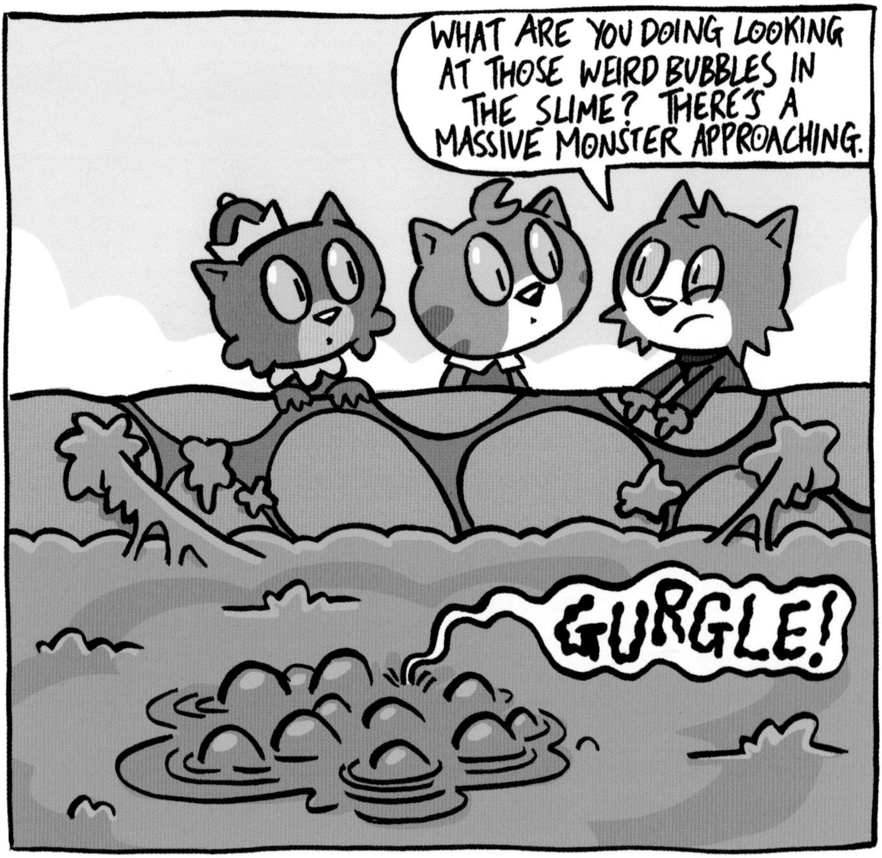
WHAT ARE YOU DOING LOOKING AT THOSE WEIRD BUBBLES IN THE SLIME? THERE'S A MASSIVE MONSTER APPROACHING.
GURGLE!

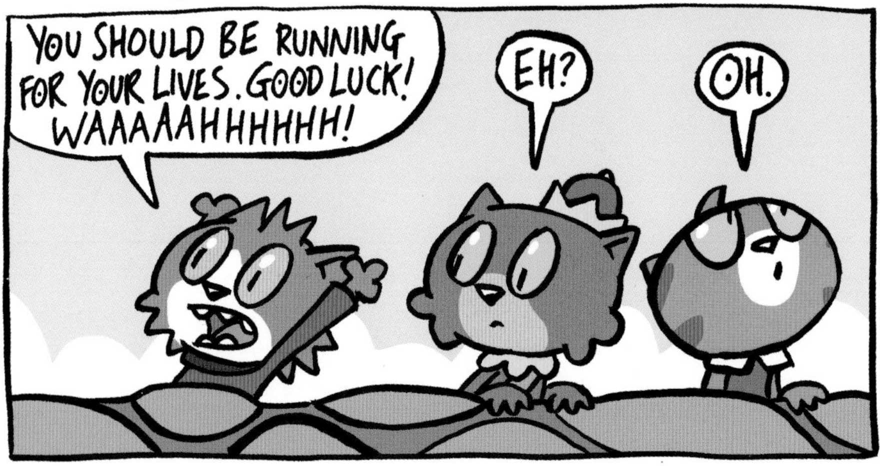
YOU SHOULD BE RUNNING FOR YOUR LIVES. GOOD LUCK! WAAAAAHHHHHH!
EH?
OH.

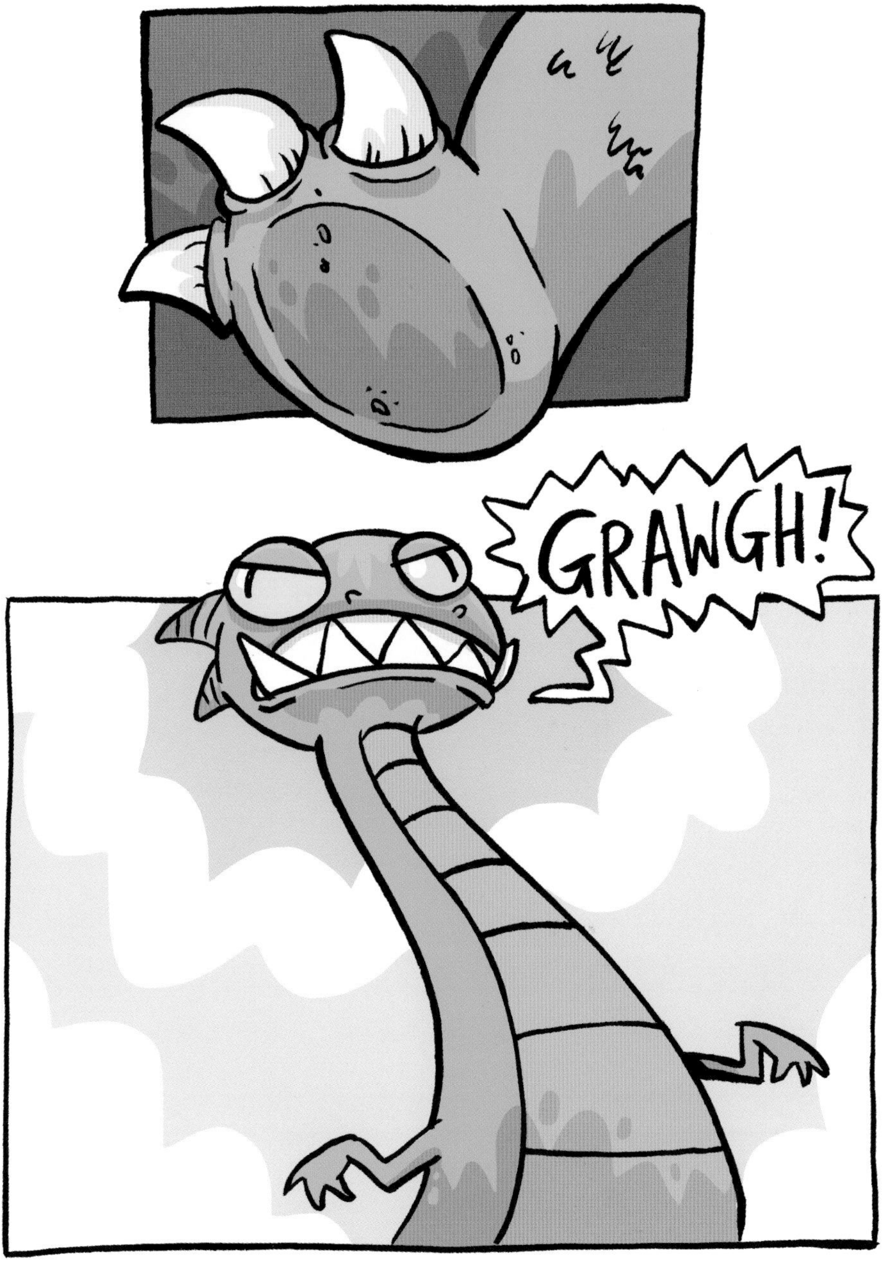
GRAWGH!

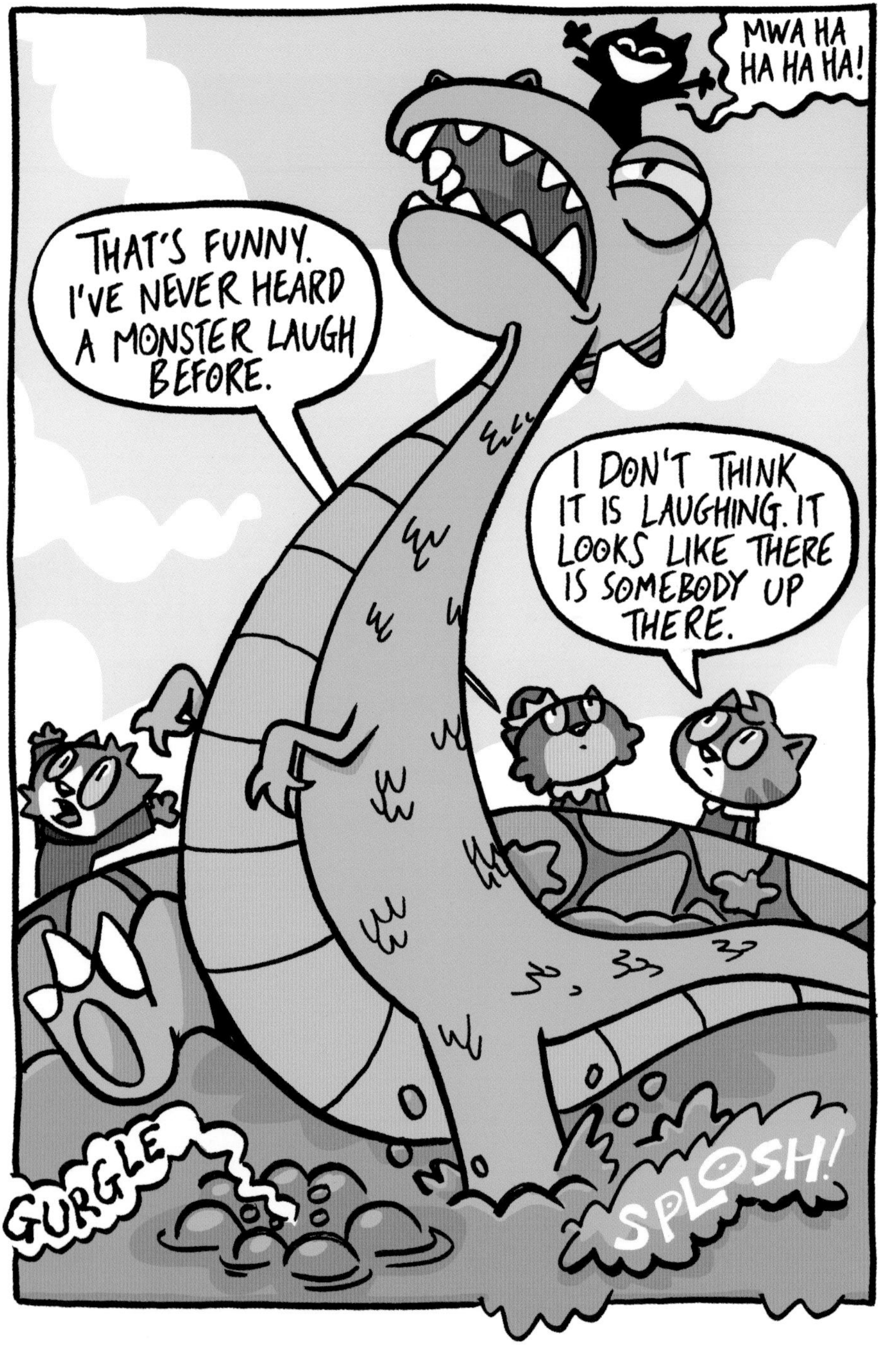
MWA HA HA HA HA!
THAT'S FUNNY. I'VE NEVER HEARD A MONSTER LAUGH BEFORE.
I DON'T THINK IT IS LAUGHING. IT LOOKS LIKE THERE IS SOMEBODY UP THERE.
GURGLE
SPLOSH!

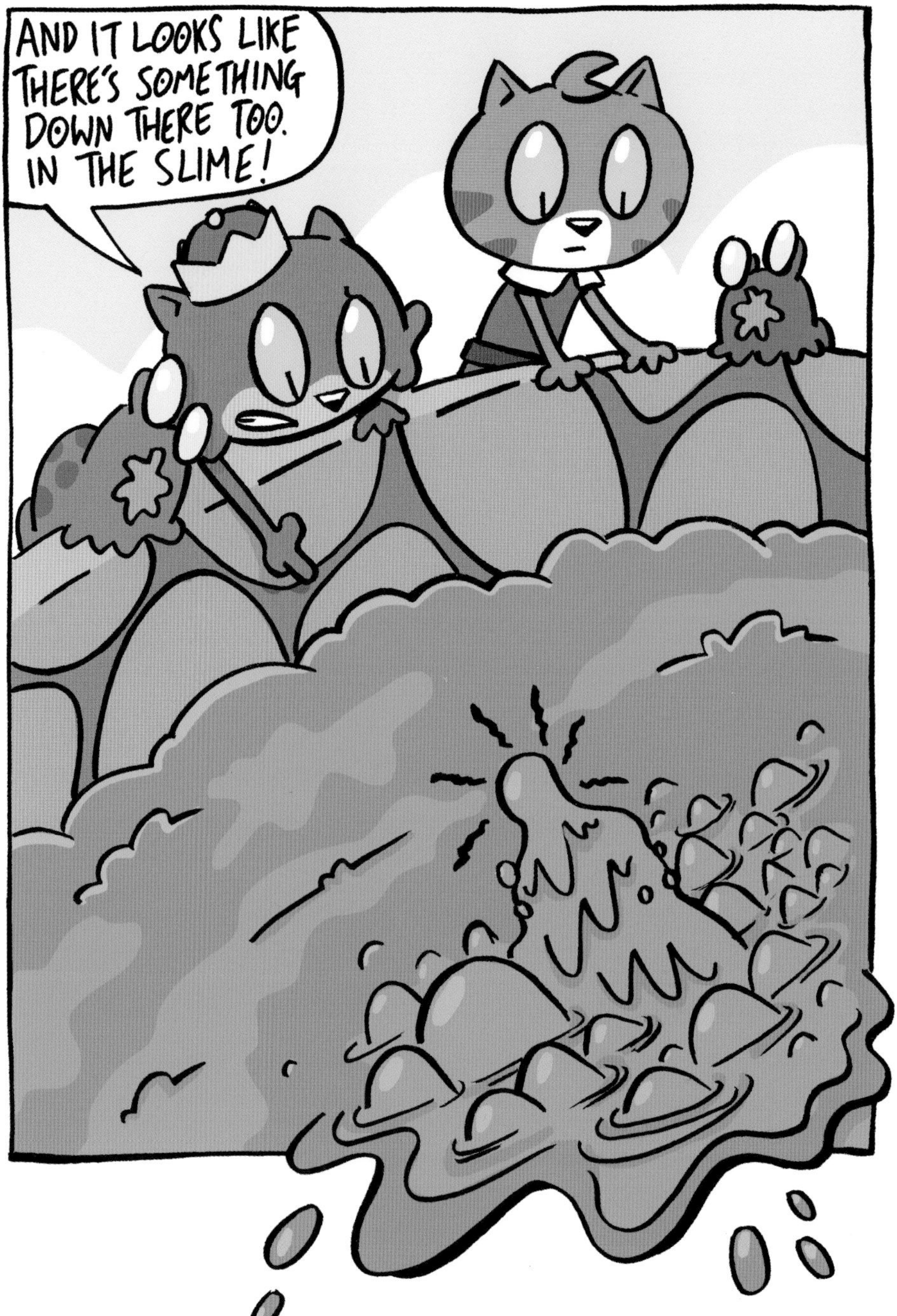
AND IT LOOKS LIKE THERE'S SOMETHING DOWN THERE TOO. IN THE SLIME!

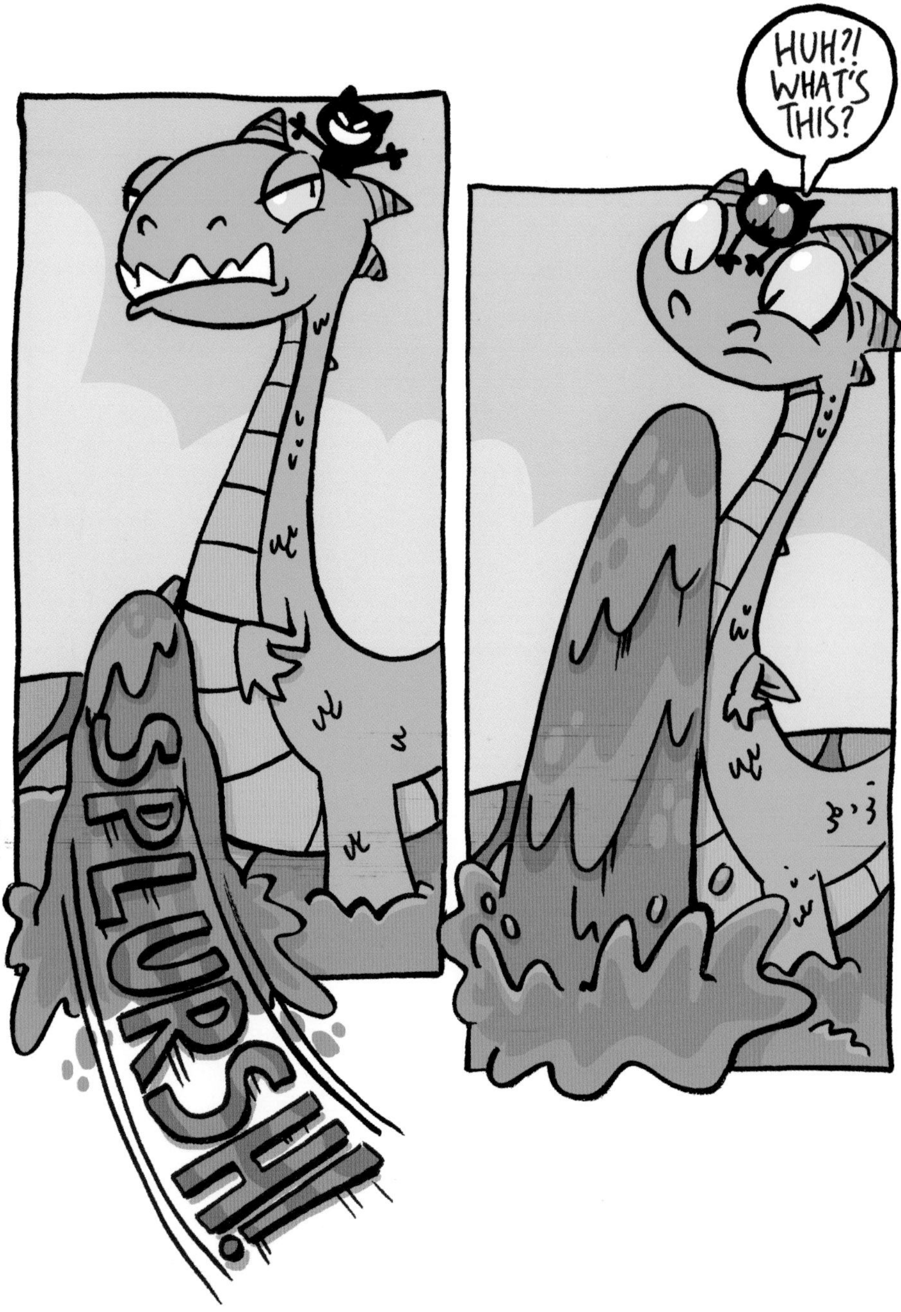
SPLURSH!
HUH?! WHAT'S THIS?

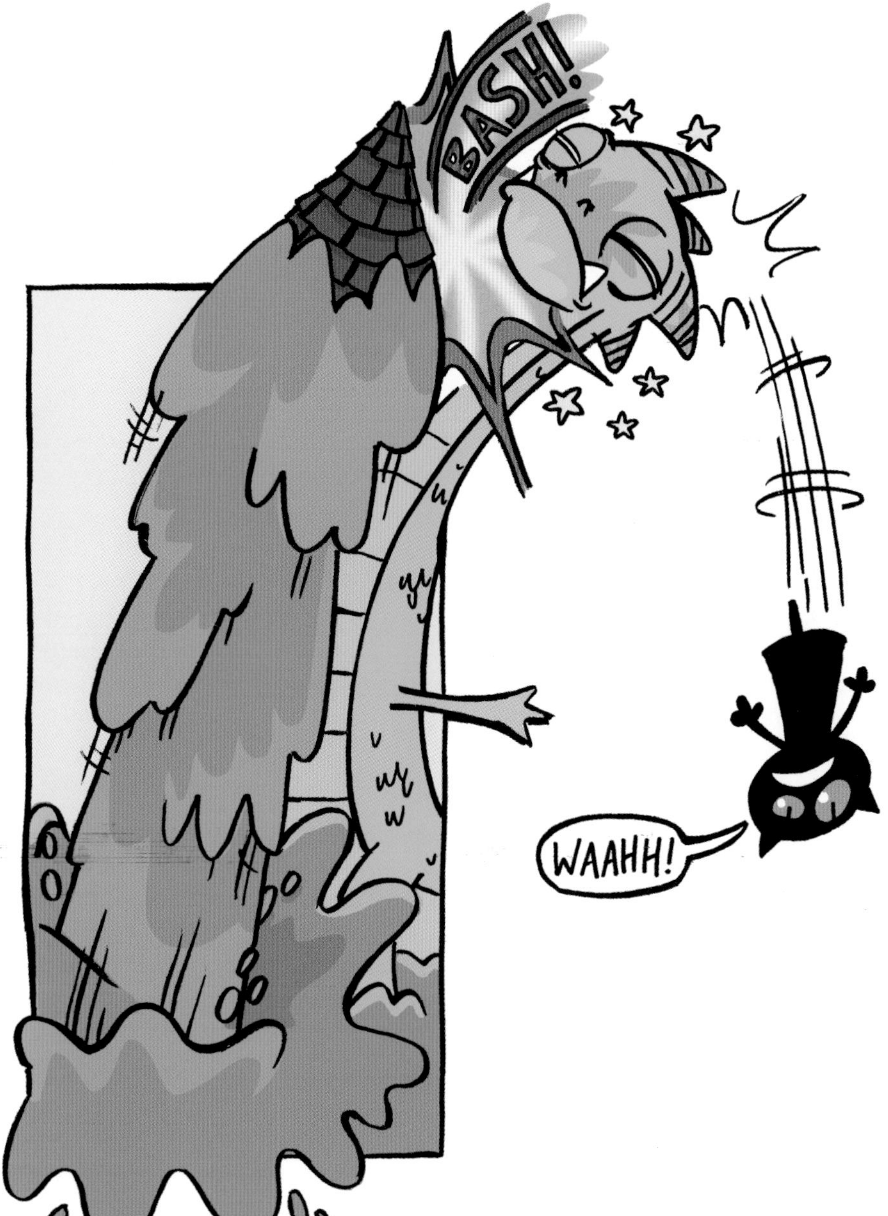
BASH!
WAAHH!

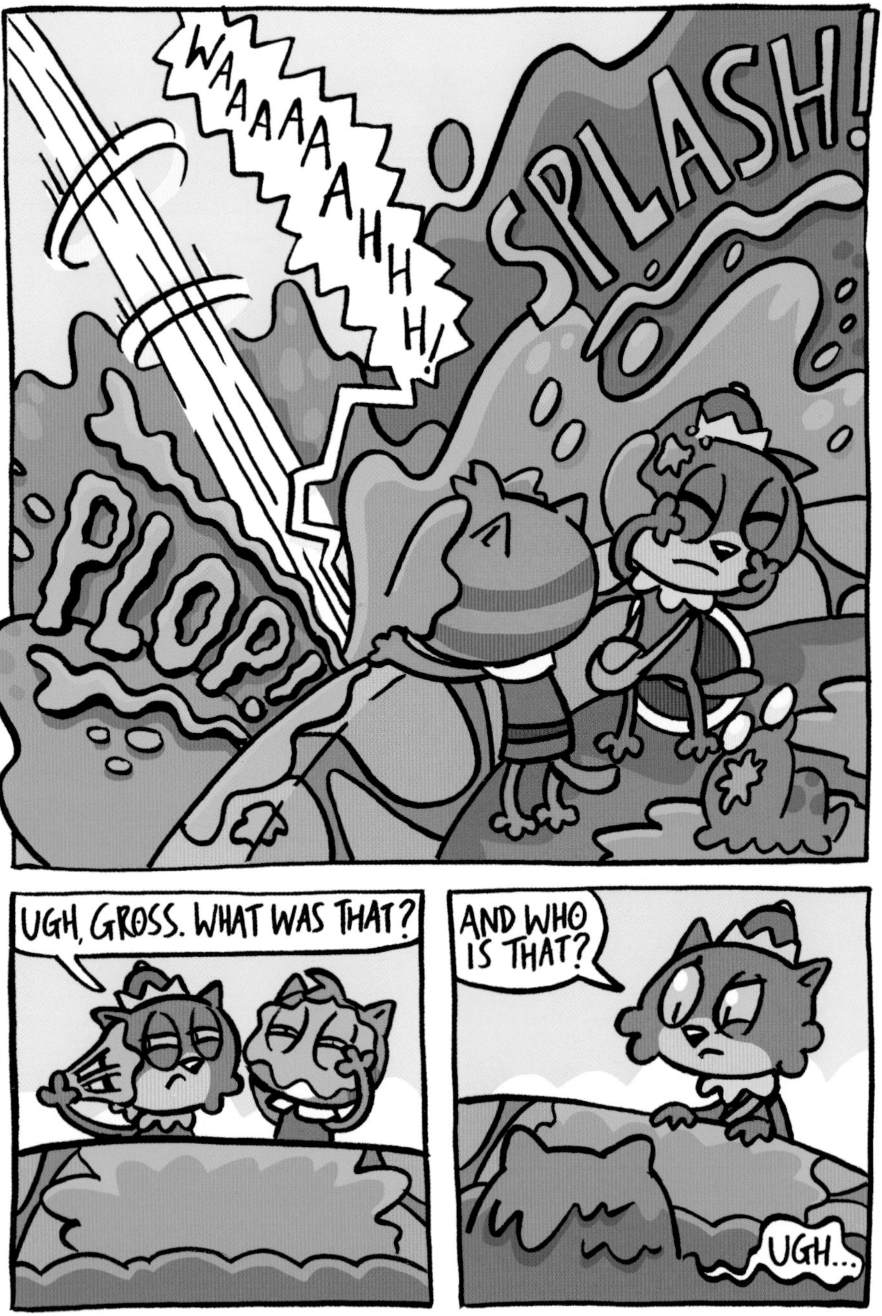
WAAAAAAHHHH!
SPLASH!
PLOP!
UGH, GROSS. WHAT WAS THAT?
AND WHO IS THAT?
UGH...

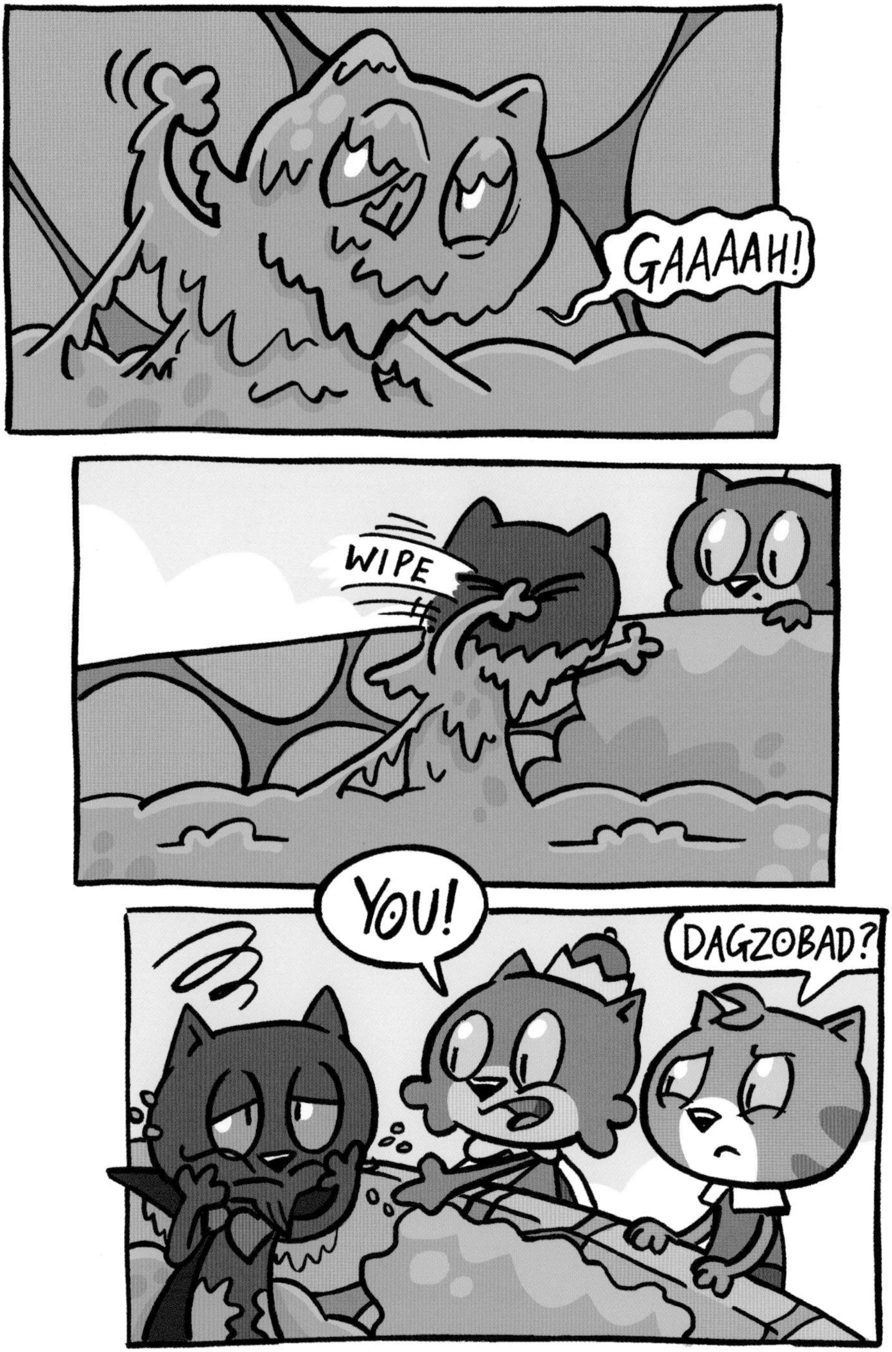
GAAAAH!
WIPE
YOU!
DAGZOBAD?

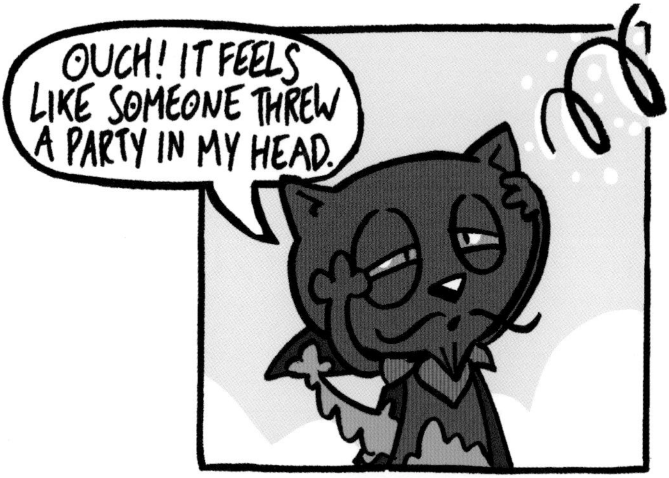
OUCH! IT FEELS LIKE SOMEONE THREW A PARTY IN MY HEAD.

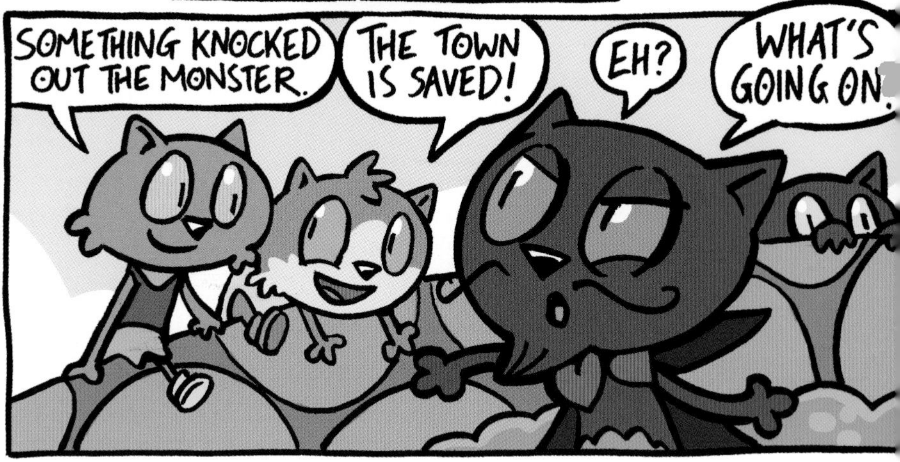
SOMETHING KNOCKED OUT THE MONSTER.
THE TOWN IS SAVED!
EH?
WHAT'S GOING ON?

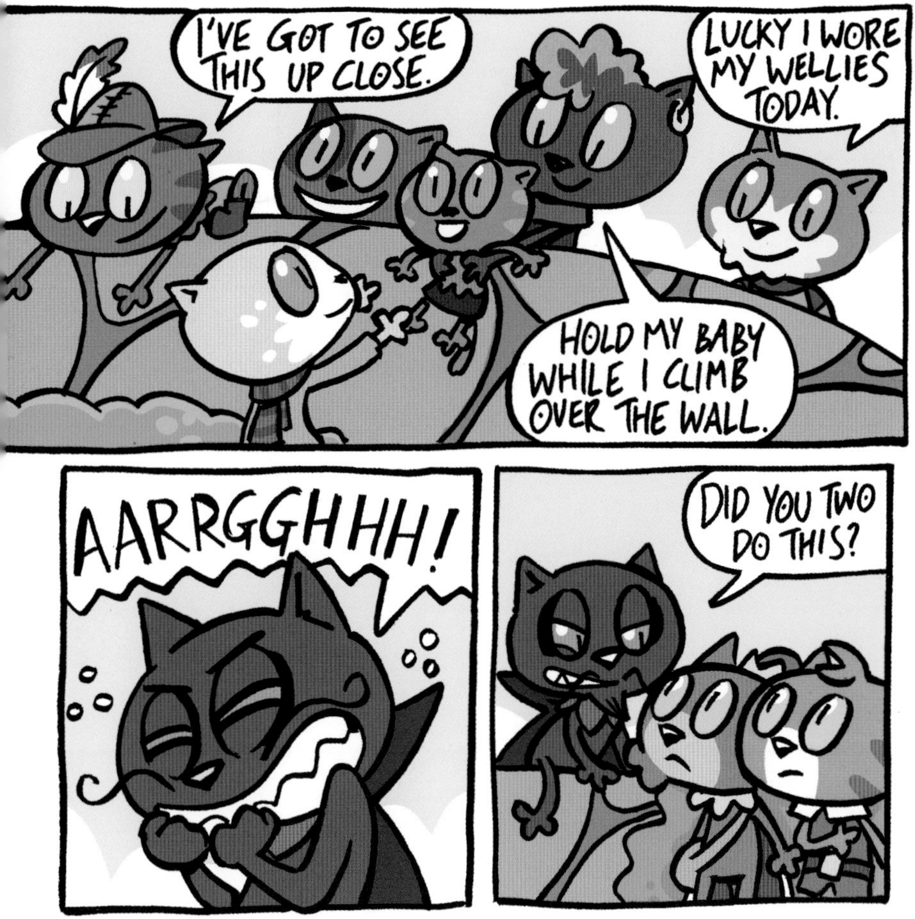
I'VE GOT TO SEE THIS UP CLOSE.
LUCKY I WORE MY WELLIES TODAY.
HOLD MY BABY WHILE I CLIMB OVER THE WALL.
AARRGGHHH!
DID YOU TWO DO THIS?

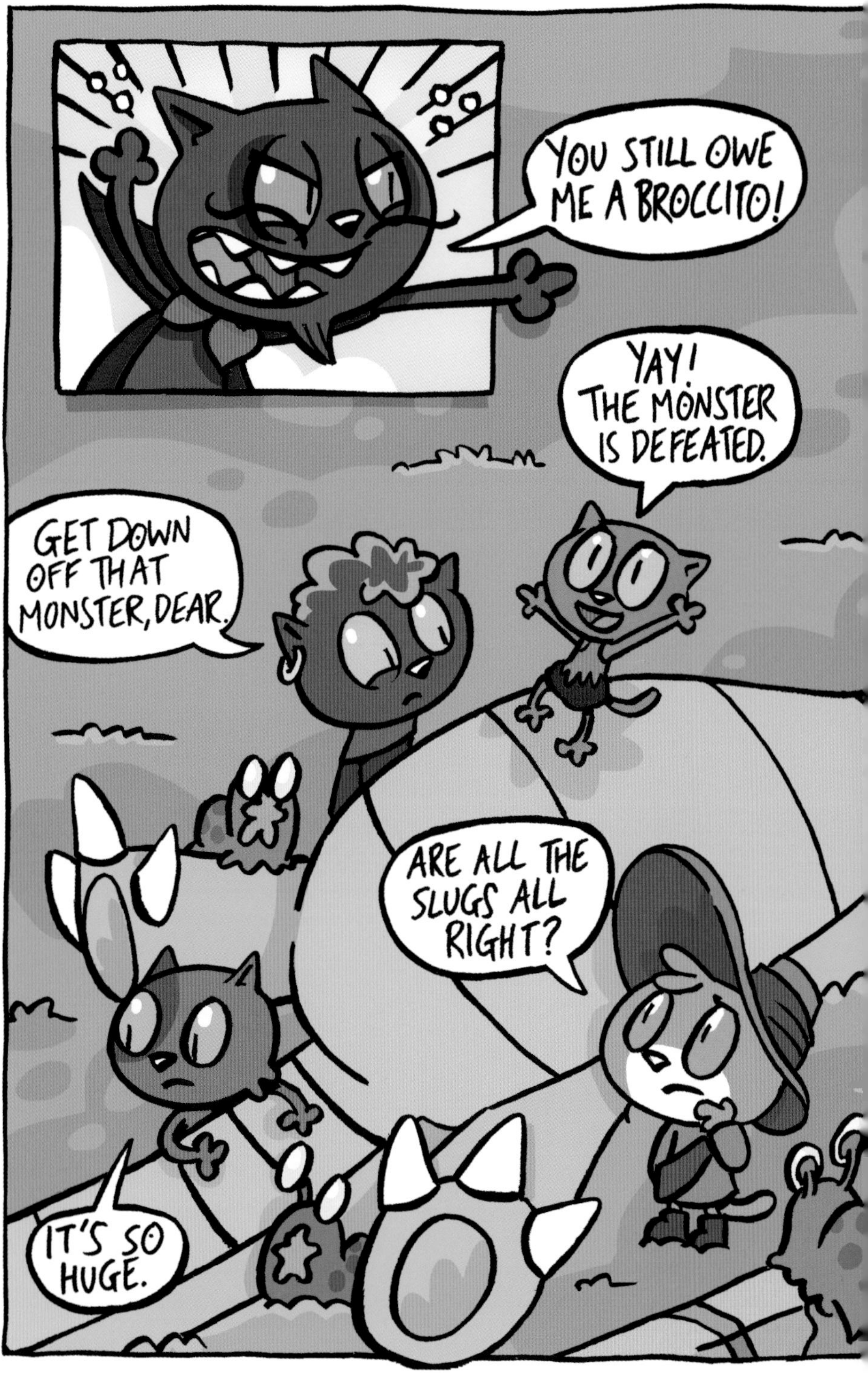
YOU STILL OWE ME A BROCCITO!
YAY! THE MONSTER IS DEFEATED.
GET DOWN OFF THAT MONSTER, DEAR.
ARE ALL THE SLUGS ALL RIGHT?
IT'S SO HUGE.

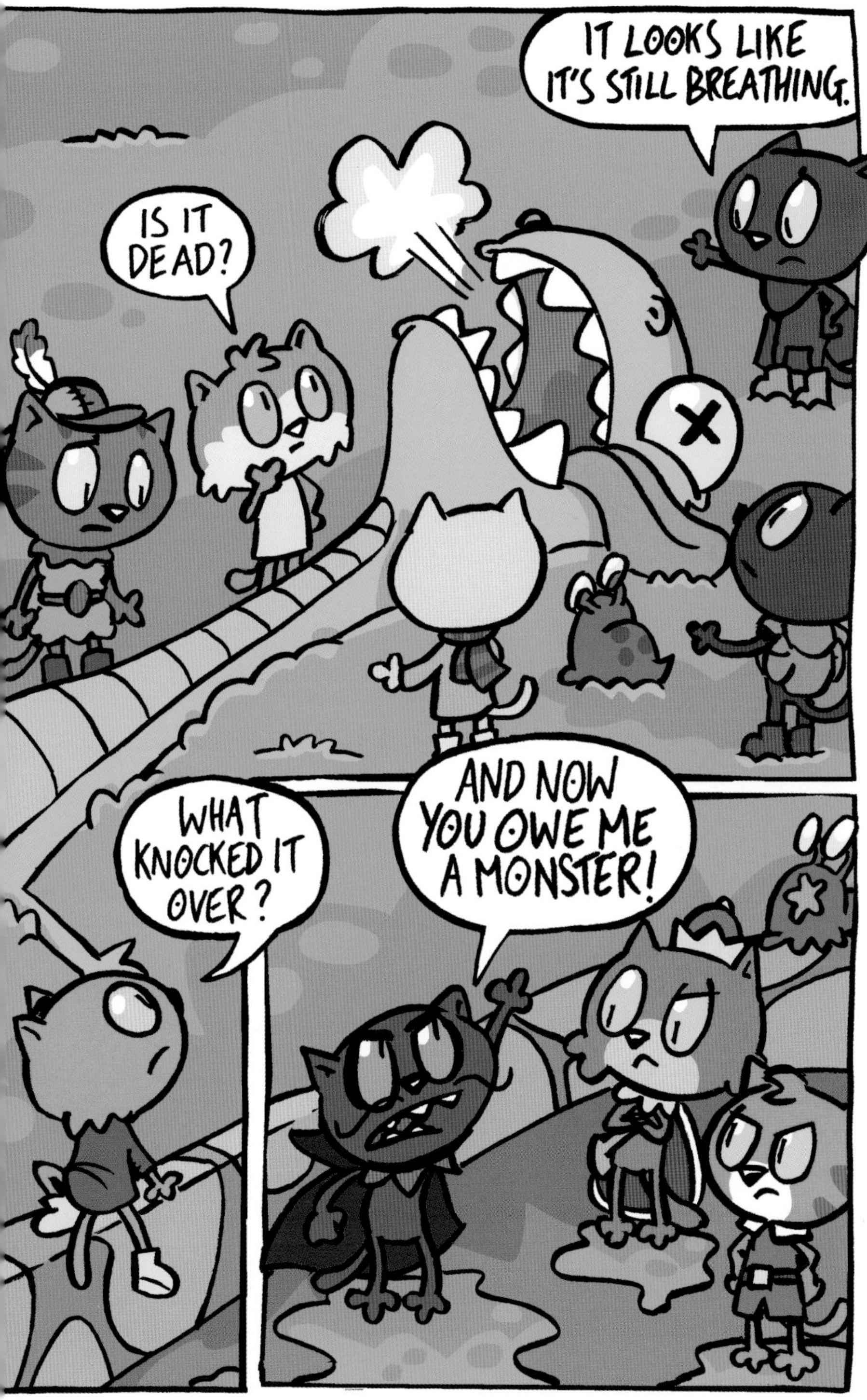
IT LOOKS LIKE IT'S STILL BREATHING.
IS IT DEAD?
WHAT KNOCKED IT OVER?
AND NOW YOU OWE ME A MONSTER!

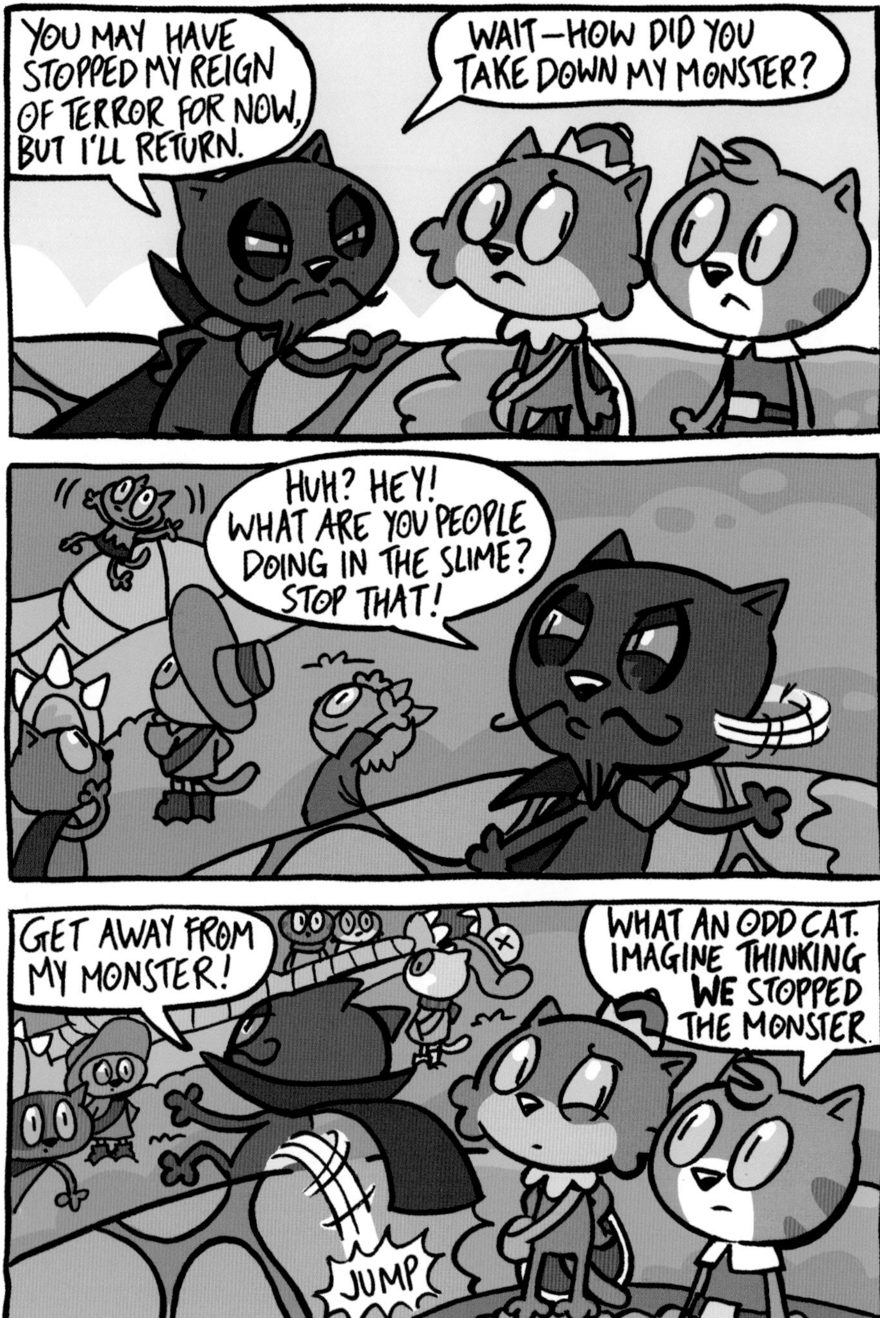
YOU MAY HAVE STOPPED MY REIGN OF TERROR FOR NOW, BUT I'LL RETURN.
WAIT—HOW DID YOU TAKE DOWN MY MONSTER?
HUH? HEY! WHAT ARE YOU PEOPLE DOING IN THE SLIME? STOP THAT!
GET AWAY FROM MY MONSTER!
WHAT AN ODD CAT. IMAGINE THINKING WE STOPPED THE MONSTER.
JUMP

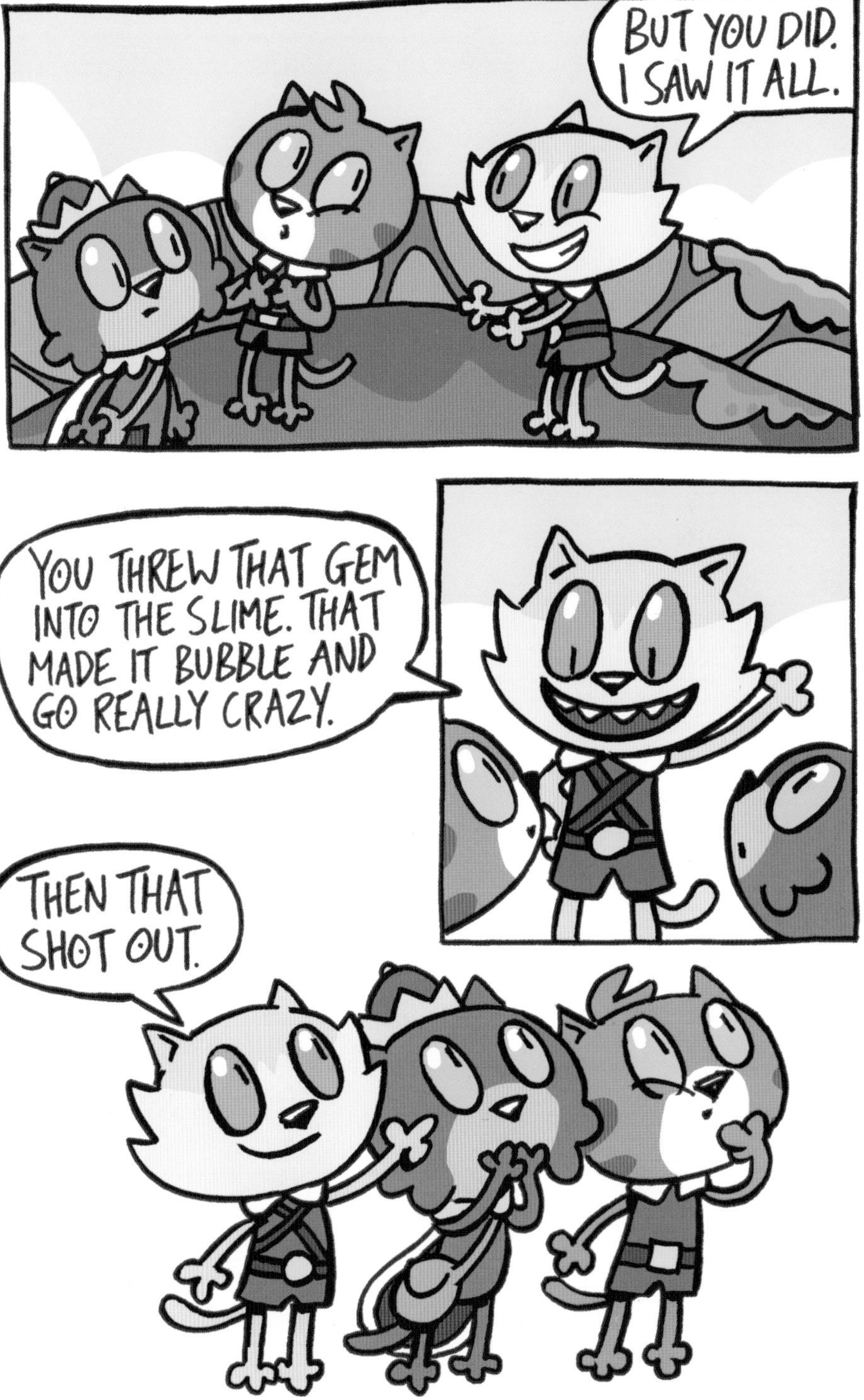
BUT YOU DID. I SAW IT ALL.
YOU THREW THAT GEM INTO THE SLIME. THAT MADE IT BUBBLE AND GO REALLY CRAZY.
THEN THAT SHOT OUT.

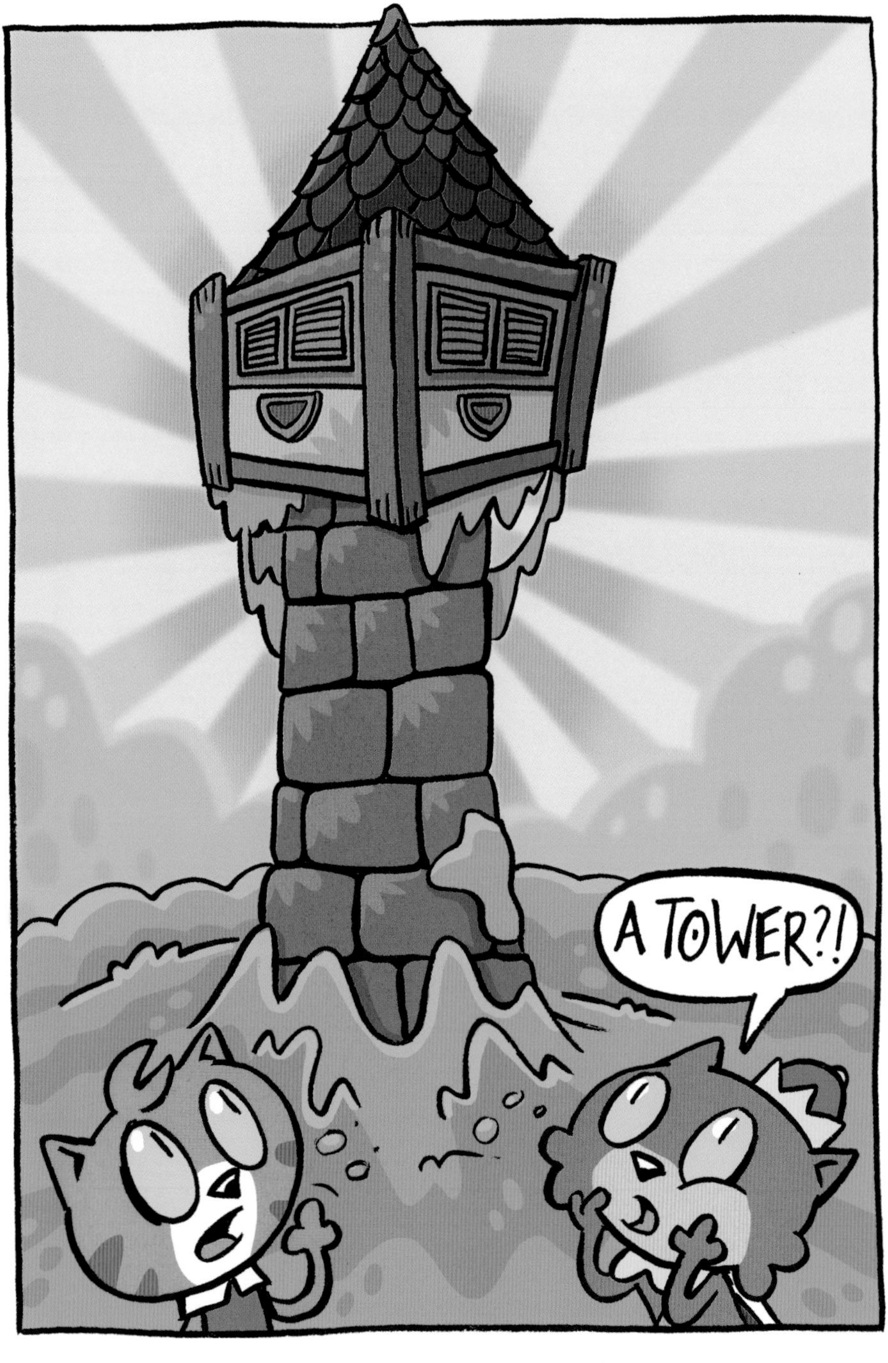
A TOWER?!

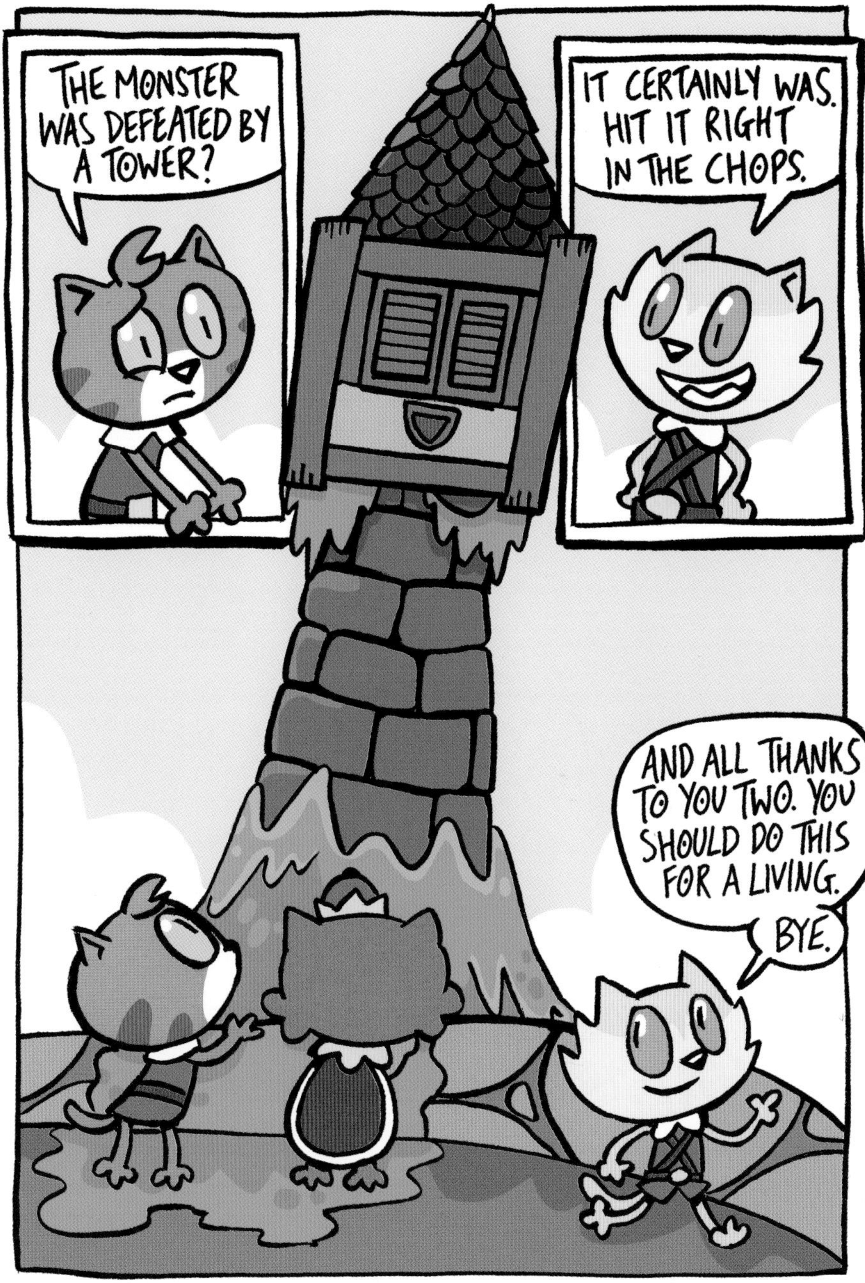
THE MONSTER WAS DEFEATED BY A TOWER?
IT CERTAINLY WAS. HIT IT RIGHT IN THE CHOPS.
AND ALL THANKS TO YOU TWO. YOU SHOULD DO THIS FOR A LIVING.
BYE.

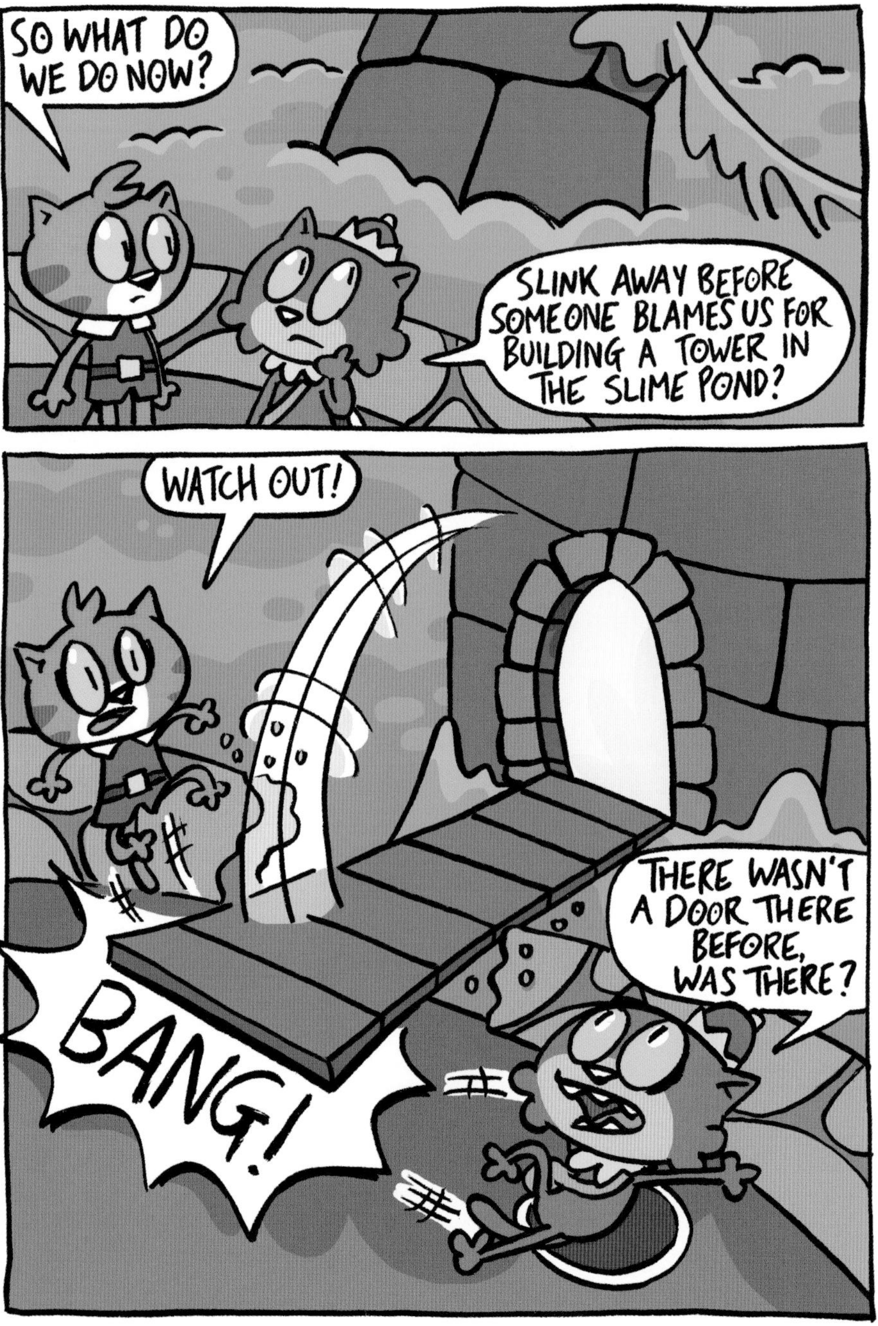
SO WHAT DO WE DO NOW?
SLINK AWAY BEFORE SOMEONE BLAMES US FOR BUILDING A TOWER IN THE SLIME POND?
WATCH OUT!
BANG!
THERE WASN'T A DOOR THERE BEFORE, WAS THERE?

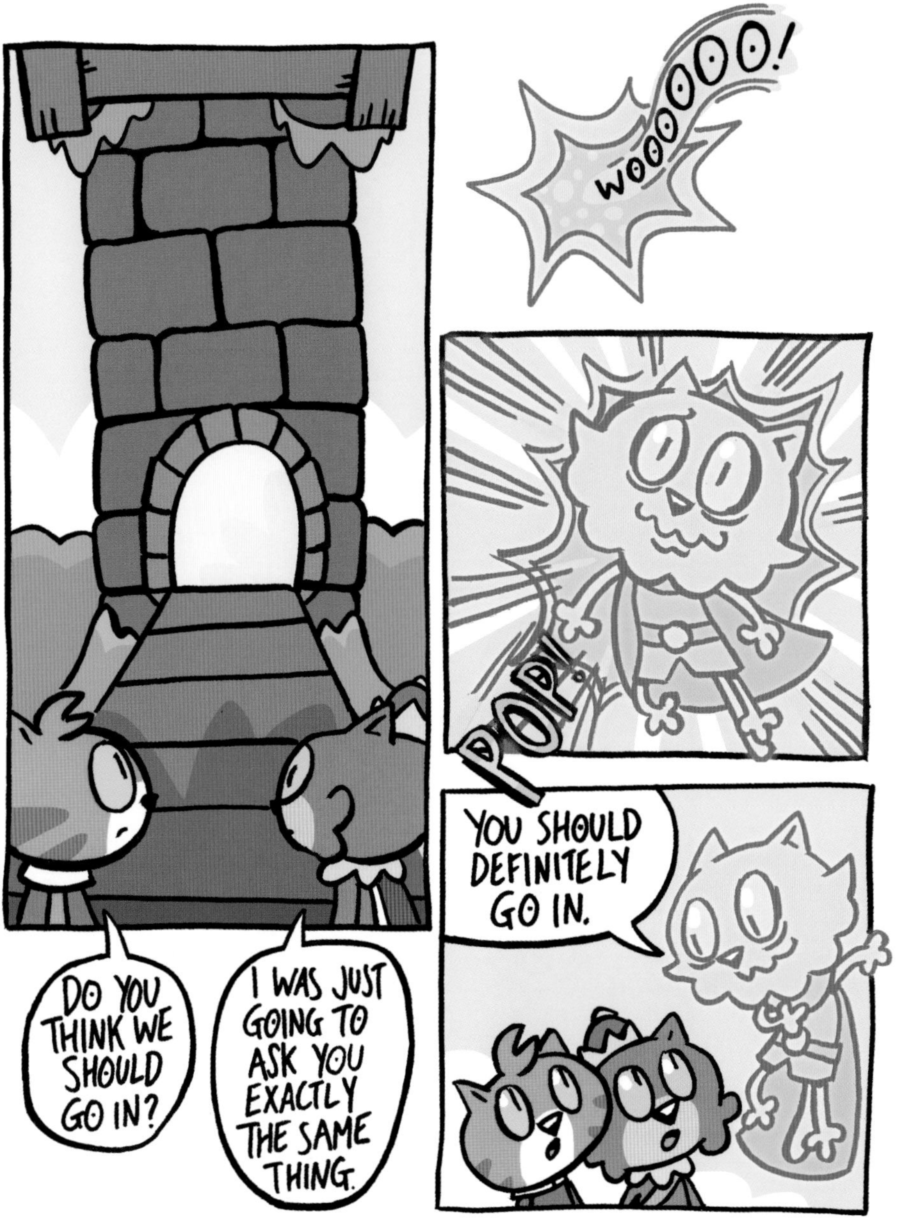
DO YOU THINK WE SHOULD GO IN?
I WAS JUST GOING TO ASK YOU EXACTLY THE SAME THING.
WOOOOOO!
POP!
YOU SHOULD DEFINITELY GO IN.

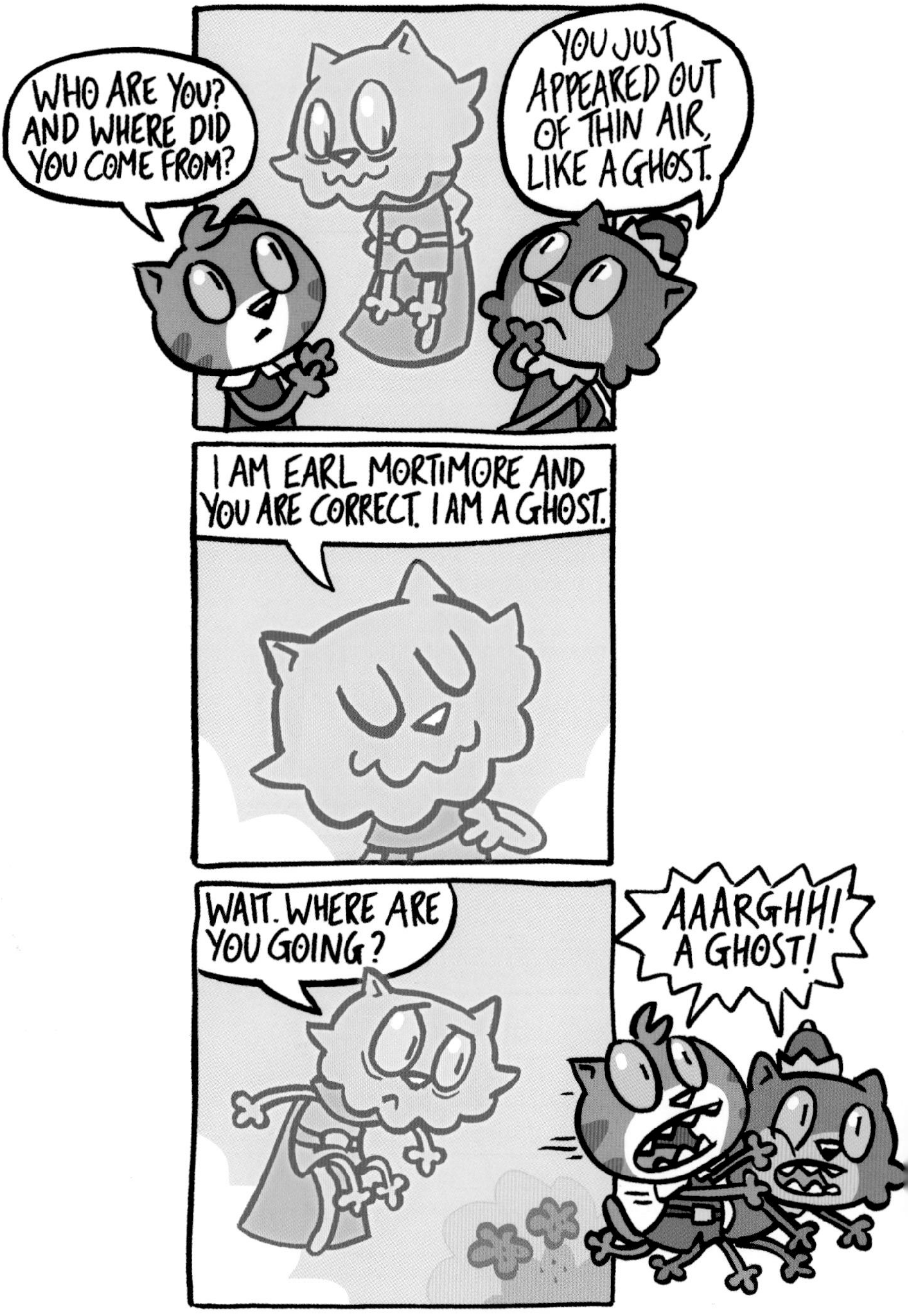
WHO ARE YOU? AND WHERE DID YOU COME FROM?
YOU JUST APPEARED OUT OF THIN AIR, LIKE A GHOST.
I AM EARL MORTIMORE AND YOU ARE CORRECT. I AM A GHOST.
WAIT. WHERE ARE YOU GOING?
AAARGHH! A GHOST!

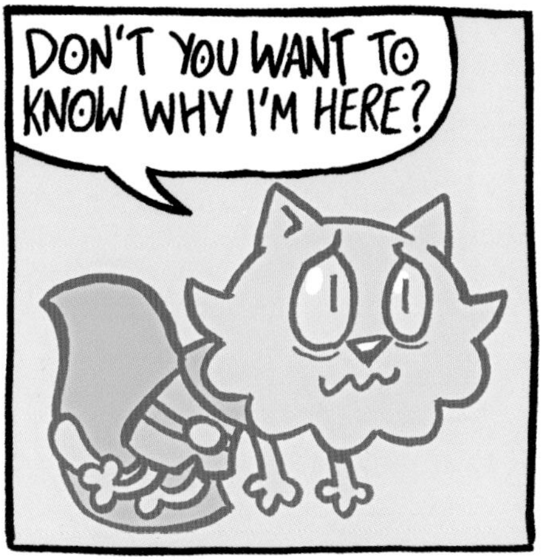
DON'T YOU WANT TO KNOW WHY I'M HERE?

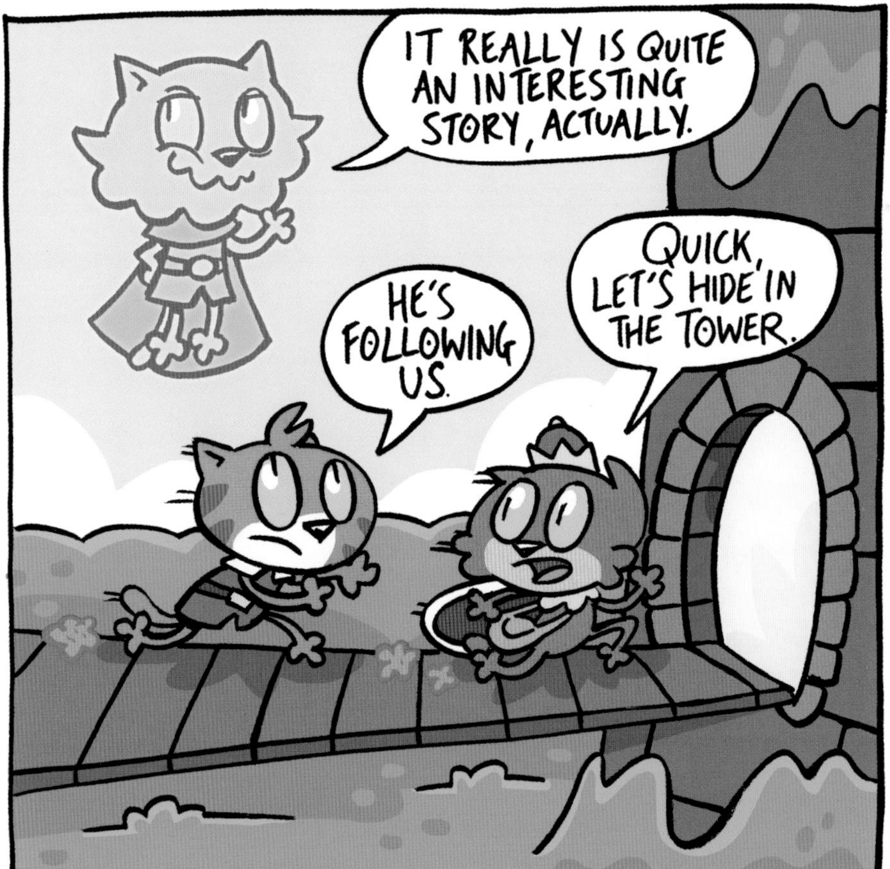
IT REALLY IS QUITE AN INTERESTING STORY, ACTUALLY.
HE'S FOLLOWING US.
QUICK, LET'S HIDE IN THE TOWER.

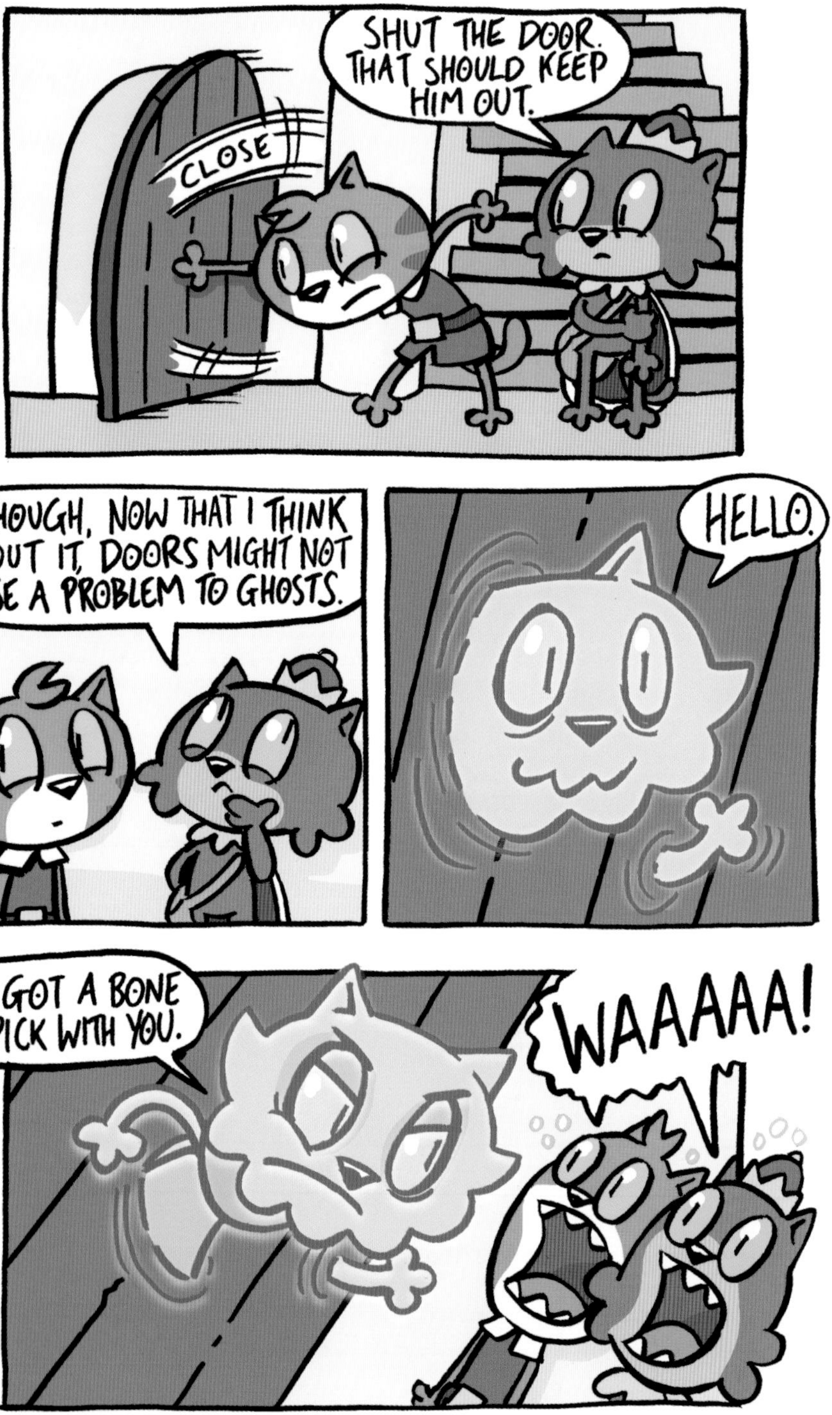
SHUT THE DOOR. THAT SHOULD KEEP HIM OUT.
CLOSE
ALTHOUGH, NOW THAT I THINK ABOUT IT, DOORS MIGHT NOT POSE A PROBLEM TO GHOSTS.
HELLO.
I'VE GOT A BONE TO PICK WITH YOU.
WAAAAA!

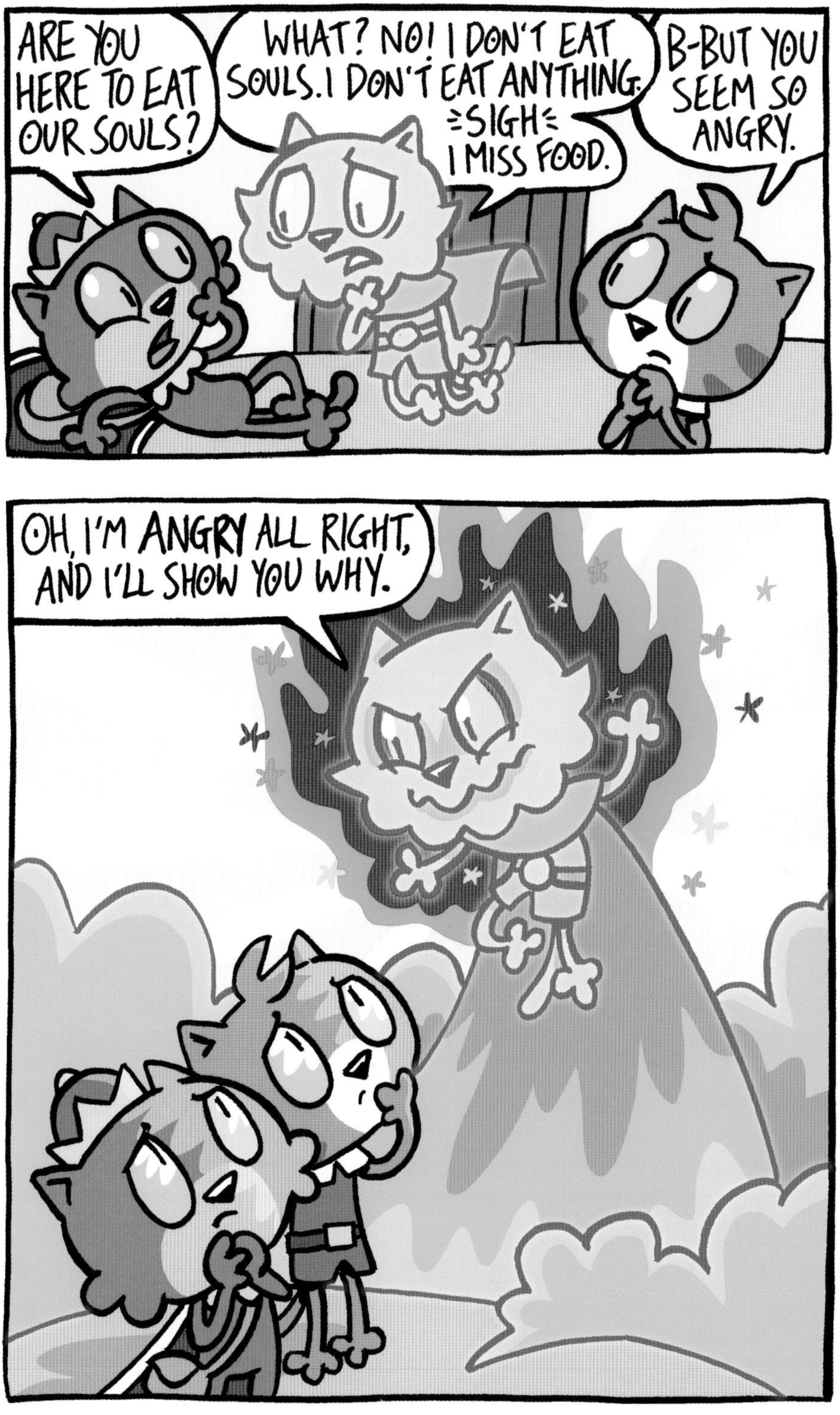
ARE YOU HERE TO EAT OUR SOULS?
WHAT? NO! I DON'T EAT SOULS. I DON'T EAT ANYTHING.
SIGH
I MISS FOOD.
B-BUT YOU SEEM SO ANGRY.
OH, I'M ANGRY ALL RIGHT, AND I'LL SHOW YOU WHY.

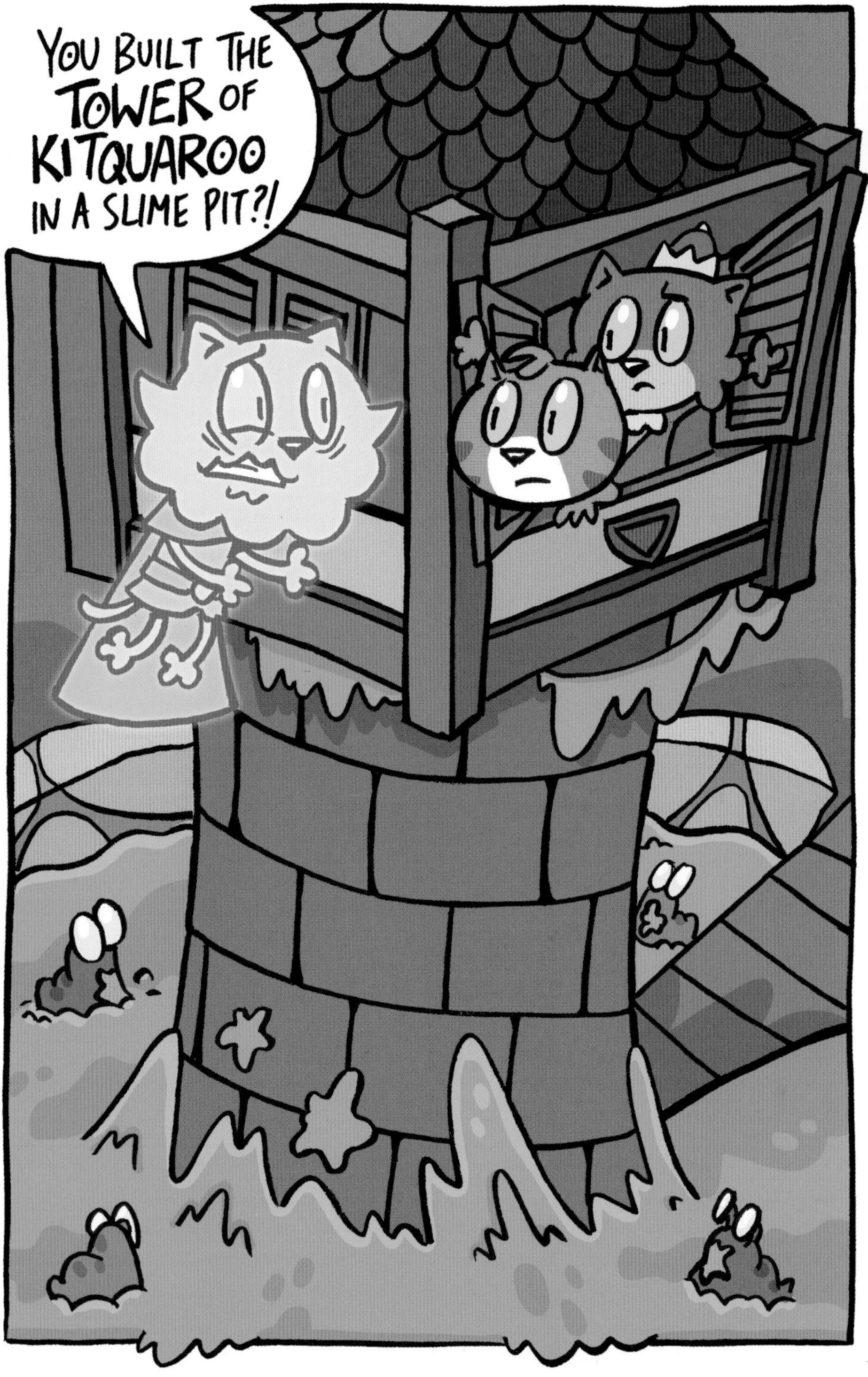
YOU BUILT THE TOWER OF KITQUAROO IN A SLIME PIT?!

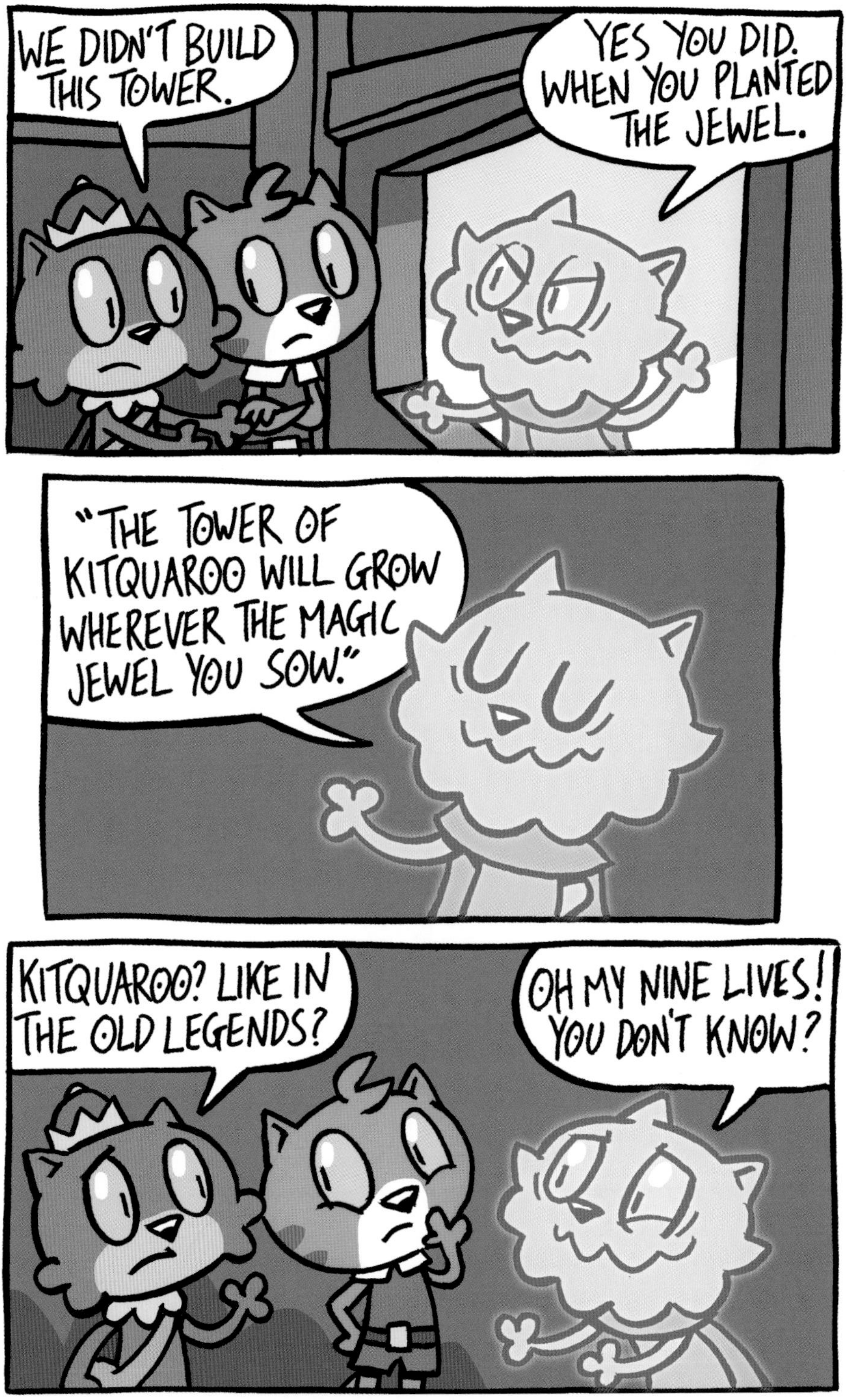
WE DIDN'T BUILD THIS TOWER.
YES YOU DID. WHEN YOU PLANTED THE JEWEL.
"THE TOWER OF KITQUAROO WILL GROW WHEREVER THE MAGIC JEWEL YOU SOW."
KITQUAROO? LIKE IN THE OLD LEGENDS?
OH MY NINE LIVES! YOU DON'T KNOW?

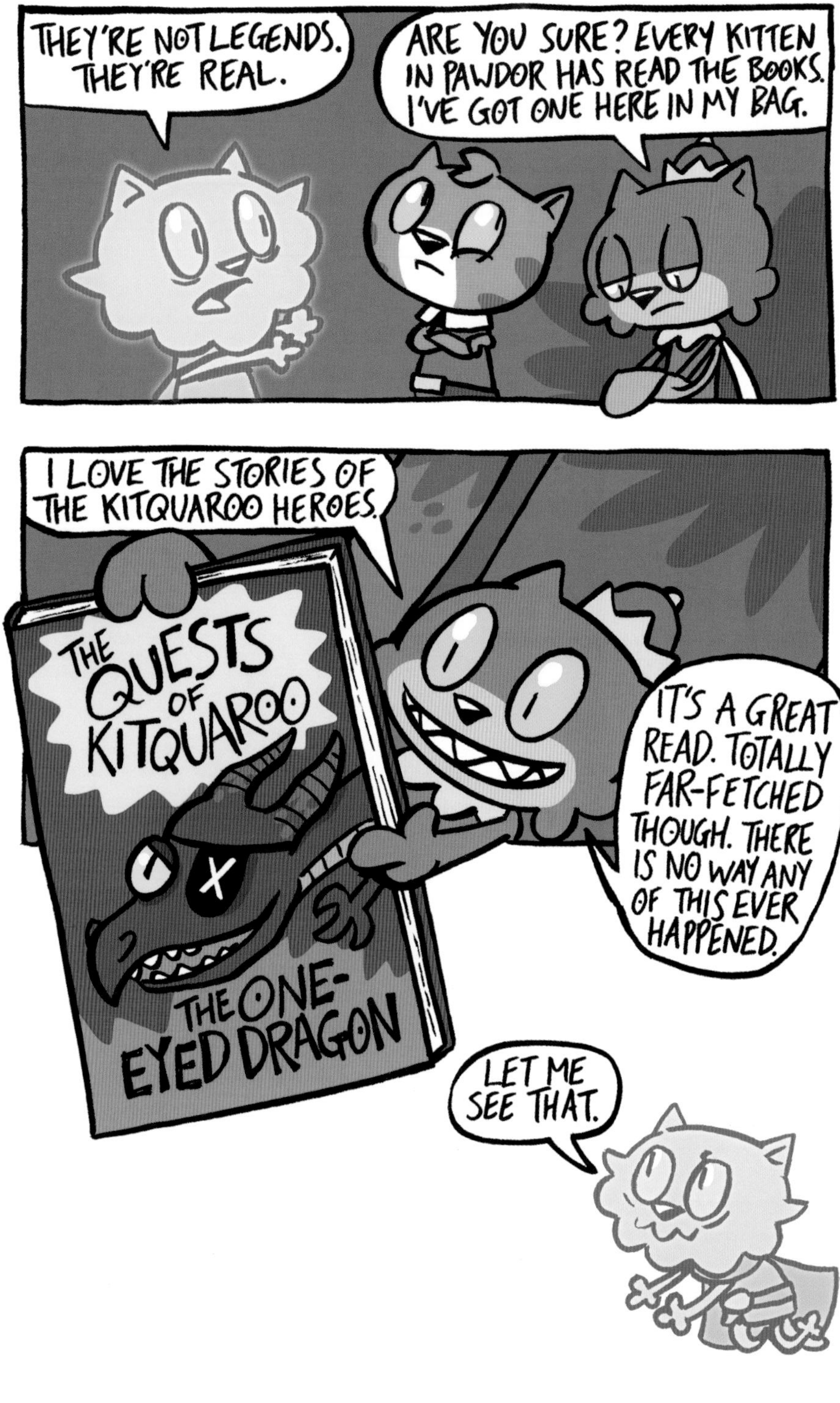
THEY'RE NOT LEGENDS. THEY'RE REAL.
ARE YOU SURE? EVERY KITTEN IN PAWDOR HAS READ THE BOOKS. I'VE GOT ONE HERE IN MY BAG.
I LOVE THE STORIES OF THE KITQUAROO HEROES.
THE QUESTS OF KITQUAROO
THE ONE-EYED DRAGON
IT'S A GREAT READ. TOTALLY FAR-FETCHED THOUGH. THERE IS NO WAY ANY OF THIS EVER HAPPENED.
LET ME SEE THAT.

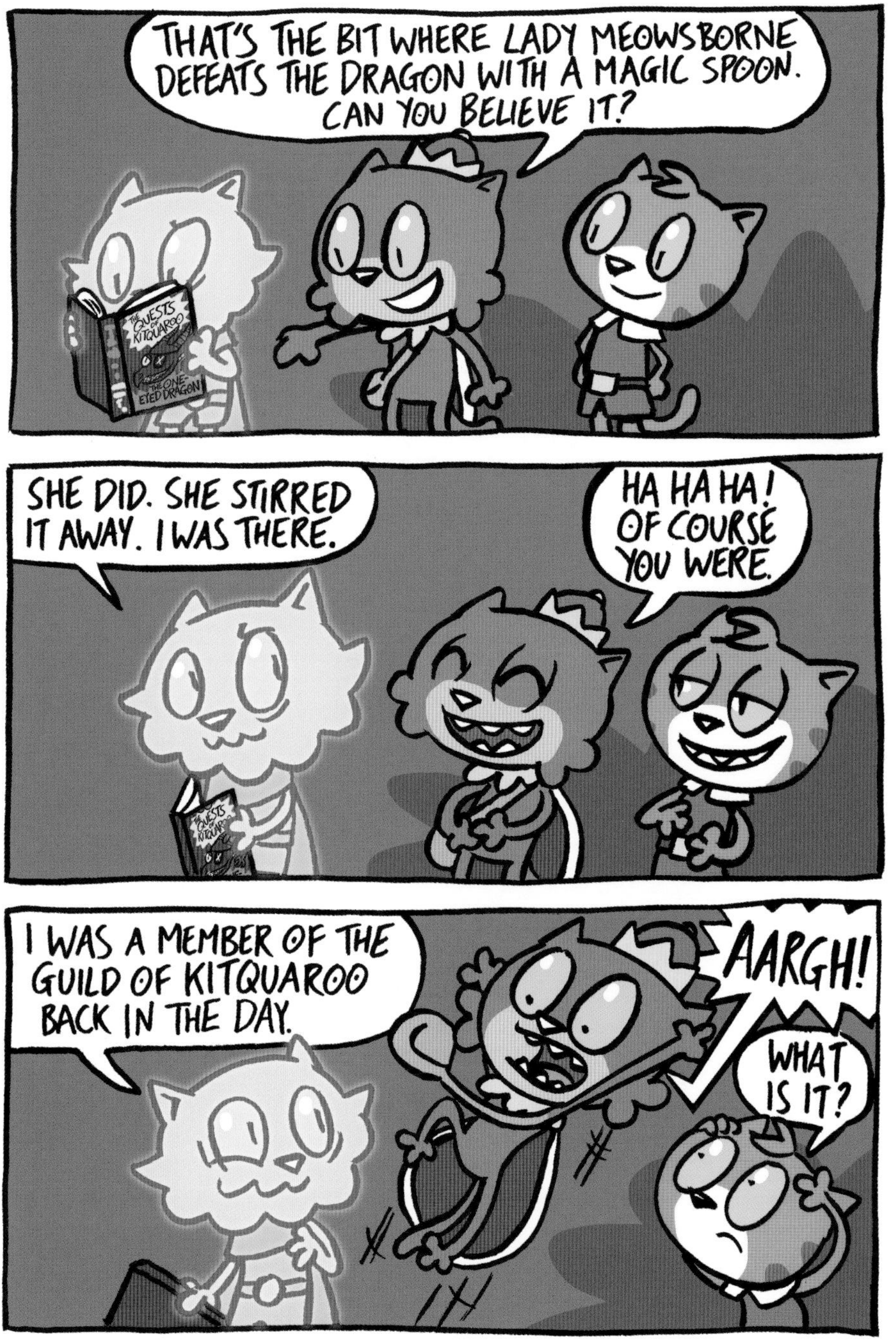
THAT'S THE BIT WHERE LADY MEOWSBORNE DEFEATS THE DRAGON WITH A MAGIC SPOON. CAN YOU BELIEVE IT?
THE QUESTS OF KITQUAROO THE ONE-EYED DRAGON
SHE DID. SHE STIRRED IT AWAY. I WAS THERE.
HA HA HA! OF COURSE YOU WERE.
I WAS A MEMBER OF THE GUILD OF KITQUAROO BACK IN THE DAY.
AARGH!
WHAT IS IT?

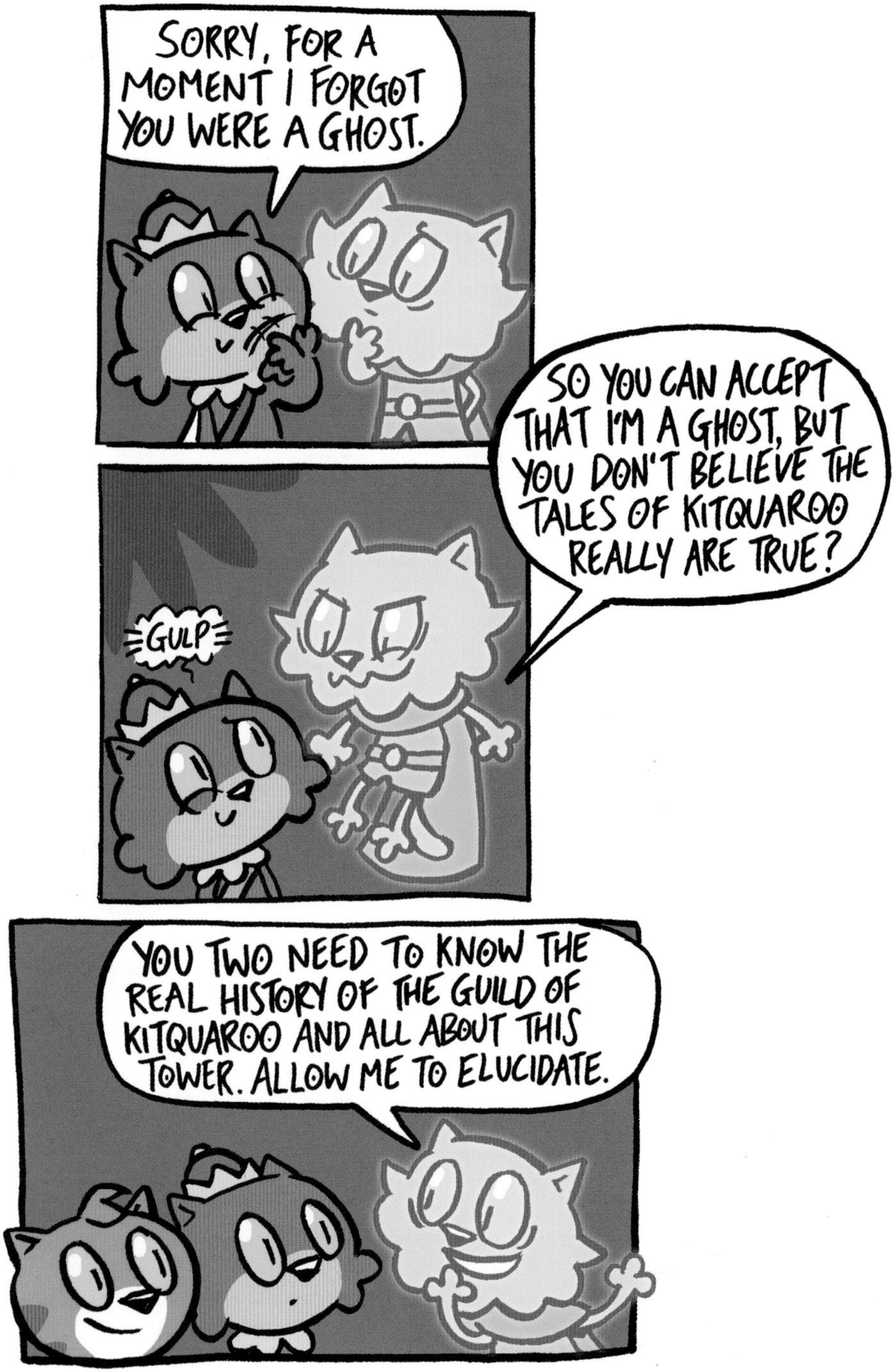
SORRY, FOR A MOMENT I FORGOT YOU WERE A GHOST.
SO YOU CAN ACCEPT THAT I'M A GHOST, BUT YOU DON'T BELIEVE THE TALES OF KITQUAROO REALLY ARE TRUE?
GULP
YOU TWO NEED TO KNOW THE REAL HISTORY OF THE GUILD OF KITQUAROO AND ALL ABOUT THIS TOWER. ALLOW ME TO ELUCIDATE.

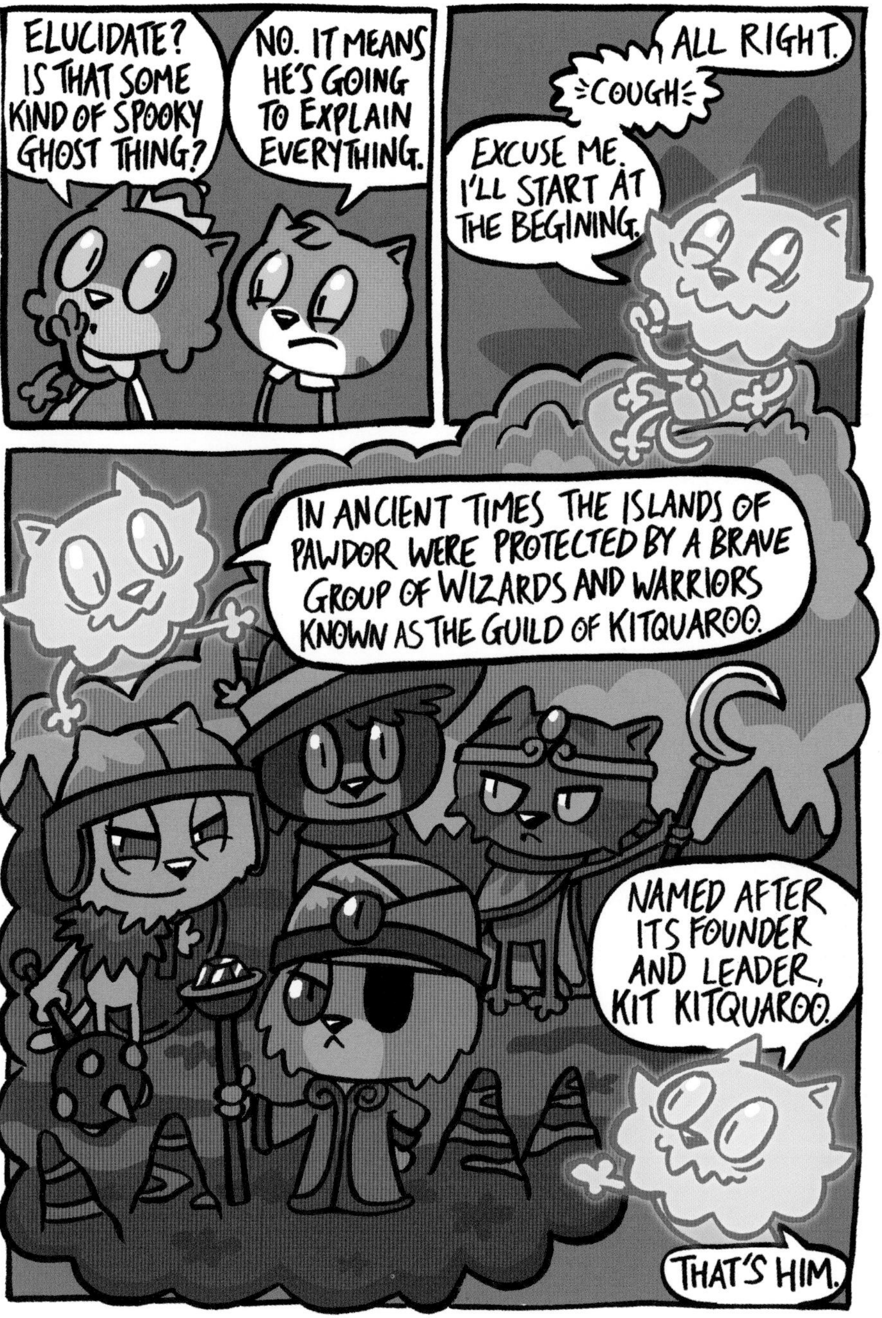
ELUCIDATE? IS THAT SOME KIND OF SPOOKY GHOST THING?
NO. IT MEANS HE'S GOING TO EXPLAIN EVERYTHING.
ALL RIGHT.
COUGH
EXCUSE ME. I'LL START AT THE BEGINING.
IN ANCIENT TIMES THE ISLANDS OF PAWDOR WERE PROTECTED BY A BRAVE GROUP OF WIZARDS AND WARRIORS KNOWN AS THE GUILD OF KITQUAROO.
NAMED AFTER ITS FOUNDER AND LEADER, KIT KITQUAROO.
THAT'S HIM.

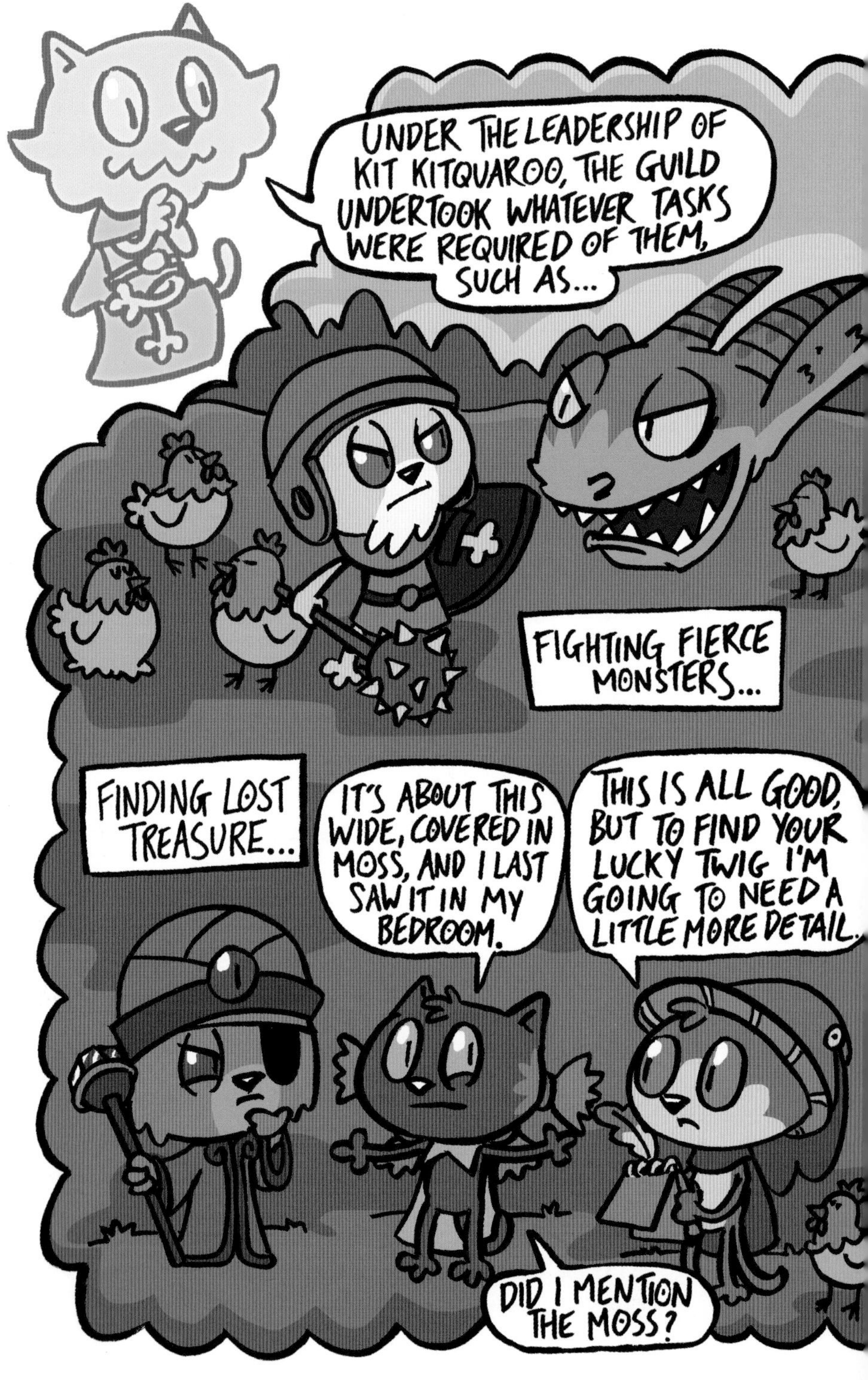
UNDER THE LEADERSHIP OF KIT KITQUAROO, THE GUILD UNDERTOOK WHATEVER TASKS WERE REQUIRED OF THEM, SUCH AS...
FIGHTING FIERCE MONSTERS...
FINDING LOST TREASURE...
IT'S ABOUT THIS WIDE, COVERED IN MOSS, AND I LAST SAW IT IN MY BEDROOM.
THIS IS ALL GOOD, BUT TO FIND YOUR LUCKY TWIG I'M GOING TO NEED A LITTLE MORE DETAIL.
DID I MENTION THE MOSS?

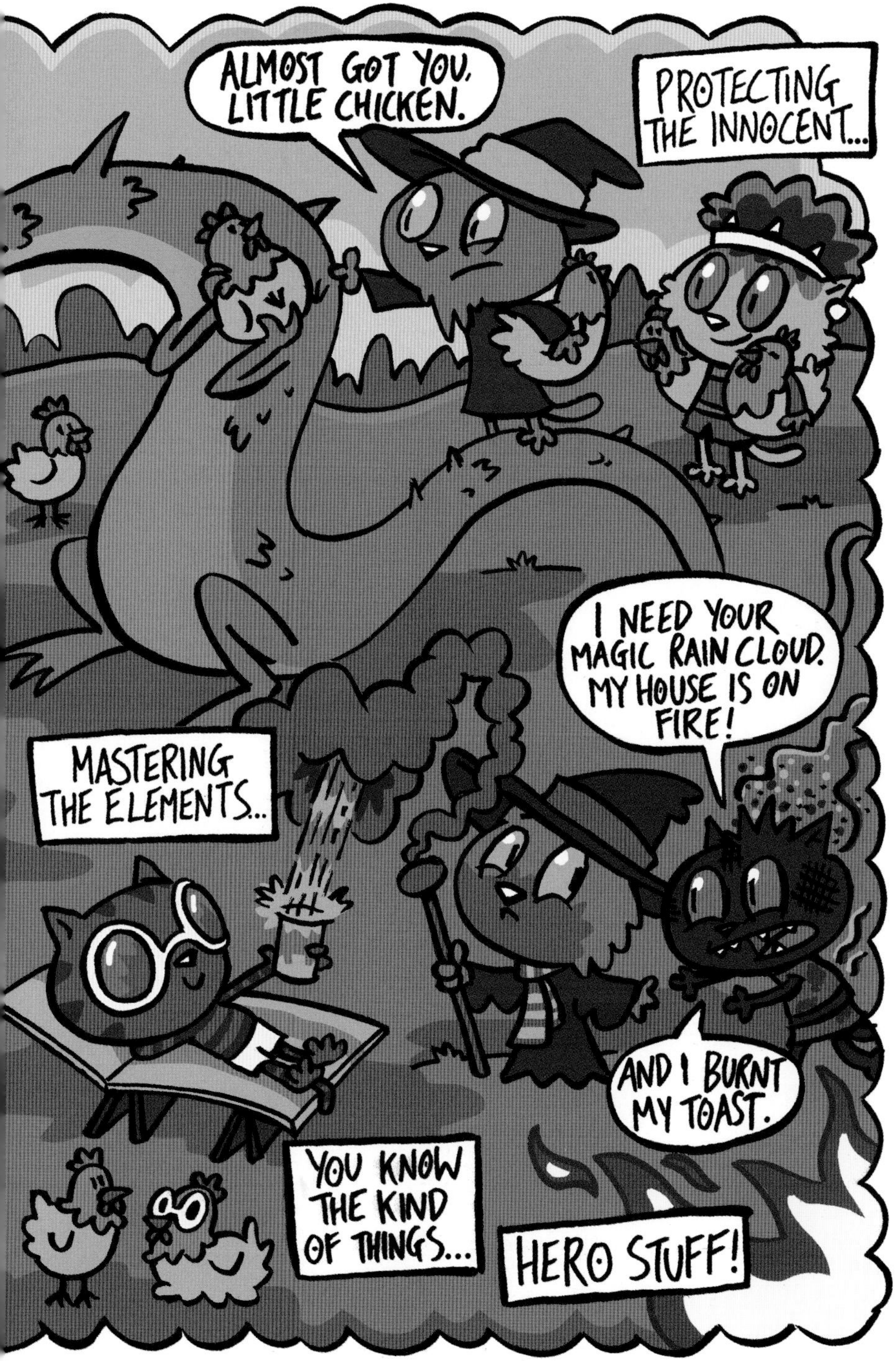
ALMOST GOT YOU, LITTLE CHICKEN.
PROTECTING THE INNOCENT...
I NEED YOUR MAGIC RAIN CLOUD. MY HOUSE IS ON FIRE!
MASTERING THE ELEMENTS...
AND I BURNT MY TOAST.
YOU KNOW THE KIND OF THINGS...
HERO STUFF!

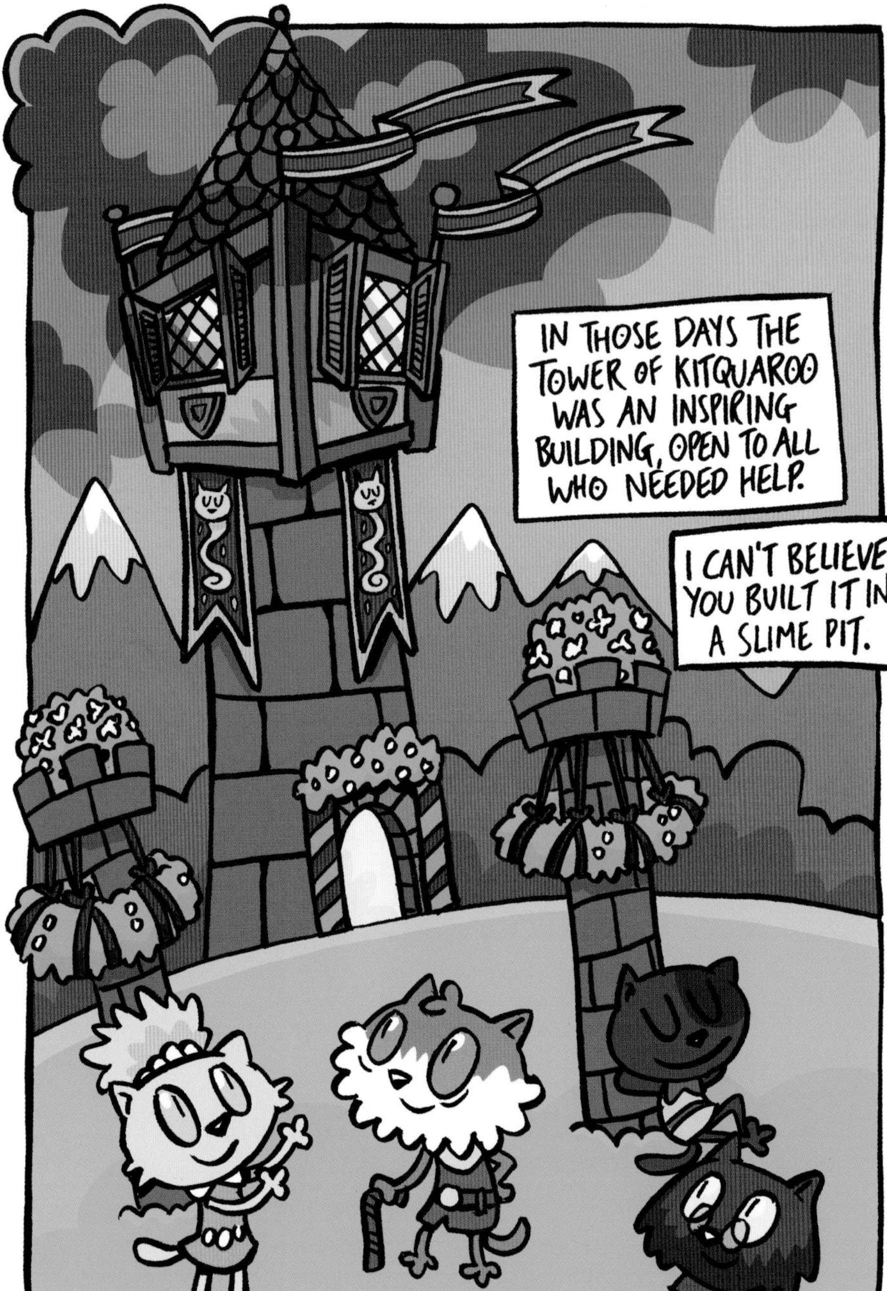
IN THOSE DAYS THE TOWER OF KITQUAROO WAS AN INSPIRING BUILDING, OPEN TO ALL WHO NEEDED HELP.
I CAN'T BELIEVE YOU BUILT IT IN A SLIME PIT.

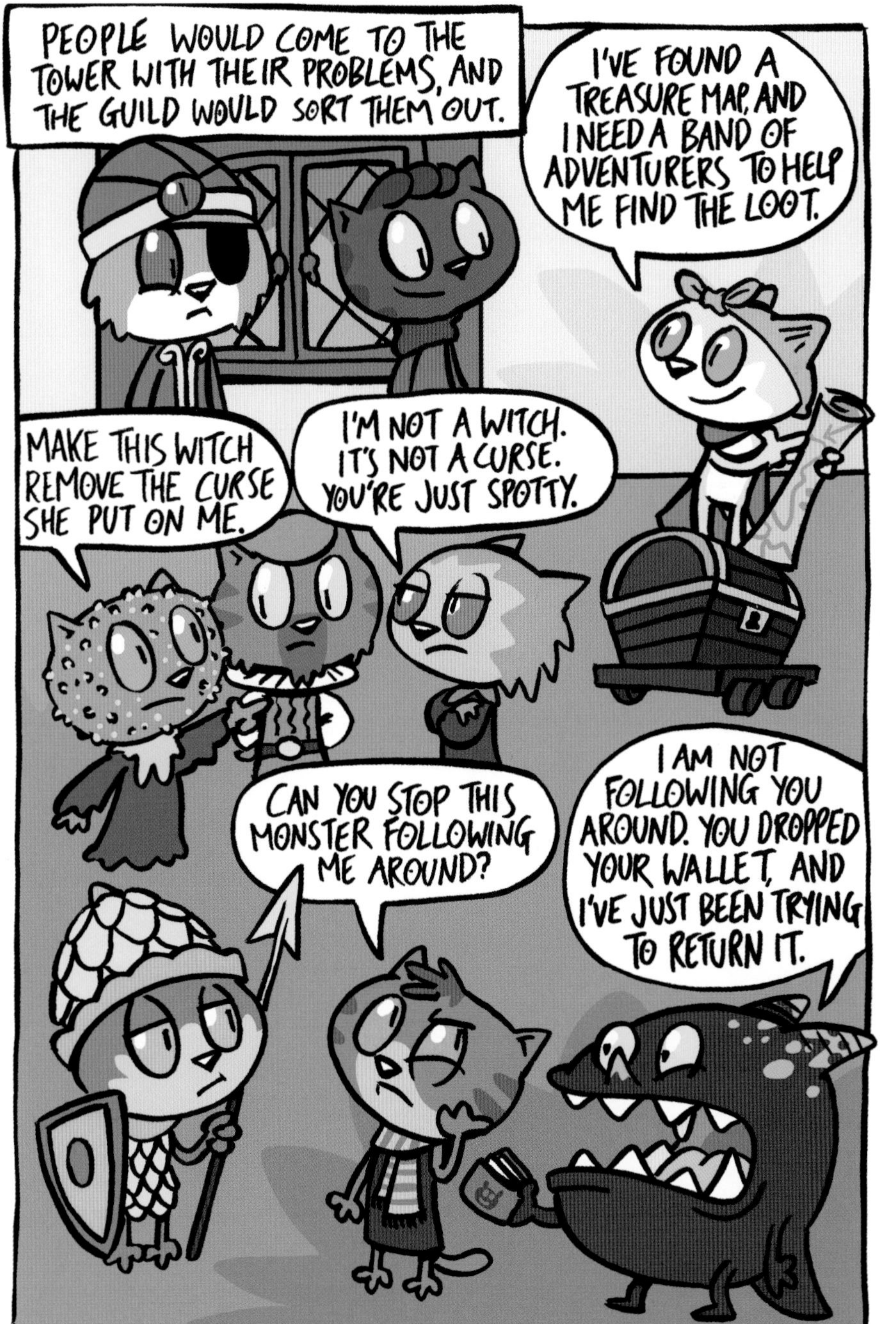
PEOPLE WOULD COME TO THE TOWER WITH THEIR PROBLEMS, AND THE GUILD WOULD SORT THEM OUT.
I'VE FOUND A TREASURE MAP, AND I NEED A BAND OF ADVENTURERS TO HELP ME FIND THE LOOT.
MAKE THIS WITCH REMOVE THE CURSE SHE PUT ON ME.
I'M NOT A WITCH. IT'S NOT A CURSE. YOU'RE JUST SPOTTY.
CAN YOU STOP THIS MONSTER FOLLOWING ME AROUND?
I AM NOT FOLLOWING YOU AROUND. YOU DROPPED YOUR WALLET, AND I'VE JUST BEEN TRYING TO RETURN IT.

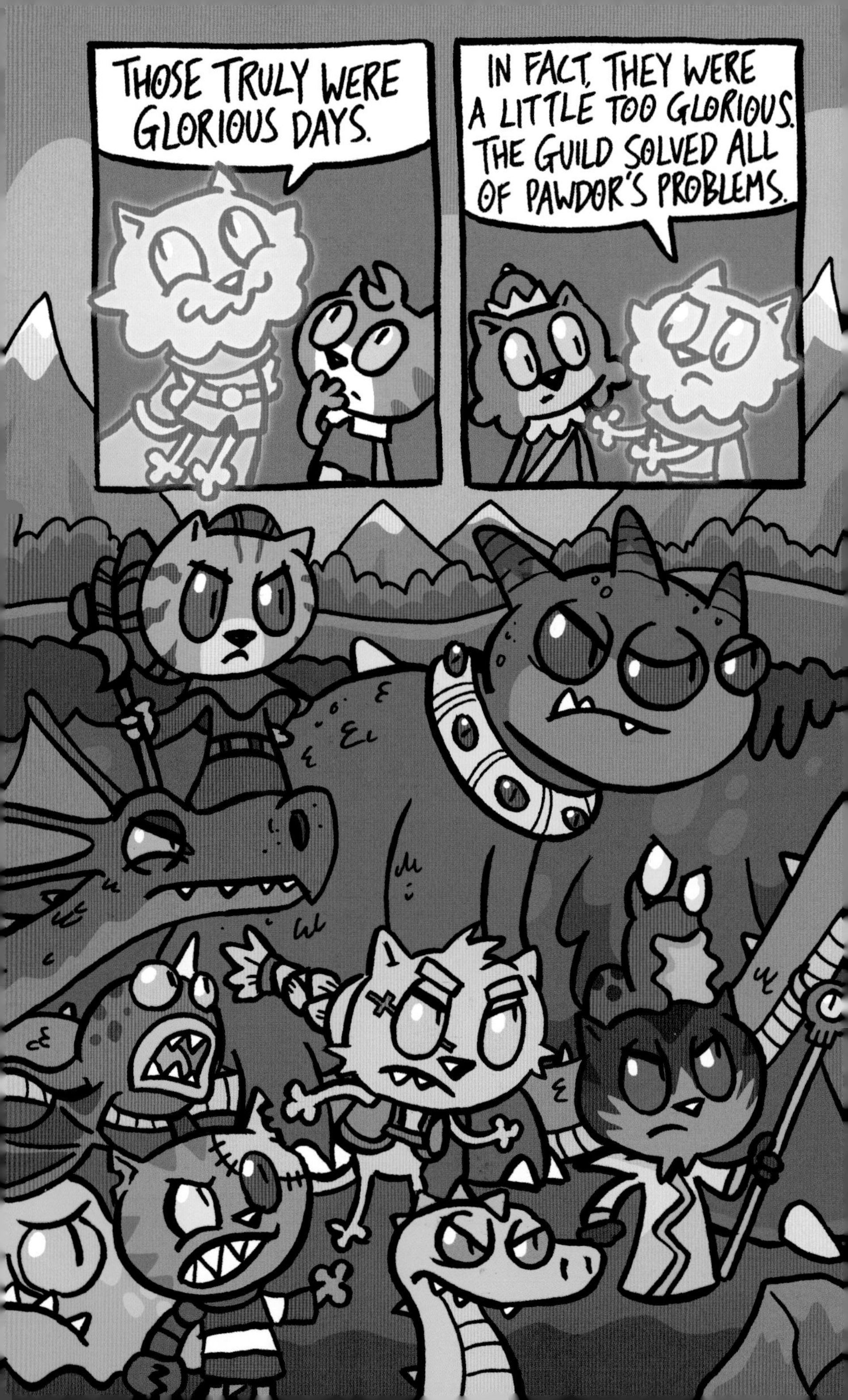
THOSE TRULY WERE GLORIOUS DAYS.
IN FACT, THEY WERE A LITTLE TOO GLORIOUS. THE GUILD SOLVED ALL OF PAWDOR'S PROBLEMS.

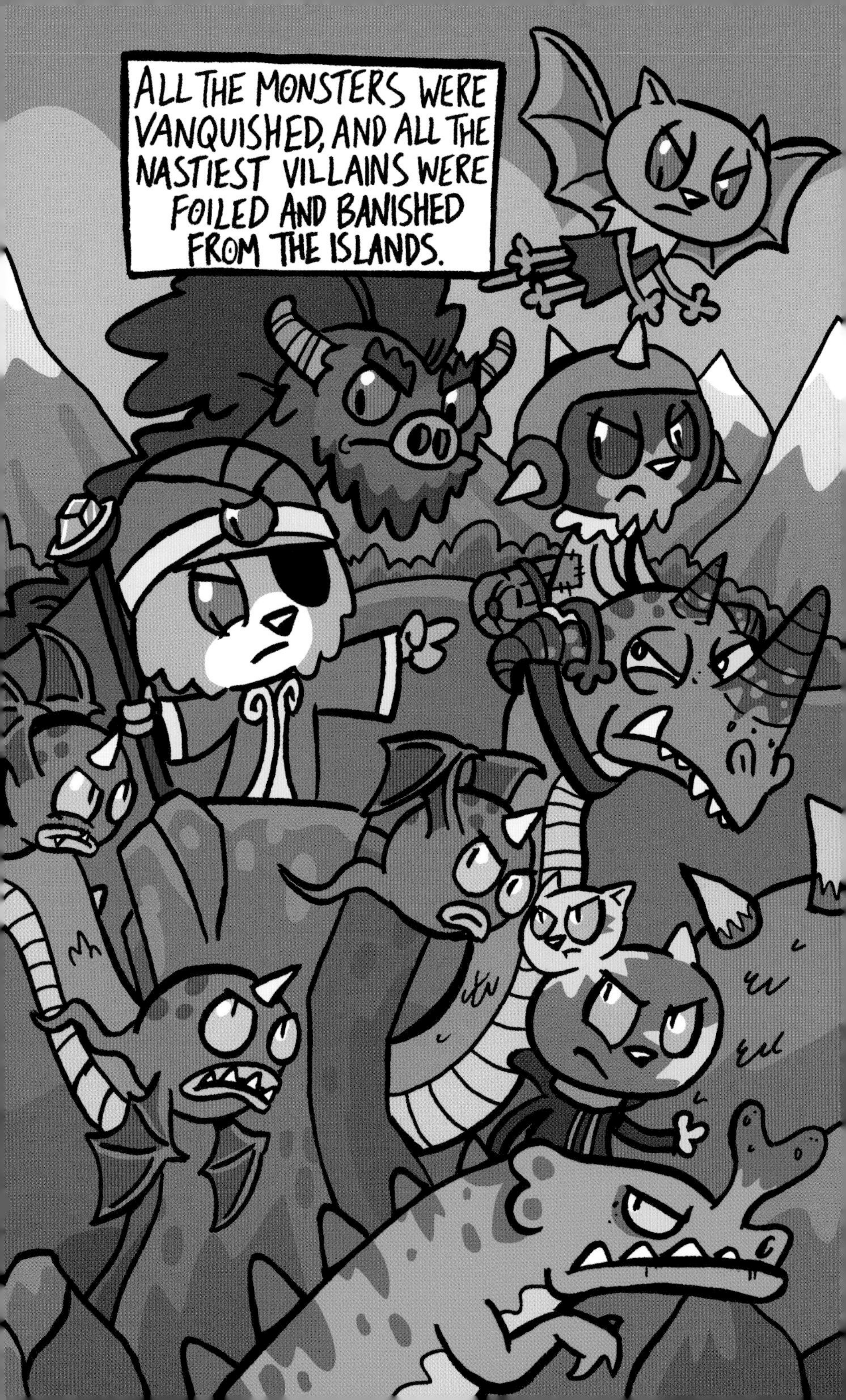
ALL THE MONSTERS WERE VANQUISHED, AND ALL THE NASTIEST VILLAINS WERE FOILED AND BANISHED FROM THE ISLANDS.

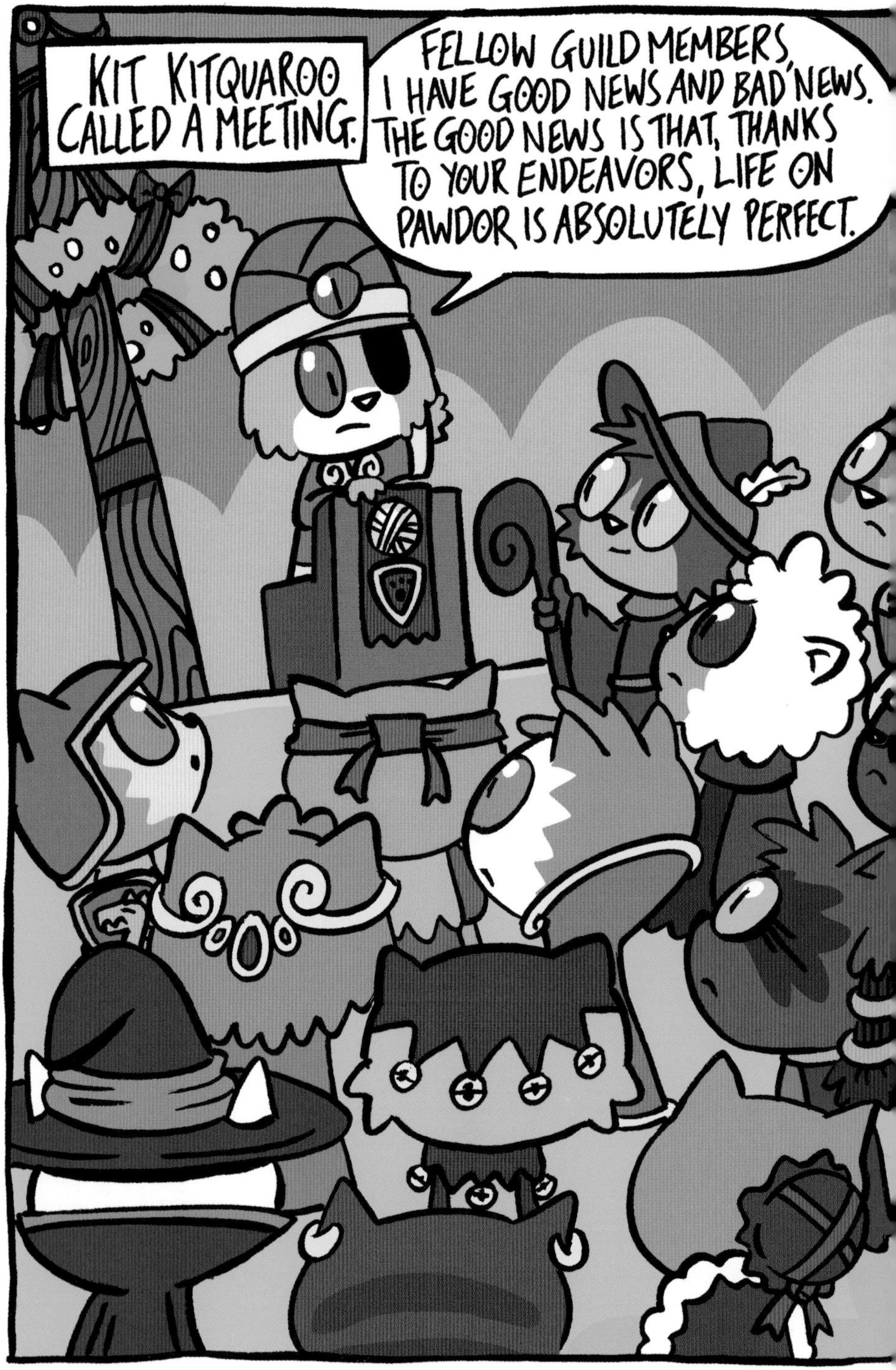
KIT KITQUAROO CALLED A MEETING.
FELLOW GUILD MEMBERS, I HAVE GOOD NEWS AND BAD NEWS. THE GOOD NEWS IS THAT, THANKS TO YOUR ENDEAVORS, LIFE ON PAWDOR IS ABSOLUTELY PERFECT.

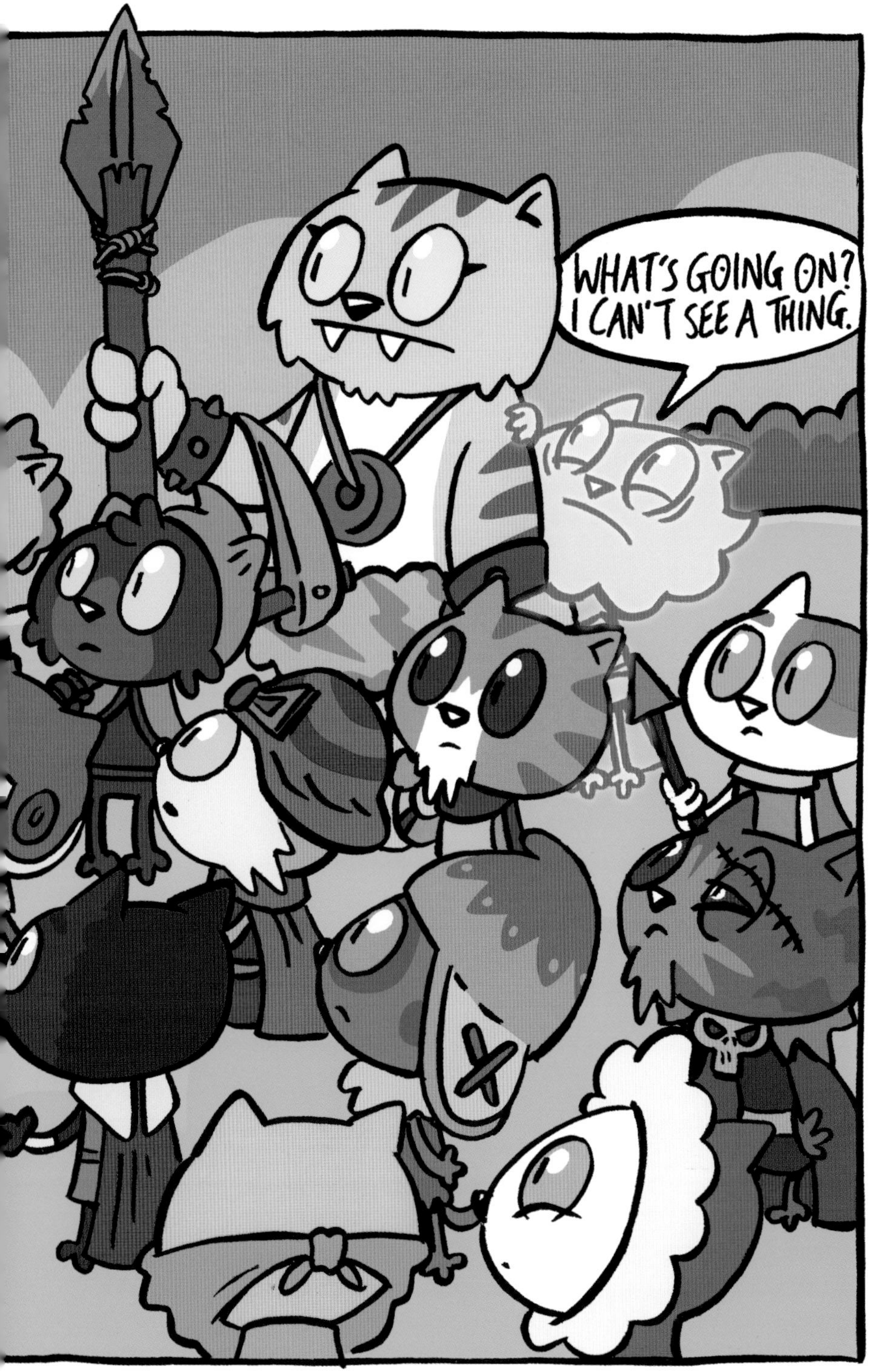
WHAT'S GOING ON? I CAN'T SEE A THING.

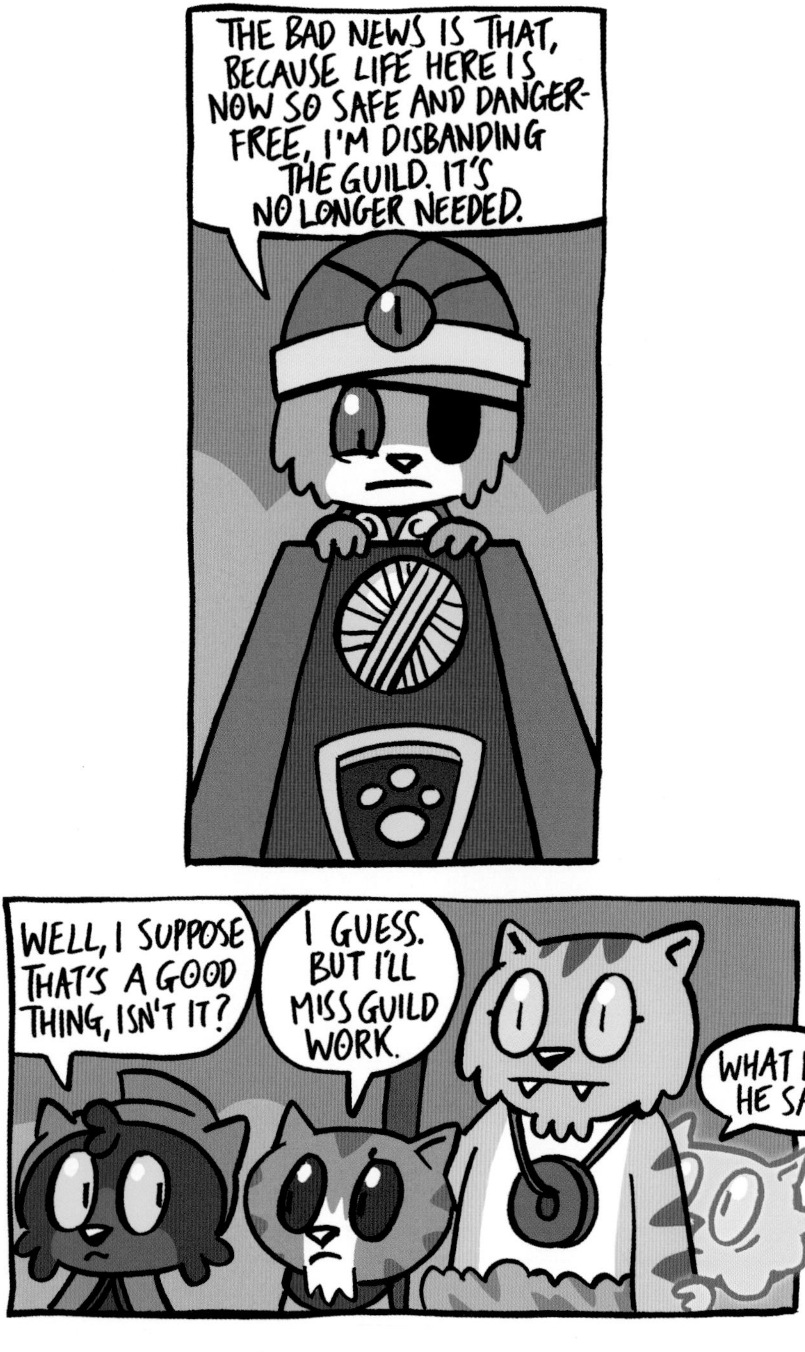
THE BAD NEWS IS THAT, BECAUSE LIFE HERE IS NOW SO SAFE AND DANGER-FREE, I'M DISBANDING THE GUILD. IT'S NO LONGER NEEDED.
WELL, I SUPPOSE THAT'S A GOOD THING, ISN'T IT?
I GUESS. BUT I'LL MISS GUILD WORK.
WHAT DID HE SAY?

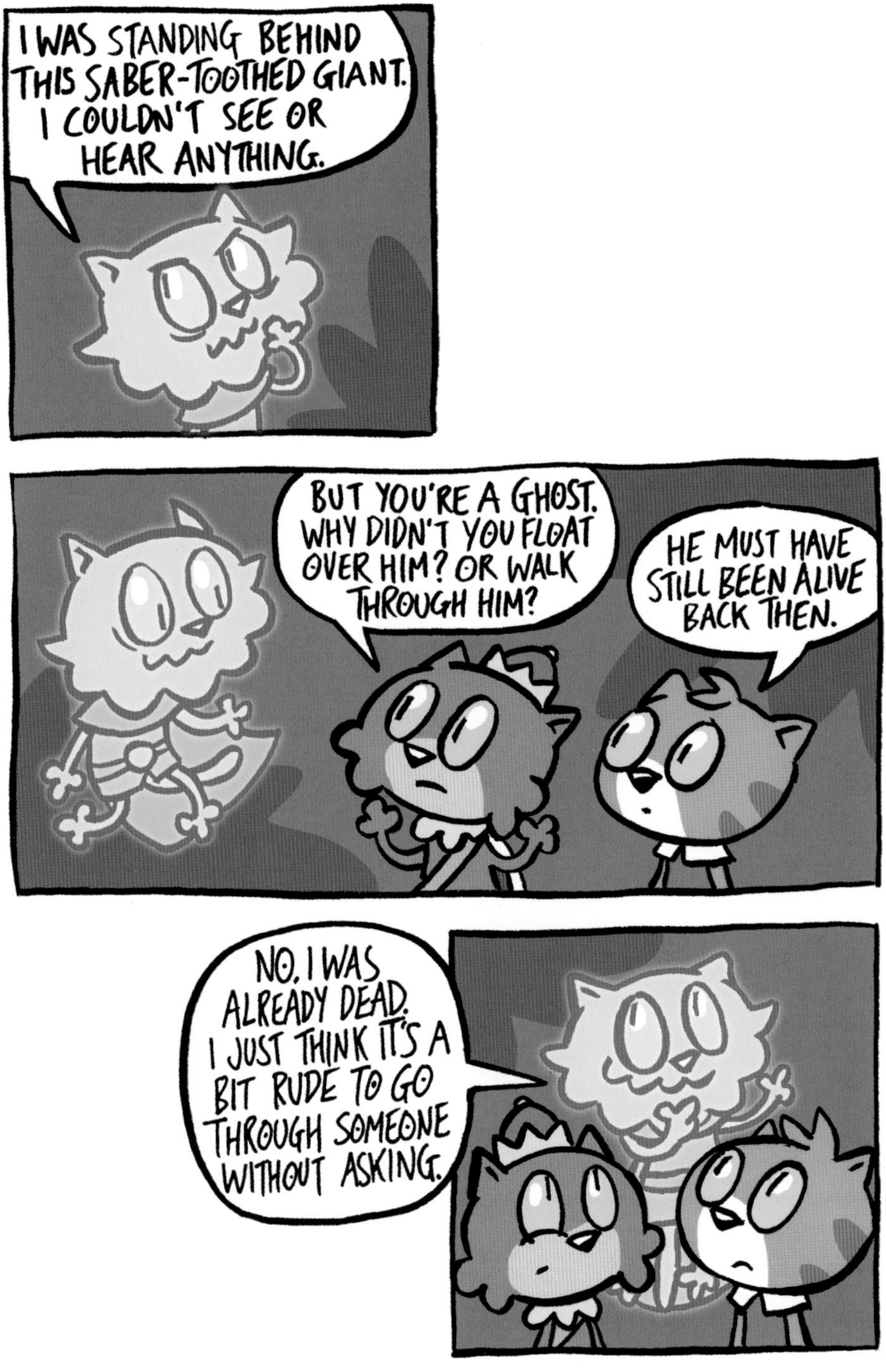
I WAS STANDING BEHIND THIS SABER-TOOTHED GIANT. I COULDN'T SEE OR HEAR ANYTHING.
BUT YOU'RE A GHOST. WHY DIDN'T YOU FLOAT OVER HIM? OR WALK THROUGH HIM?
HE MUST HAVE STILL BEEN ALIVE BACK THEN.
NO, I WAS ALREADY DEAD. I JUST THINK IT'S A BIT RUDE TO GO THROUGH SOMEONE WITHOUT ASKING.

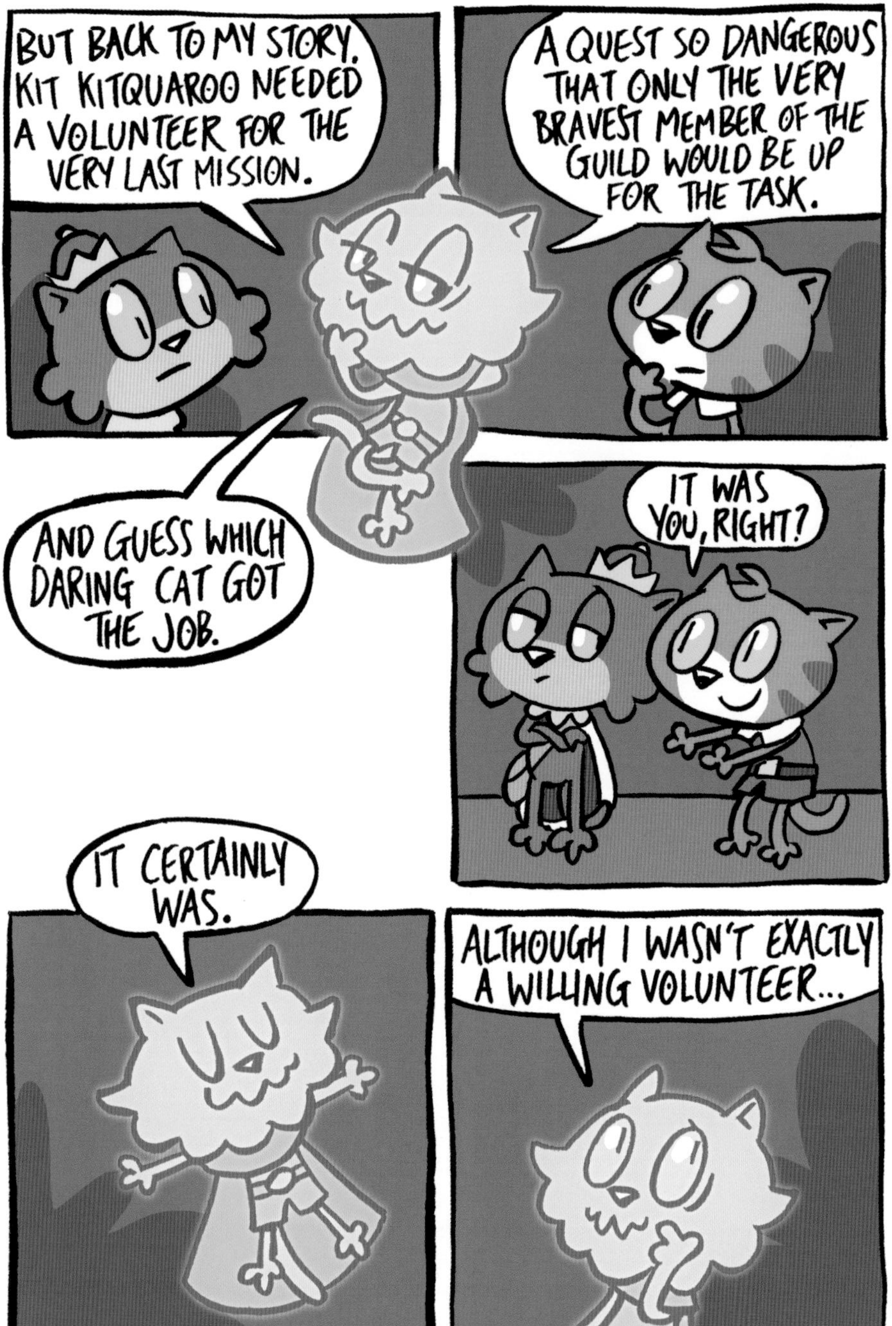
BUT BACK TO MY STORY. KIT KITQUAROO NEEDED A VOLUNTEER FOR THE VERY LAST MISSION.
A QUEST SO DANGEROUS THAT ONLY THE VERY BRAVEST MEMBER OF THE GUILD WOULD BE UP FOR THE TASK.
AND GUESS WHICH DARING CAT GOT THE JOB.
IT WAS YOU, RIGHT?
IT CERTAINLY WAS.
ALTHOUGH I WASN'T EXACTLY A WILLING VOLUNTEER...

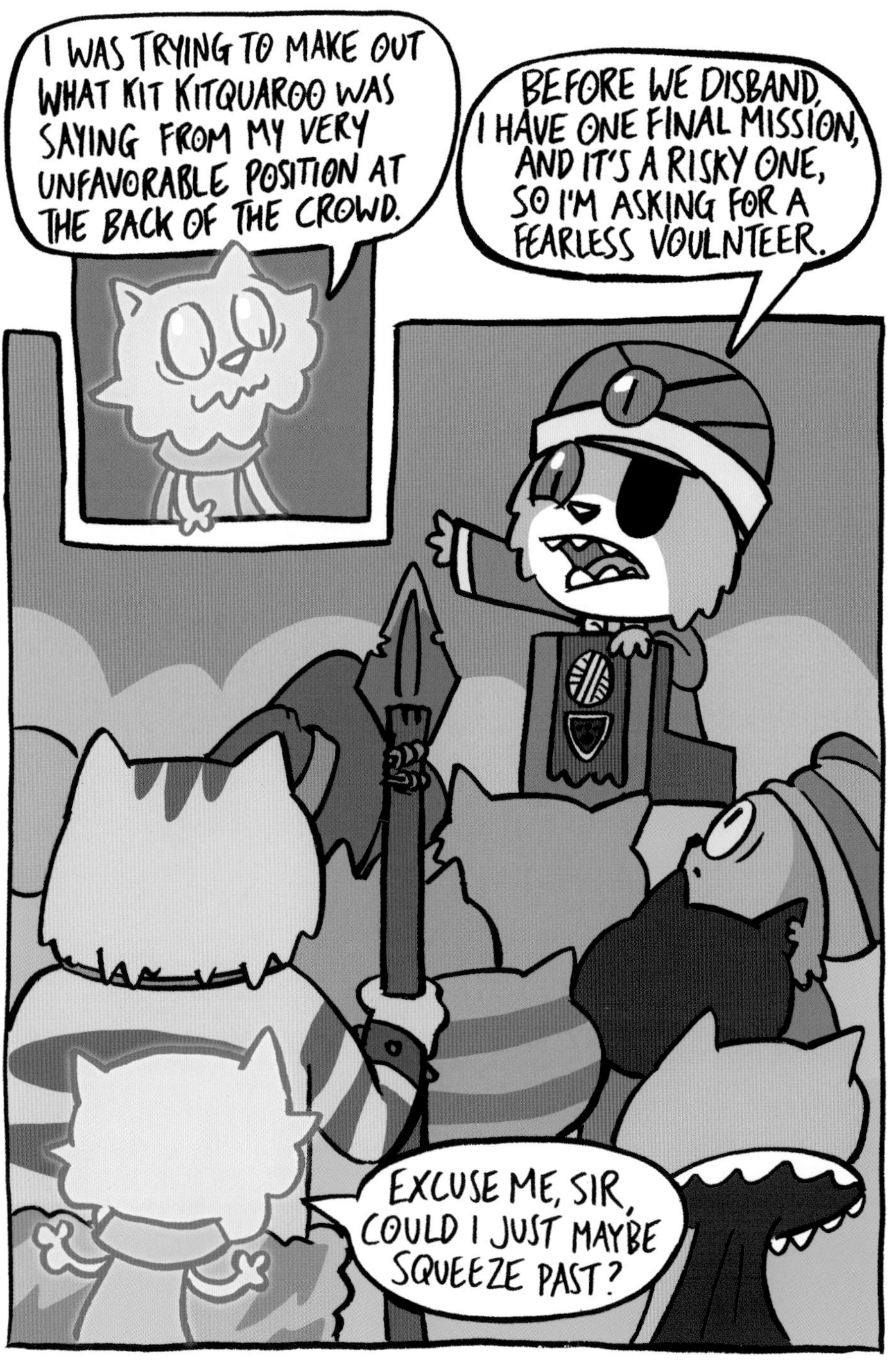
I WAS TRYING TO MAKE OUT WHAT KIT KITQUAROO WAS SAYING FROM MY VERY UNFAVORABLE POSITION AT THE BACK OF THE CROWD.
BEFORE WE DISBAND, I HAVE ONE FINAL MISSION, AND IT'S A RISKY ONE, SO I'M ASKING FOR A FEARLESS VOULNTEER.
EXCUSE ME, SIR, COULD I JUST MAYBE SQUEEZE PAST?

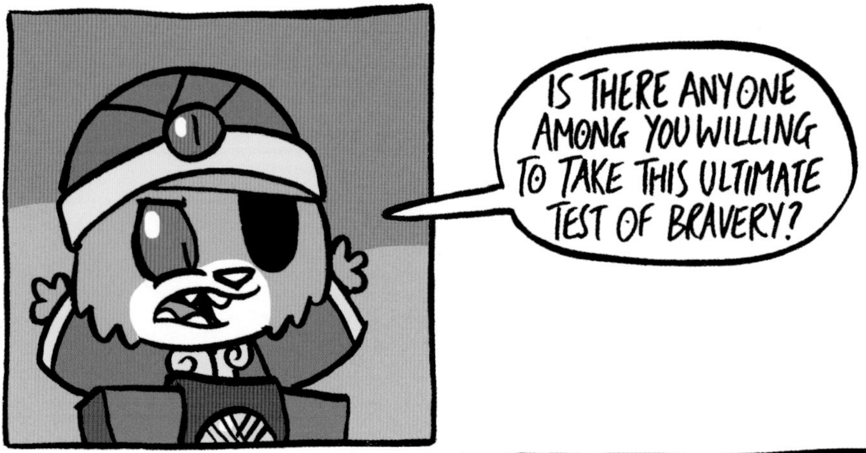
IS THERE ANYONE AMONG YOU WILLING TO TAKE THIS ULTIMATE TEST OF BRAVERY?

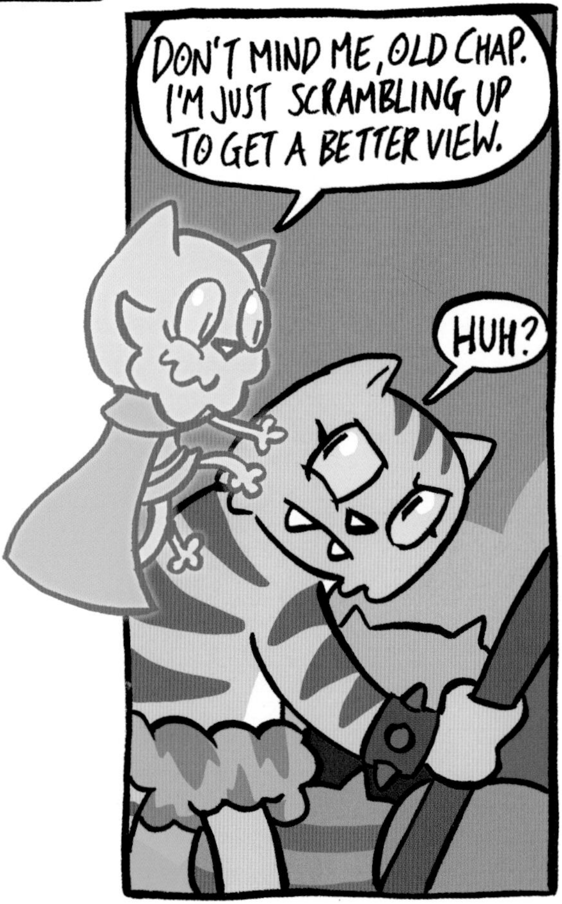
DON'T MIND ME, OLD CHAP. I'M JUST SCRAMBLING UP TO GET A BETTER VIEW.
HUH?

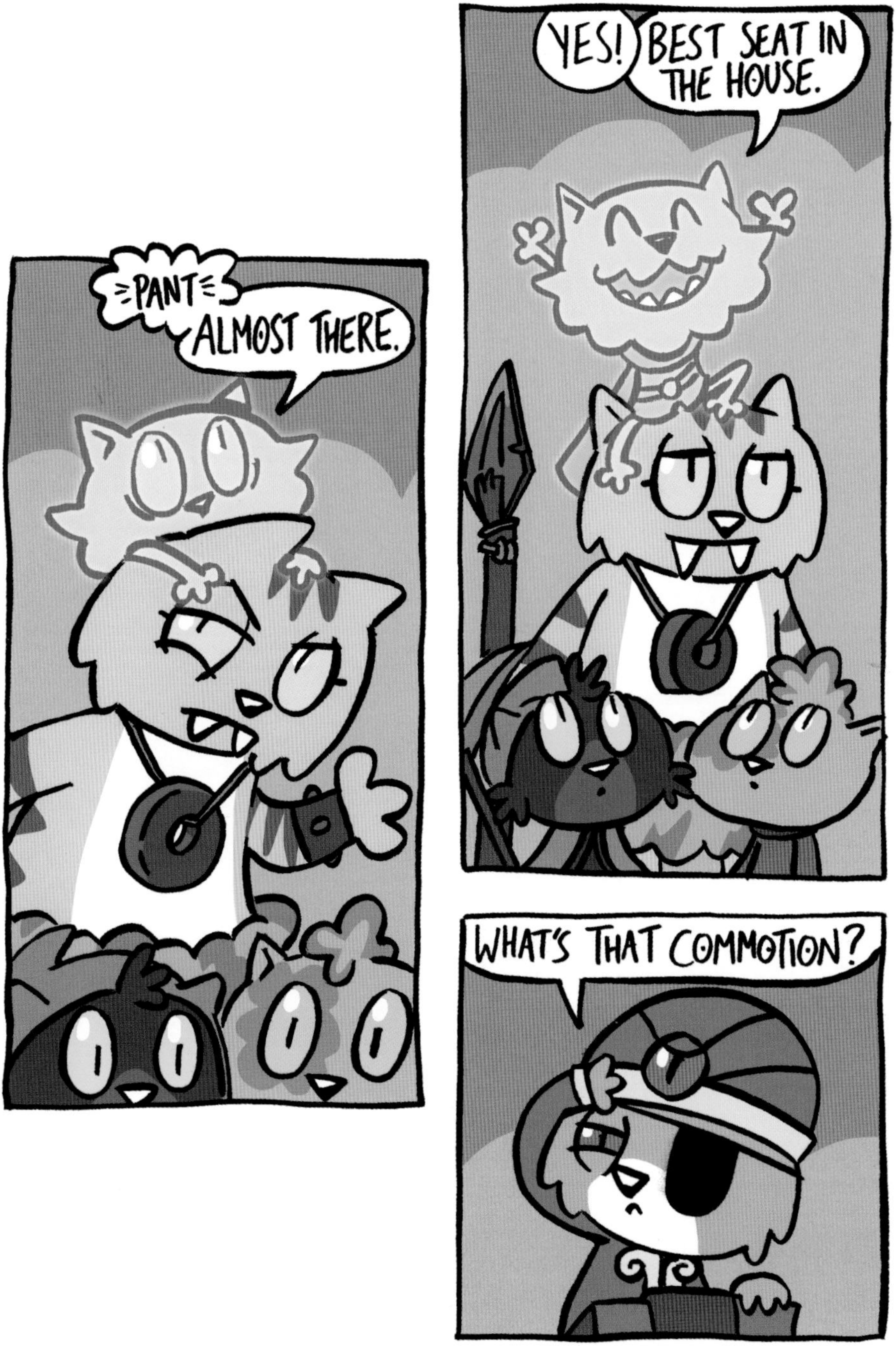
PANT
ALMOST THERE.
YES!
BEST SEAT IN THE HOUSE.
WHAT'S THAT COMMOTION?

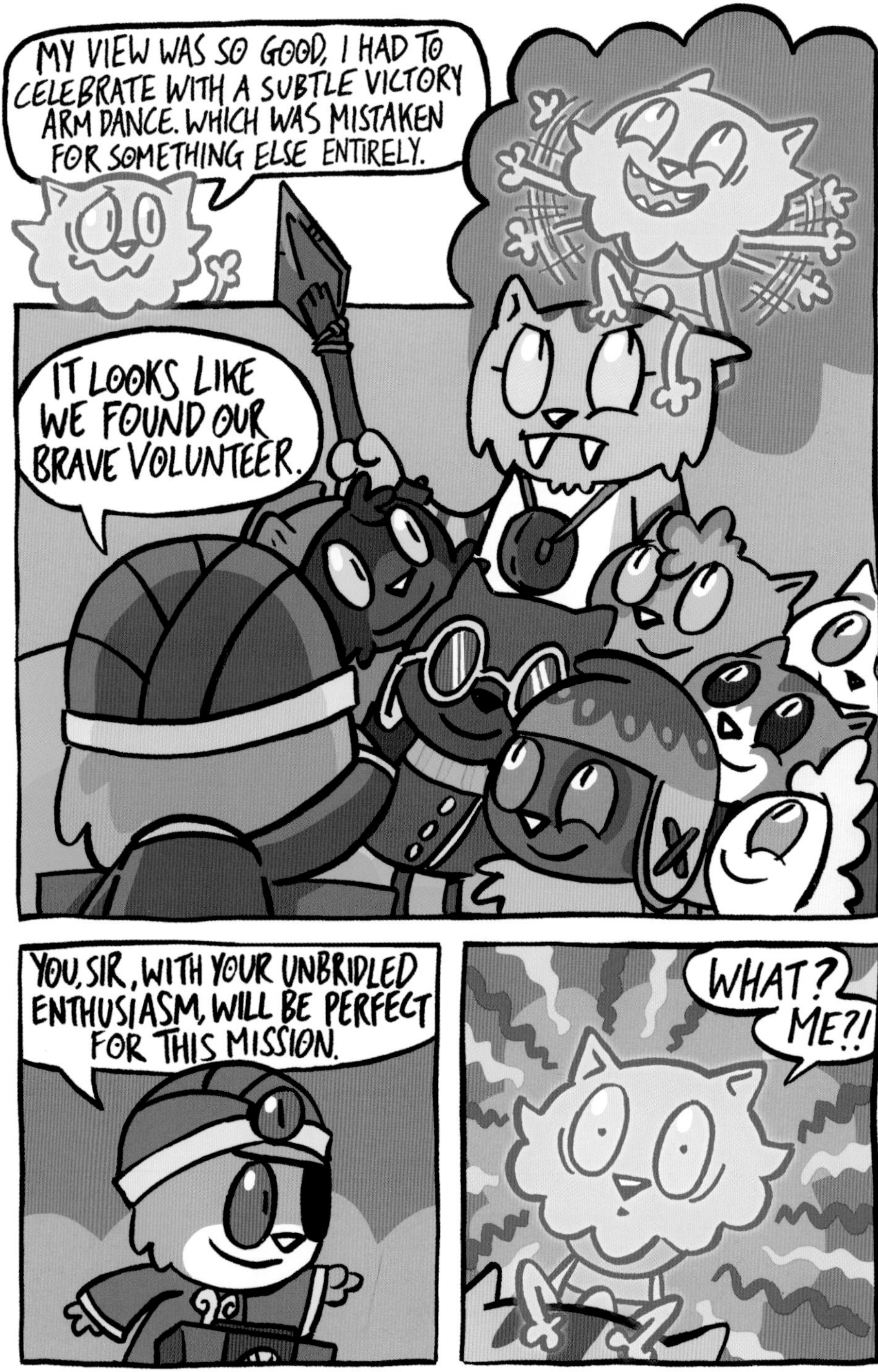
MY VIEW WAS SO GOOD, I HAD TO CELEBRATE WITH A SUBTLE VICTORY ARM DANCE. WHICH WAS MISTAKEN FOR SOMETHING ELSE ENTIRELY.
IT LOOKS LIKE WE FOUND OUR BRAVE VOLUNTEER.
YOU, SIR, WITH YOUR UNBRIDLED ENTHUSIASM, WILL BE PERFECT FOR THIS MISSION.
WHAT? ME?!

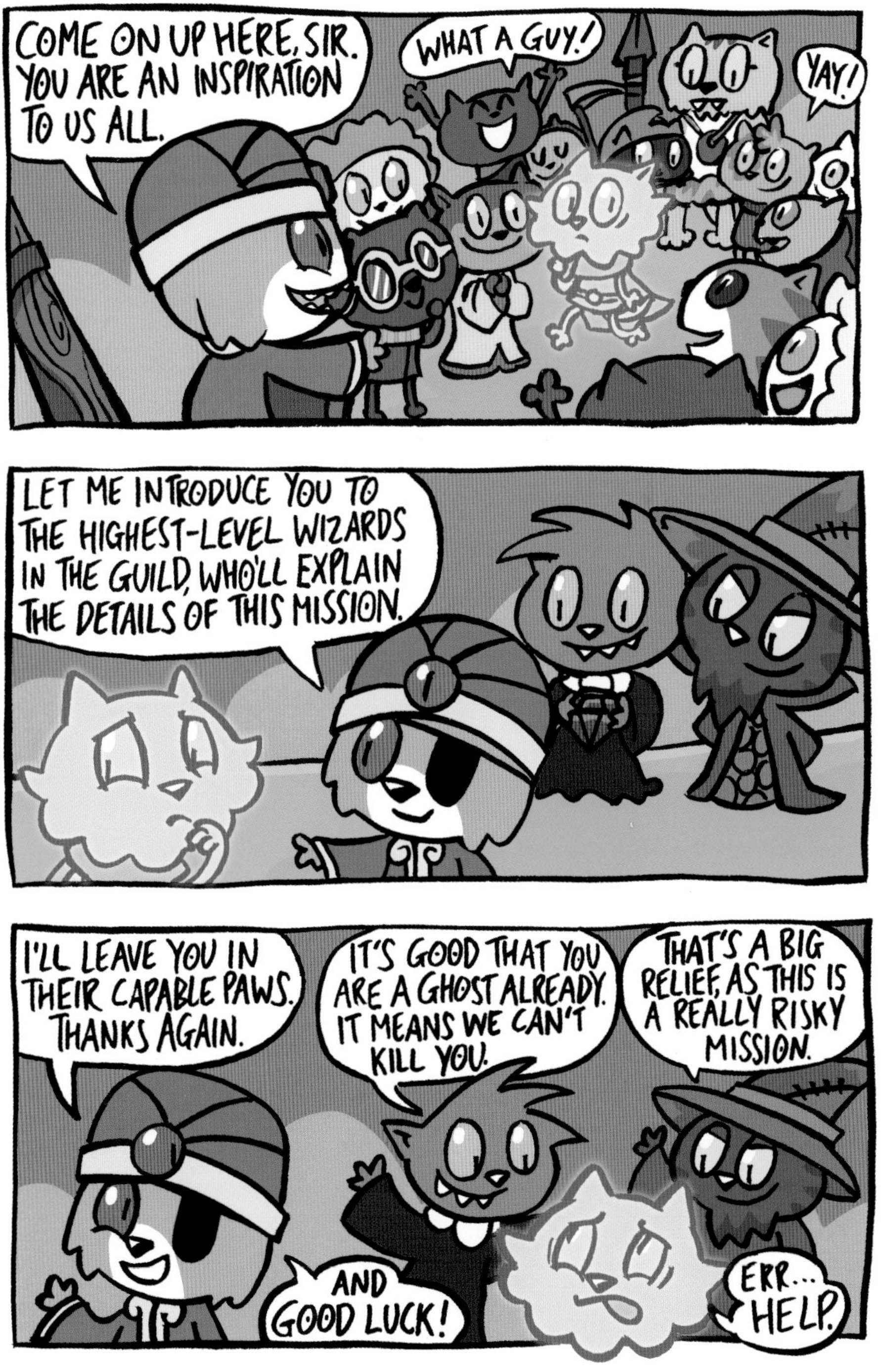
COME ON UP HERE, SIR. YOU ARE AN INSPIRATION TO US ALL.
WHAT A GUY!
YAY!
LET ME INTRODUCE YOU TO THE HIGHEST-LEVEL WIZARDS IN THE GUILD, WHO'LL EXPLAIN THE DETAILS OF THIS MISSION.
I'LL LEAVE YOU IN THEIR CAPABLE PAWS. THANKS AGAIN.
IT'S GOOD THAT YOU ARE A GHOST ALREADY. IT MEANS WE CAN'T KILL YOU.
THAT'S A BIG RELIEF, AS THIS IS A REALLY RISKY MISSION.
AND GOOD LUCK!
ERR... HELP.

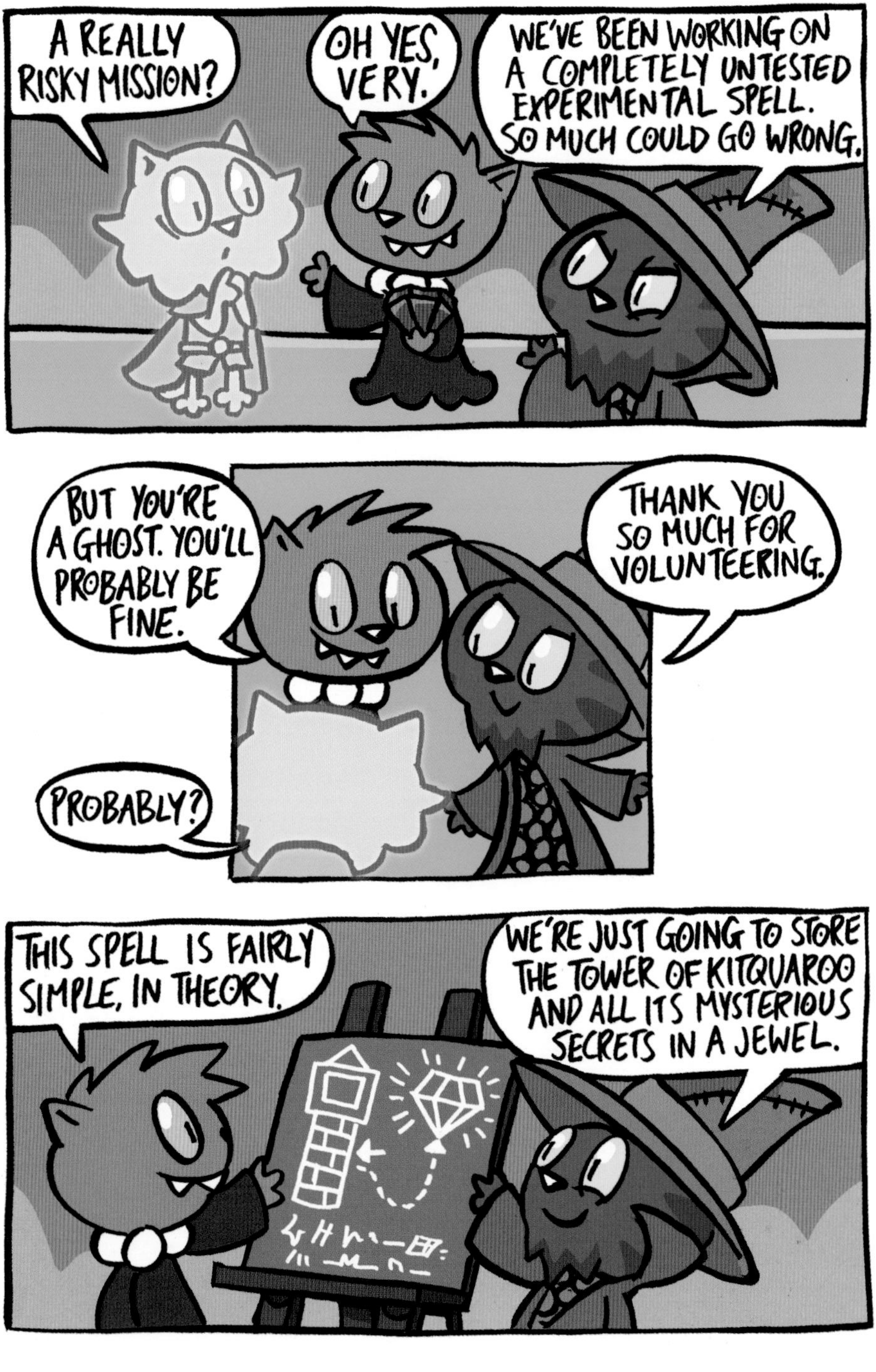
A REALLY RISKY MISSION?
OH YES, VERY.
WE'VE BEEN WORKING ON A COMPLETELY UNTESTED EXPERIMENTAL SPELL. SO MUCH COULD GO WRONG.
BUT YOU'RE A GHOST. YOU'LL PROBABLY BE FINE.
THANK YOU SO MUCH FOR VOLUNTEERING.
PROBABLY?
THIS SPELL IS FAIRLY SIMPLE, IN THEORY.
WE'RE JUST GOING TO STORE THE TOWER OF KITQUAROO AND ALL ITS MYSTERIOUS SECRETS IN A JEWEL.

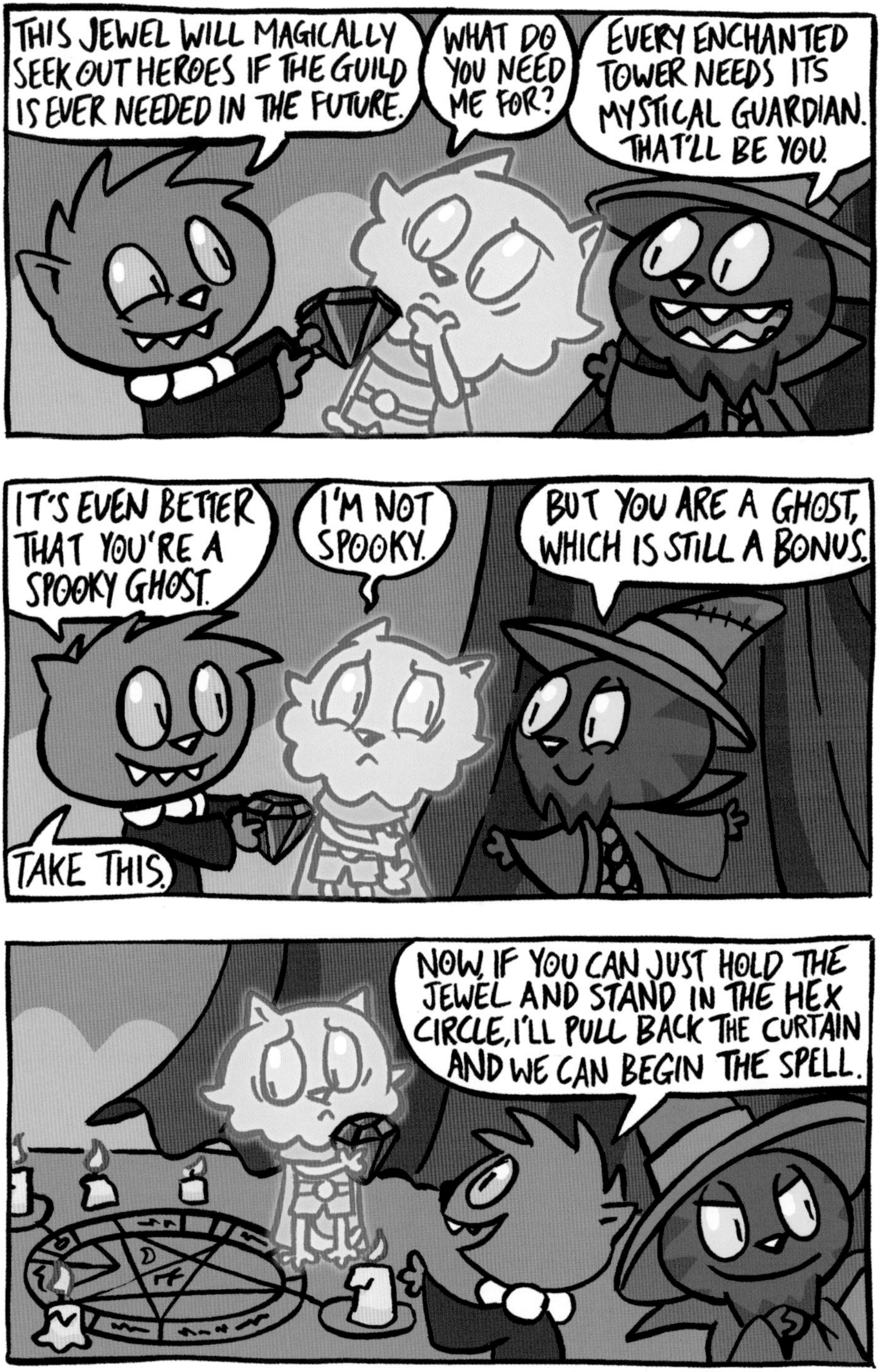
THIS JEWEL WILL MAGICALLY SEEK OUT HEROES IF THE GUILD IS EVER NEEDED IN THE FUTURE.
WHAT DO YOU NEED ME FOR?
EVERY ENCHANTED TOWER NEEDS ITS MYSTICAL GUARDIAN. THAT'LL BE YOU.
IT'S EVEN BETTER THAT YOU'RE A SPOOKY GHOST.
TAKE THIS.
I'M NOT SPOOKY.
BUT YOU ARE A GHOST, WHICH IS STILL A BONUS.
NOW, IF YOU CAN JUST HOLD THE JEWEL AND STAND IN THE HEX CIRCLE, I'LL PULL BACK THE CURTAIN AND WE CAN BEGIN THE SPELL.

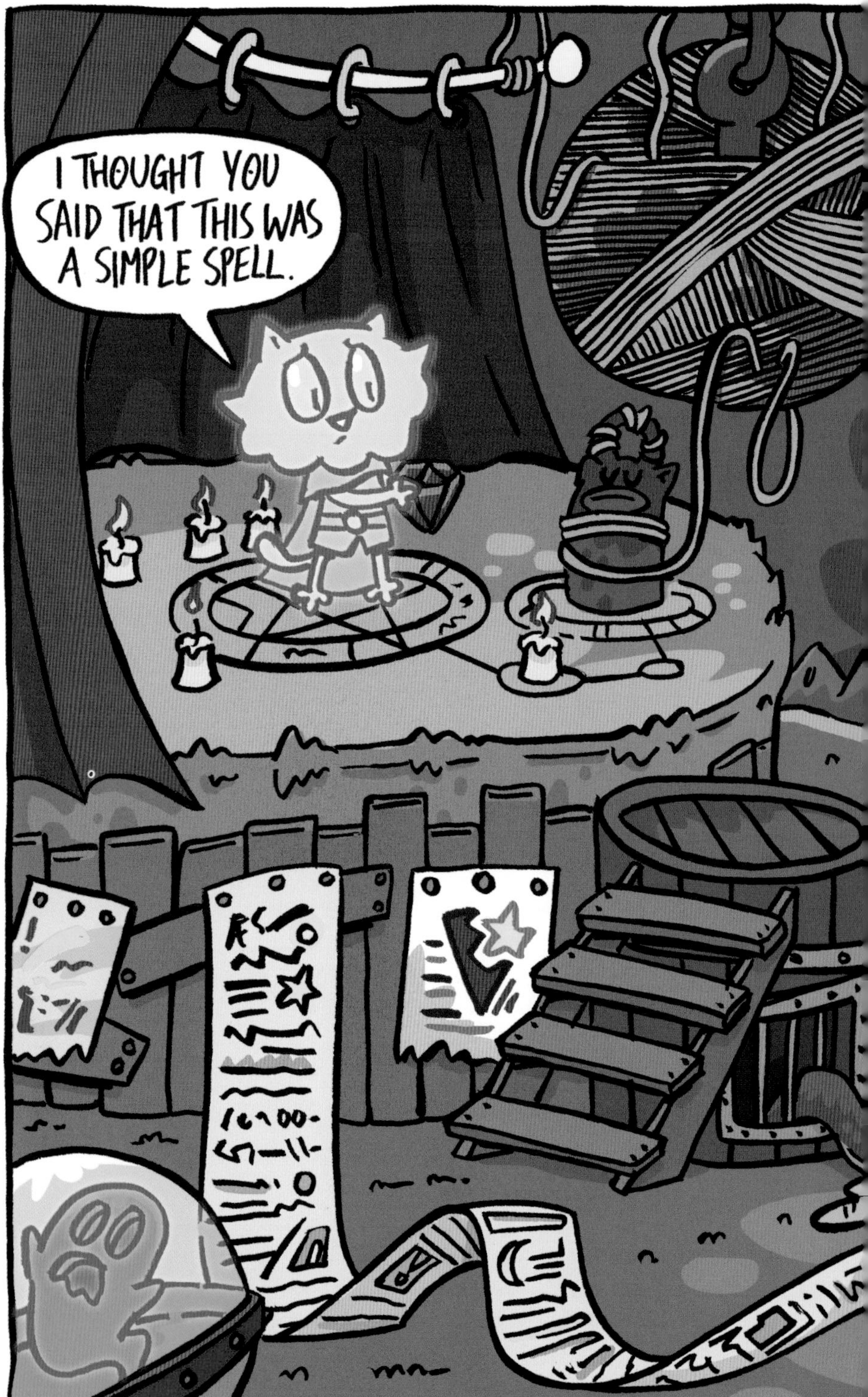
I THOUGHT YOU SAID THAT THIS WAS A SIMPLE SPELL.

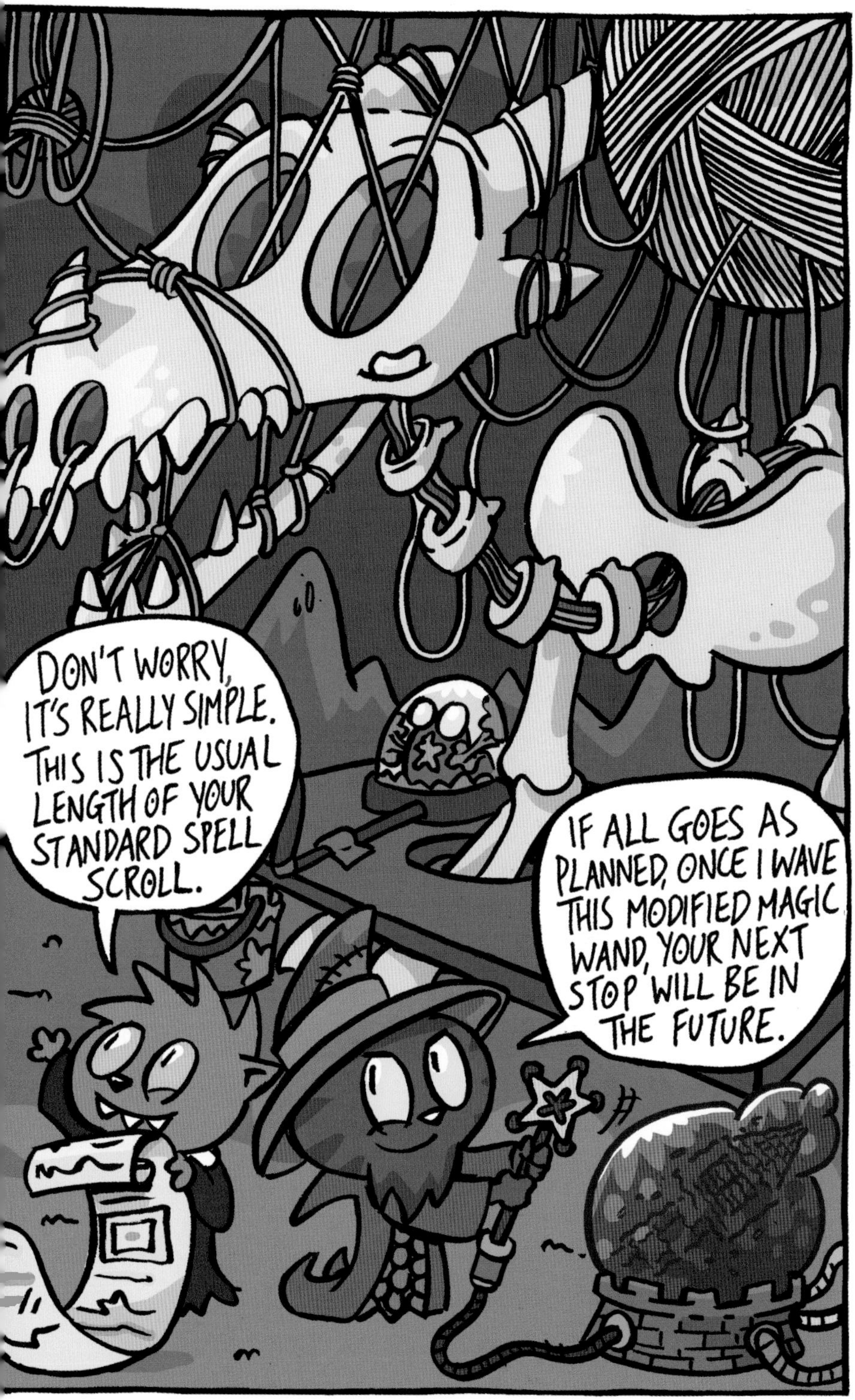
DON'T WORRY, IT'S REALLY SIMPLE. THIS IS THE USUAL LENGTH OF YOUR STANDARD SPELL SCROLL.
IF ALL GOES AS PLANNED, ONCE I WAVE THIS MODIFIED MAGIC WAND, YOUR NEXT STOP WILL BE IN THE FUTURE.

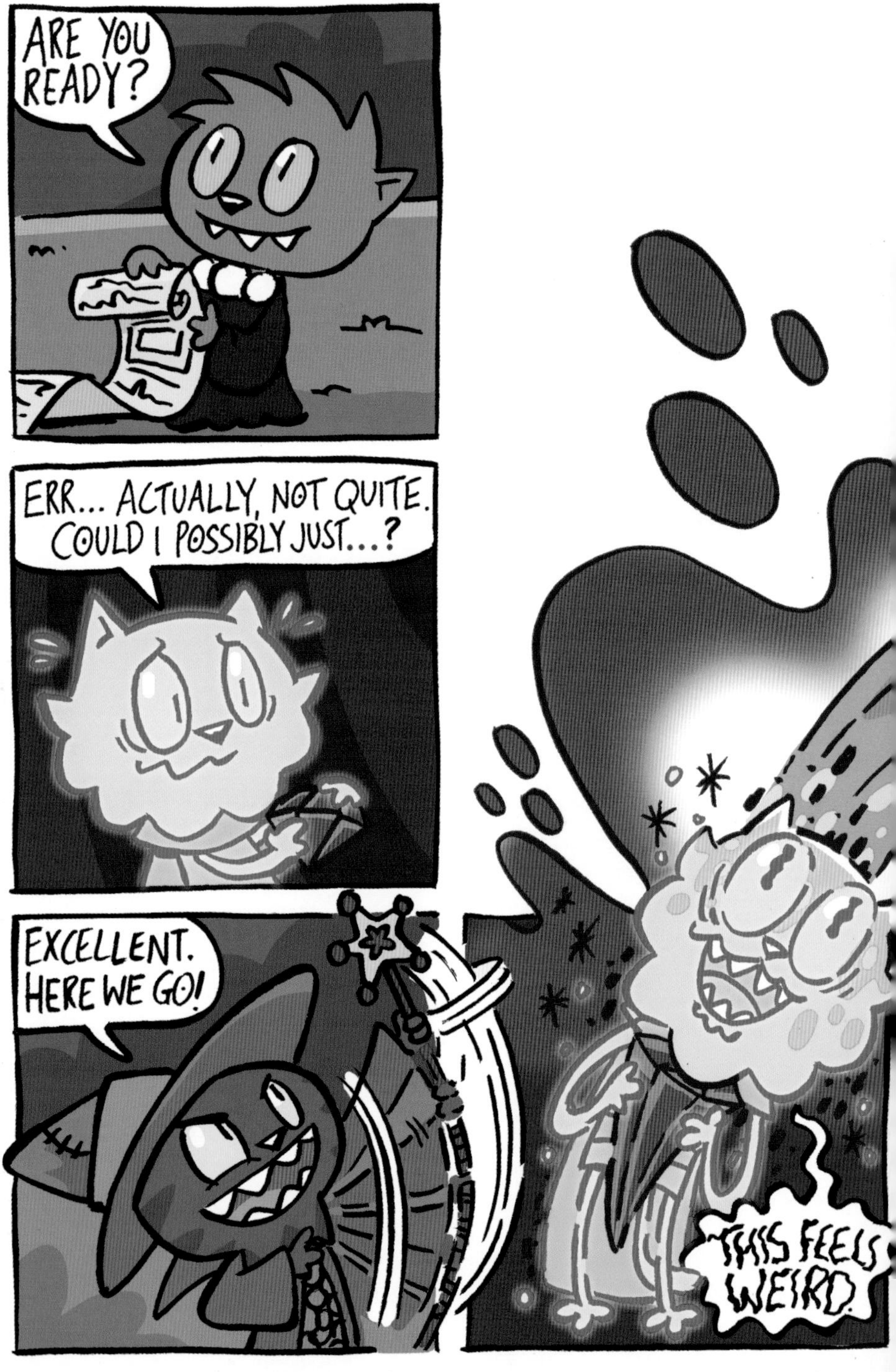
ARE YOU READY?
ERR... ACTUALLY, NOT QUITE. COULD I POSSIBLY JUST...?
EXCELLENT. HERE WE GO!
THIS FEELS WEIRD.

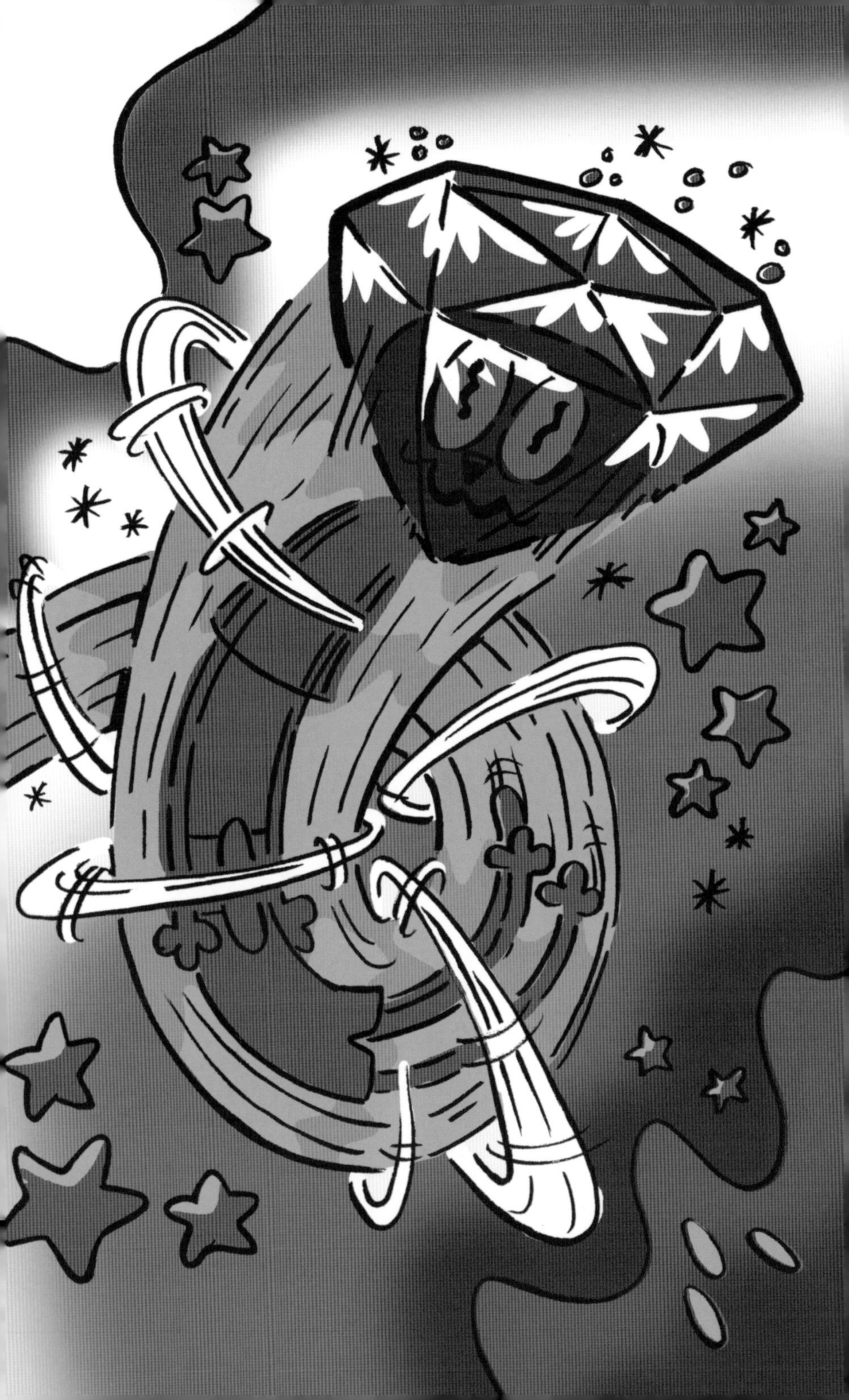

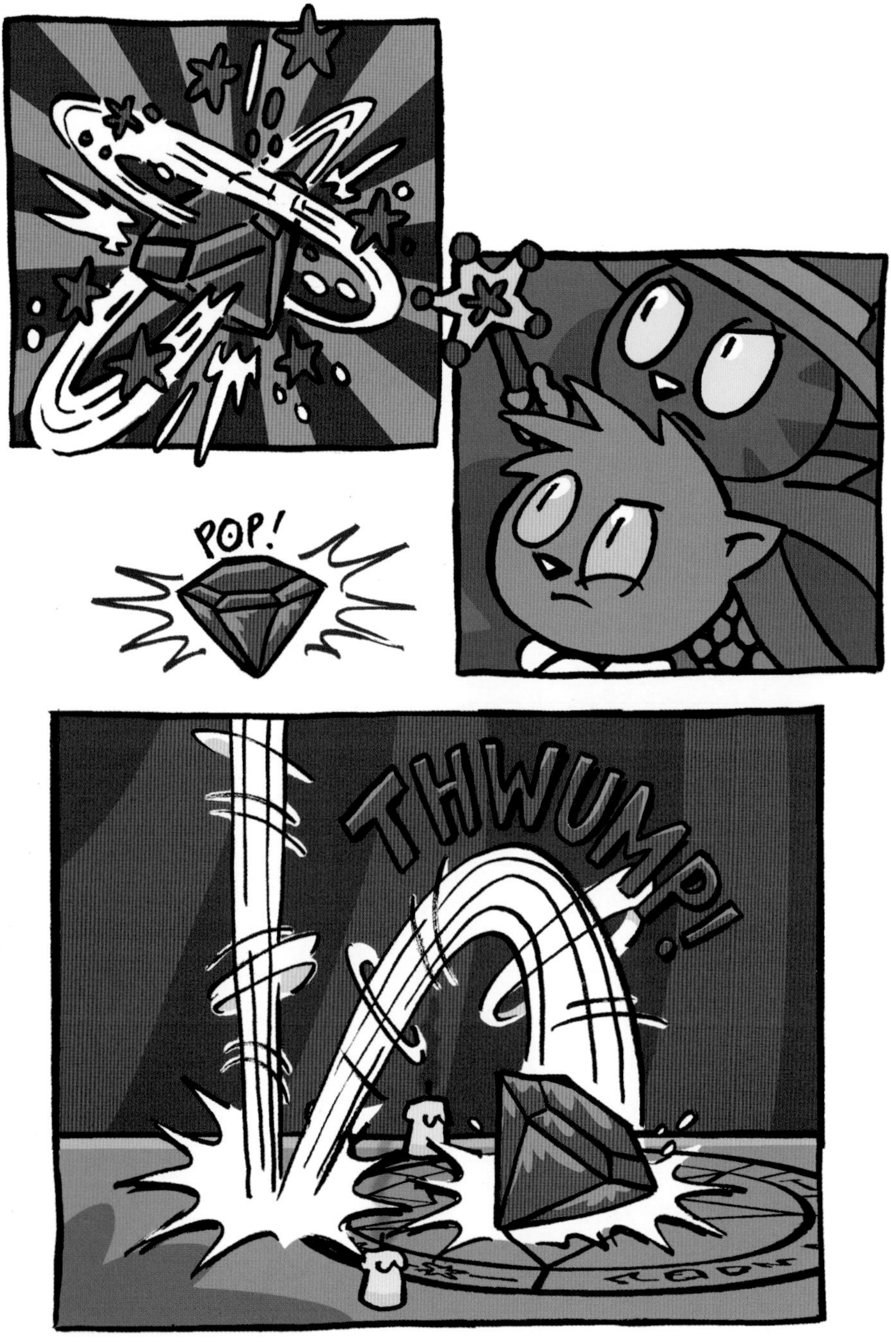
POP!
THWUMP!

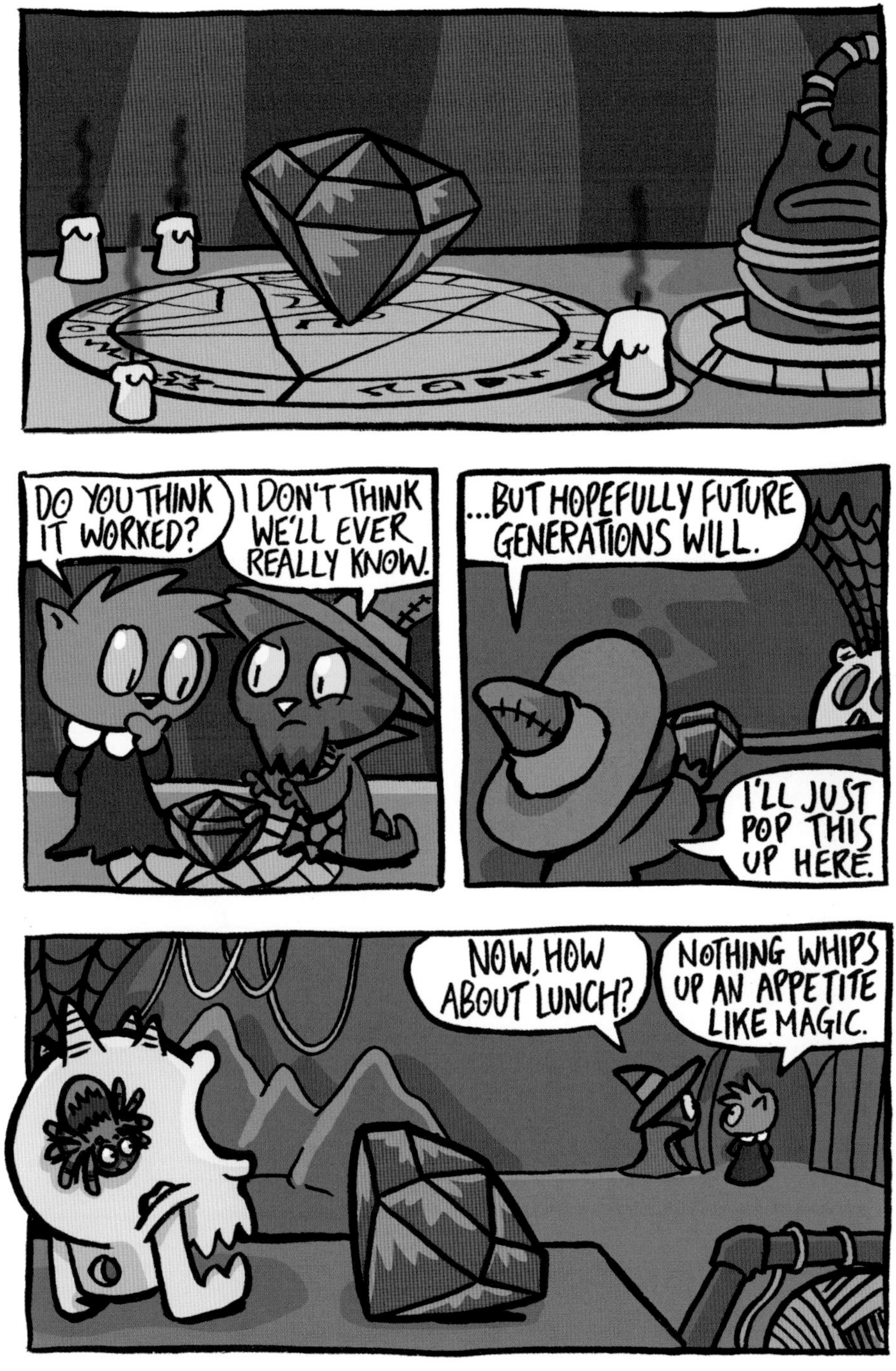
DO YOU THINK IT WORKED?
I DON'T THINK WE'LL EVER REALLY KNOW.
...BUT HOPEFULLY FUTURE GENERATIONS WILL.
I'LL JUST POP THIS UP HERE.
NOW, HOW ABOUT LUNCH?
NOTHING WHIPS UP AN APPETITE LIKE MAGIC.

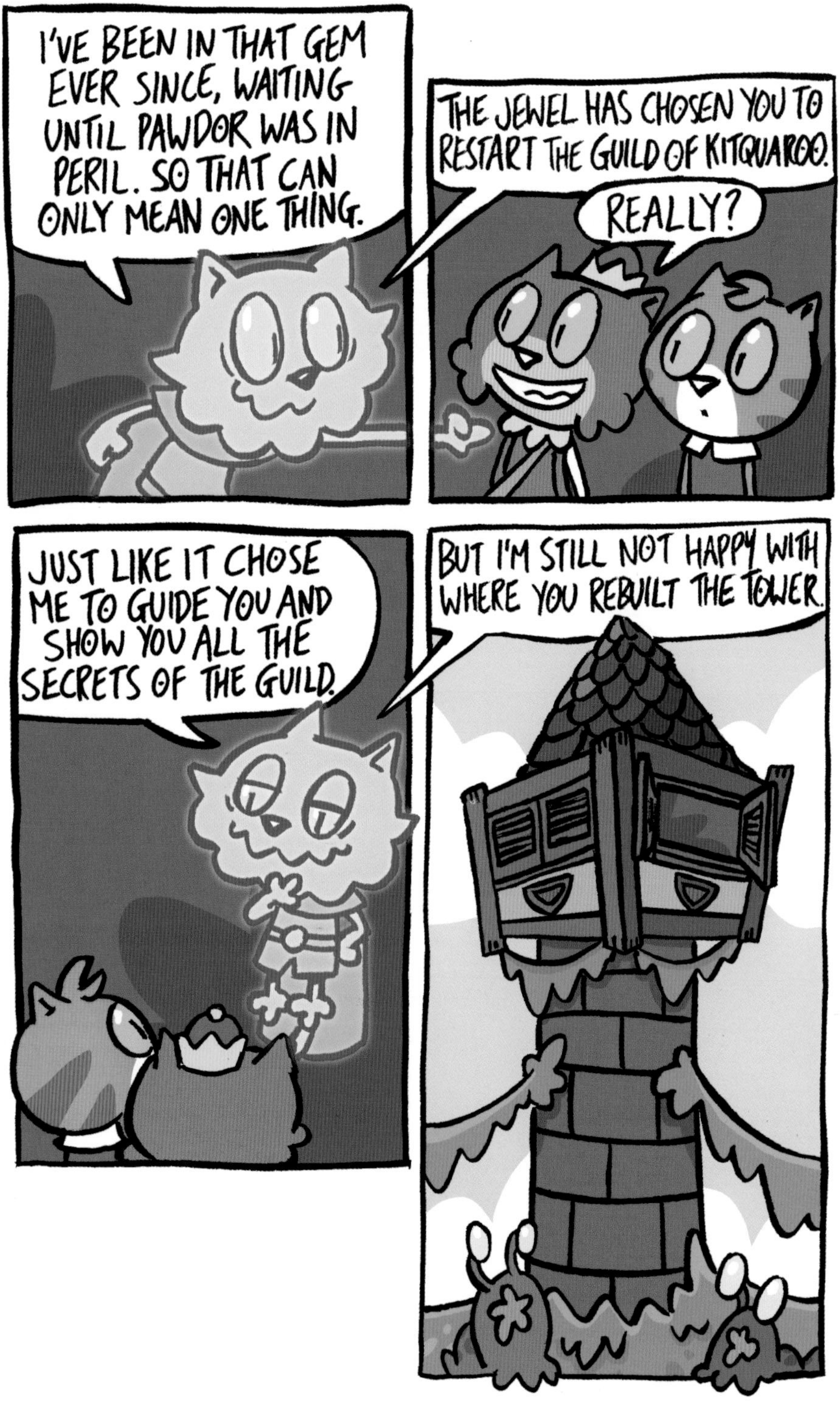
I'VE BEEN IN THAT GEM EVER SINCE, WAITING UNTIL PAWDOR WAS IN PERIL. SO THAT CAN ONLY MEAN ONE THING.
THE JEWEL HAS CHOSEN YOU TO RESTART THE GUILD OF KITQUAROO.
REALLY?
JUST LIKE IT CHOSE ME TO GUIDE YOU AND SHOW YOU ALL THE SECRETS OF THE GUILD.
BUT I'M STILL NOT HAPPY WITH WHERE YOU REBUILT THE TOWER.

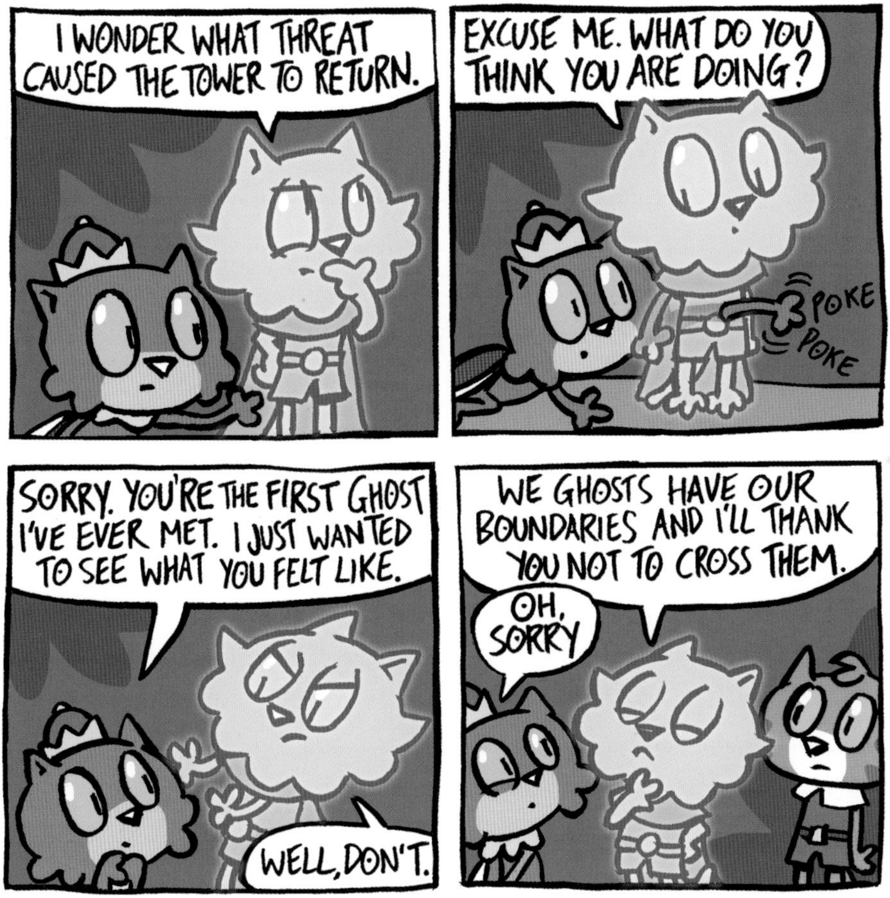
I WONDER WHAT THREAT CAUSED THE TOWER TO RETURN.
EXCUSE ME. WHAT DO YOU THINK YOU ARE DOING?
POKE
POKE
SORRY. YOU'RE THE FIRST GHOST I'VE EVER MET. I JUST WANTED TO SEE WHAT YOU FELT LIKE.
WELL, DON'T.
WE GHOSTS HAVE OUR BOUNDARIES AND I'LL THANK YOU NOT TO CROSS THEM.
OH, SORRY

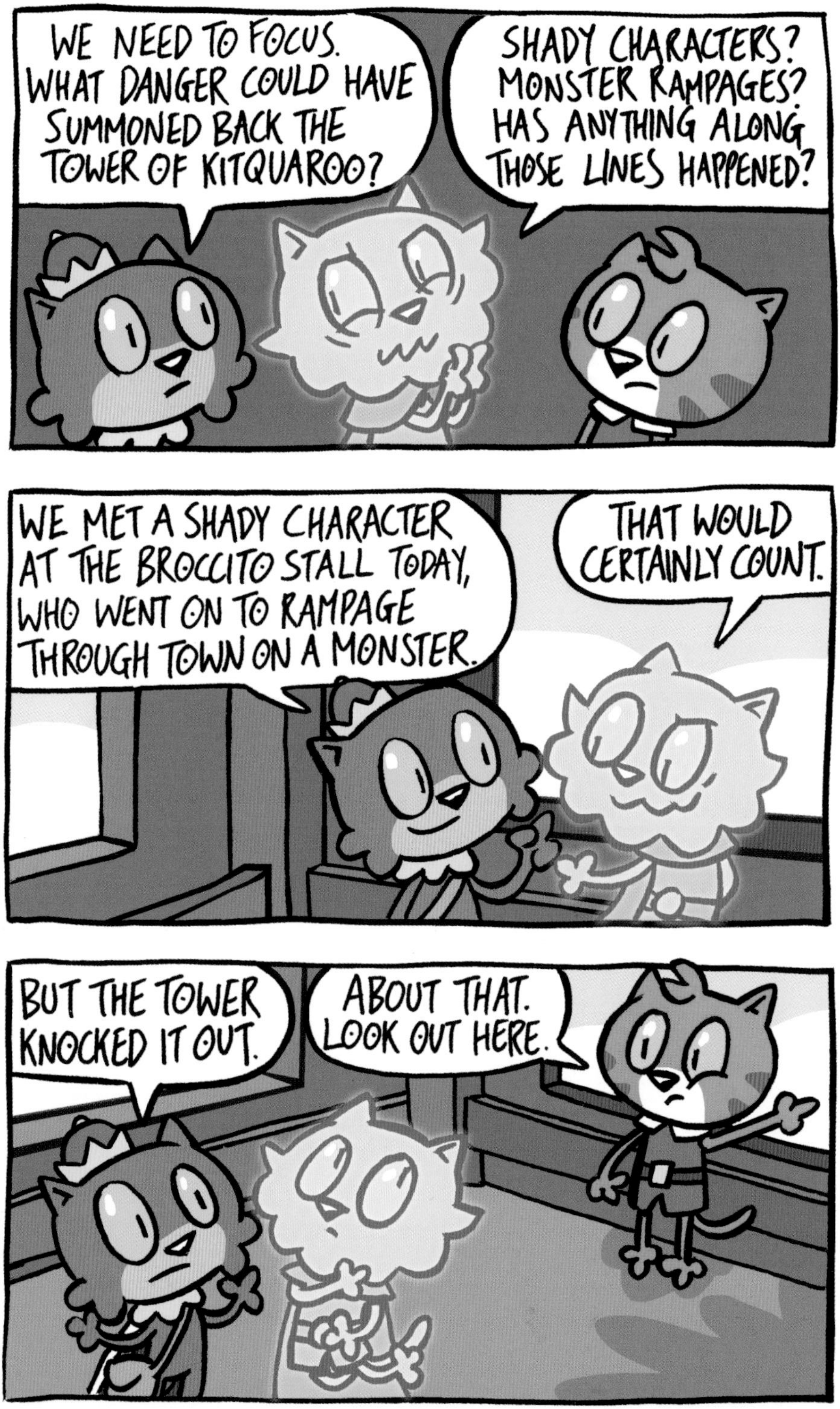
WE NEED TO FOCUS. WHAT DANGER COULD HAVE SUMMONED BACK THE TOWER OF KITQUAROO?
SHADY CHARACTERS? MONSTER RAMPAGES? HAS ANYTHING ALONG THOSE LINES HAPPENED?
WE MET A SHADY CHARACTER AT THE BROCCITO STALL TODAY, WHO WENT ON TO RAMPAGE THROUGH TOWN ON A MONSTER.
THAT WOULD CERTAINLY COUNT.
BUT THE TOWER KNOCKED IT OUT.
ABOUT THAT. LOOK OUT HERE.

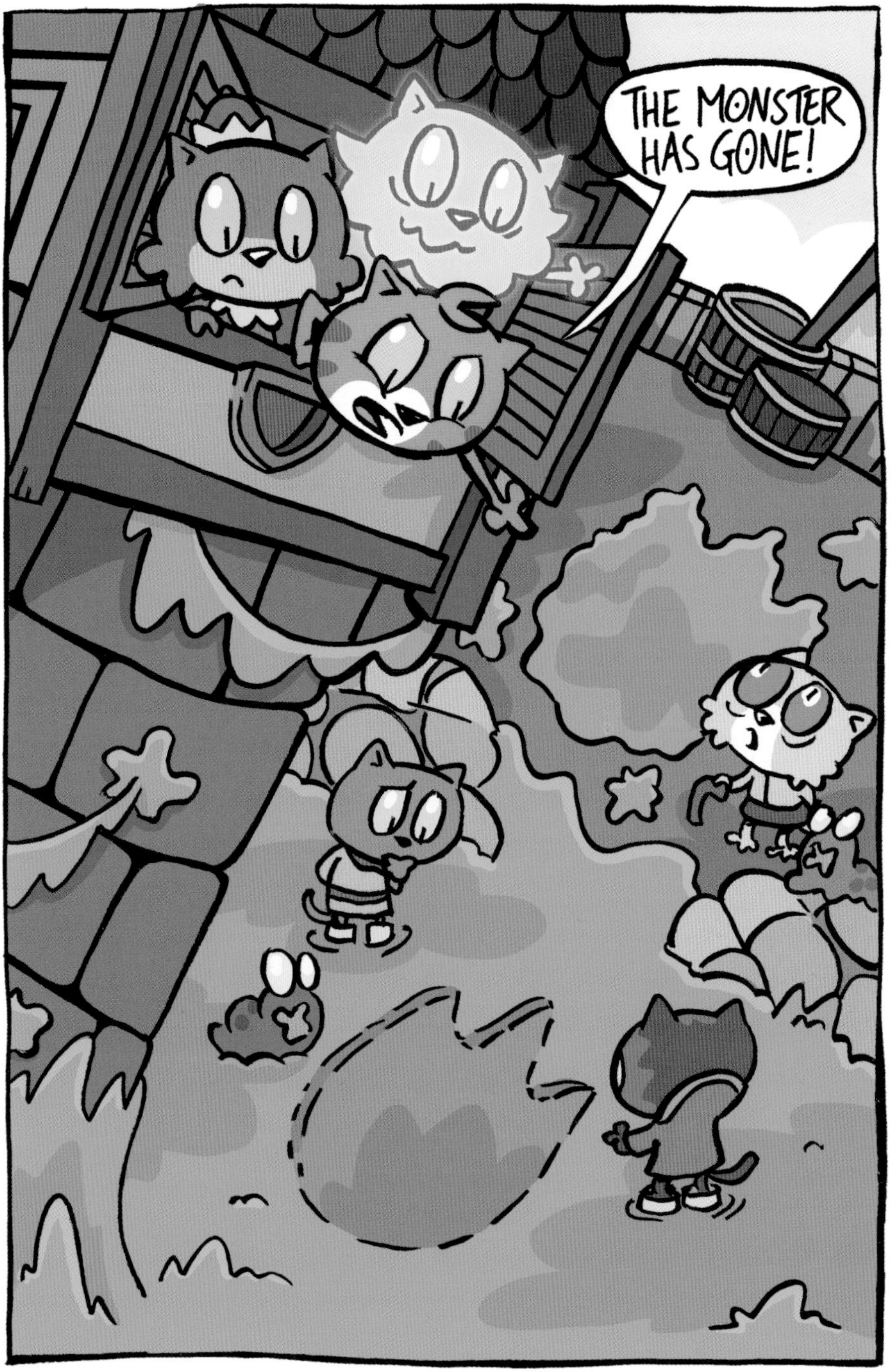
THE MONSTER HAS GONE!

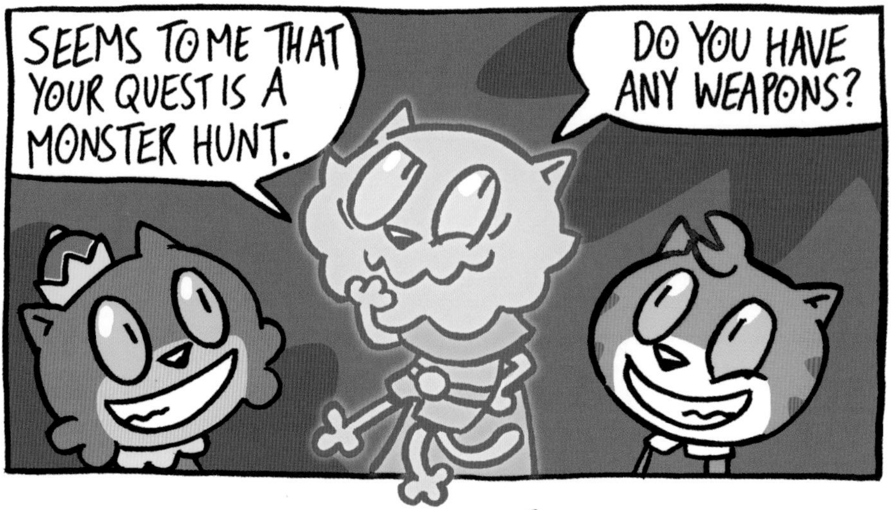
SEEMS TO ME THAT YOUR QUEST IS A MONSTER HUNT.
DO YOU HAVE ANY WEAPONS?

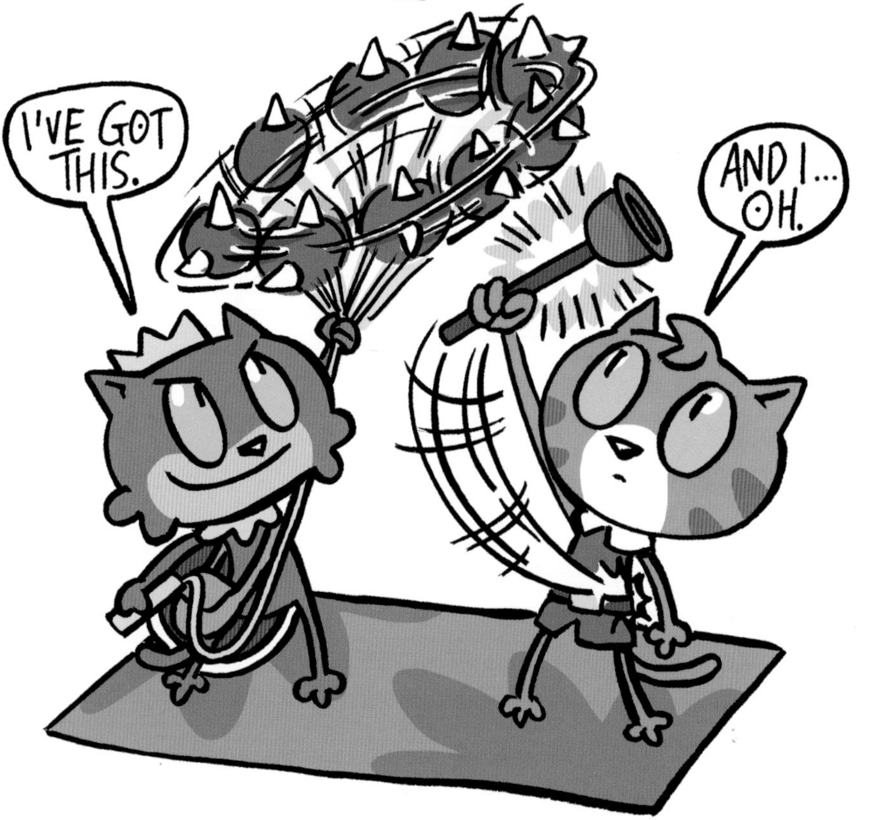
I'VE GOT THIS.
AND I... OH.

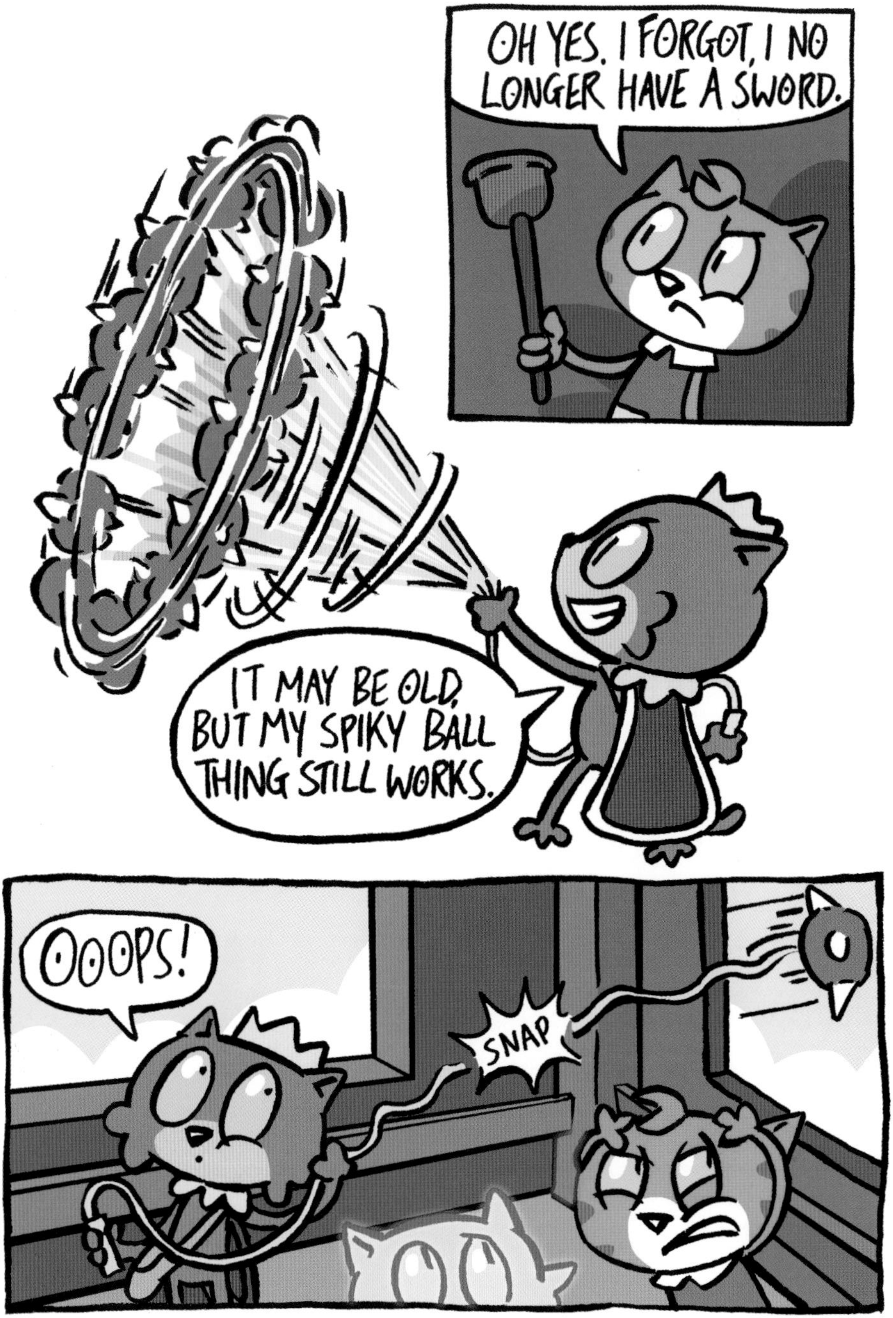
OH YES. I FORGOT, I NO LONGER HAVE A SWORD.
IT MAY BE OLD, BUT MY SPIKY BALL THING STILL WORKS.
OOOPS!
SNAP

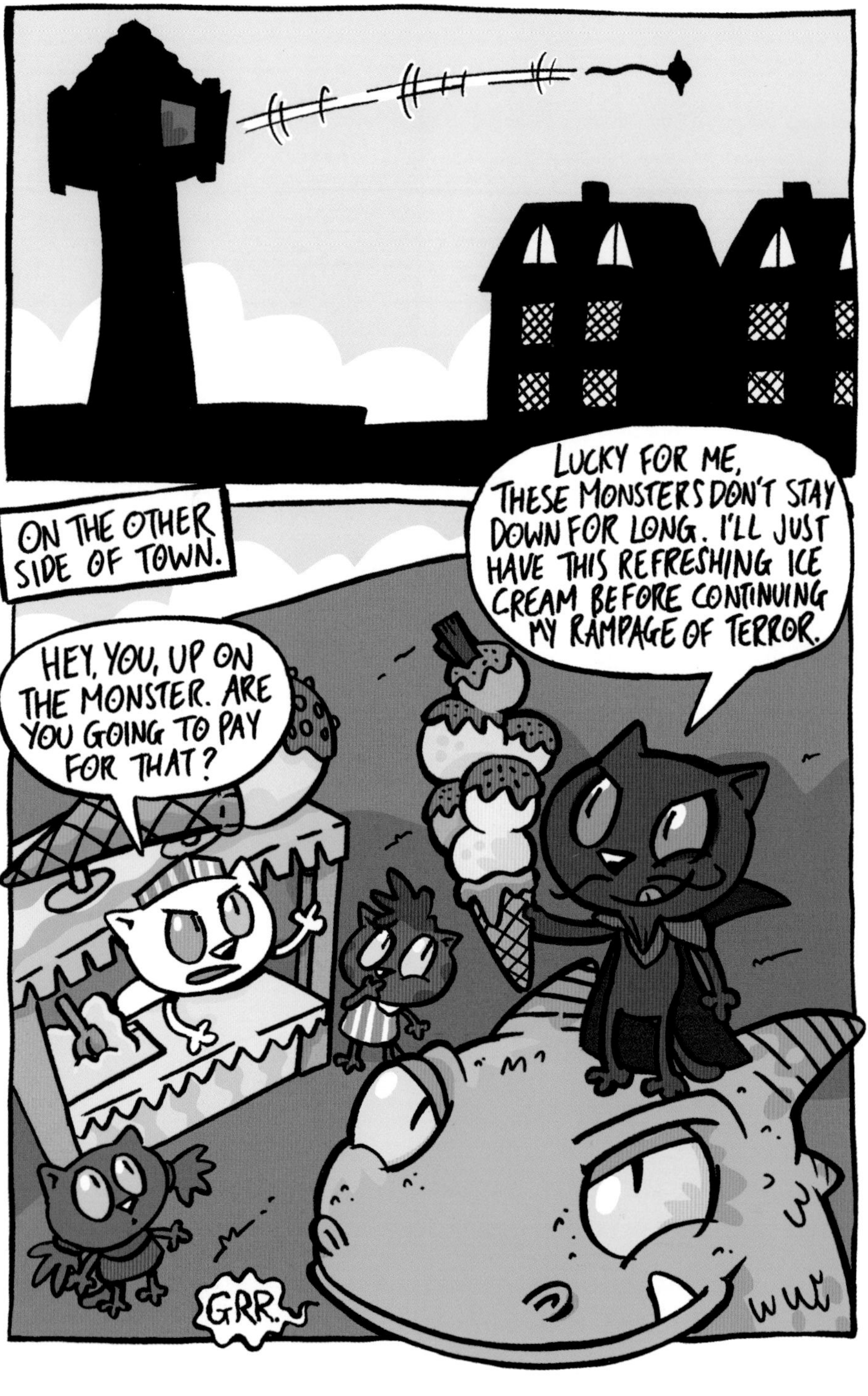
ON THE OTHER SIDE OF TOWN.
LUCKY FOR ME, THESE MONSTERS DON'T STAY DOWN FOR LONG. I'LL JUST HAVE THIS REFRESHING ICE CREAM BEFORE CONTINUING MY RAMPAGE OF TERROR.
HEY, YOU, UP ON THE MONSTER. ARE YOU GOING TO PAY FOR THAT?
GRR.

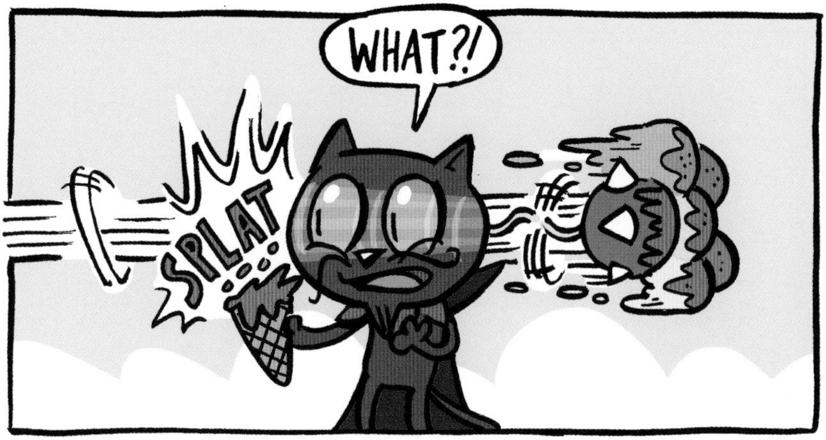
WHAT?!
SPLAT

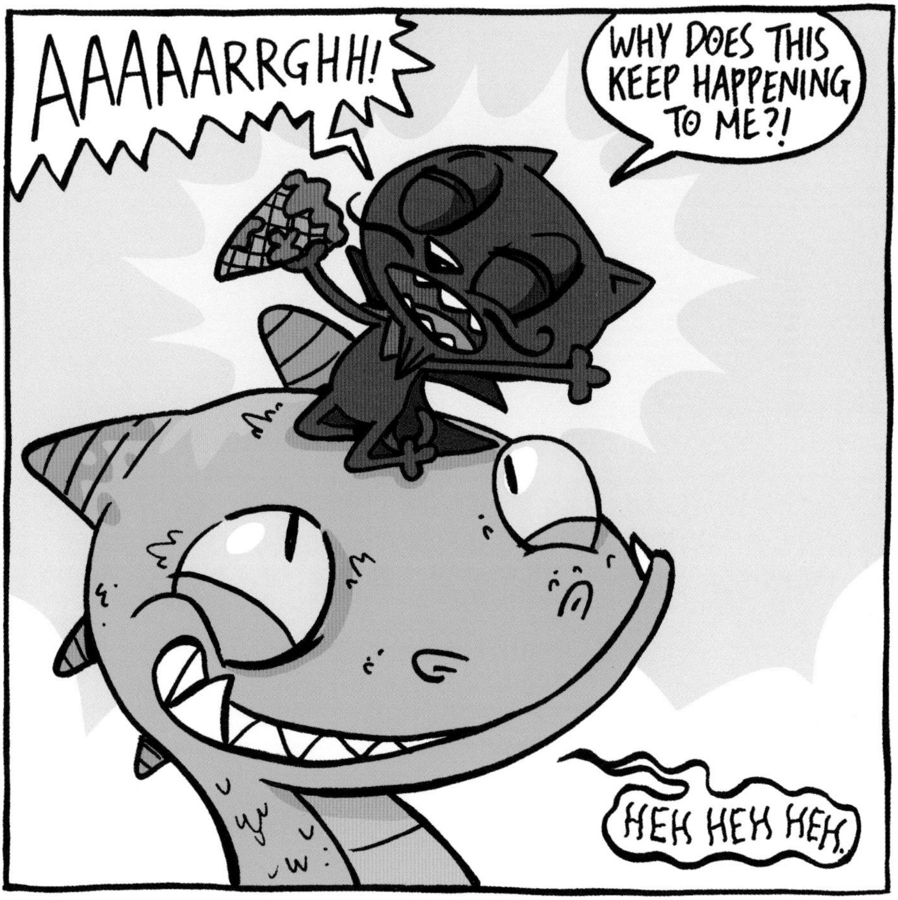
AAAAARRGHH!
WHY DOES THIS KEEP HAPPENING TO ME?!
HEH HEH HEH.

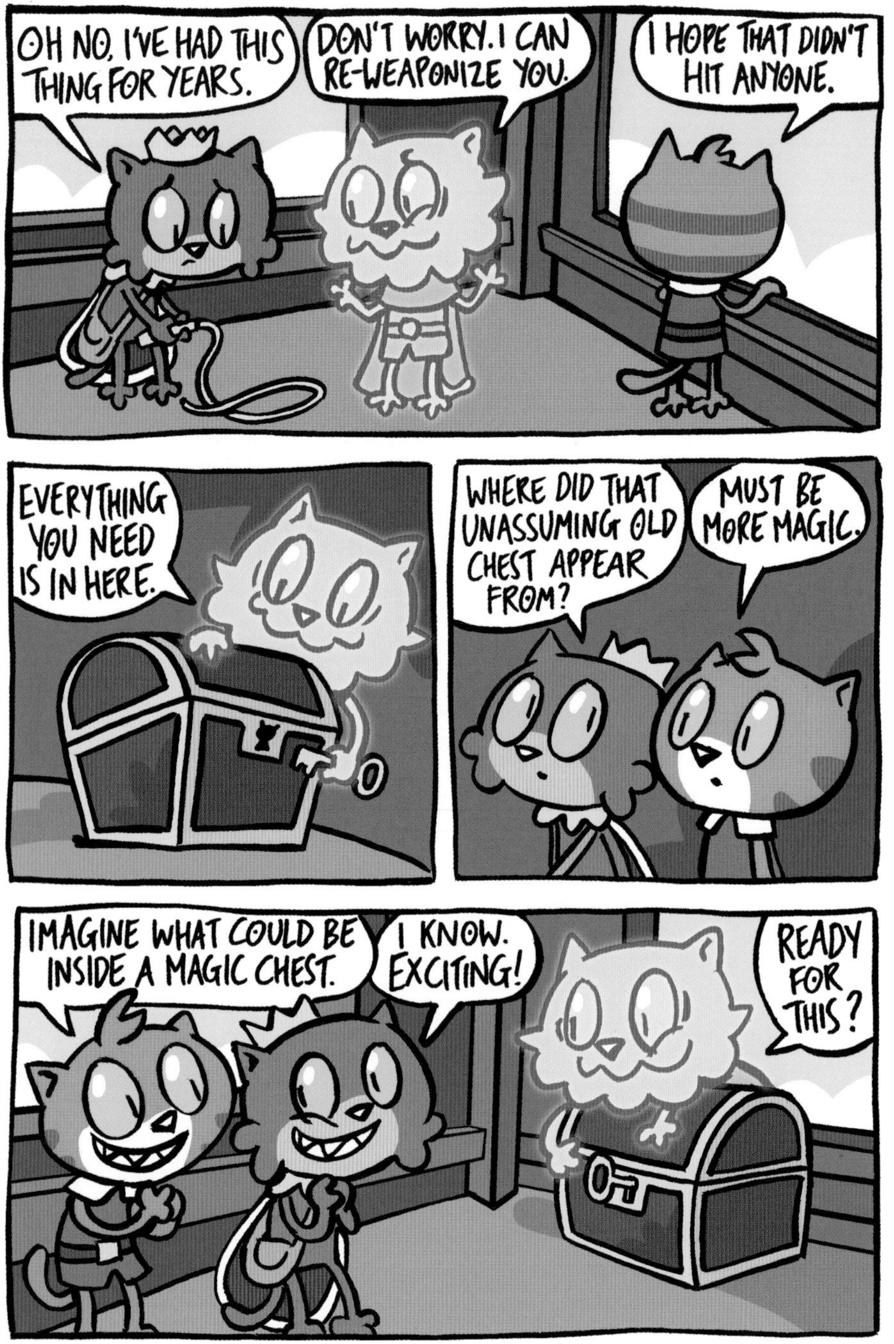
OH NO, I'VE HAD THIS THING FOR YEARS.
DON'T WORRY. I CAN RE-WEAPONIZE YOU.
I HOPE THAT DIDN'T HIT ANYONE.
EVERYTHING YOU NEED IS IN HERE.
WHERE DID THAT UNASSUMING OLD CHEST APPEAR FROM?
MUST BE MORE MAGIC.
IMAGINE WHAT COULD BE INSIDE A MAGIC CHEST.
I KNOW. EXCITING!
READY FOR THIS?

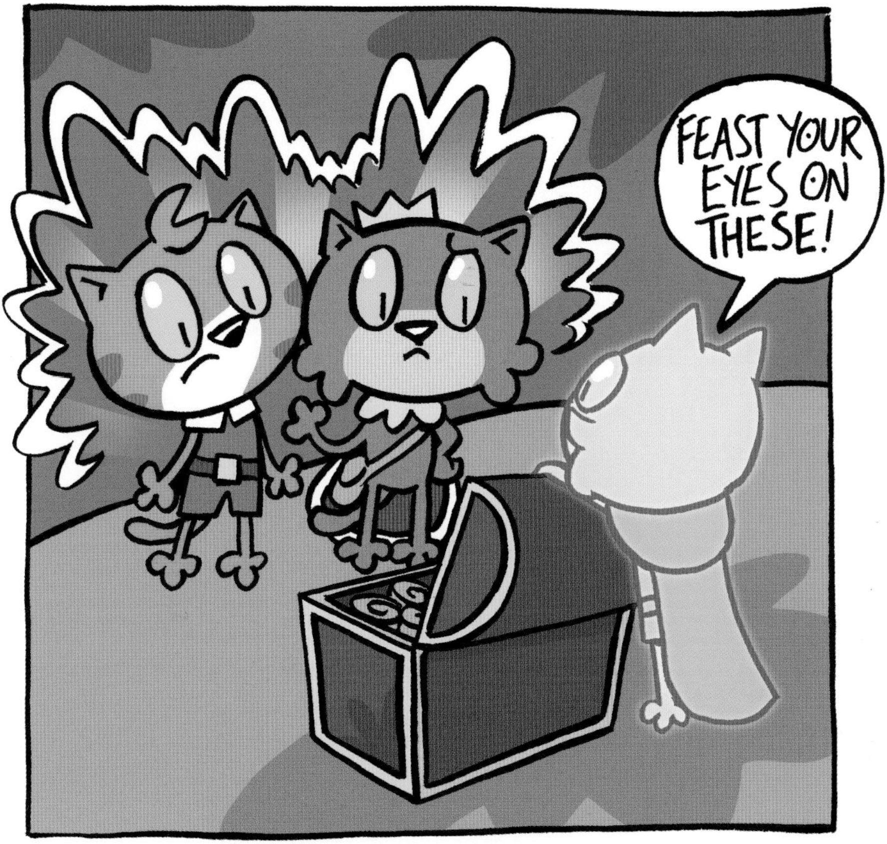
FEAST YOUR EYES ON THESE!

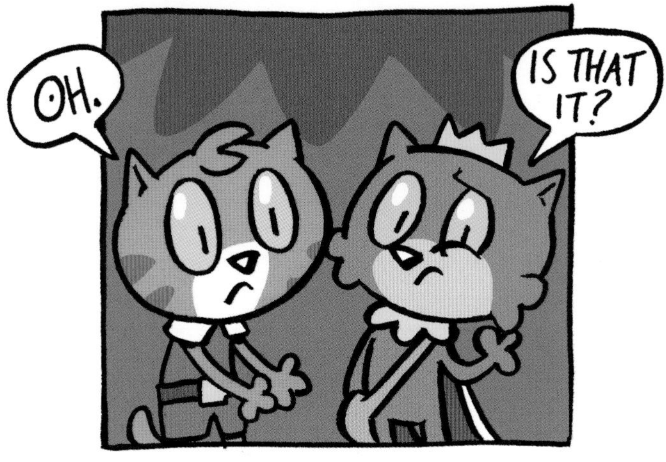
OH.
IS THAT IT?

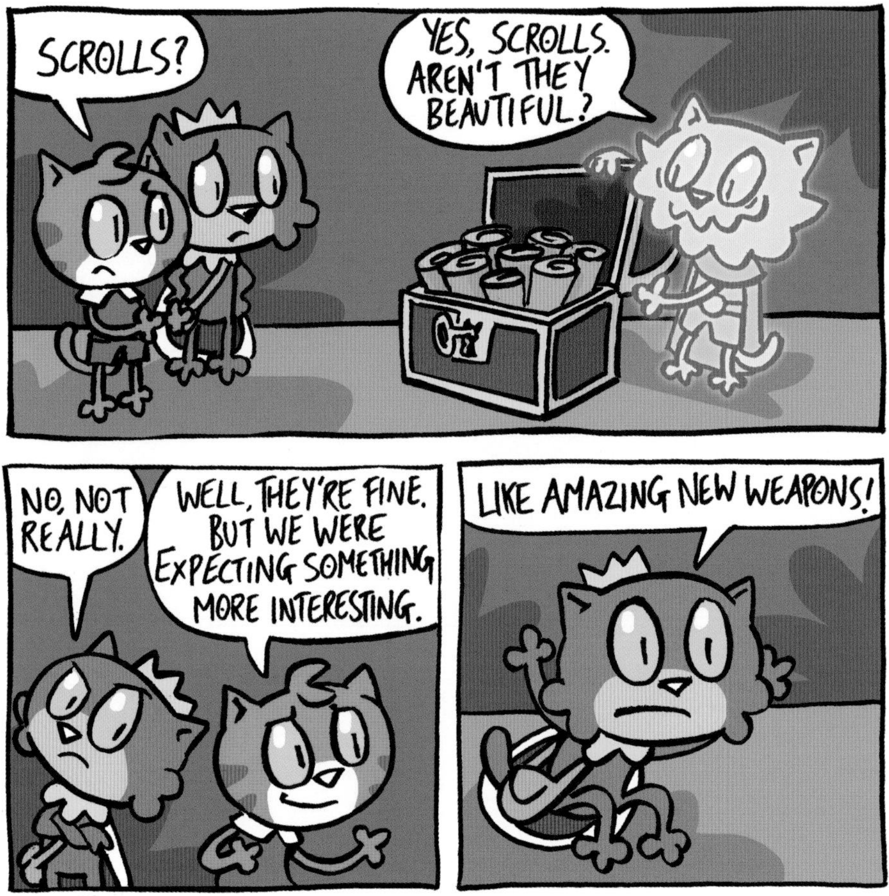
SCROLLS?
YES, SCROLLS. AREN'T THEY BEAUTIFUL?
NO, NOT REALLY.
WELL, THEY'RE FINE. BUT WE WERE EXPECTING SOMETHING MORE INTERESTING.
LIKE AMAZING NEW WEAPONS!

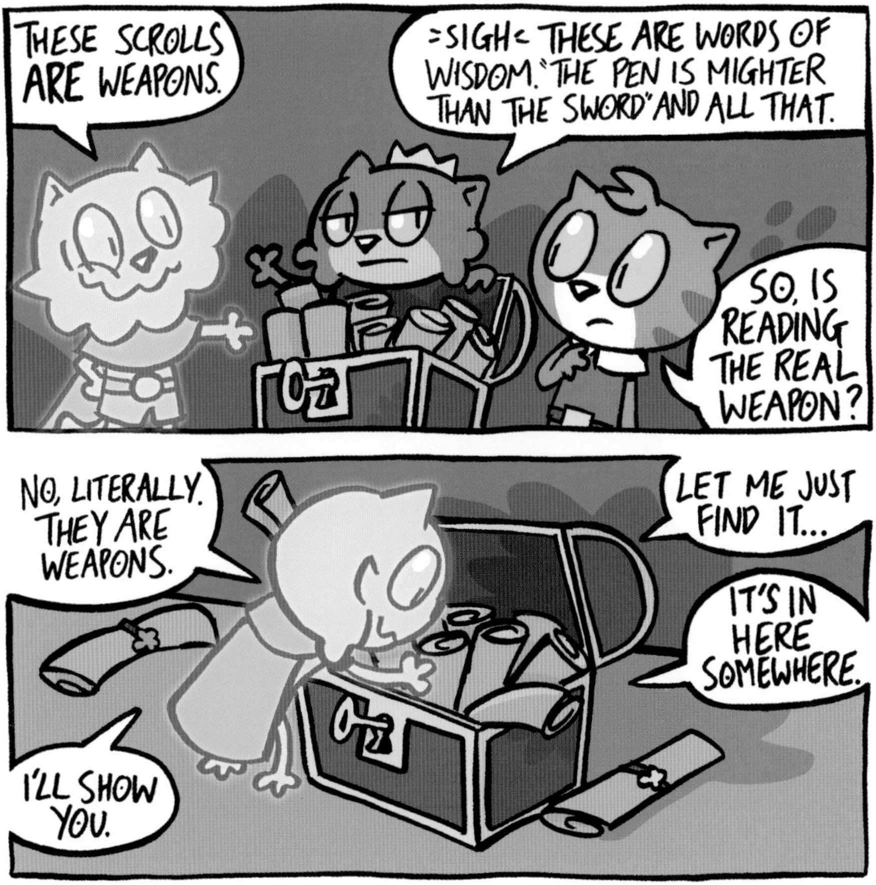
THESE SCROLLS ARE WEAPONS.
=SIGH= THESE ARE WORDS OF WISDOM. "THE PEN IS MIGHTER THAN THE SWORD" AND ALL THAT.
SO, IS READING THE REAL WEAPON?
NO, LITERALLY. THEY ARE WEAPONS.
LET ME JUST FIND IT...
IT'S IN HERE SOMEWHERE.
I'LL SHOW YOU.

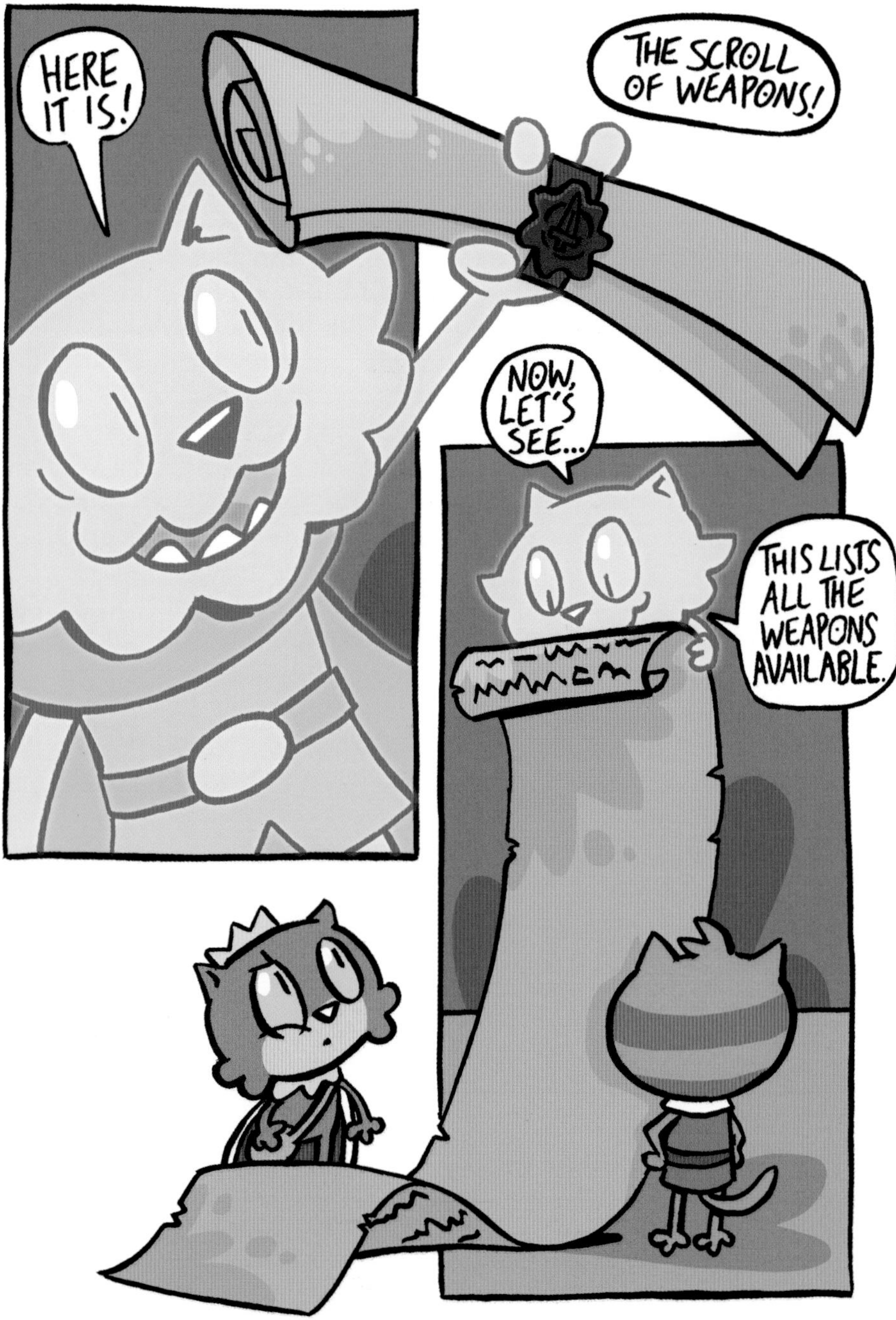
HERE IT IS!
THE SCROLL OF WEAPONS!
NOW, LET'S SEE...
THIS LISTS ALL THE WEAPONS AVAILABLE.

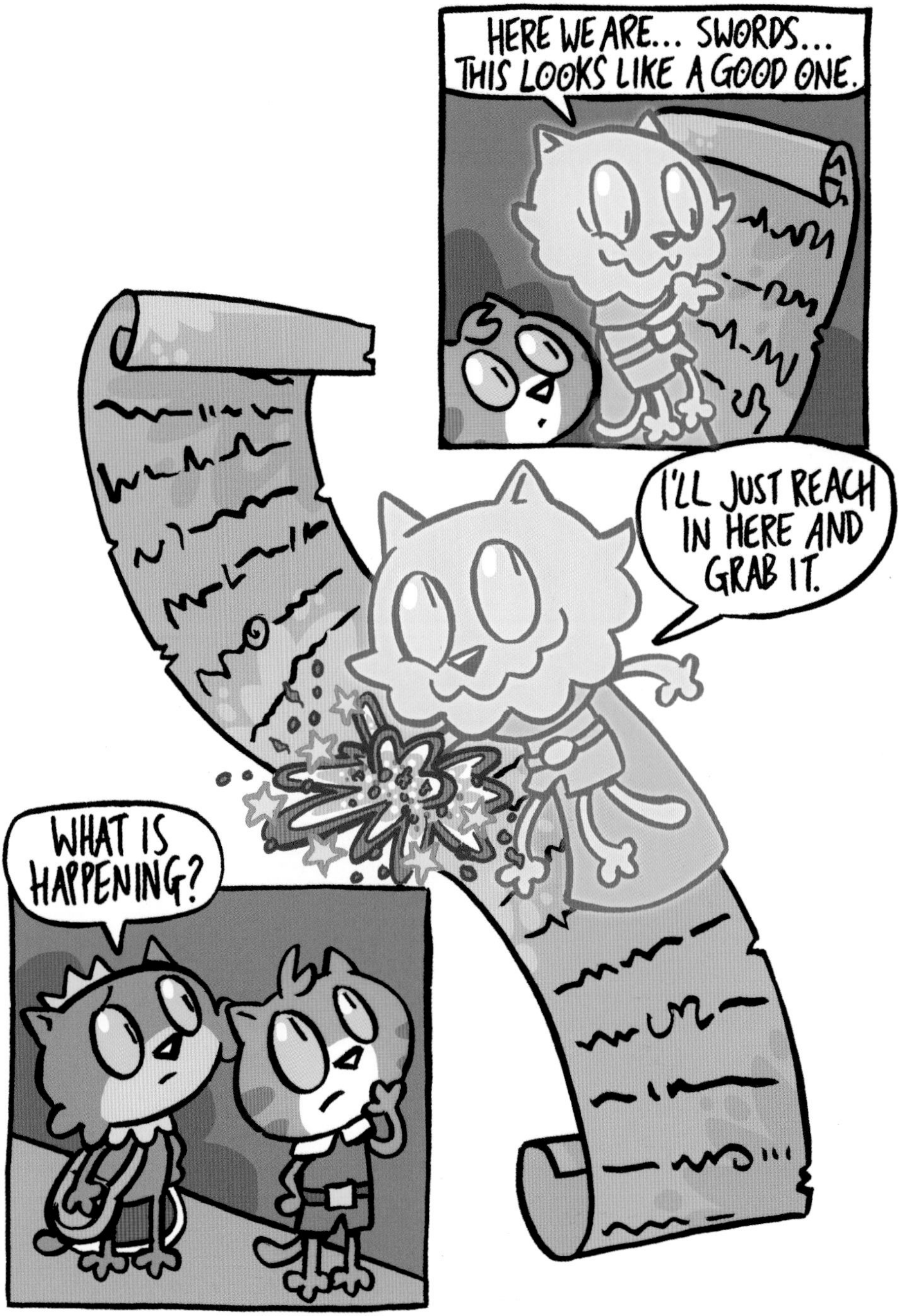
HERE WE ARE... SWORDS... THIS LOOKS LIKE A GOOD ONE.
I'LL JUST REACH IN HERE AND GRAB IT.
WHAT IS HAPPENING?

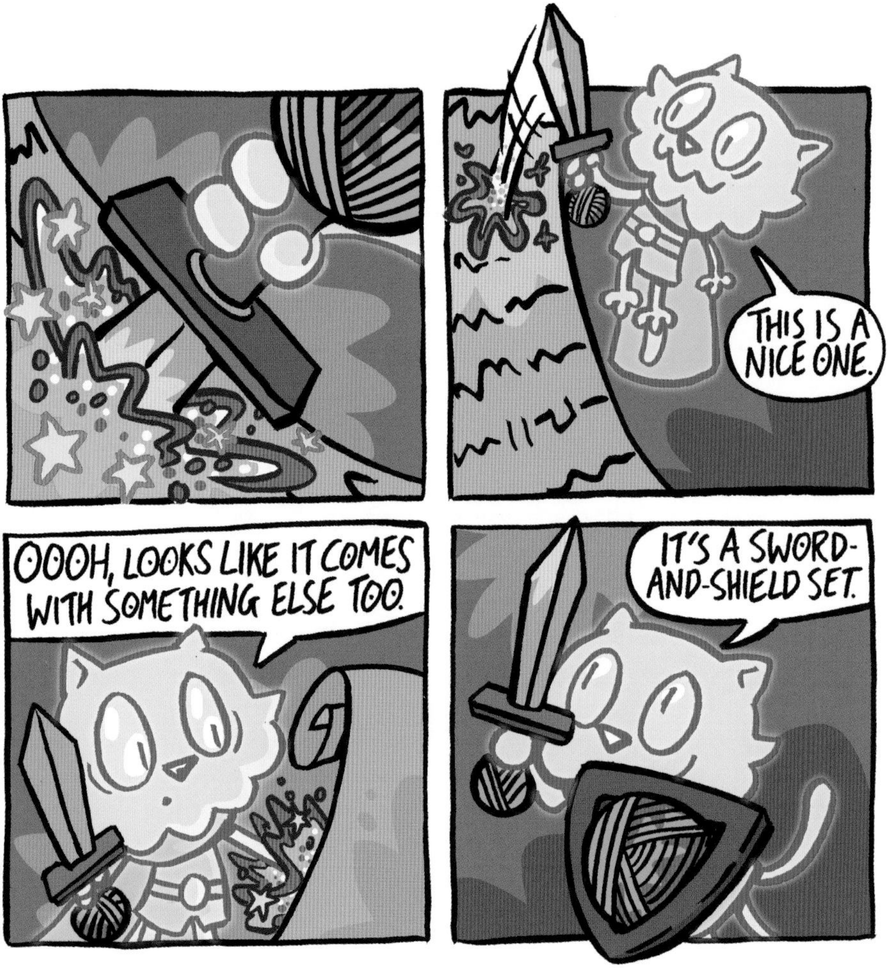
THIS IS A NICE ONE.
OOOH, LOOKS LIKE IT COMES WITH SOMETHING ELSE TOO.
IT'S A SWORD-AND-SHIELD SET.

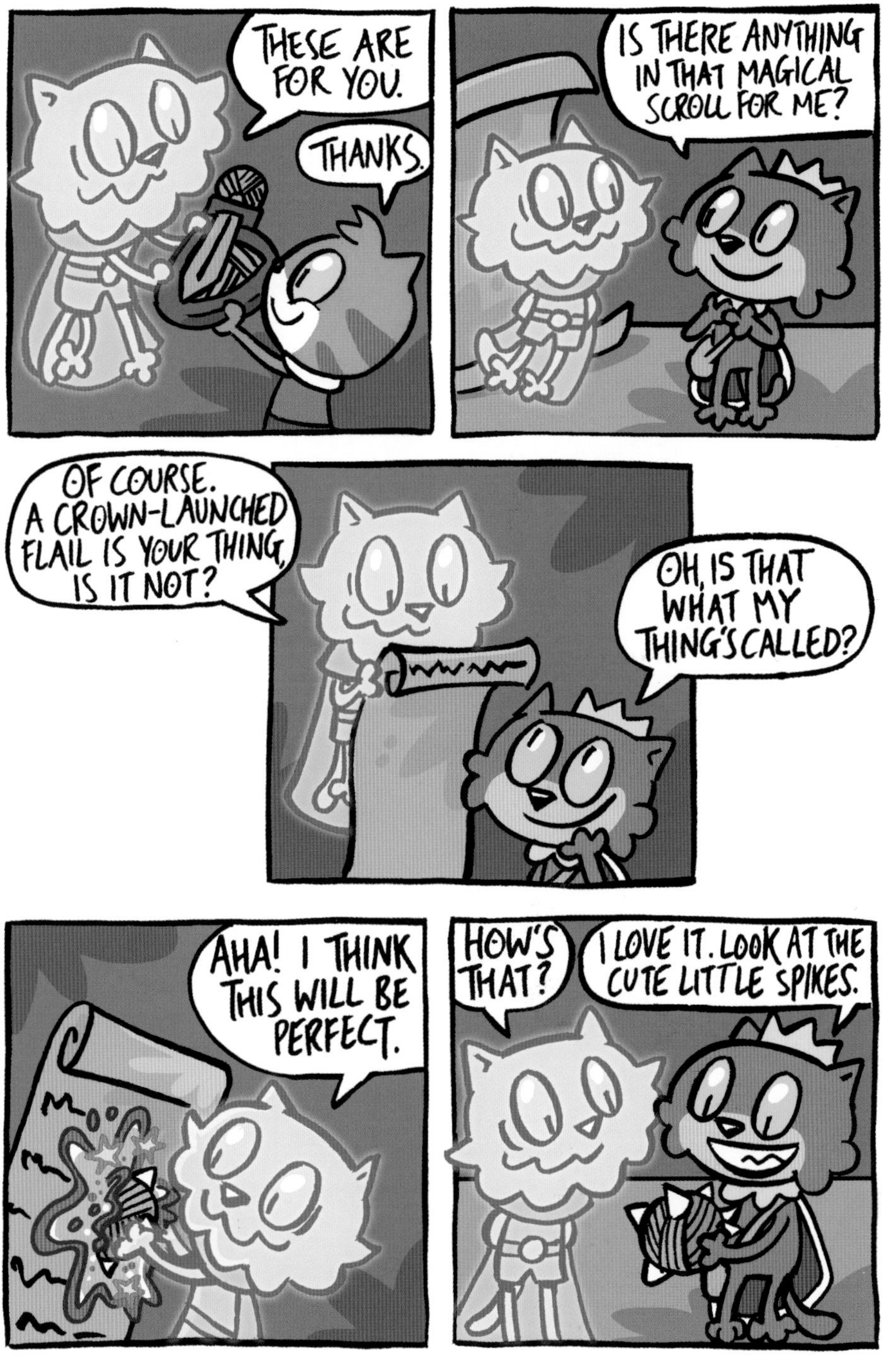
THESE ARE FOR YOU.
THANKS.
IS THERE ANYTHING IN THAT MAGICAL SCROLL FOR ME?
OF COURSE. A CROWN-LAUNCHED FLAIL IS YOUR THING, IS IT NOT?
OH, IS THAT WHAT MY THING'S CALLED?
AHA! I THINK THIS WILL BE PERFECT.
HOW'S THAT?
I LOVE IT. LOOK AT THE CUTE LITTLE SPIKES.

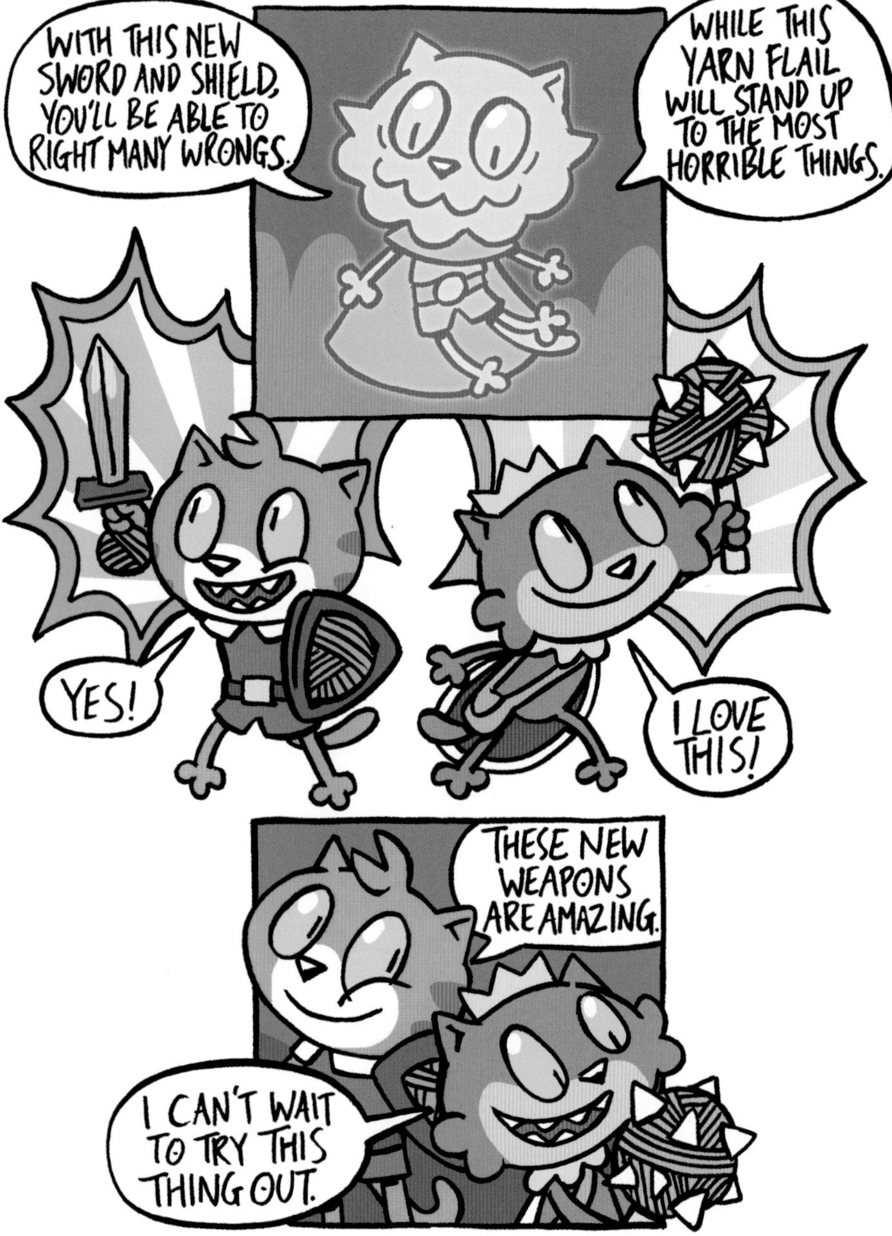
WITH THIS NEW SWORD AND SHIELD, YOU'LL BE ABLE TO RIGHT MANY WRONGS.
WHILE THIS YARN FLAIL WILL STAND UP TO THE MOST HORRIBLE THINGS.
YES!
I LOVE THIS!
THESE NEW WEAPONS ARE AMAZING.
I CAN'T WAIT TO TRY THIS THING OUT.

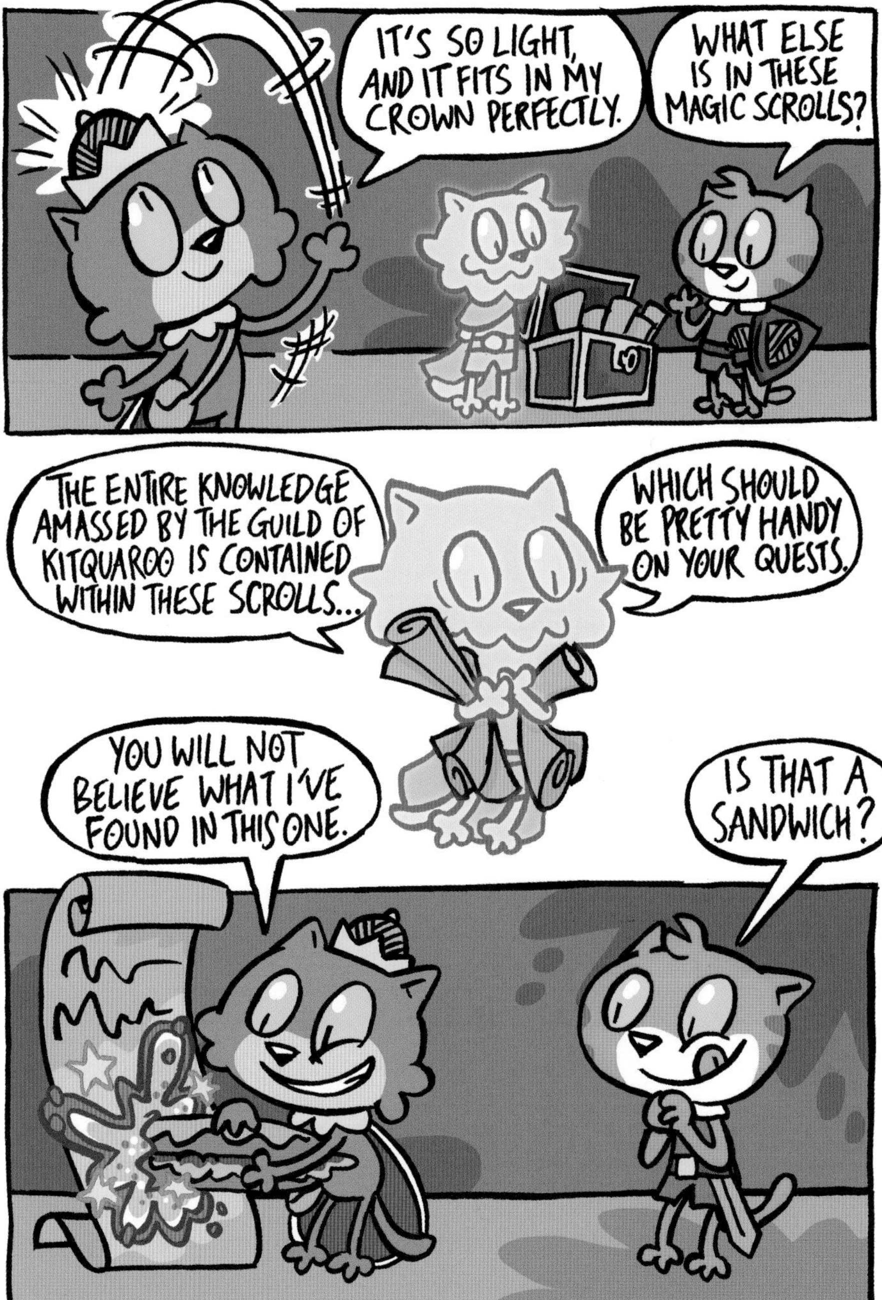
IT'S SO LIGHT, AND IT FITS IN MY CROWN PERFECTLY.
WHAT ELSE IS IN THESE MAGIC SCROLLS?
THE ENTIRE KNOWLEDGE AMASSED BY THE GUILD OF KITQUAROO IS CONTAINED WITHIN THESE SCROLLS...
WHICH SHOULD BE PRETTY HANDY ON YOUR QUESTS.
YOU WILL NOT BELIEVE WHAT I'VE FOUND IN THIS ONE.
IS THAT A SANDWICH?

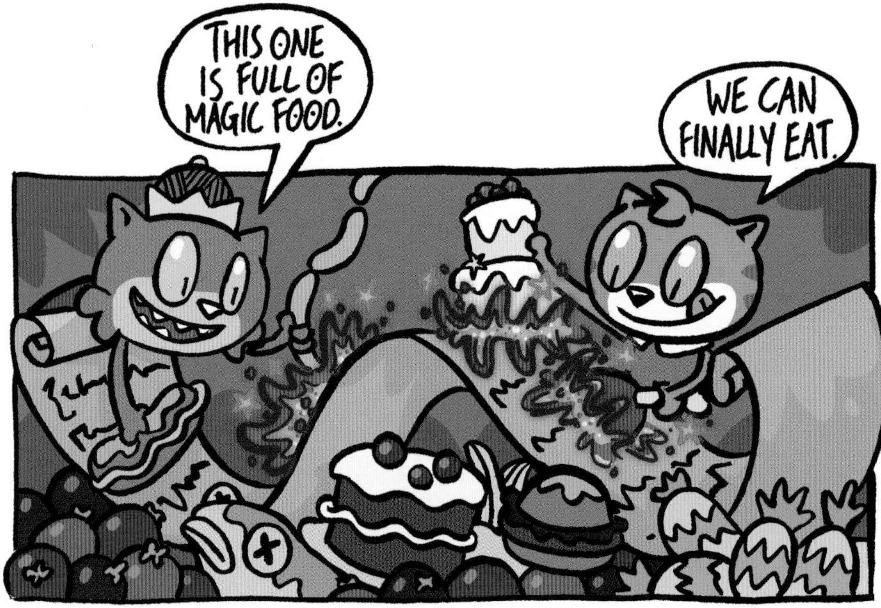
THIS ONE IS FULL OF MAGIC FOOD.
WE CAN FINALLY EAT.

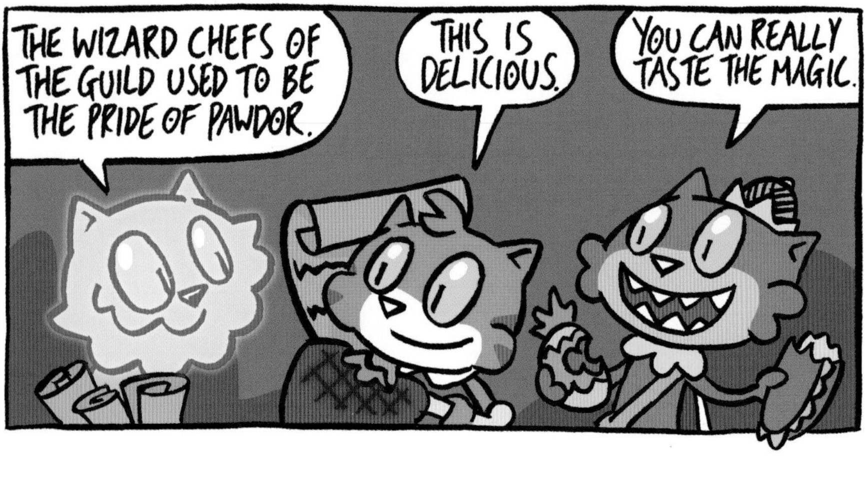
THE WIZARD CHEFS OF THE GUILD USED TO BE THE PRIDE OF PAWDOR.
THIS IS DELICIOUS.
YOU CAN REALLY TASTE THE MAGIC.

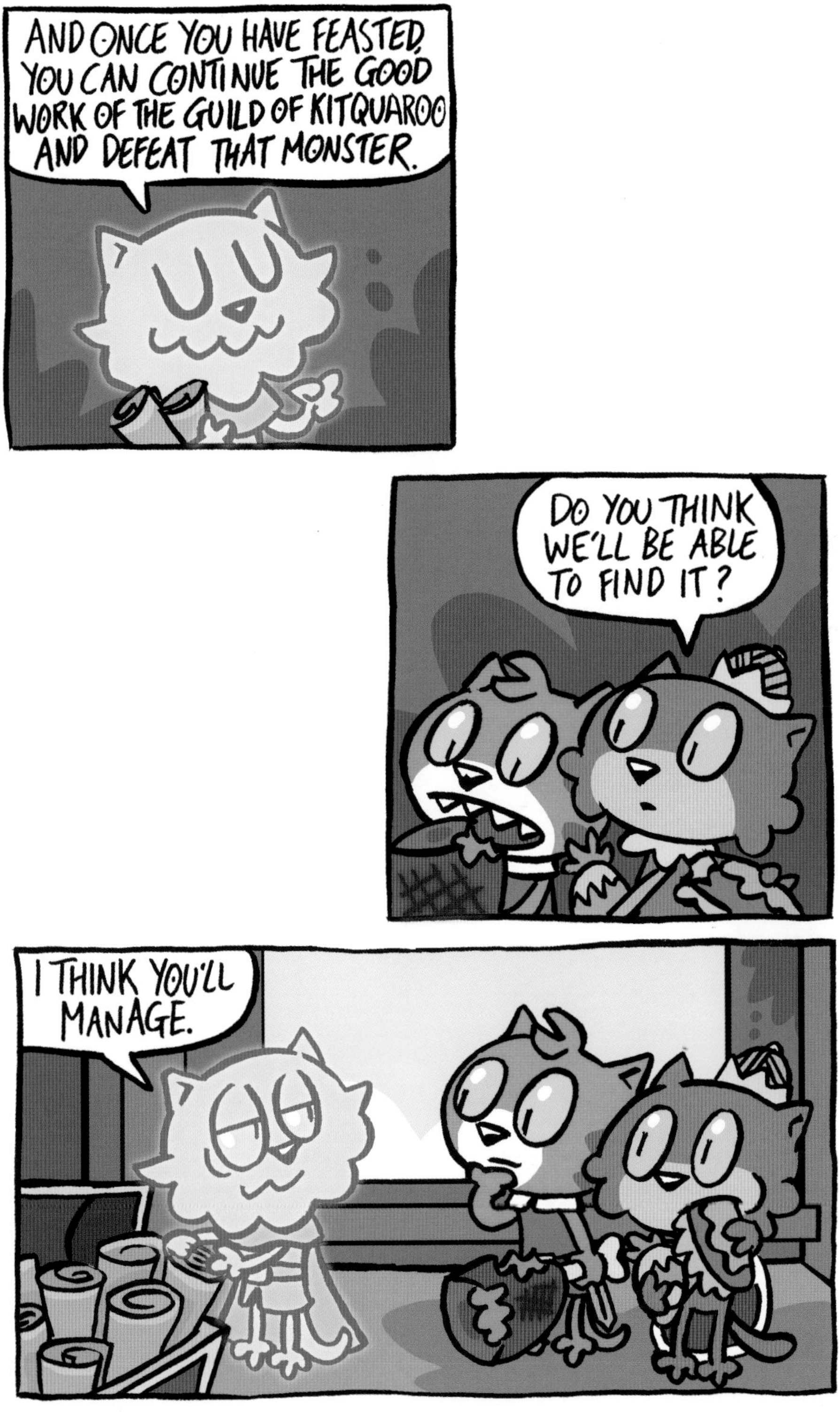
AND ONCE YOU HAVE FEASTED, YOU CAN CONTINUE THE GOOD WORK OF THE GUILD OF KITQUAROO AND DEFEAT THAT MONSTER.
DO YOU THINK WE'LL BE ABLE TO FIND IT?
I THINK YOU'LL MANAGE.

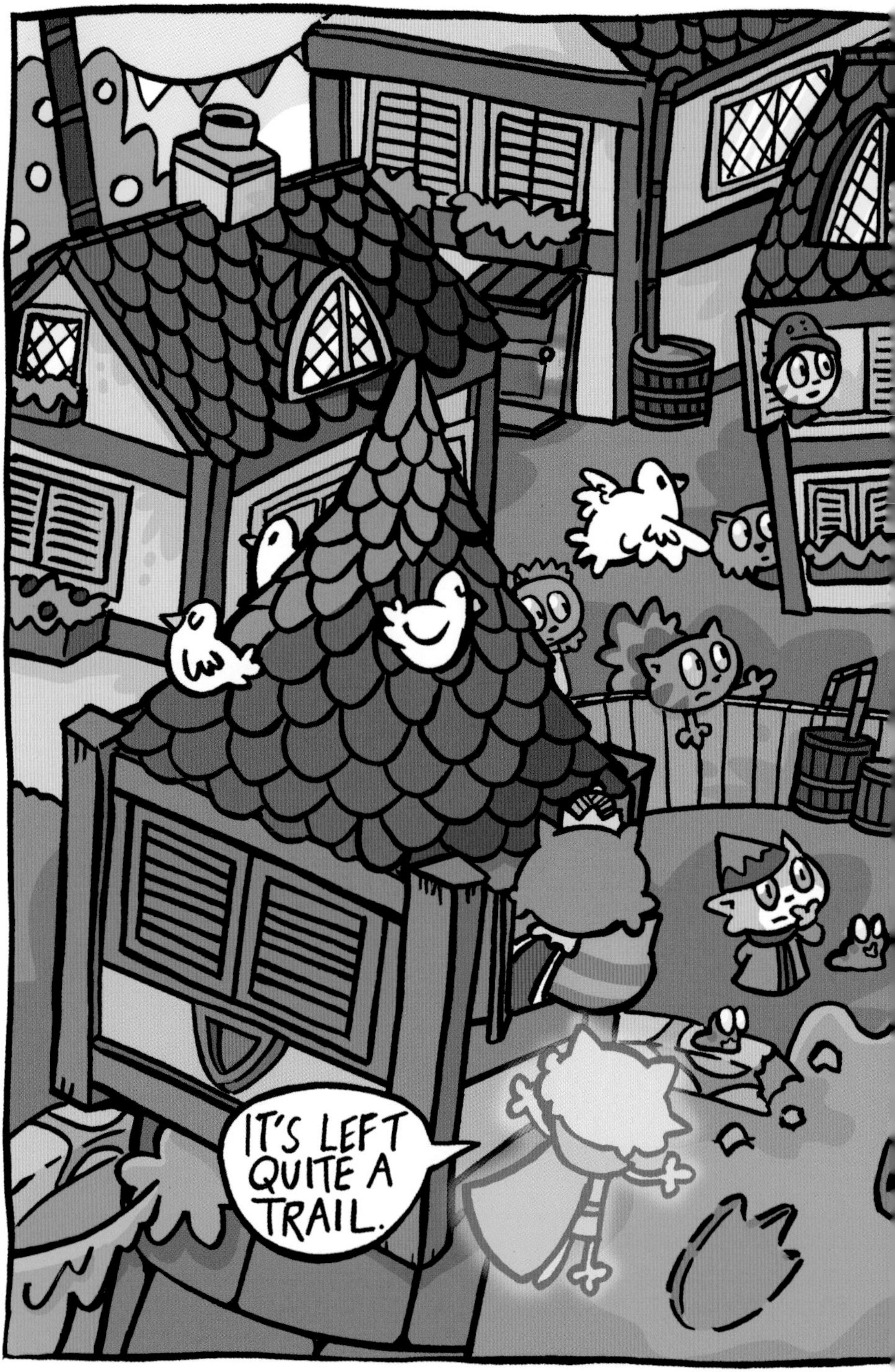
IT'S LEFT QUITE A TRAIL.

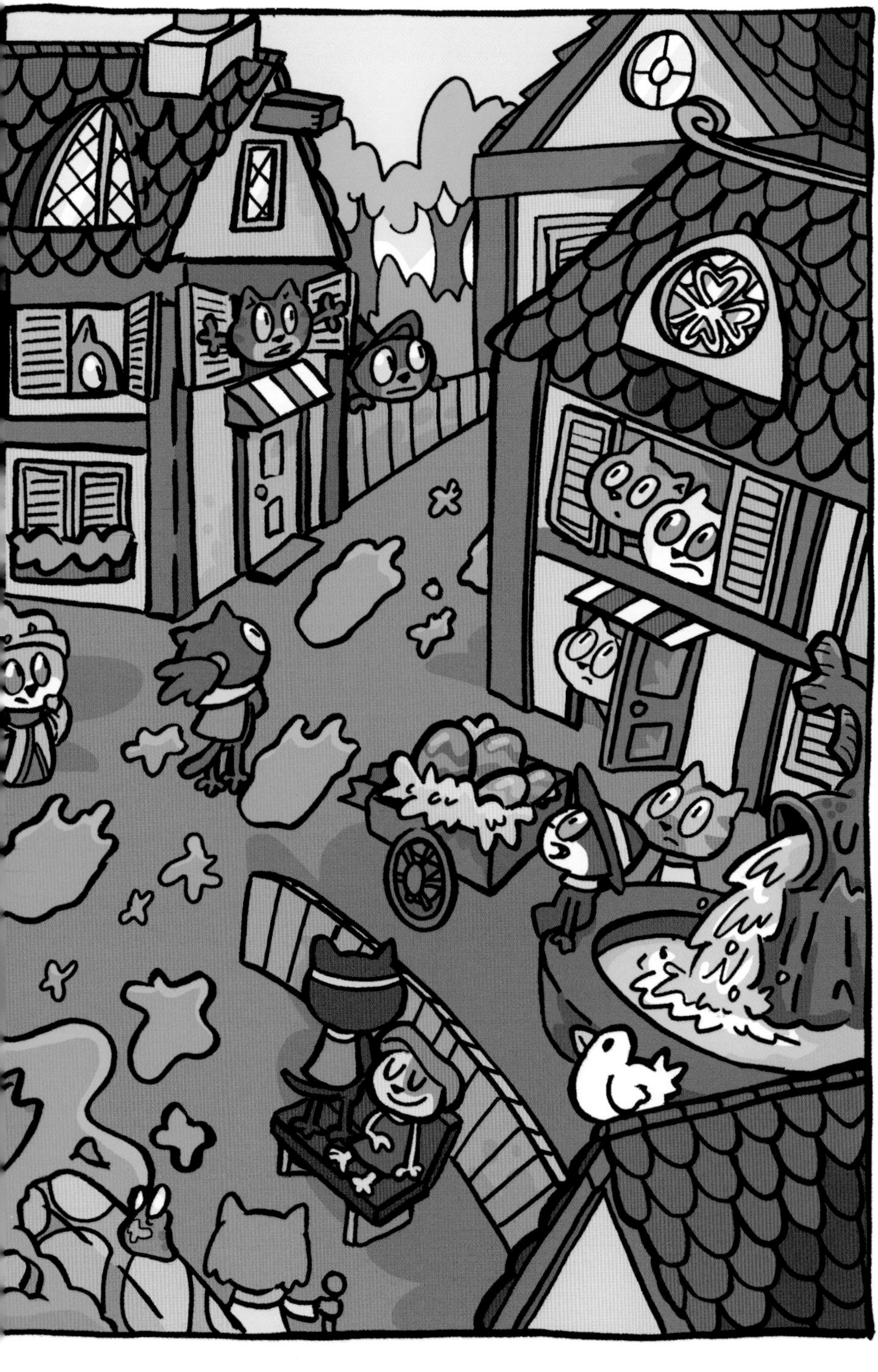

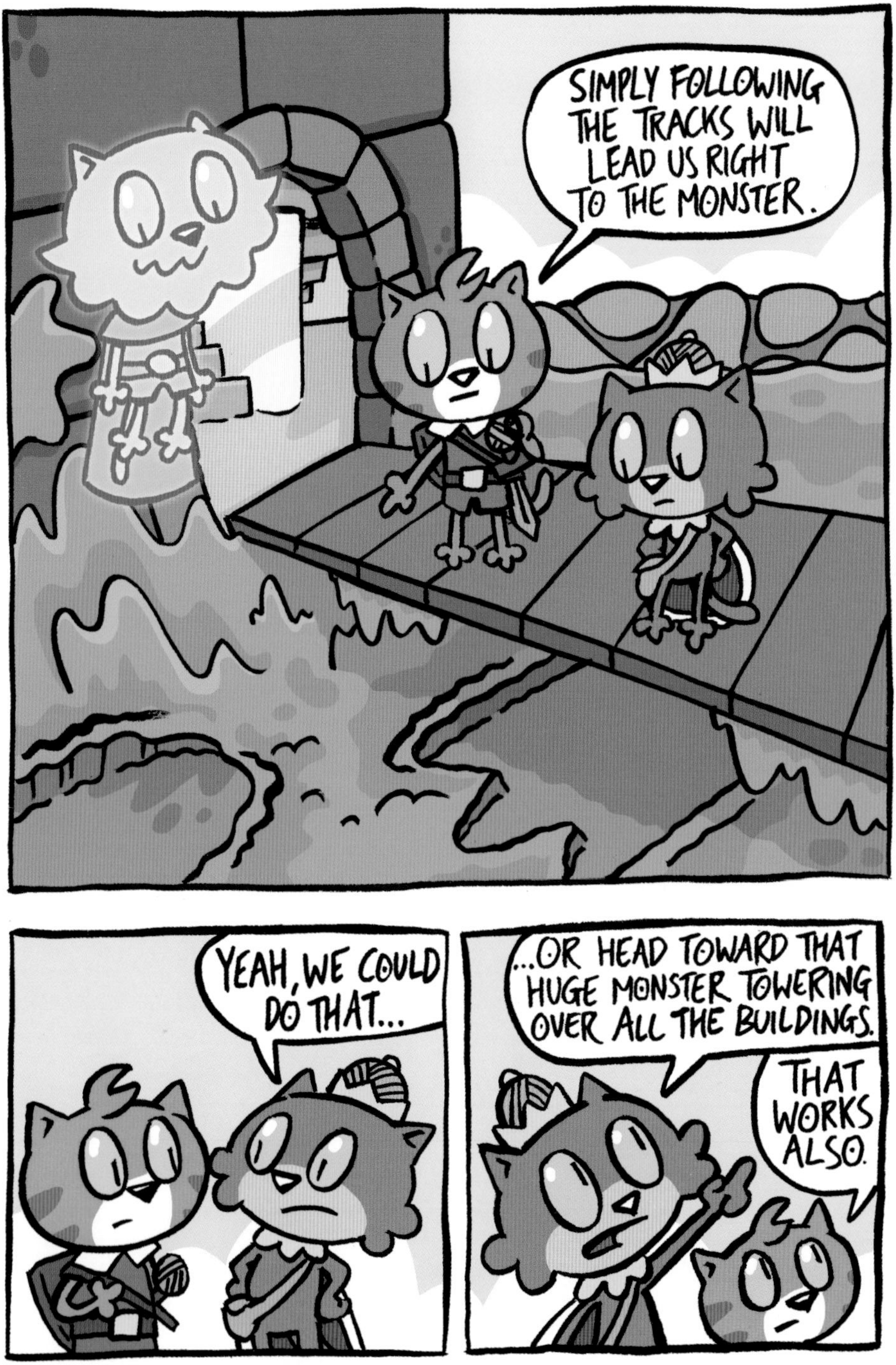
SIMPLY FOLLOWING THE TRACKS WILL LEAD US RIGHT TO THE MONSTER.
YEAH, WE COULD DO THAT...
...OR HEAD TOWARD THAT HUGE MONSTER TOWERING OVER ALL THE BUILDINGS.
THAT WORKS ALSO.

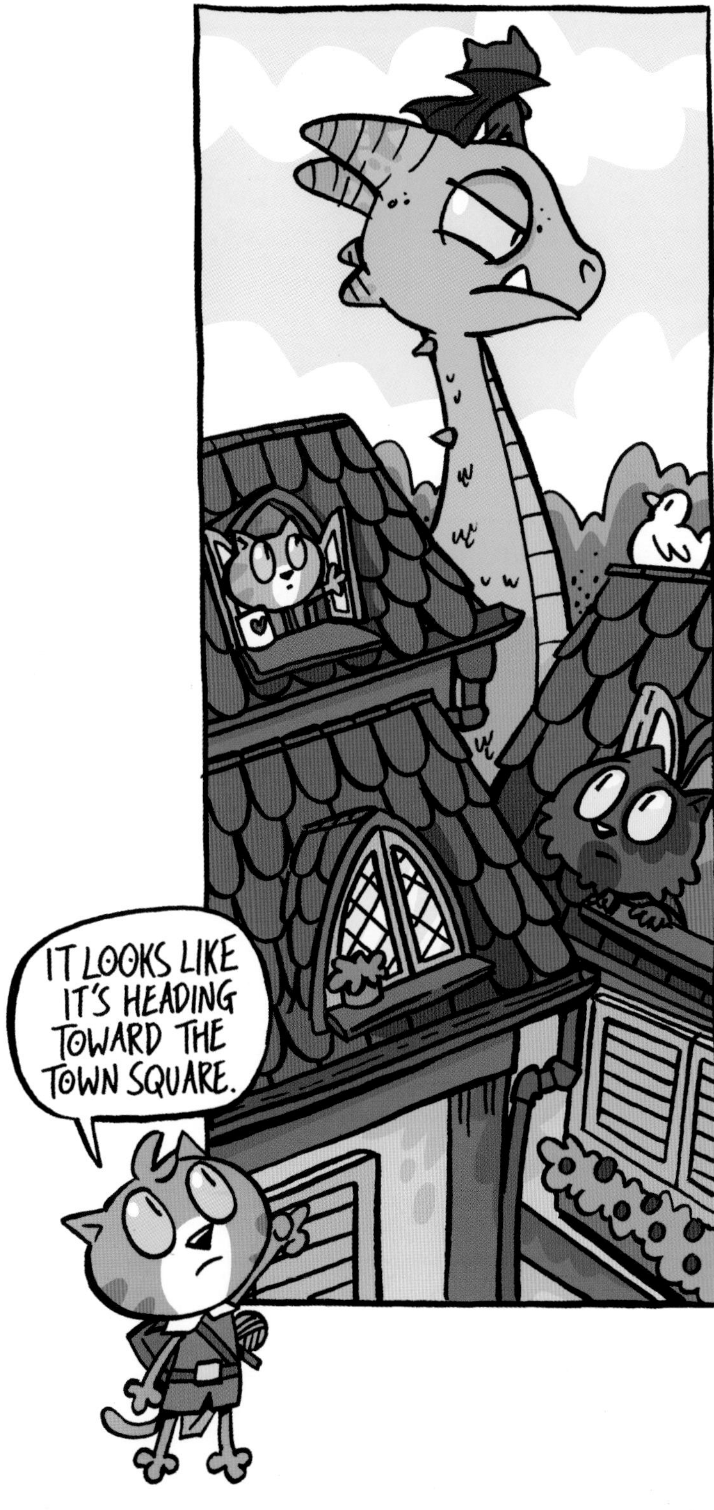
IT LOOKS LIKE IT'S HEADING TOWARD THE TOWN SQUARE.

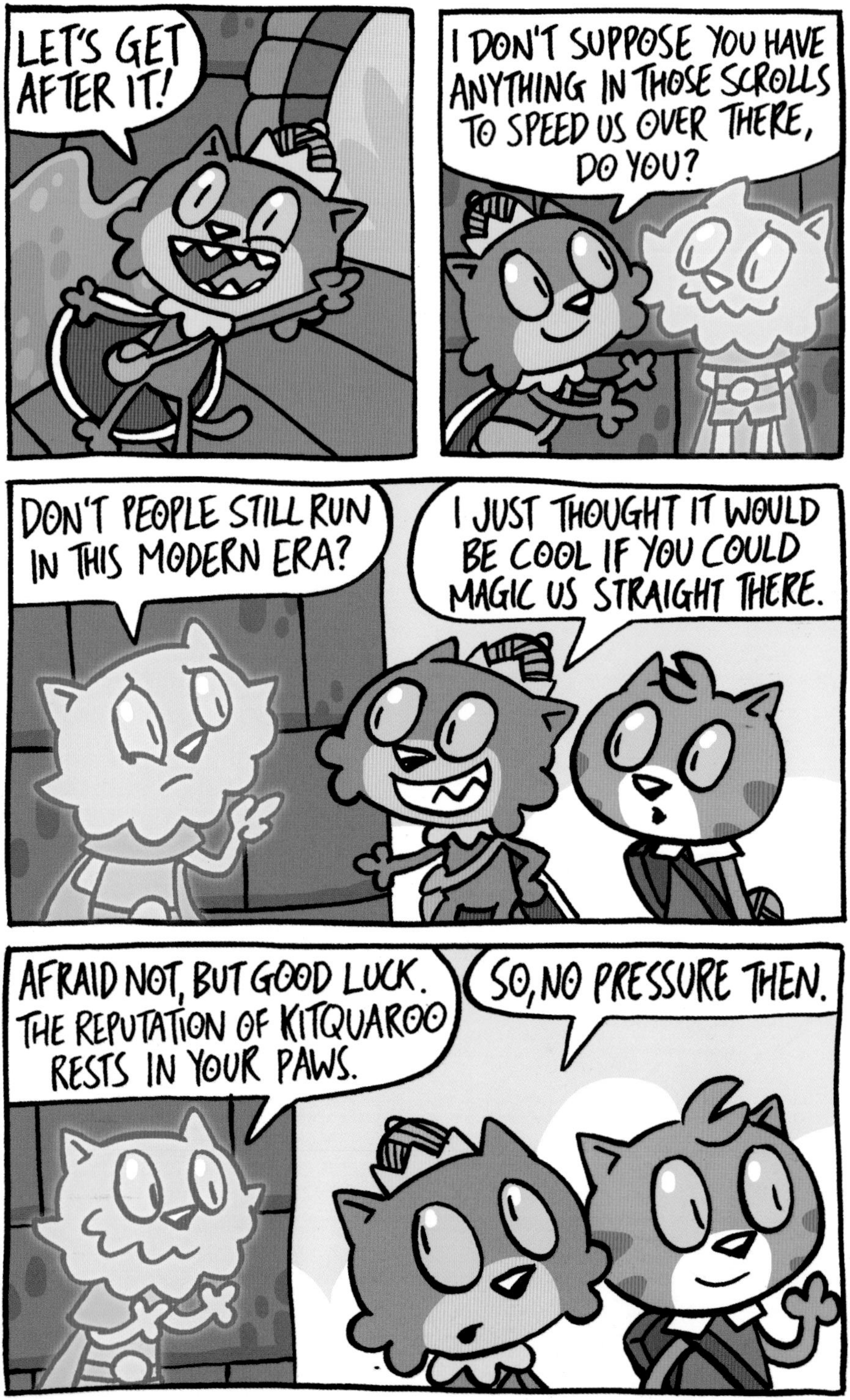
LET'S GET AFTER IT!
I DON'T SUPPOSE YOU HAVE ANYTHING IN THOSE SCROLLS TO SPEED US OVER THERE, DO YOU?
DON'T PEOPLE STILL RUN IN THIS MODERN ERA?
I JUST THOUGHT IT WOULD BE COOL IF YOU COULD MAGIC US STRAIGHT THERE.
AFRAID NOT, BUT GOOD LUCK. THE REPUTATION OF KITQUAROO RESTS IN YOUR PAWS.
SO, NO PRESSURE THEN.

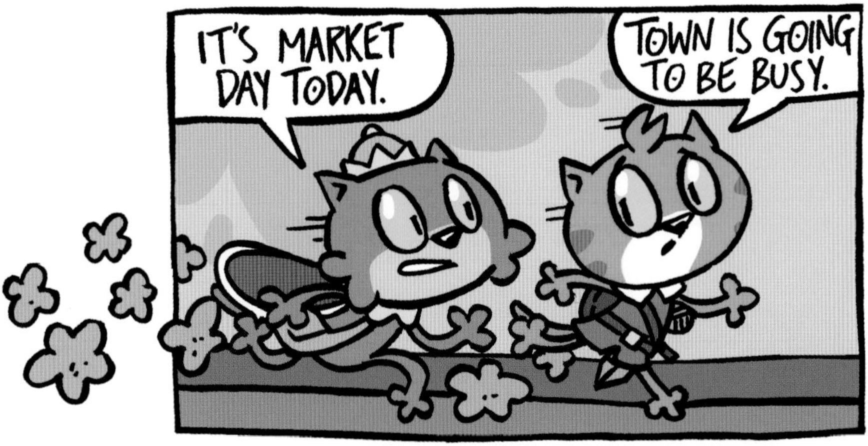
IT'S MARKET DAY TODAY.
TOWN IS GOING TO BE BUSY.

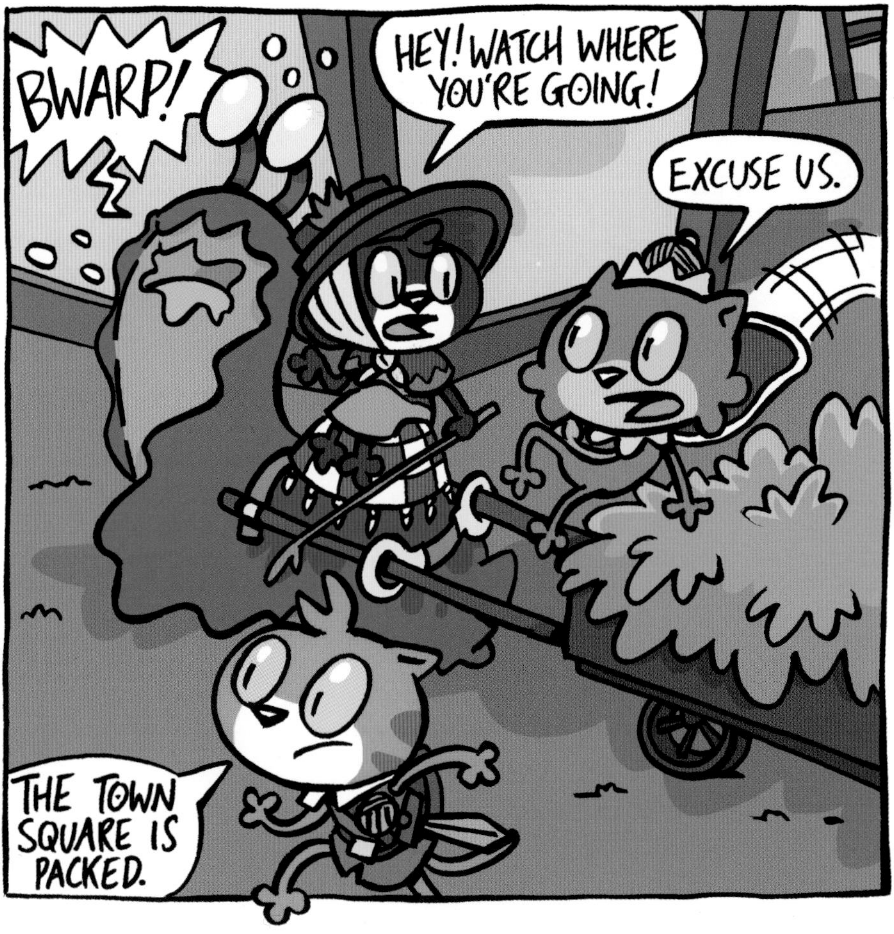
BWARP!
HEY! WATCH WHERE YOU'RE GOING!
EXCUSE US.
THE TOWN SQUARE IS PACKED.

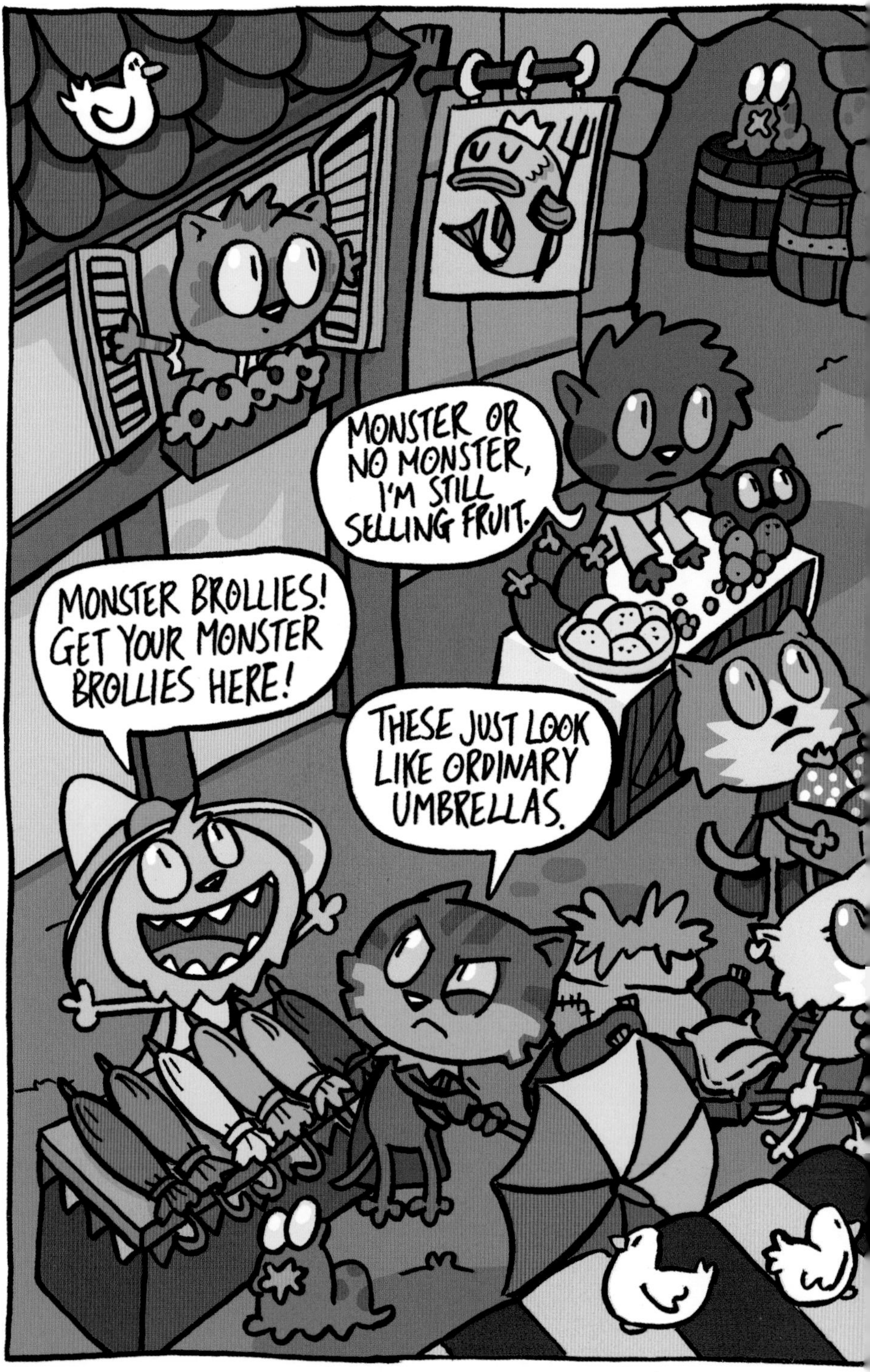
MONSTER OR NO MONSTER, I'M STILL SELLING FRUIT.
MONSTER BROLLIES! GET YOUR MONSTER BROLLIES HERE!
THESE JUST LOOK LIKE ORDINARY UMBRELLAS.

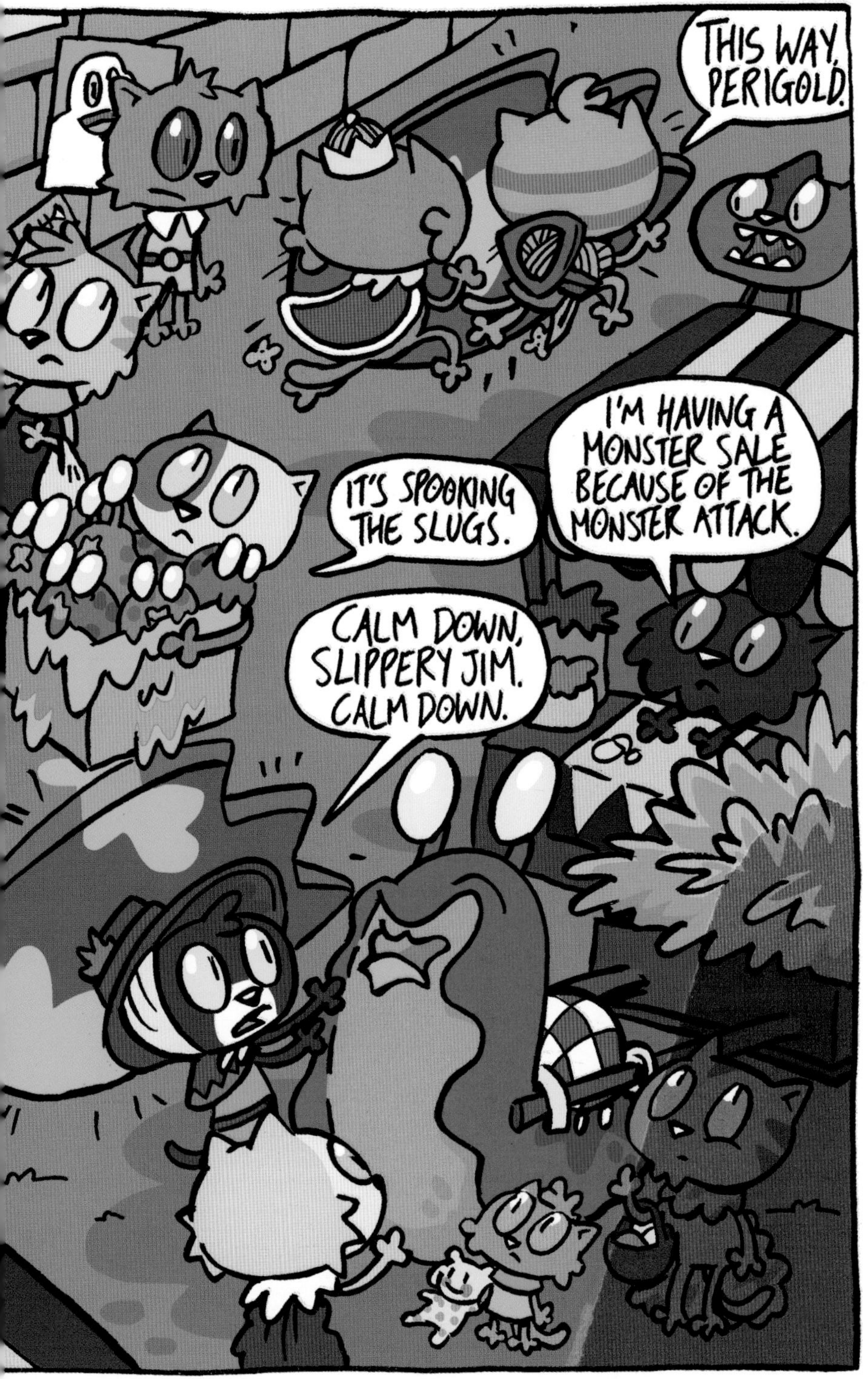
THIS WAY, PERIGOLD.
I'M HAVING A MONSTER SALE BECAUSE OF THE MONSTER ATTACK.
IT'S SPOOKING THE SLUGS.
CALM DOWN, SLIPPERY JIM. CALM DOWN.

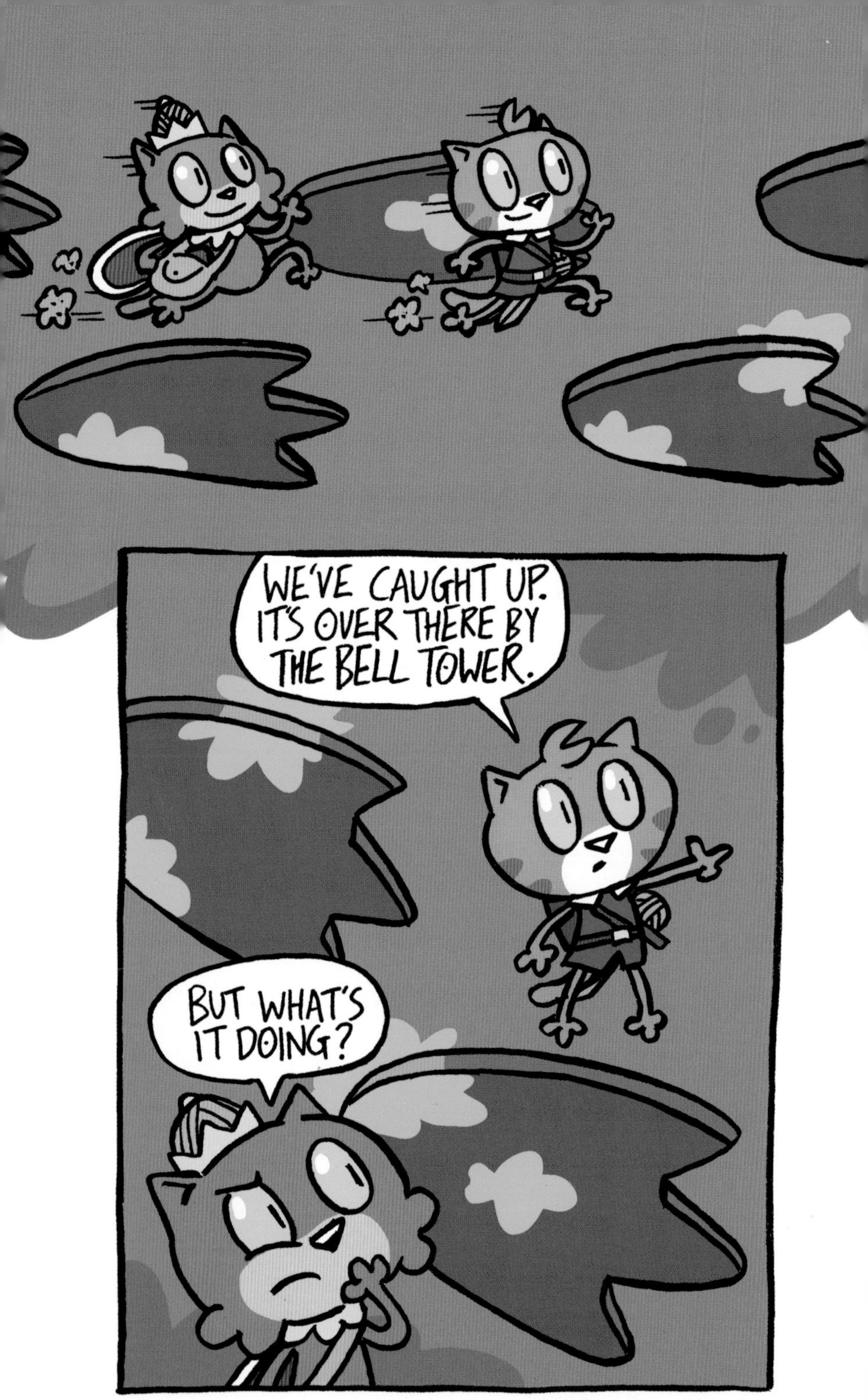
WE'VE CAUGHT UP. IT'S OVER THERE BY THE BELL TOWER.
BUT WHAT'S IT DOING?

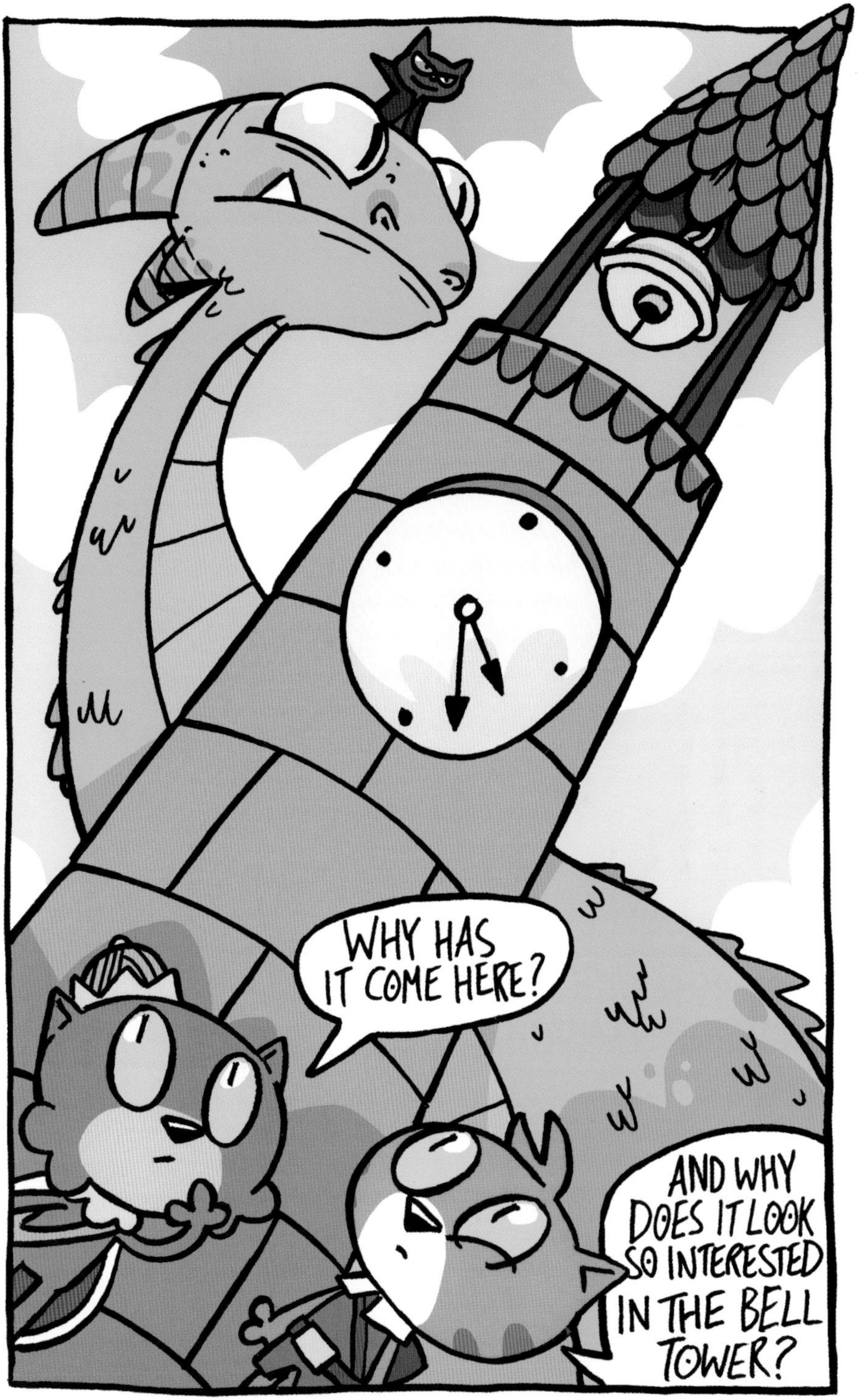
WHY HAS IT COME HERE?
AND WHY DOES IT LOOK SO INTERESTED IN THE BELL TOWER?

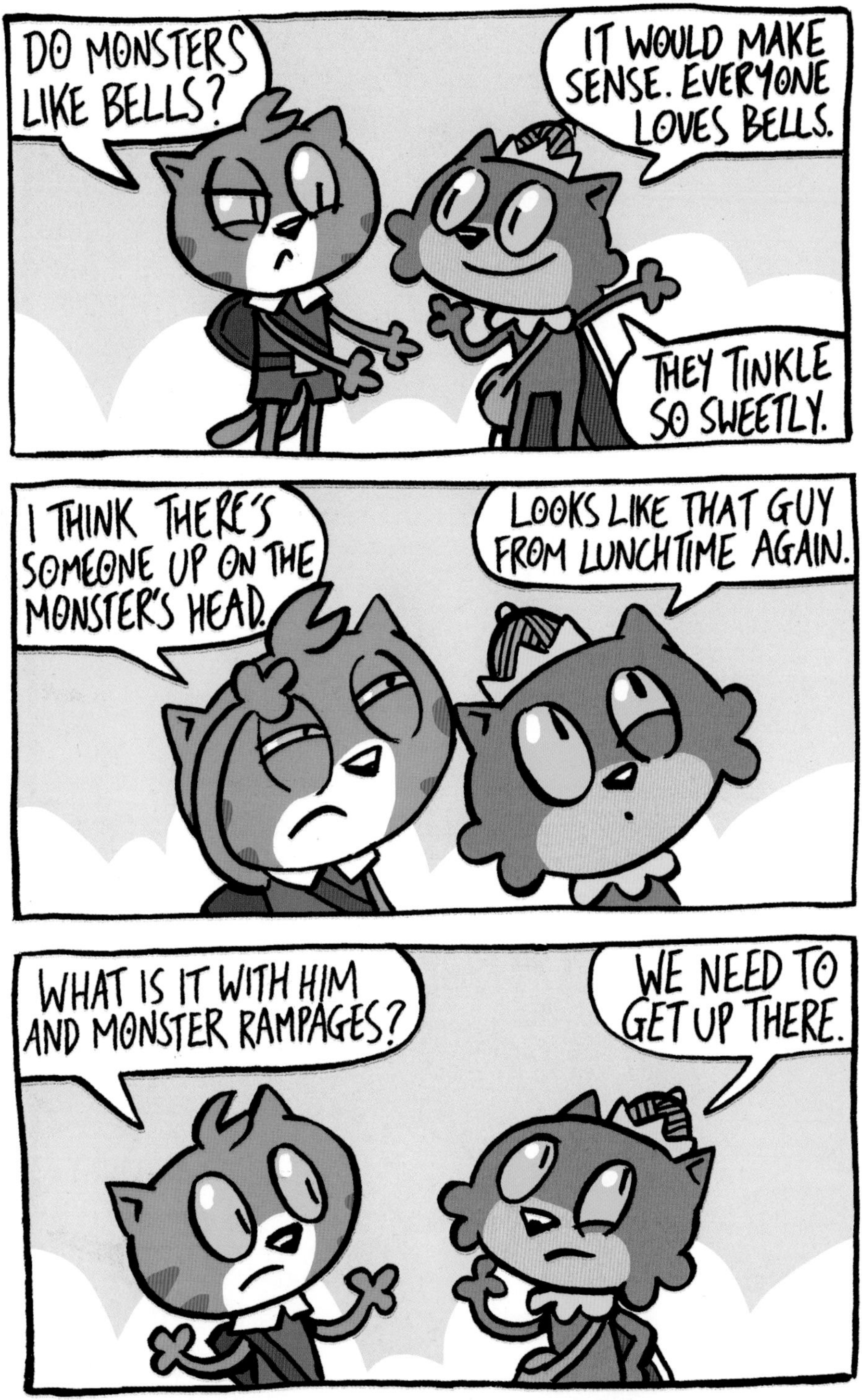
DO MONSTERS LIKE BELLS?
IT WOULD MAKE SENSE. EVERYONE LOVES BELLS.
THEY TINKLE SO SWEETLY.
I THINK THERE'S SOMEONE UP ON THE MONSTER'S HEAD.
LOOKS LIKE THAT GUY FROM LUNCHTIME AGAIN.
WHAT IS IT WITH HIM AND MONSTER RAMPAGES?
WE NEED TO GET UP THERE.

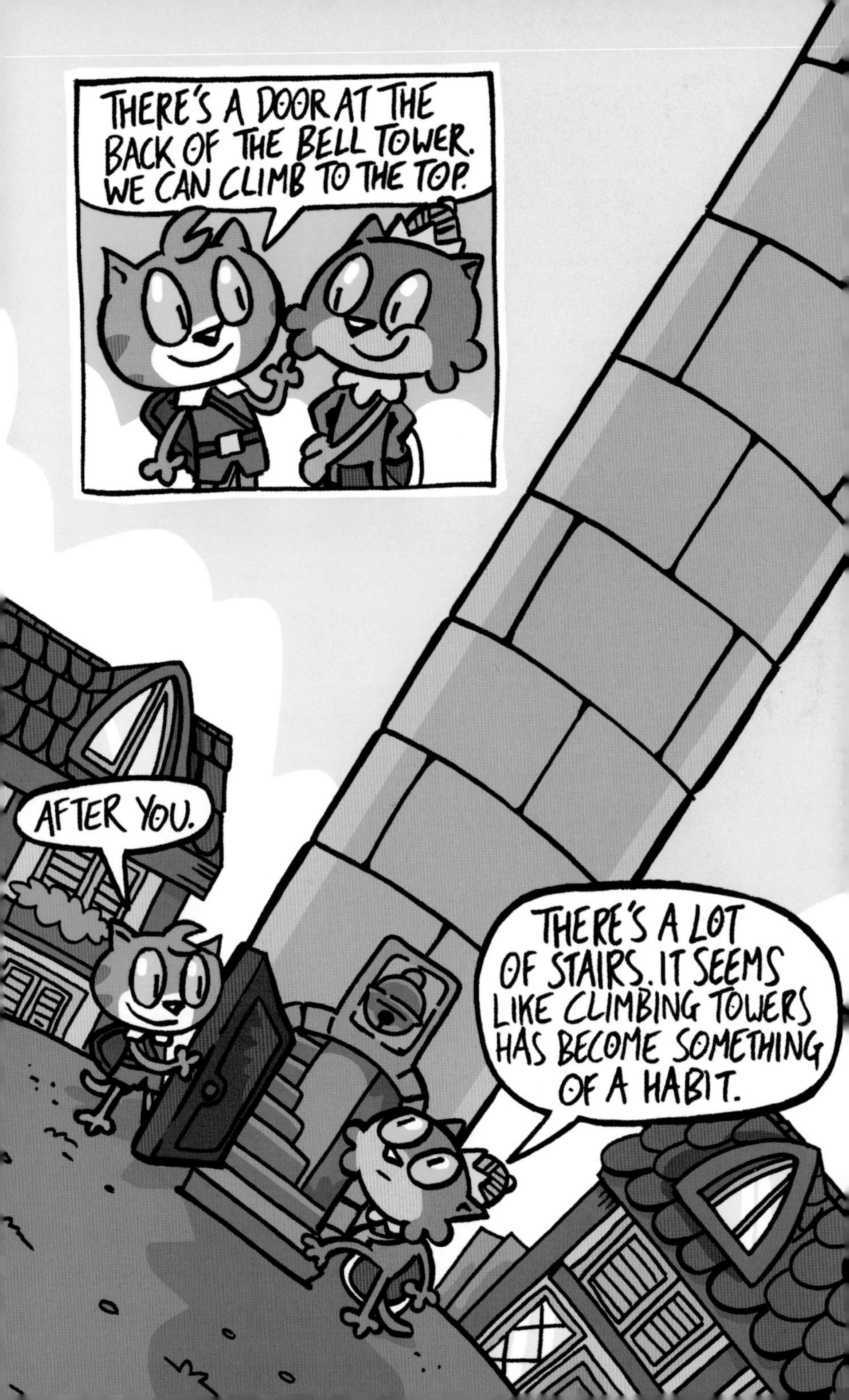
THERE'S A DOOR AT THE BACK OF THE BELL TOWER. WE CAN CLIMB TO THE TOP.
AFTER YOU.
THERE'S A LOT OF STAIRS. IT SEEMS LIKE CLIMBING TOWERS HAS BECOME SOMETHING OF A HABIT.

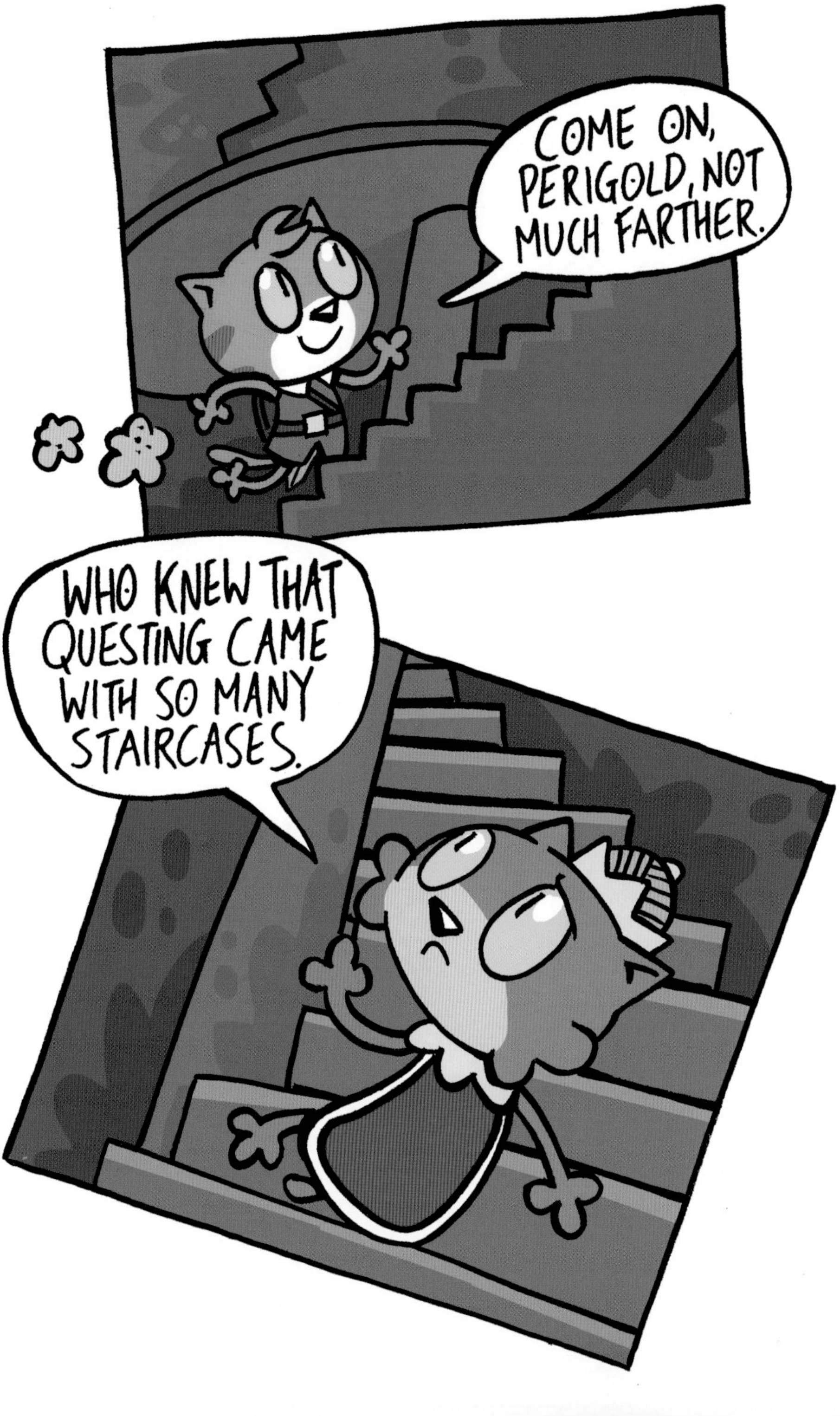
COME ON, PERIGOLD, NOT MUCH FARTHER.
WHO KNEW THAT QUESTING CAME WITH SO MANY STAIRCASES.

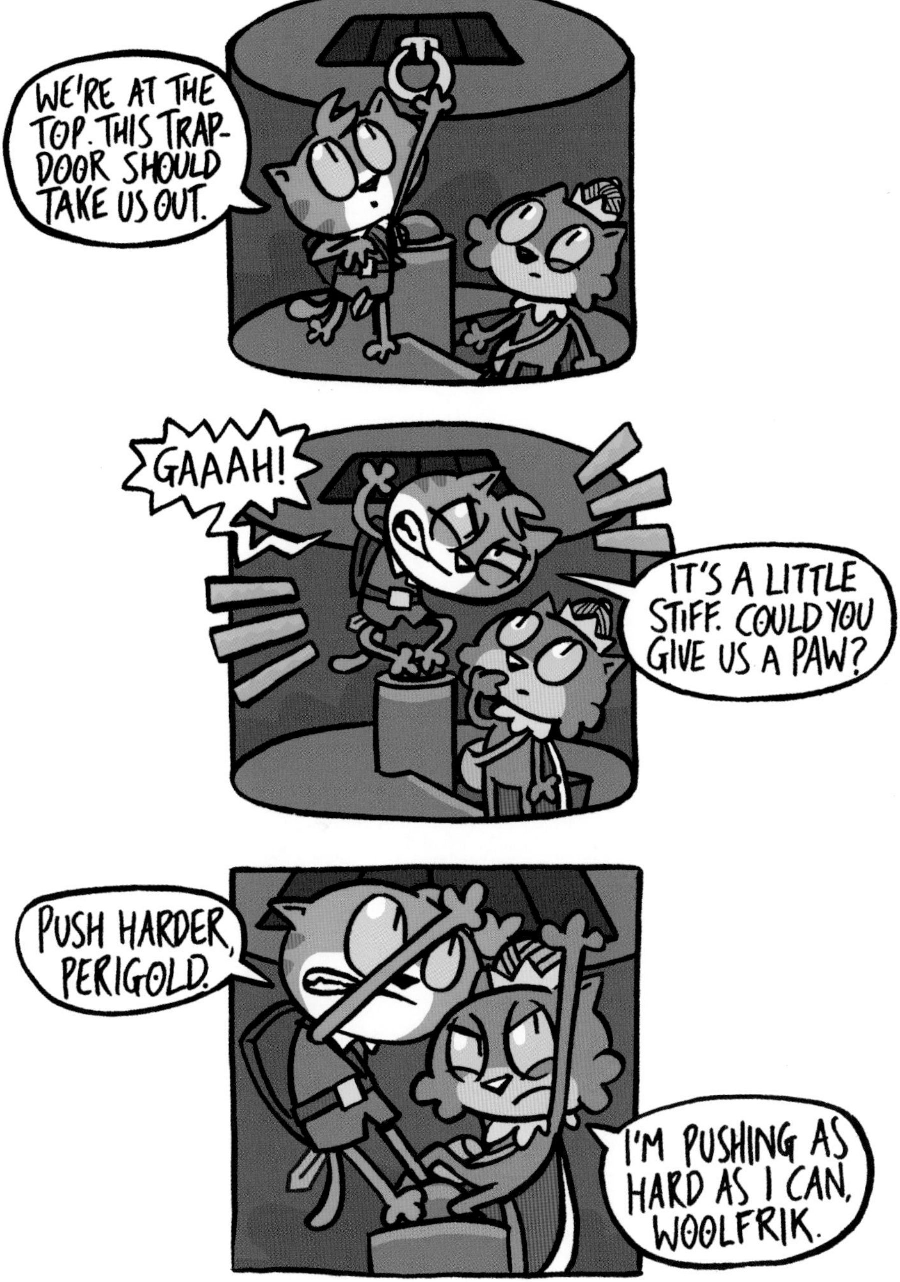
WE'RE AT THE TOP. THIS TRAP-DOOR SHOULD TAKE US OUT.
GAAAH!
IT'S A LITTLE STIFF. COULD YOU GIVE US A PAW?
PUSH HARDER, PERIGOLD.
I'M PUSHING AS HARD AS I CAN, WOOLFRIK.

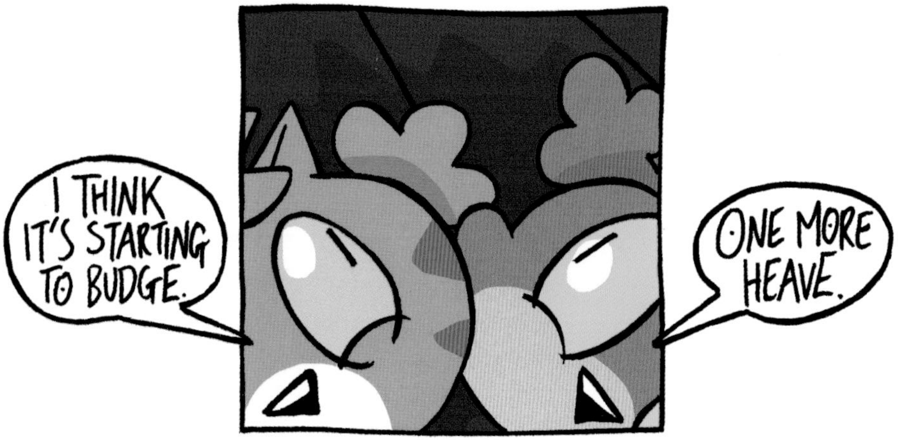
I THINK IT'S STARTING TO BUDGE.
ONE MORE HEAVE.

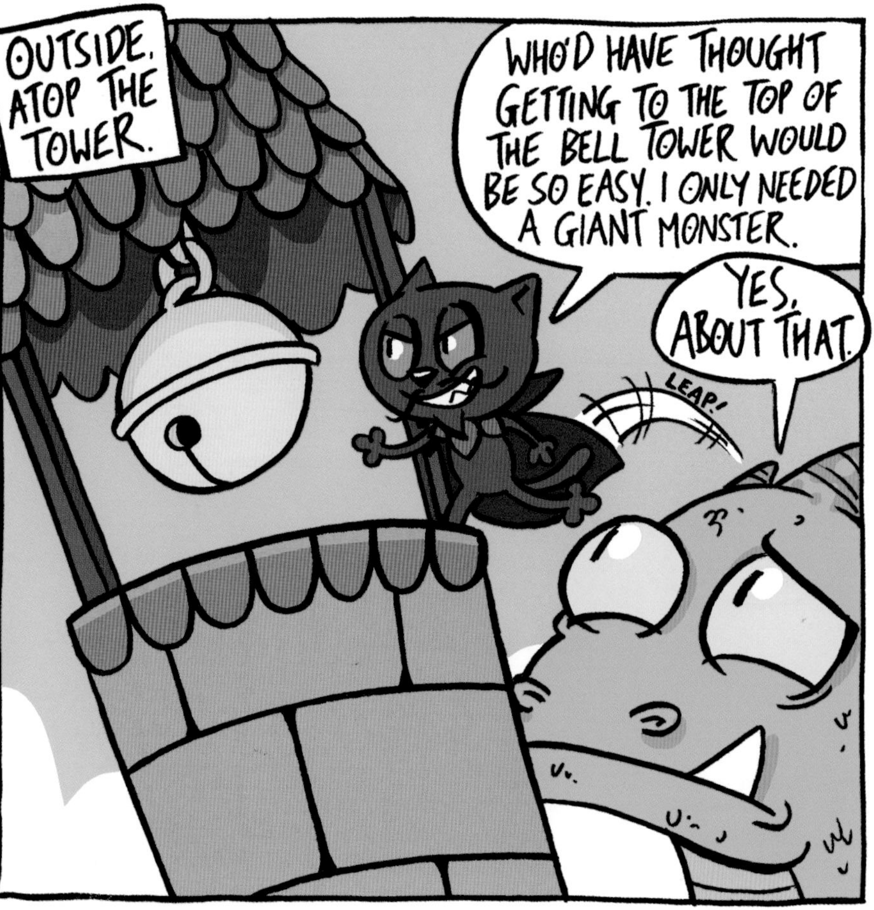
OUTSIDE, ATOP THE TOWER.
WHO'D HAVE THOUGHT GETTING TO THE TOP OF THE BELL TOWER WOULD BE SO EASY. I ONLY NEEDED A GIANT MONSTER.
YES, ABOUT THAT.
LEAP!

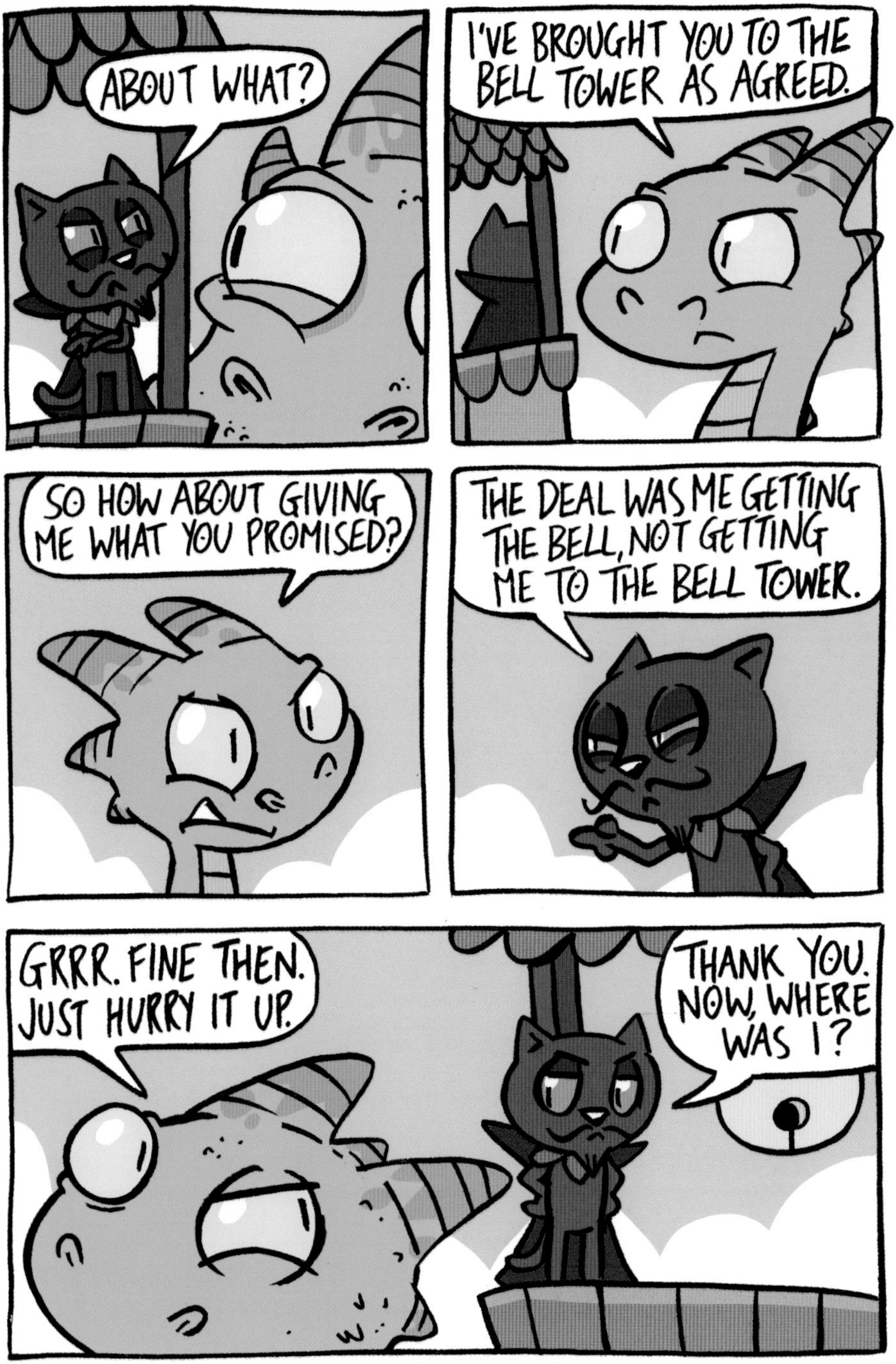
ABOUT WHAT?
I'VE BROUGHT YOU TO THE BELL TOWER AS AGREED.
SO HOW ABOUT GIVING ME WHAT YOU PROMISED?
THE DEAL WAS ME GETTING THE BELL, NOT GETTING ME TO THE BELL TOWER.
GRRR. FINE THEN. JUST HURRY IT UP.
THANK YOU. NOW, WHERE WAS I?

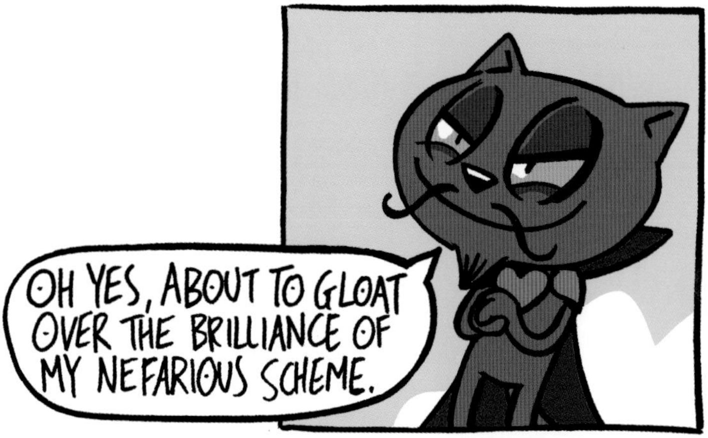
OH YES, ABOUT TO GLOAT OVER THE BRILLIANCE OF MY NEFARIOUS SCHEME.

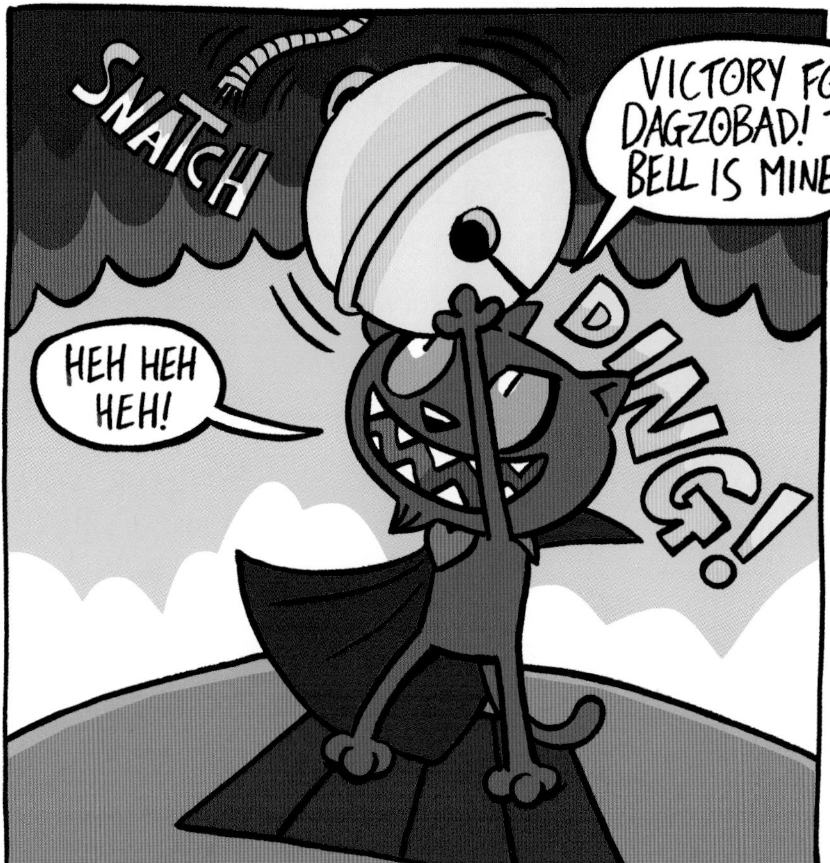
SNATCH
VICTORY FOR DAGZOBAD! THE BELL IS MINE!
HEH HEH HEH!
DING!

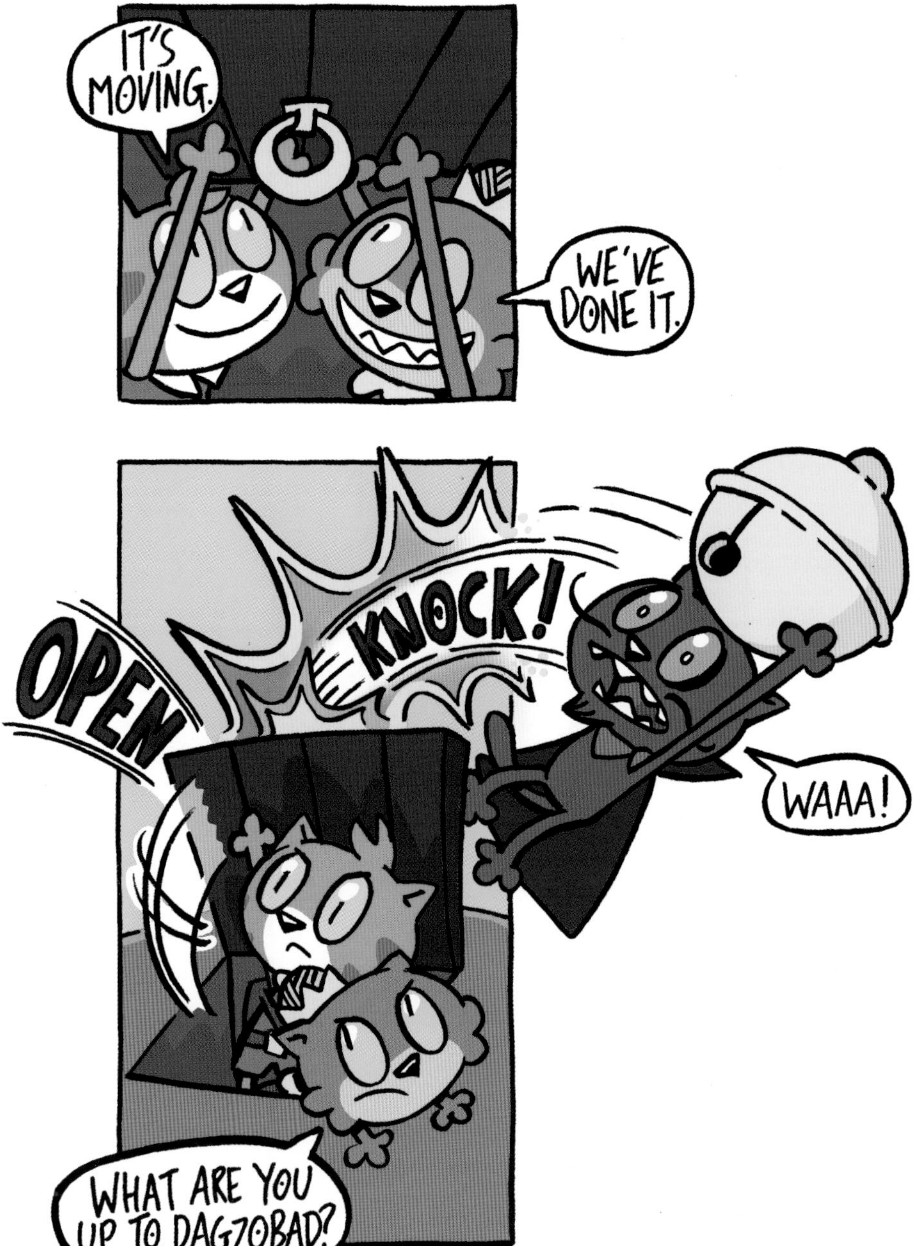
IT'S MOVING.
WE'VE DONE IT.
OPEN
KNOCK!
WAAA!
WHAT ARE YOU UP TO, DAGZOBAD?

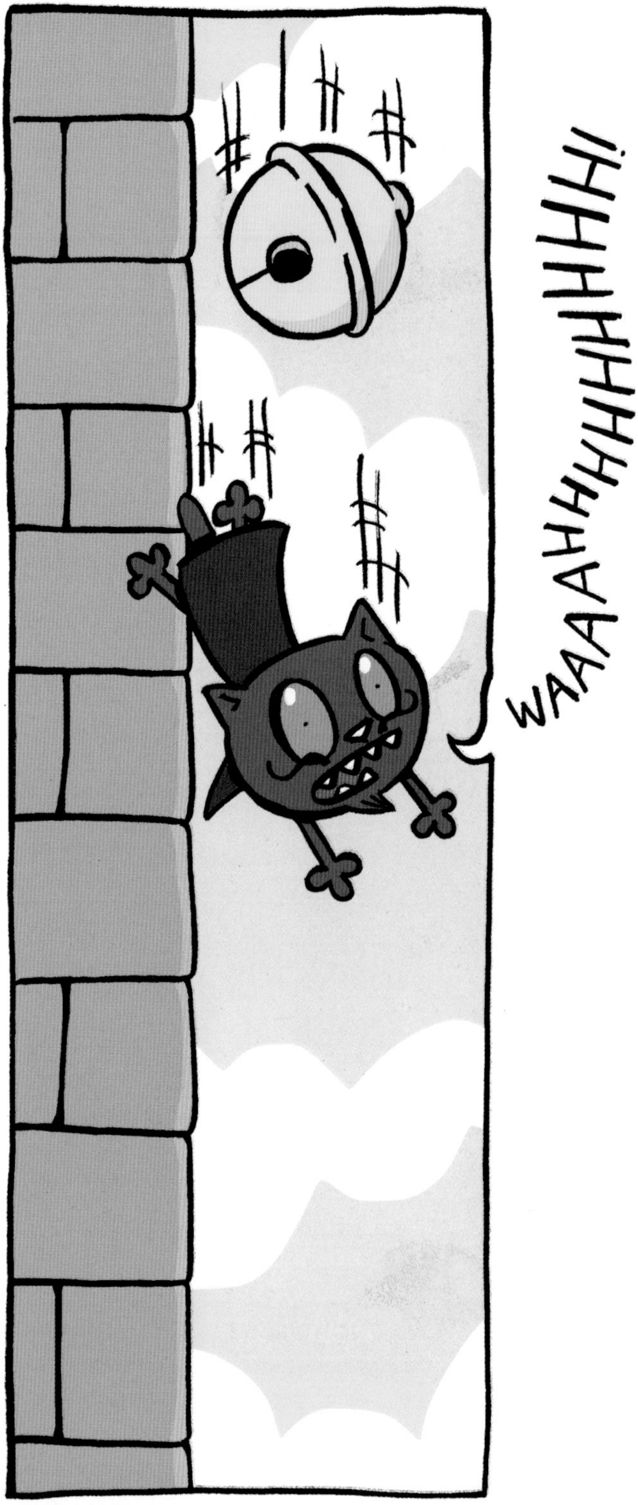
WAAAHHHHHHHHHH!

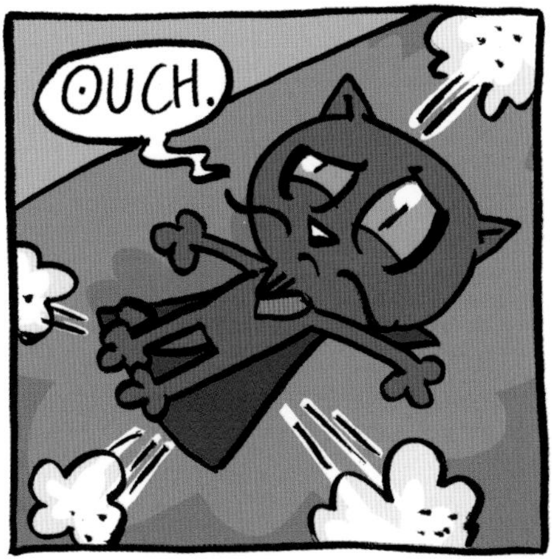
OUCH.

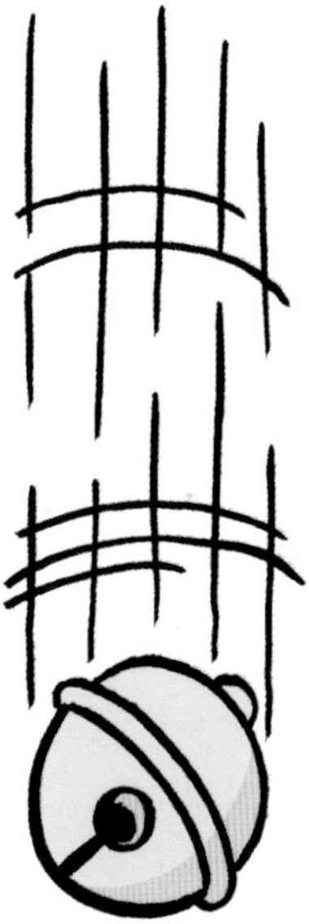

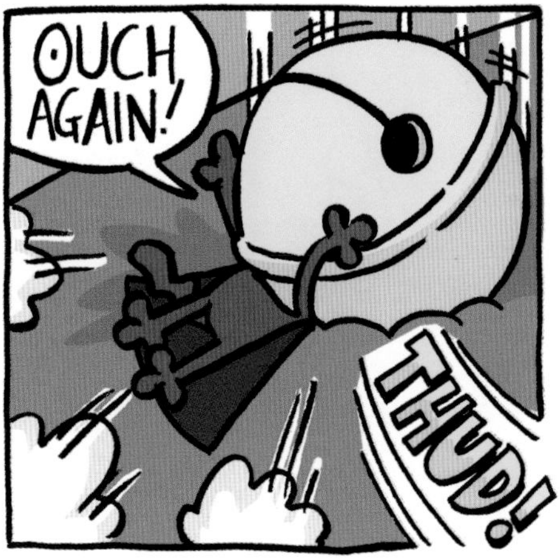
OUCH, AGAIN!
THUD!

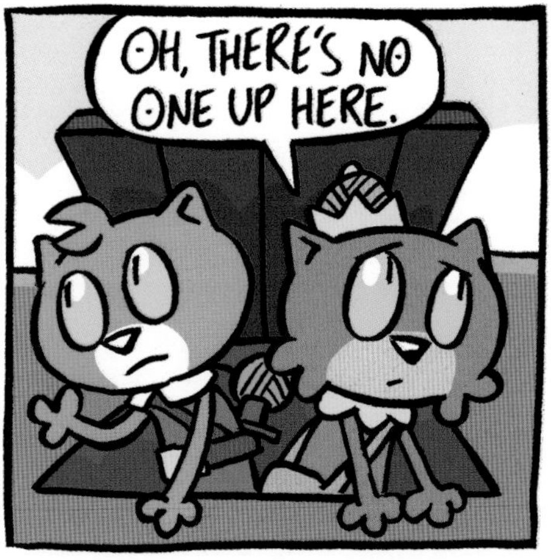
OH, THERE'S NO ONE UP HERE.

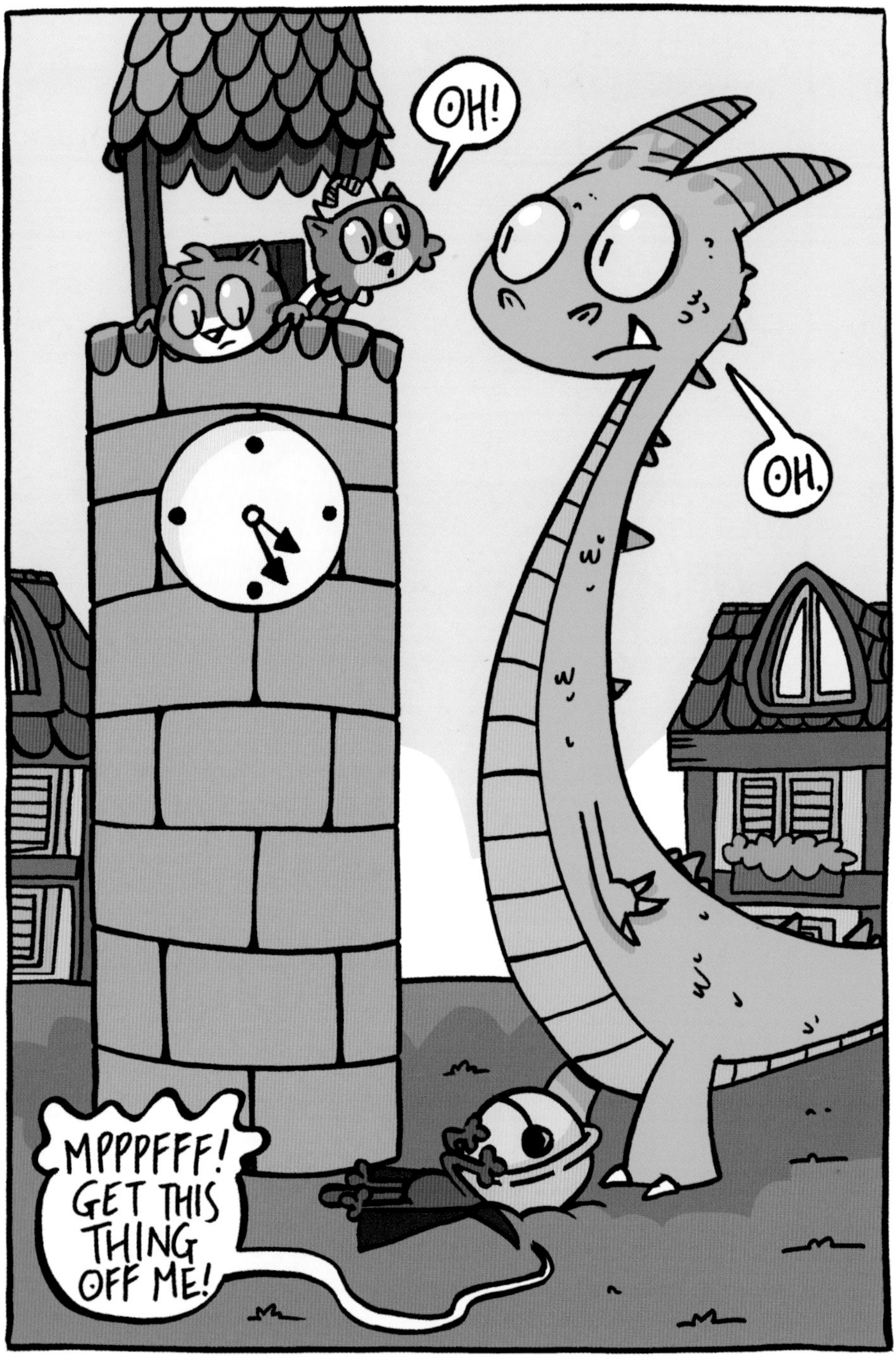
OH!
OH.
MPPPFFF! GET THIS THING OFF ME!

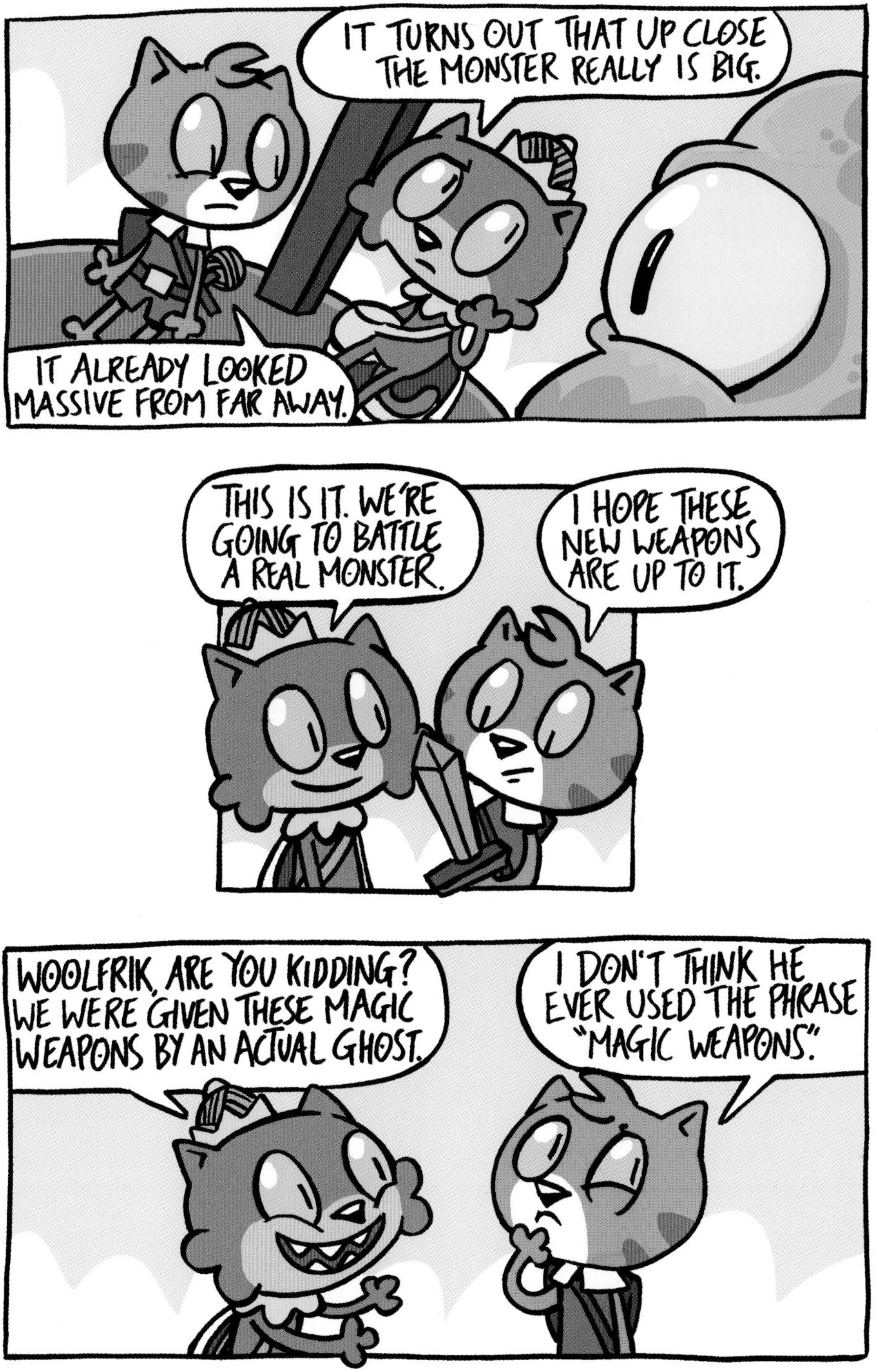
IT ALREADY LOOKED MASSIVE FROM FAR AWAY.
IT TURNS OUT THAT UP CLOSE THE MONSTER REALLY IS BIG.
THIS IS IT. WE'RE GOING TO BATTLE A REAL MONSTER.
I HOPE THESE NEW WEAPONS ARE UP TO IT.
WOOLFRIK, ARE YOU KIDDING? WE WERE GIVEN THESE MAGIC WEAPONS BY AN ACTUAL GHOST.
I DON'T THINK HE EVER USED THE PHRASE "MAGIC WEAPONS".

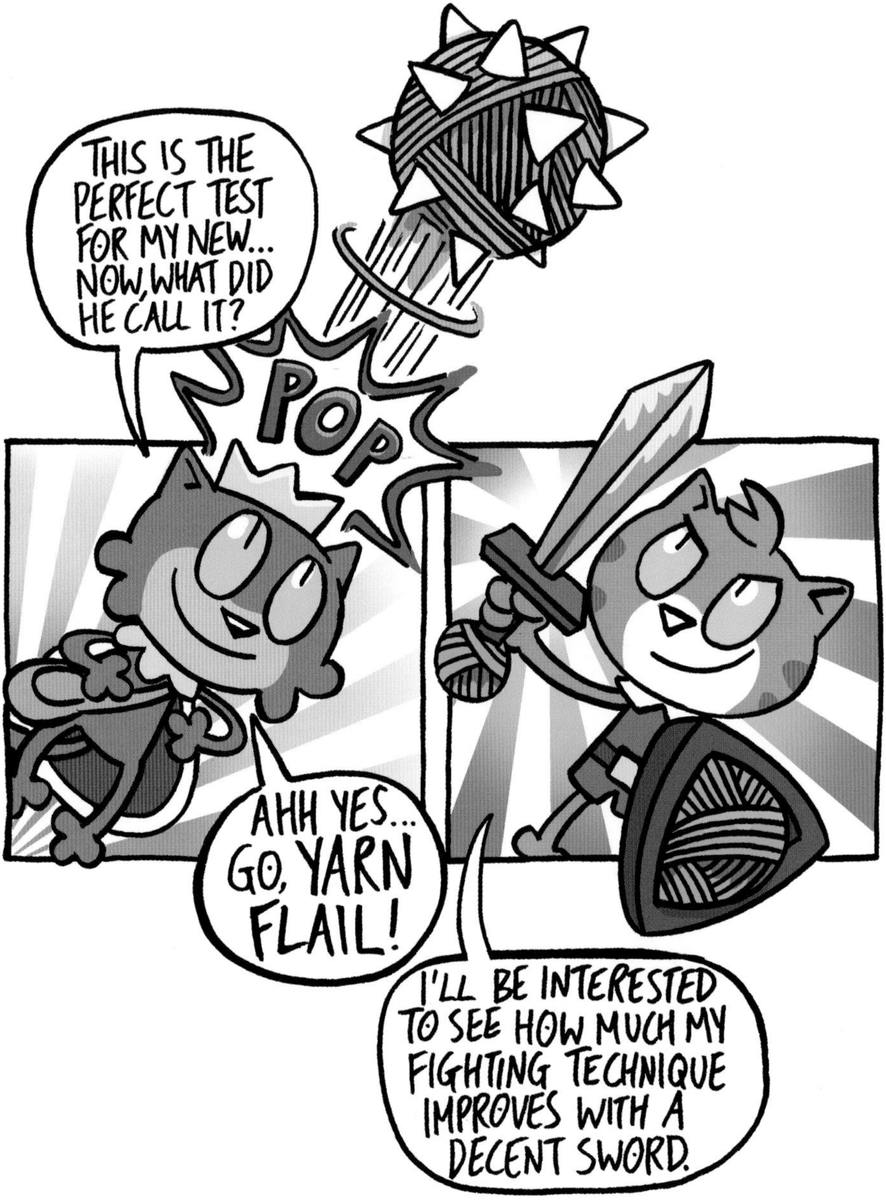
THIS IS THE PERFECT TEST FOR MY NEW... NOW, WHAT DID HE CALL IT?
POP
AHH YES... GO, YARN FLAIL!
I'LL BE INTERESTED TO SEE HOW MUCH MY FIGHTING TECHNIQUE IMPROVES WITH A DECENT SWORD.

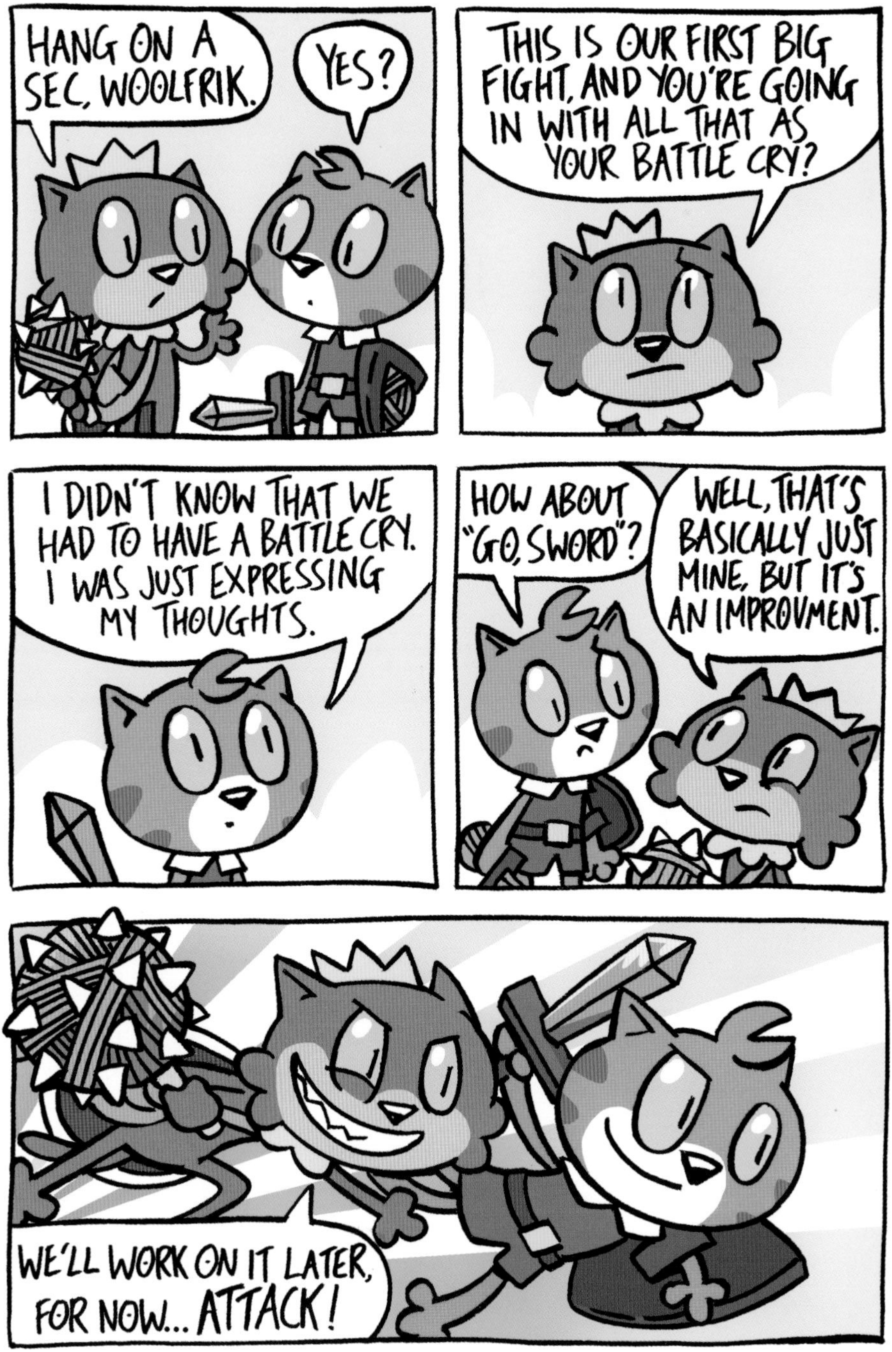
HANG ON A SEC, WOOLFRIK.
YES?
THIS IS OUR FIRST BIG FIGHT, AND YOU'RE GOING IN WITH ALL THAT AS YOUR BATTLE CRY?
I DIDN'T KNOW THAT WE HAD TO HAVE A BATTLE CRY. I WAS JUST EXPRESSING MY THOUGHTS.
HOW ABOUT "GO, SWORD"?
WELL, THAT'S BASICALLY JUST MINE, BUT IT'S AN IMPROVMENT.
WE'LL WORK ON IT LATER, FOR NOW... ATTACK!

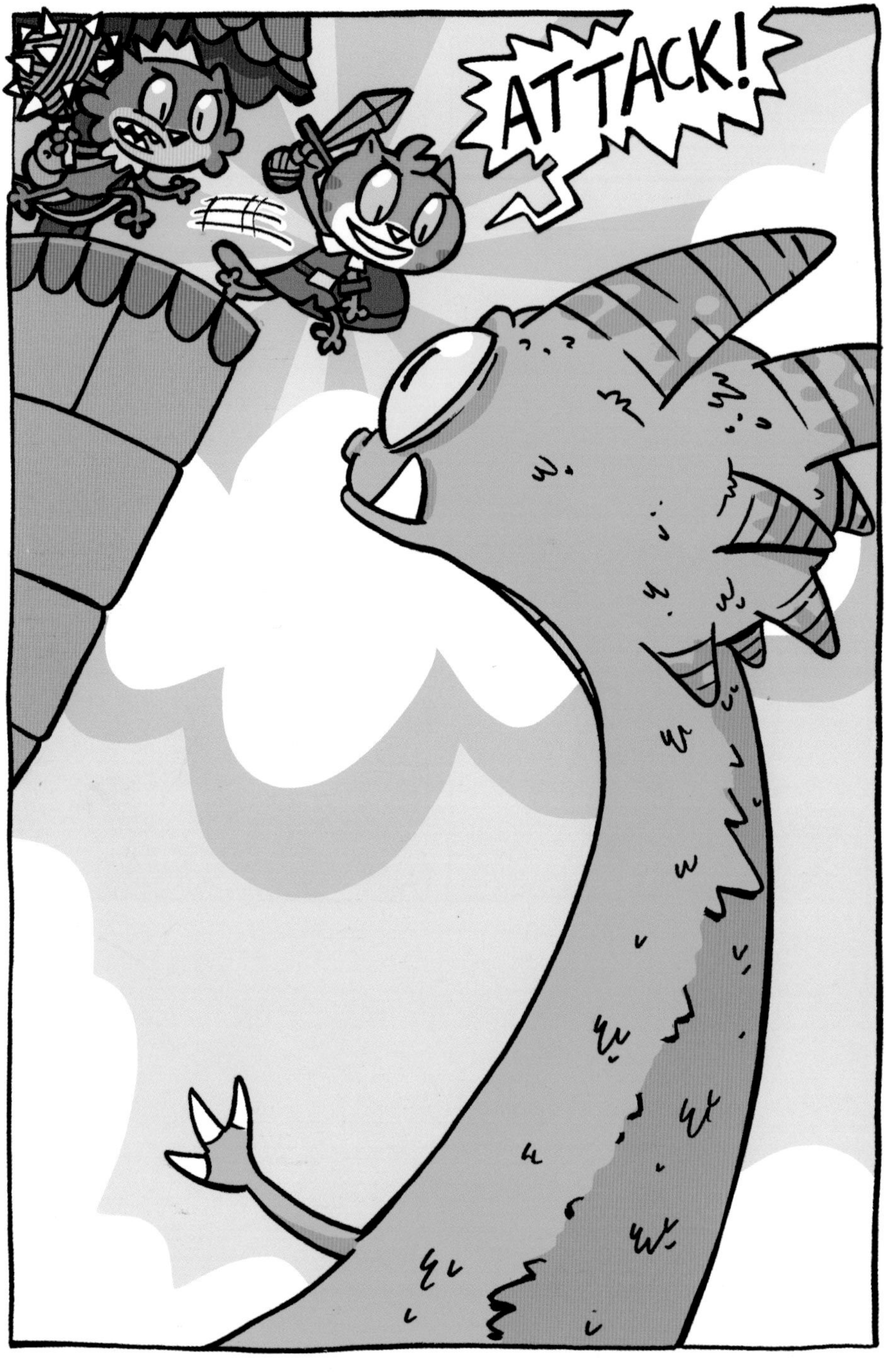
ATTACK!

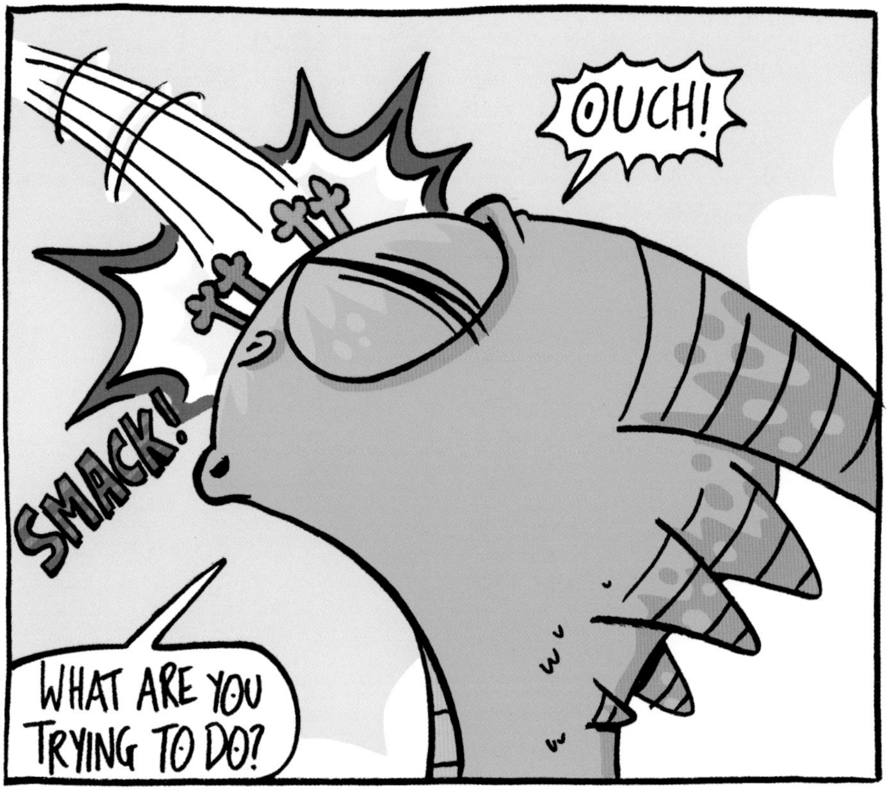
SMACK!
OUCH!
WHAT ARE YOU TRYING TO DO?
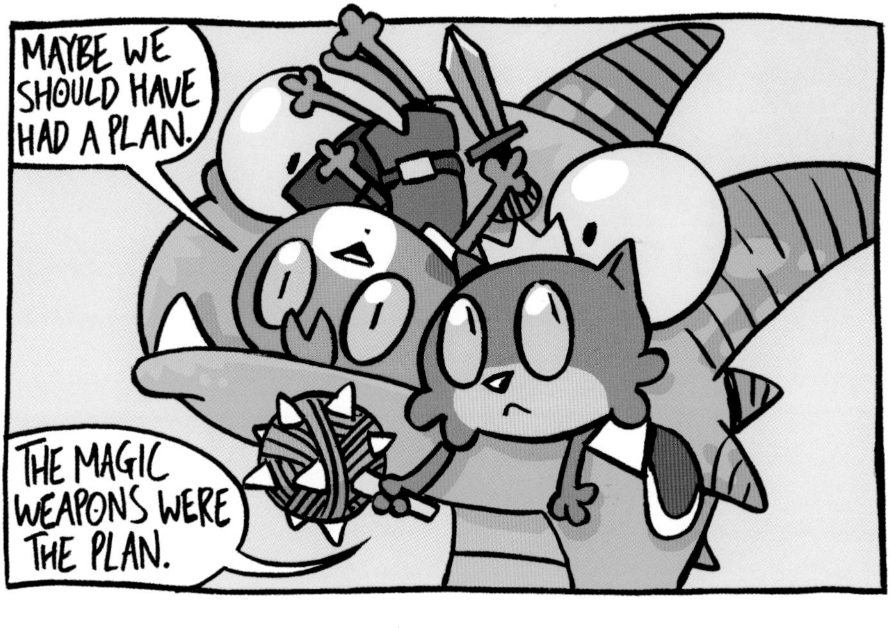
MAYBE WE SHOULD HAVE HAD A PLAN.
THE MAGIC WEAPONS WERE THE PLAN.

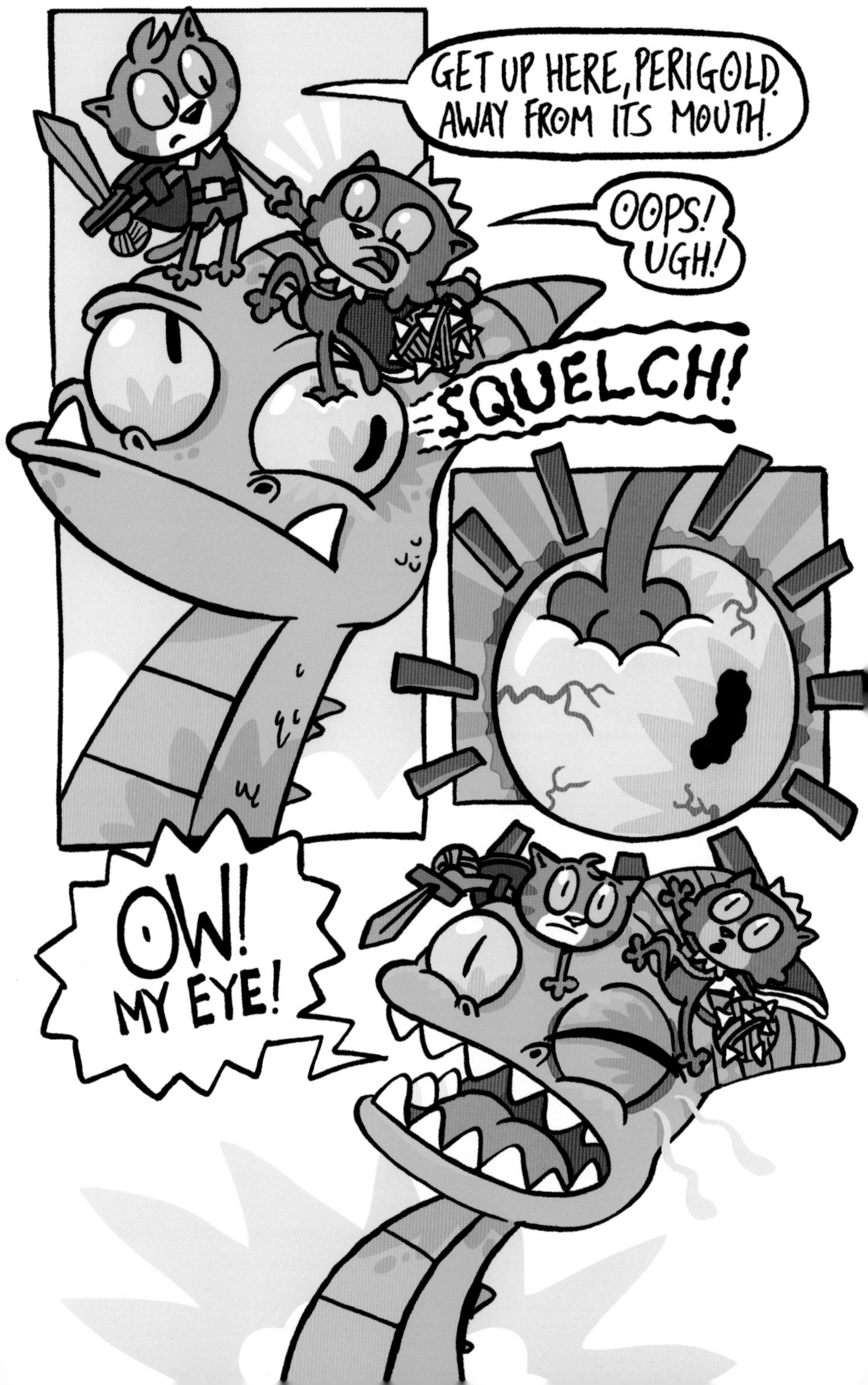
GET UP HERE, PERIGOLD. AWAY FROM ITS MOUTH.
OOPS! UGH!
SQUELCH!
OW! MY EYE!

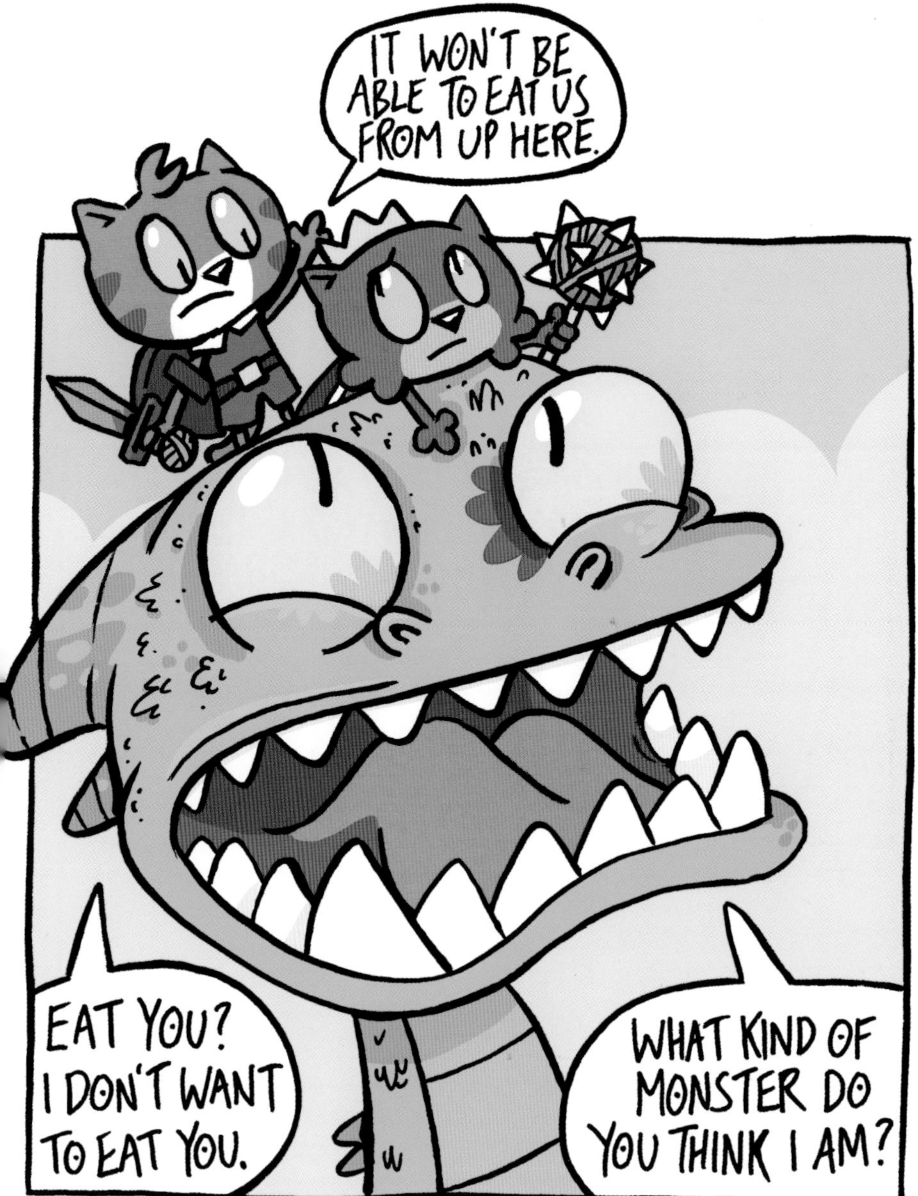
IT WON'T BE ABLE TO EAT US FROM UP HERE.
EAT YOU? I DON'T WANT TO EAT YOU.
WHAT KIND OF MONSTER DO YOU THINK I AM?

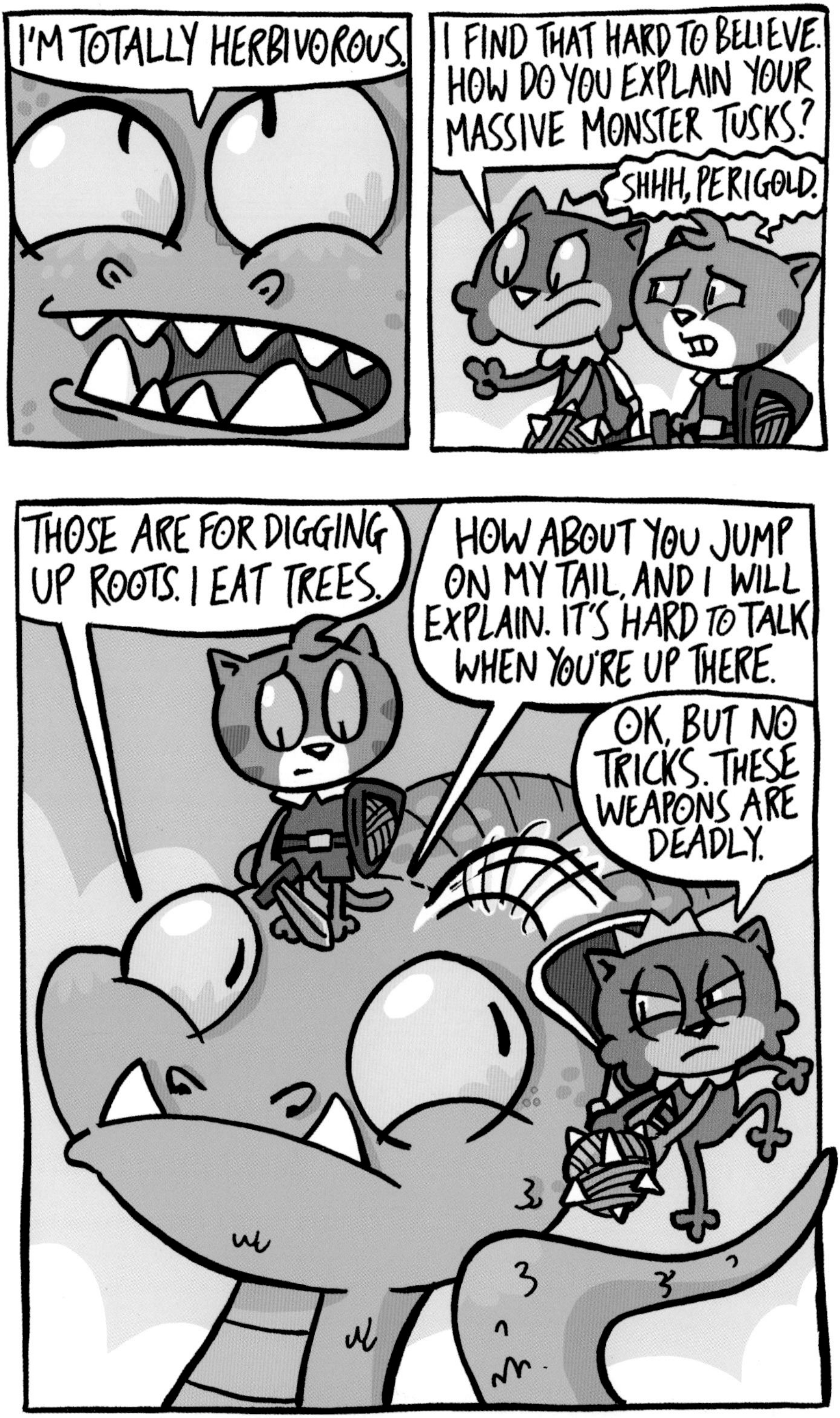
I'M TOTALLY HERBIVOROUS.
I FIND THAT HARD TO BELIEVE. HOW DO YOU EXPLAIN YOUR MASSIVE MONSTER TUSKS?
SHHH, PERIGOLD.
THOSE ARE FOR DIGGING UP ROOTS. I EAT TREES.
HOW ABOUT YOU JUMP ON MY TAIL, AND I WILL EXPLAIN. IT'S HARD TO TALK WHEN YOU'RE UP THERE.
OK, BUT NO TRICKS. THESE WEAPONS ARE DEADLY.

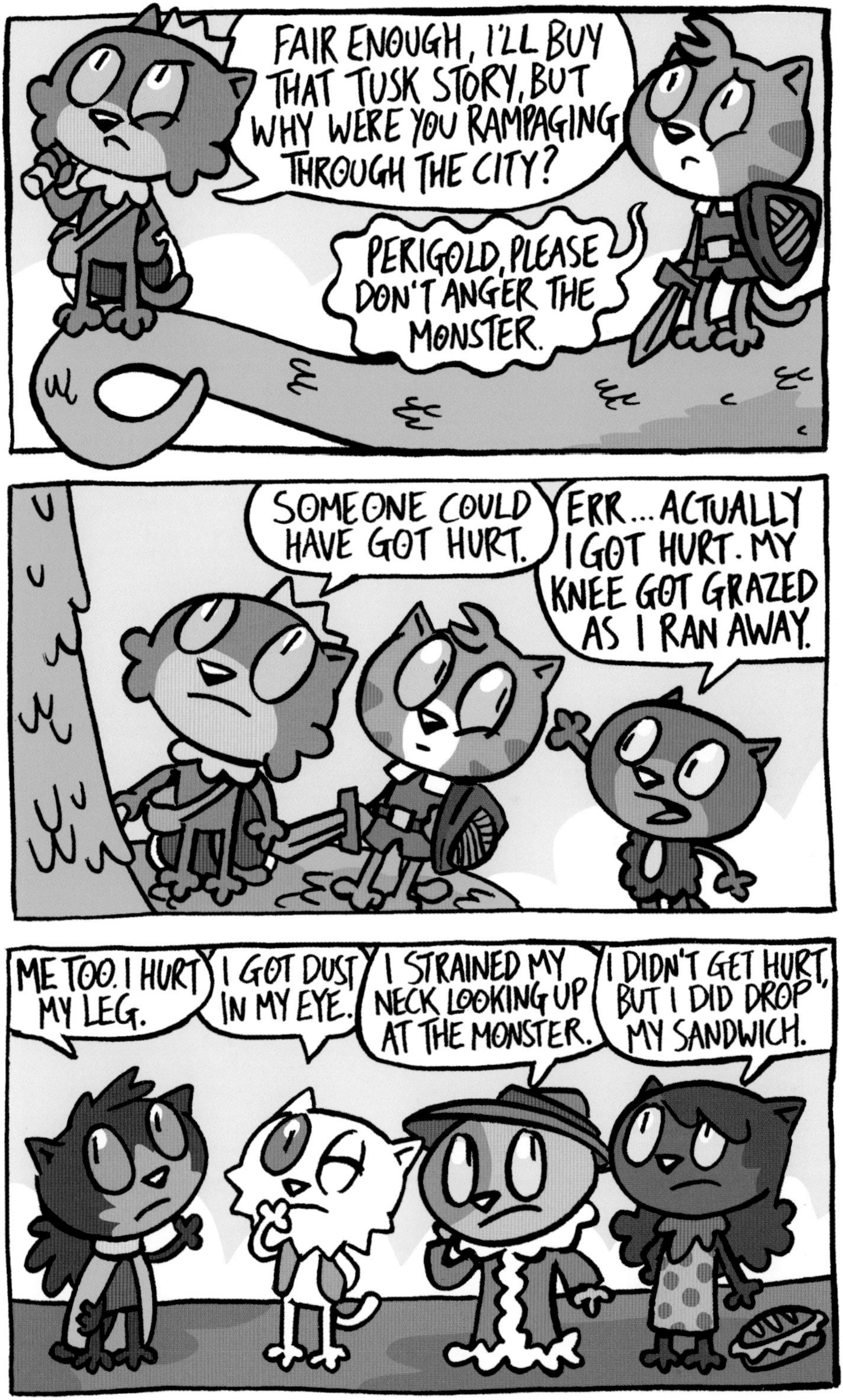
FAIR ENOUGH, I'LL BUY THAT TUSK STORY, BUT WHY WERE YOU RAMPAGING THROUGH THE CITY?
PERIGOLD, PLEASE DON'T ANGER THE MONSTER.
SOMEONE COULD HAVE GOT HURT.
ERR... ACTUALLY I GOT HURT. MY KNEE GOT GRAZED AS I RAN AWAY.
ME TOO. I HURT MY LEG.
I GOT DUST IN MY EYE.
I STRAINED MY NECK LOOKING UP AT THE MONSTER.
I DIDN'T GET HURT, BUT I DID DROP MY SANDWICH.

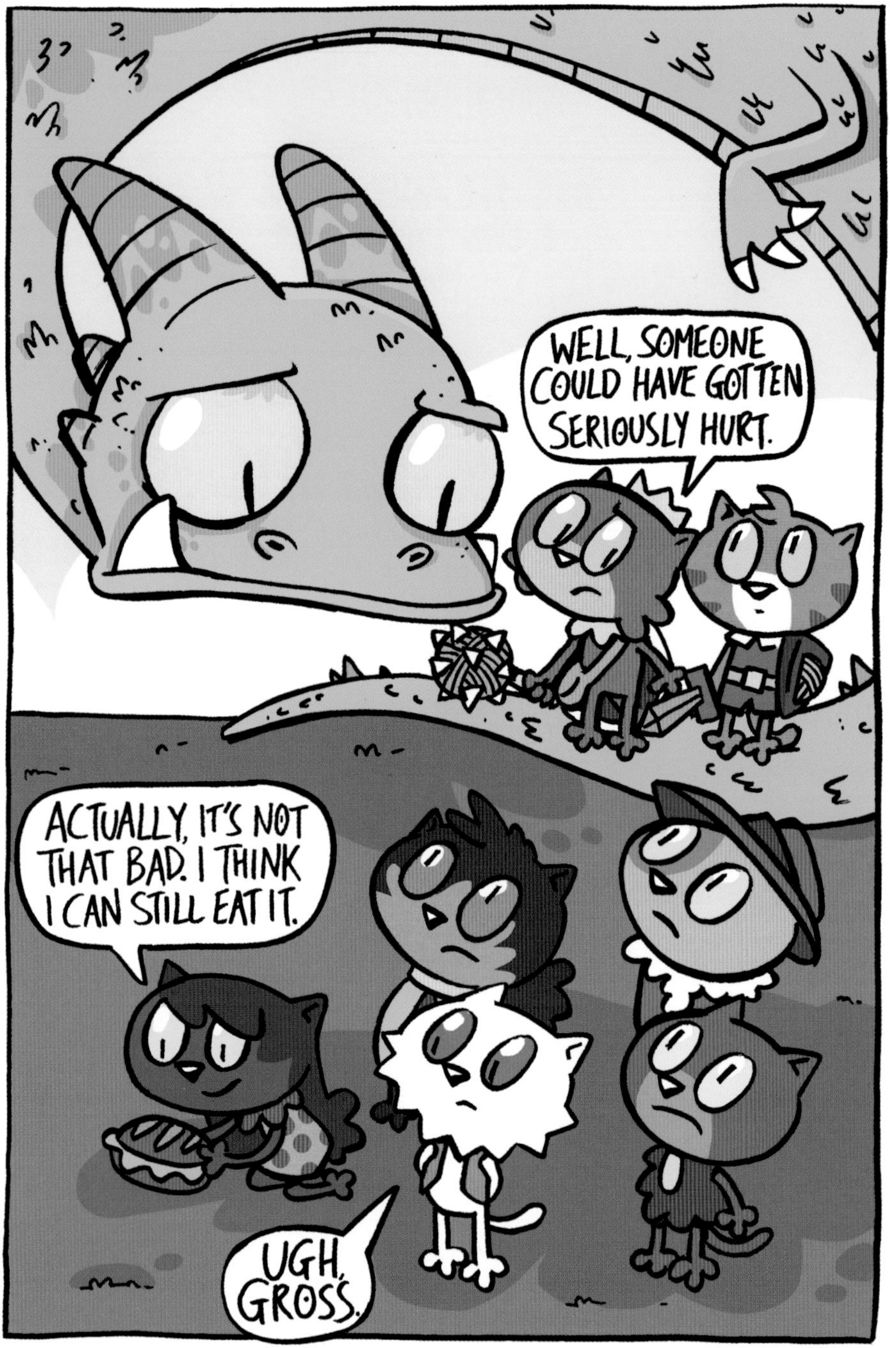
WELL, SOMEONE COULD HAVE GOTTEN SERIOUSLY HURT.
ACTUALLY, IT'S NOT THAT BAD. I THINK I CAN STILL EAT IT.
UGH, GROSS.

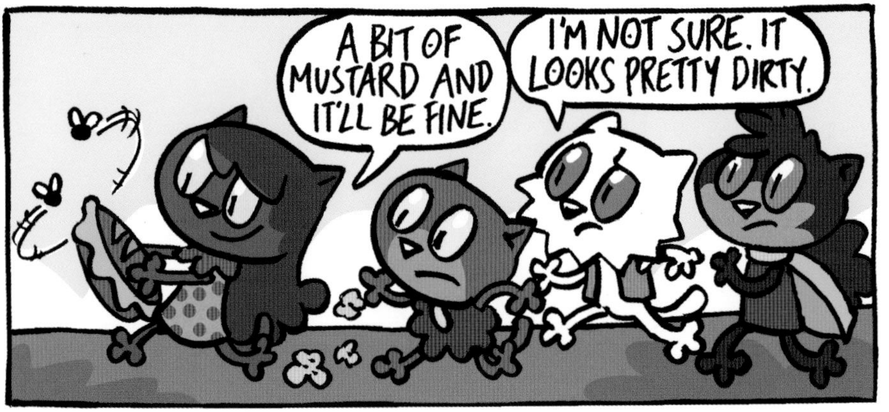
A BIT OF MUSTARD AND IT'LL BE FINE.
I'M NOT SURE. IT LOOKS PRETTY DIRTY.

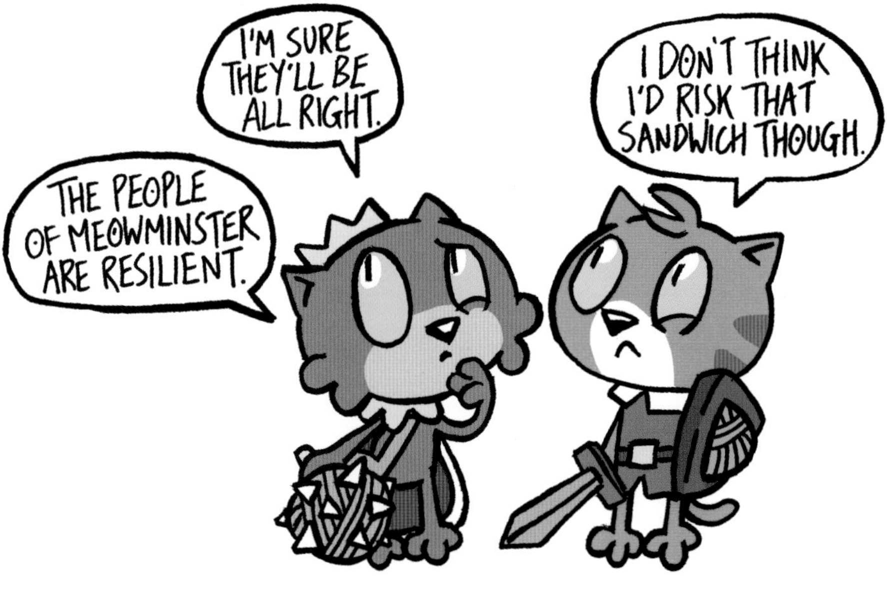
THE PEOPLE OF MEOWMINSTER ARE RESILIENT.
I'M SURE THEY'LL BE ALL RIGHT.
I DON'T THINK I'D RISK THAT SANDWICH THOUGH.

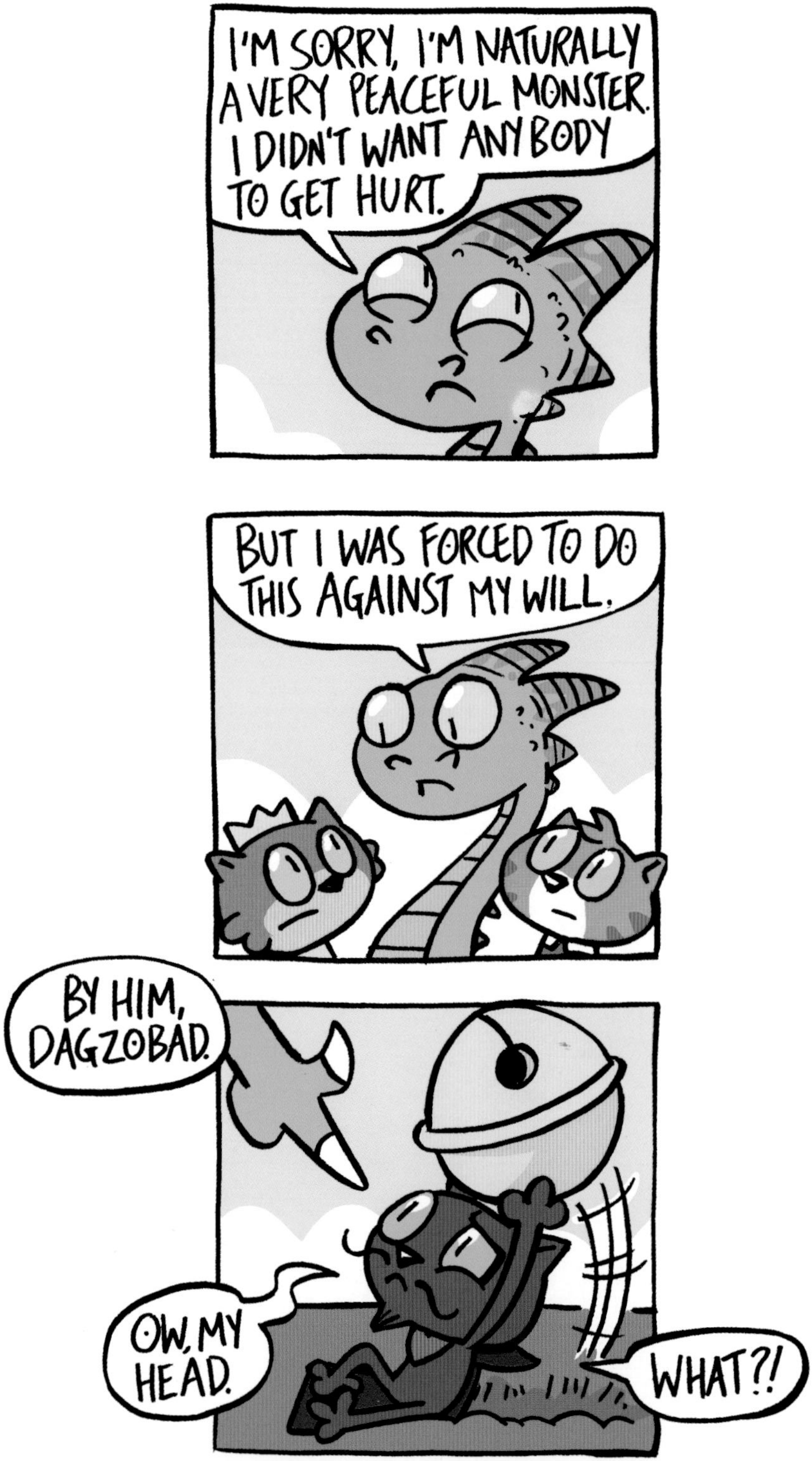
I'M SORRY, I'M NATURALLY A VERY PEACEFUL MONSTER. I DIDN'T WANT ANYBODY TO GET HURT.
BUT I WAS FORCED TO DO THIS AGAINST MY WILL.
BY HIM, DAGZOBAD.
OW, MY HEAD.
WHAT?!

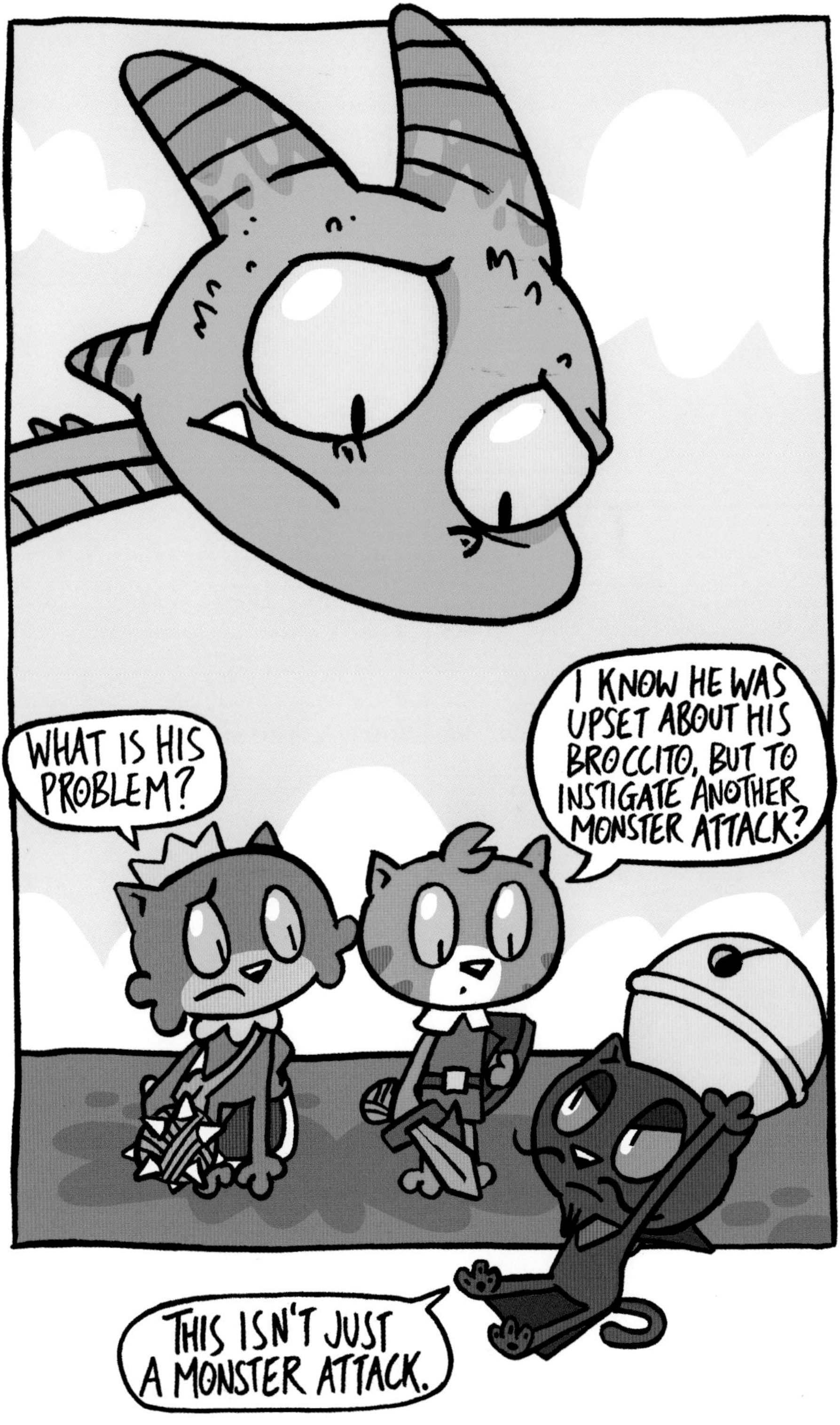
WHAT IS HIS PROBLEM?
I KNOW HE WAS UPSET ABOUT HIS BROCCITO, BUT TO INSTIGATE ANOTHER MONSTER ATTACK?
THIS ISN'T JUST A MONSTER ATTACK.

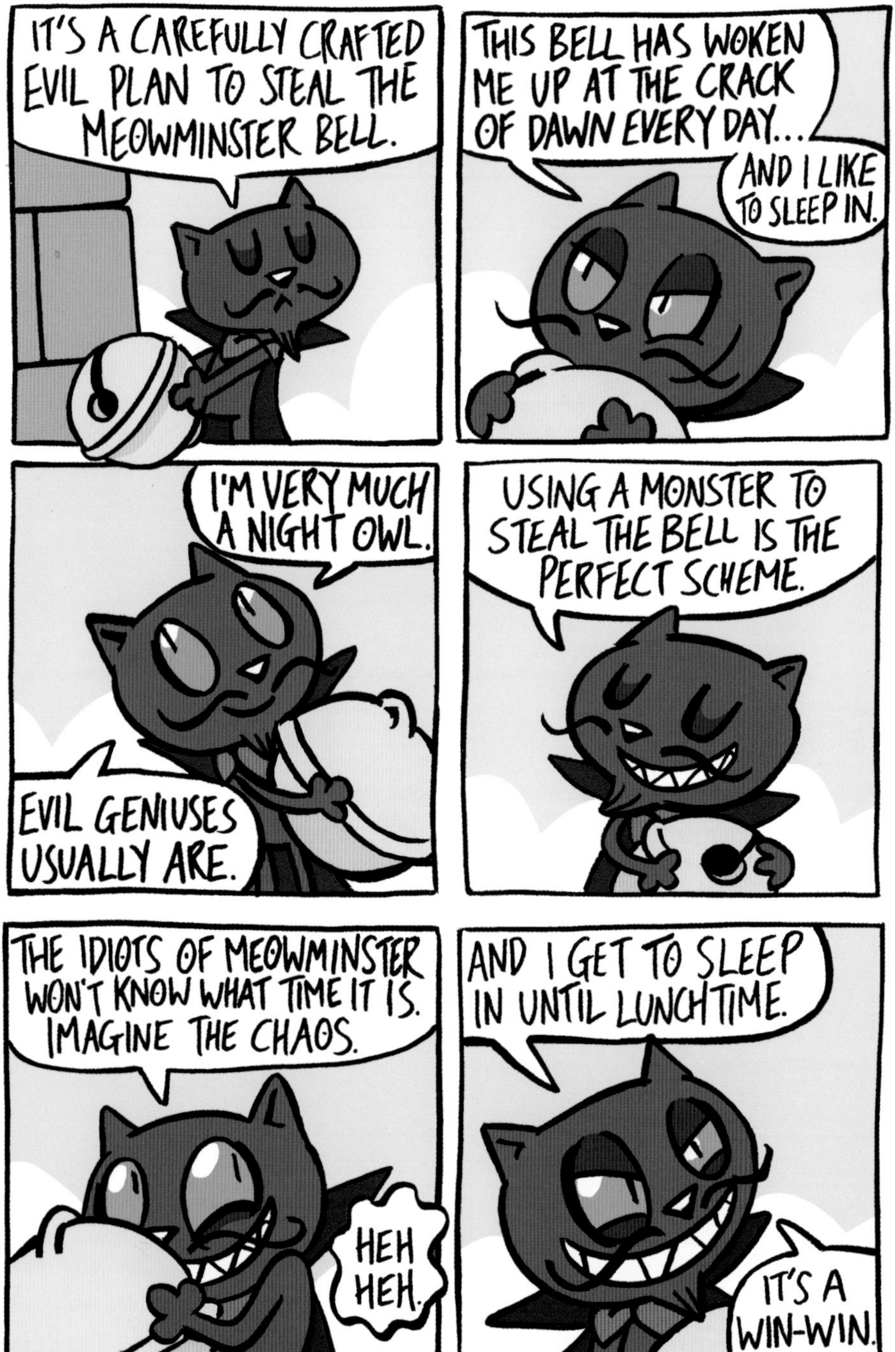
IT'S A CAREFULLY CRAFTED EVIL PLAN TO STEAL THE MEOWMINSTER BELL.
THIS BELL HAS WOKEN ME UP AT THE CRACK OF DAWN EVERY DAY...
AND I LIKE TO SLEEP IN.
I'M VERY MUCH A NIGHT OWL.
EVIL GENIUSES USUALLY ARE.
USING A MONSTER TO STEAL THE BELL IS THE PERFECT SCHEME.
THE IDIOTS OF MEOWMINSTER WON'T KNOW WHAT TIME IT IS. IMAGINE THE CHAOS.
HEH HEH.
AND I GET TO SLEEP IN UNTIL LUNCHTIME.
IT'S A WIN-WIN.

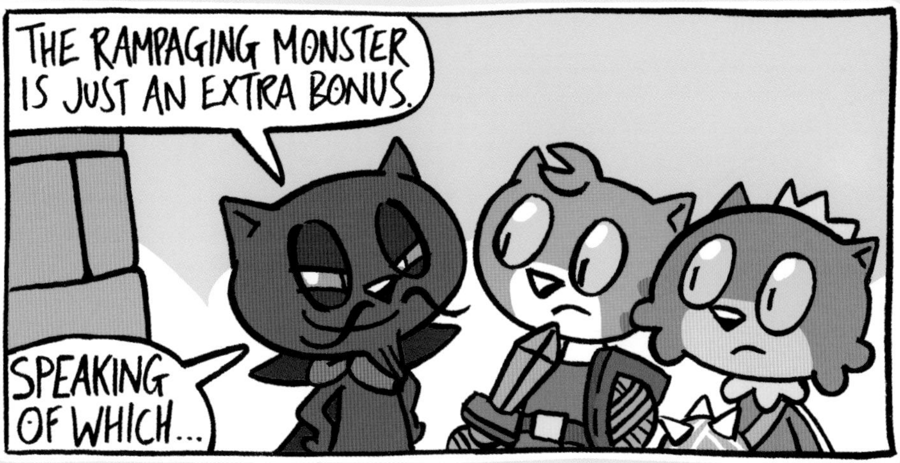
THE RAMPAGING MONSTER IS JUST AN EXTRA BONUS.
SPEAKING OF WHICH...

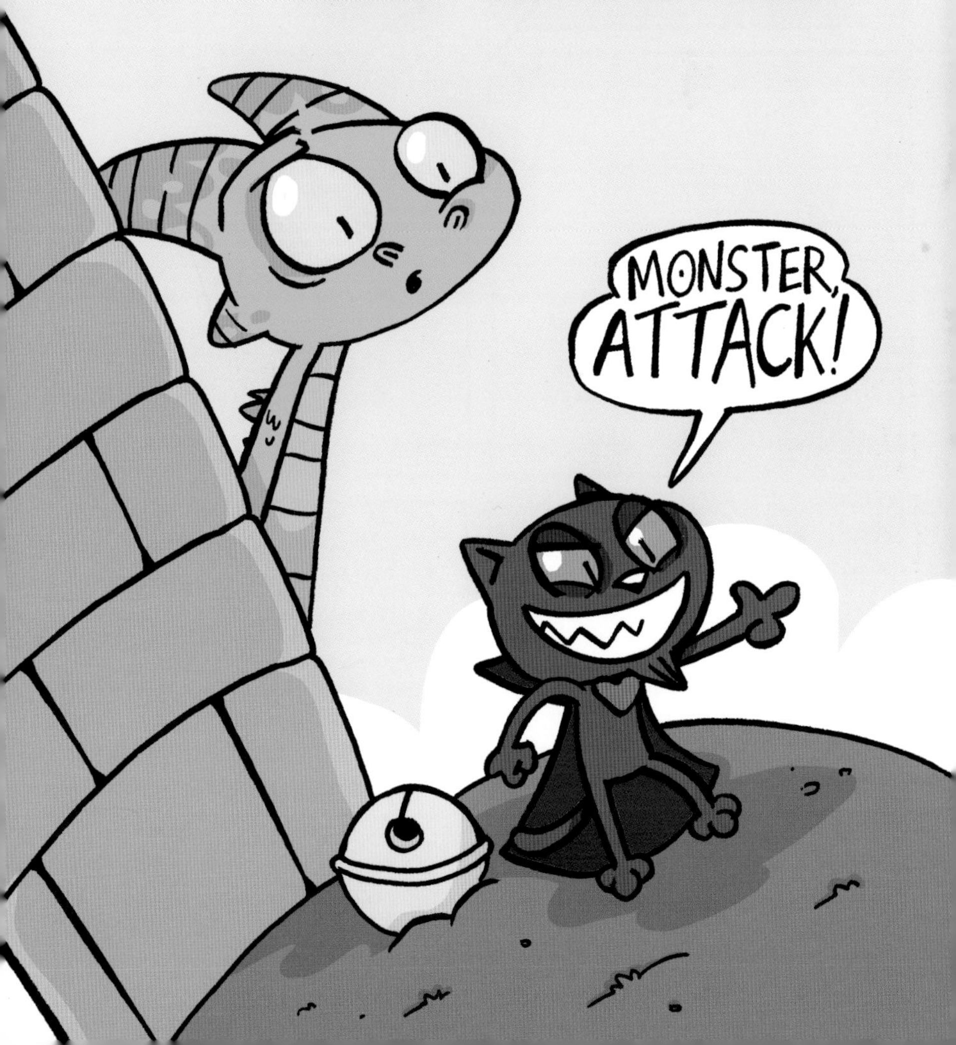
MONSTER, ATTACK!

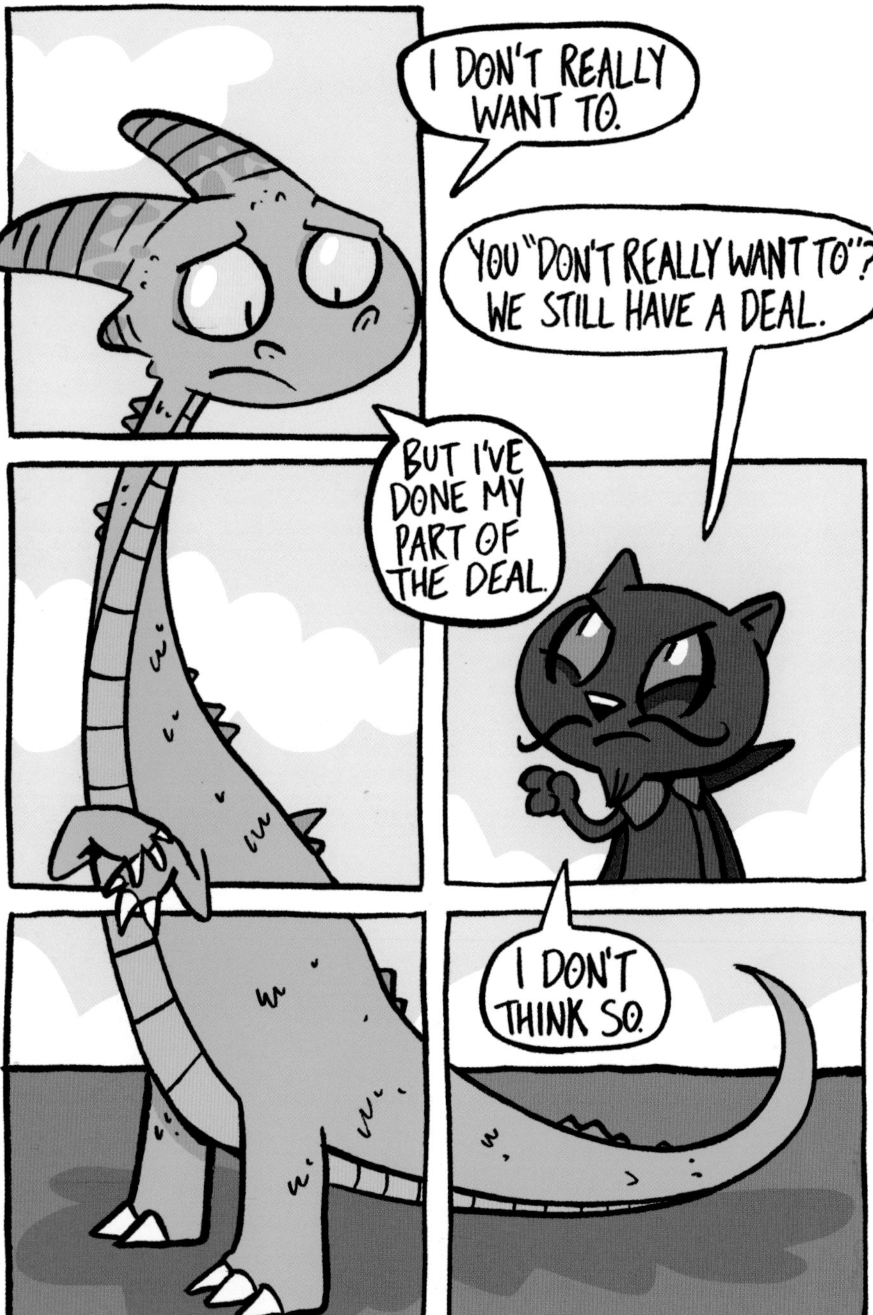
I DON'T REALLY WANT TO.
YOU "DON'T REALLY WANT TO"? WE STILL HAVE A DEAL.
BUT I'VE DONE MY PART OF THE DEAL.
I DON'T THINK SO.

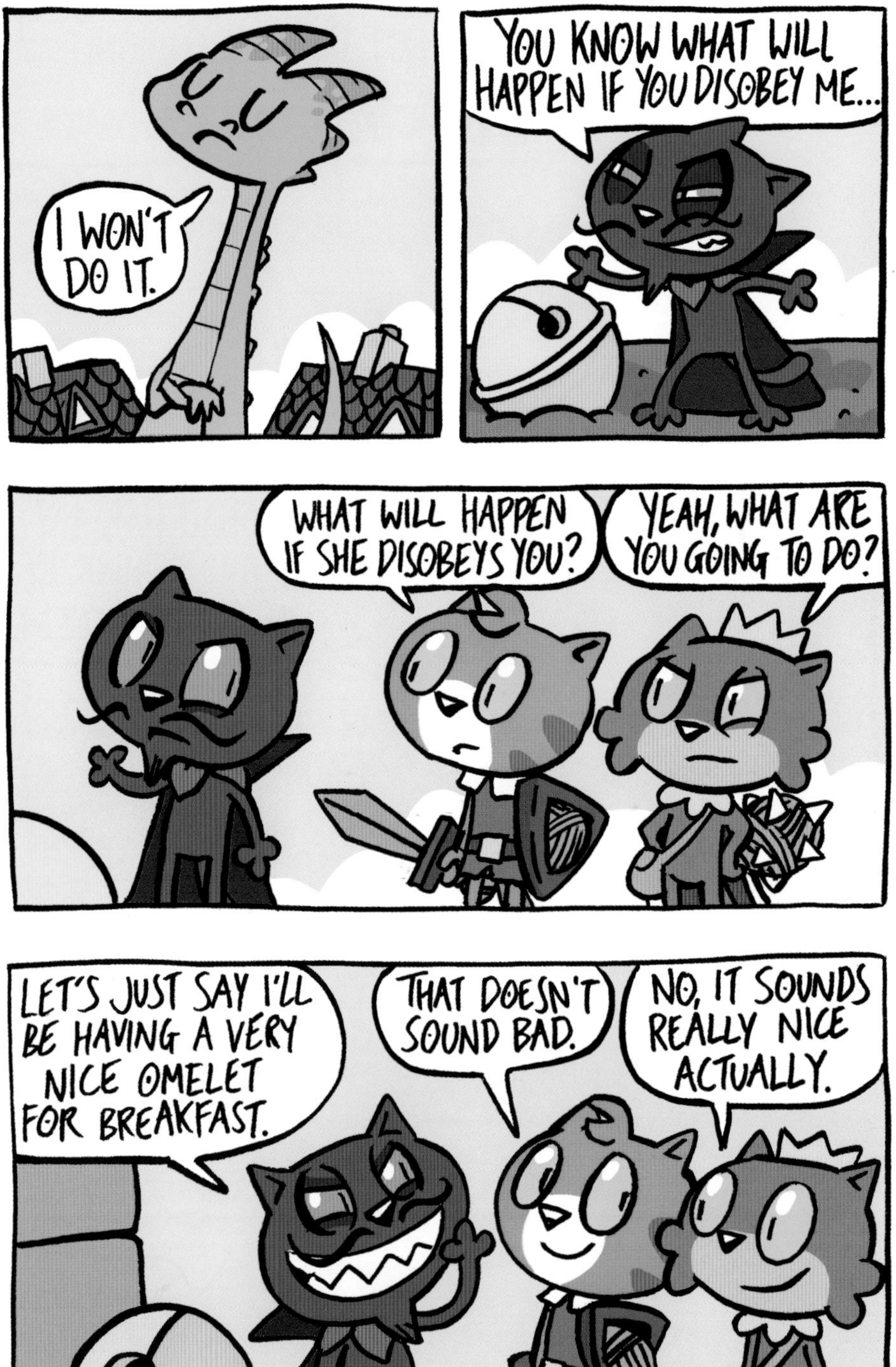
I WON'T DO IT.
YOU KNOW WHAT WILL HAPPEN IF YOU DISOBEY ME...
WHAT WILL HAPPEN IF SHE DISOBEYS YOU?
YEAH, WHAT ARE YOU GOING TO DO?
LET'S JUST SAY I'LL BE HAVING A VERY NICE OMELET FOR BREAKFAST.
THAT DOESN'T SOUND BAD.
NO, IT SOUNDS REALLY NICE ACTUALLY.

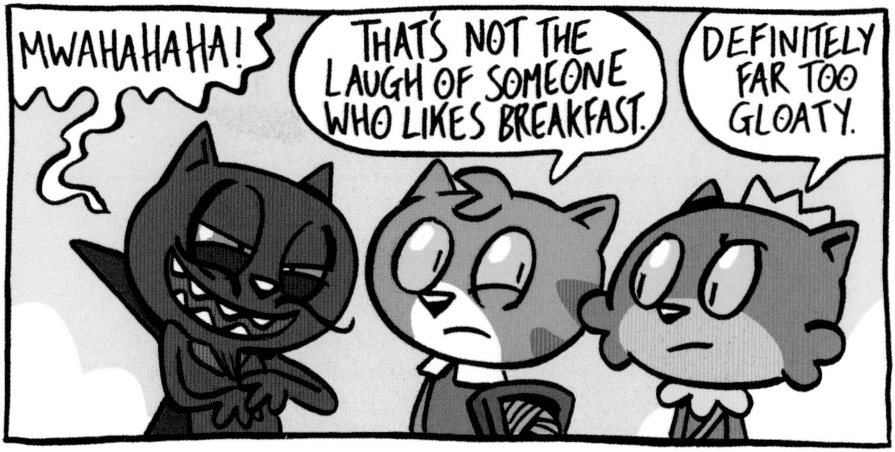
MWAHAHAHA!
THAT'S NOT THE LAUGH OF SOMEONE WHO LIKES BREAKFAST.
DEFINITELY FAR TOO GLOATY.

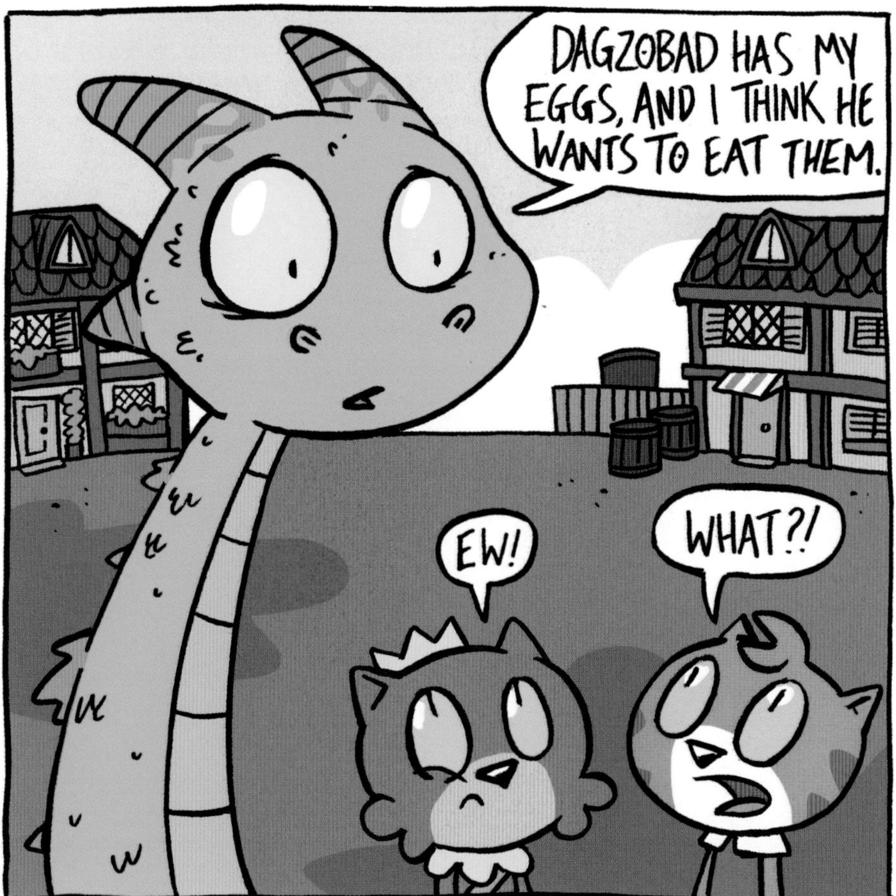
DAGZOBAD HAS MY EGGS, AND I THINK HE WANTS TO EAT THEM.
EW!
WHAT?!

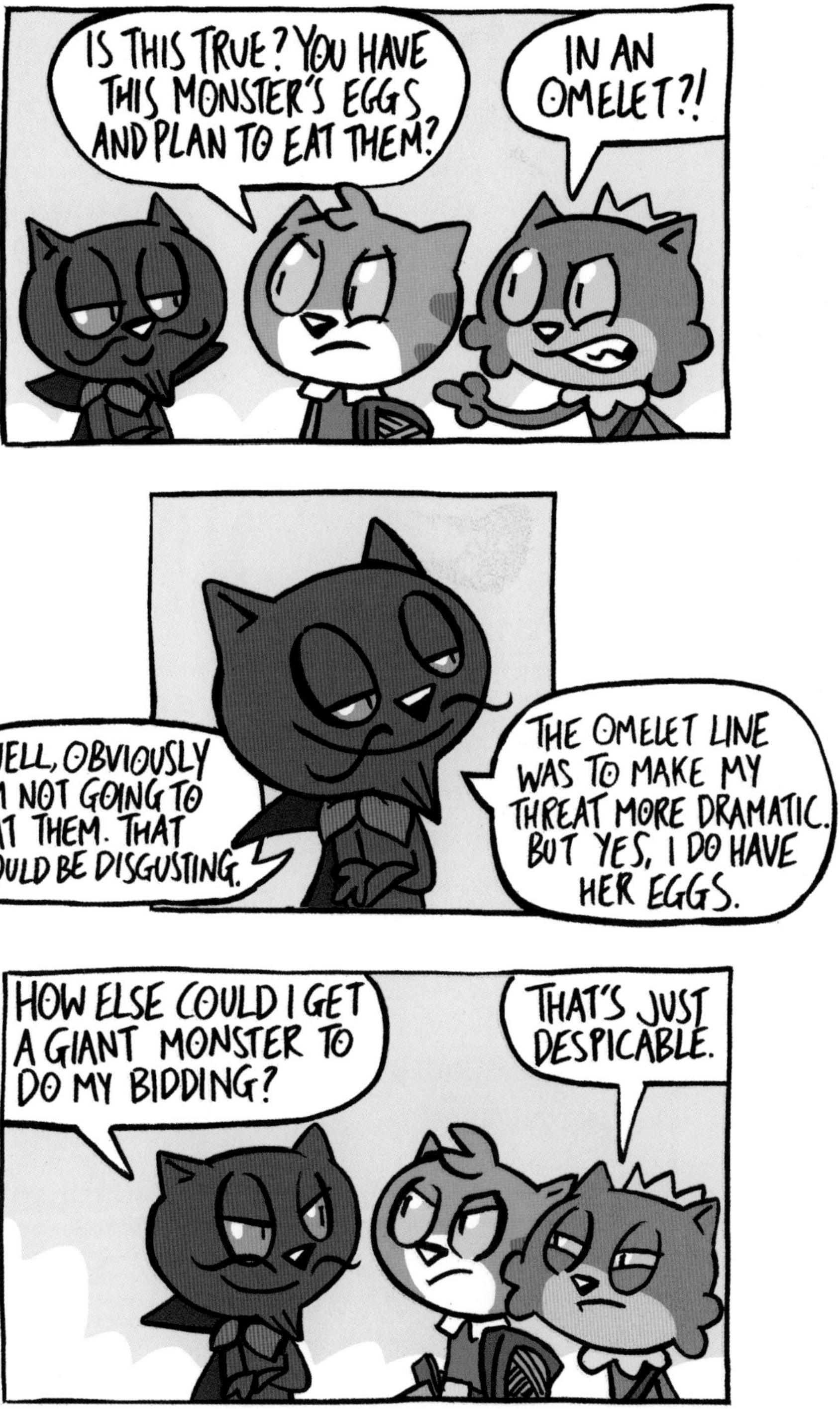
IS THIS TRUE? YOU HAVE THIS MONSTER'S EGGS AND PLAN TO EAT THEM?
IN AN OMELET?!
WELL, OBVIOUSLY I'M NOT GOING TO EAT THEM. THAT WOULD BE DISGUSTING.
THE OMELET LINE WAS TO MAKE MY THREAT MORE DRAMATIC. BUT YES, I DO HAVE HER EGGS.
HOW ELSE COULD I GET A GIANT MONSTER TO DO MY BIDDING?
THAT'S JUST DESPICABLE.

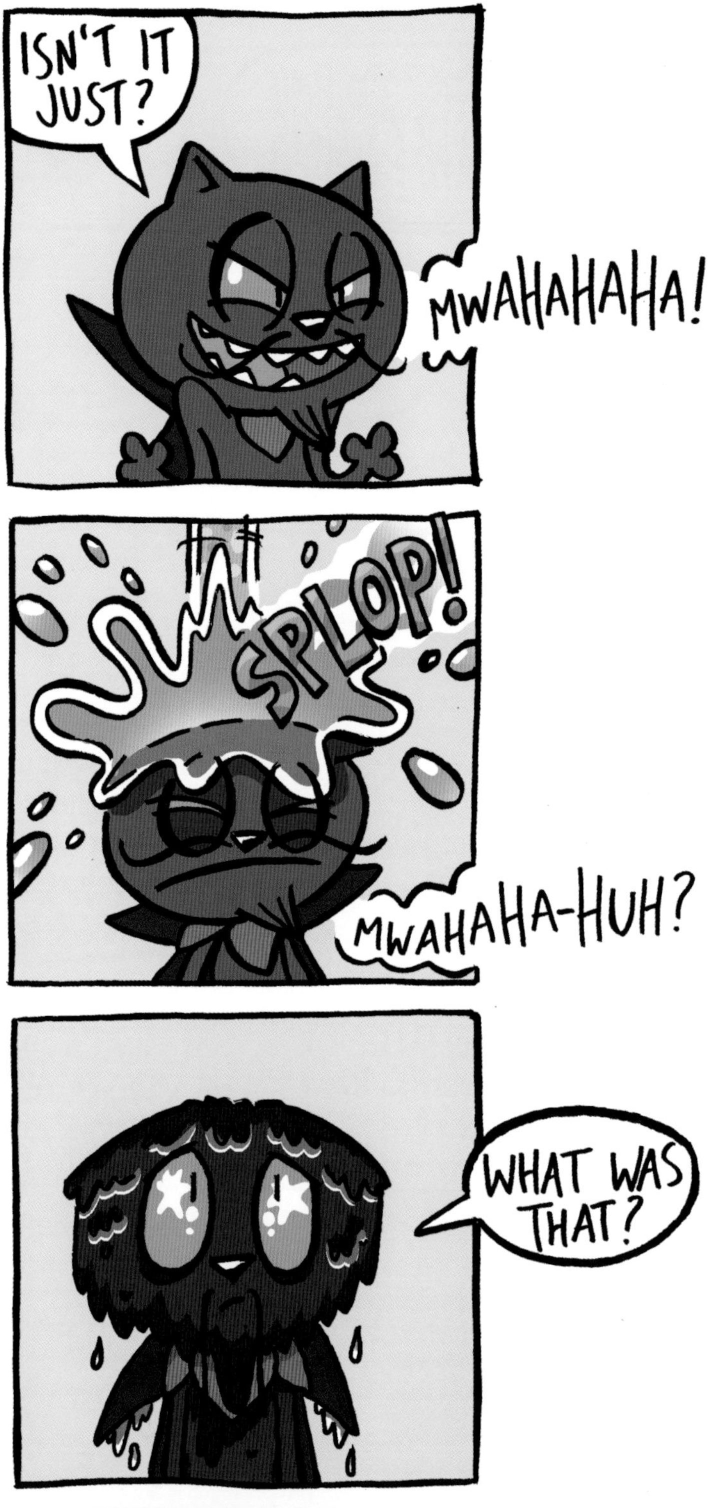
ISN'T IT JUST?
MWAHAHAHA!
SPLOP!
MWAHAHA-HUH?
WHAT WAS THAT?

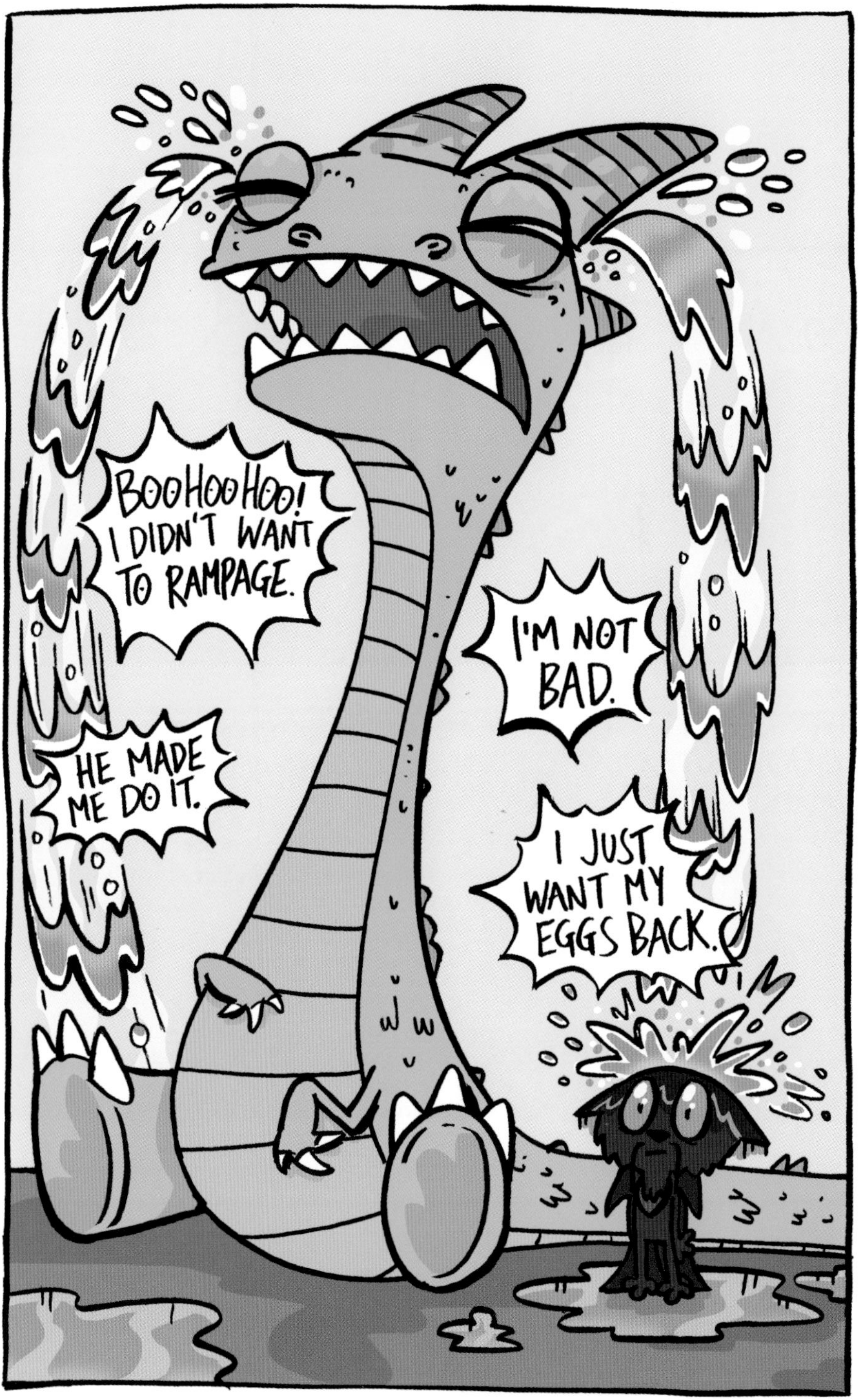
BOOHOOHOO! I DIDN'T WANT TO RAMPAGE.
HE MADE ME DO IT.
I'M NOT BAD.
I JUST WANT MY EGGS BACK.

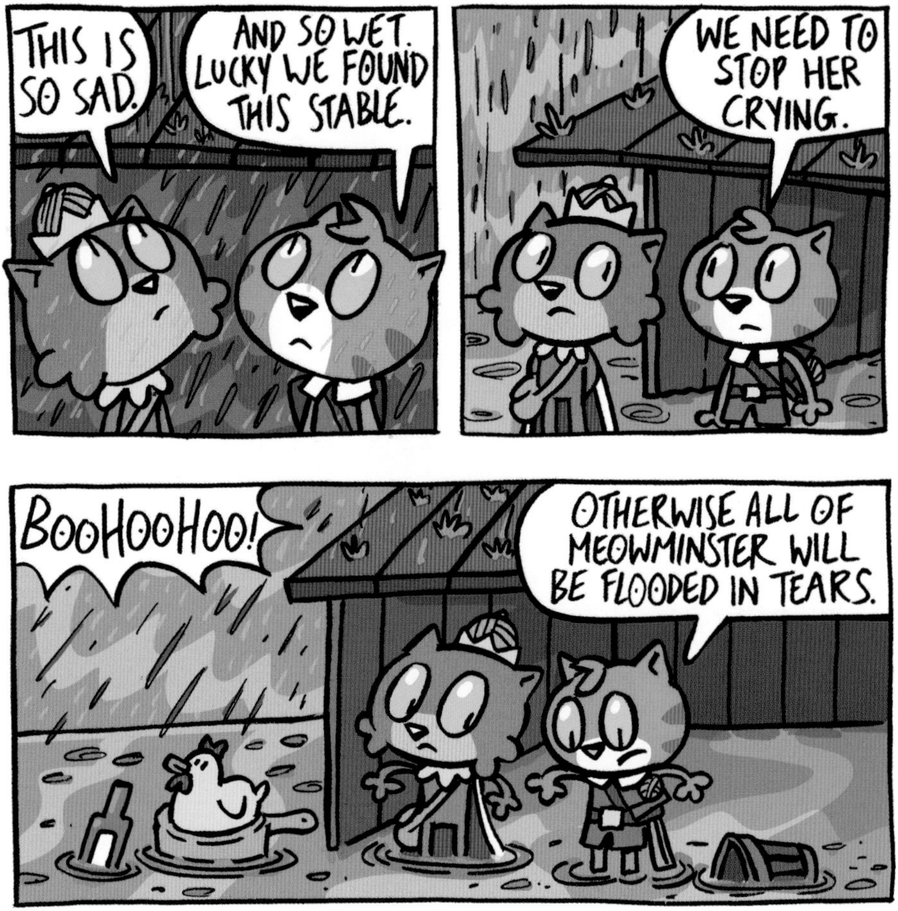
THIS IS SO SAD.
AND SO WET. LUCKY WE FOUND THIS STABLE.
WE NEED TO STOP HER CRYING.
BOOHOOHOO!
OTHERWISE ALL OF MEOWMINSTER WILL BE FLOODED IN TEARS.

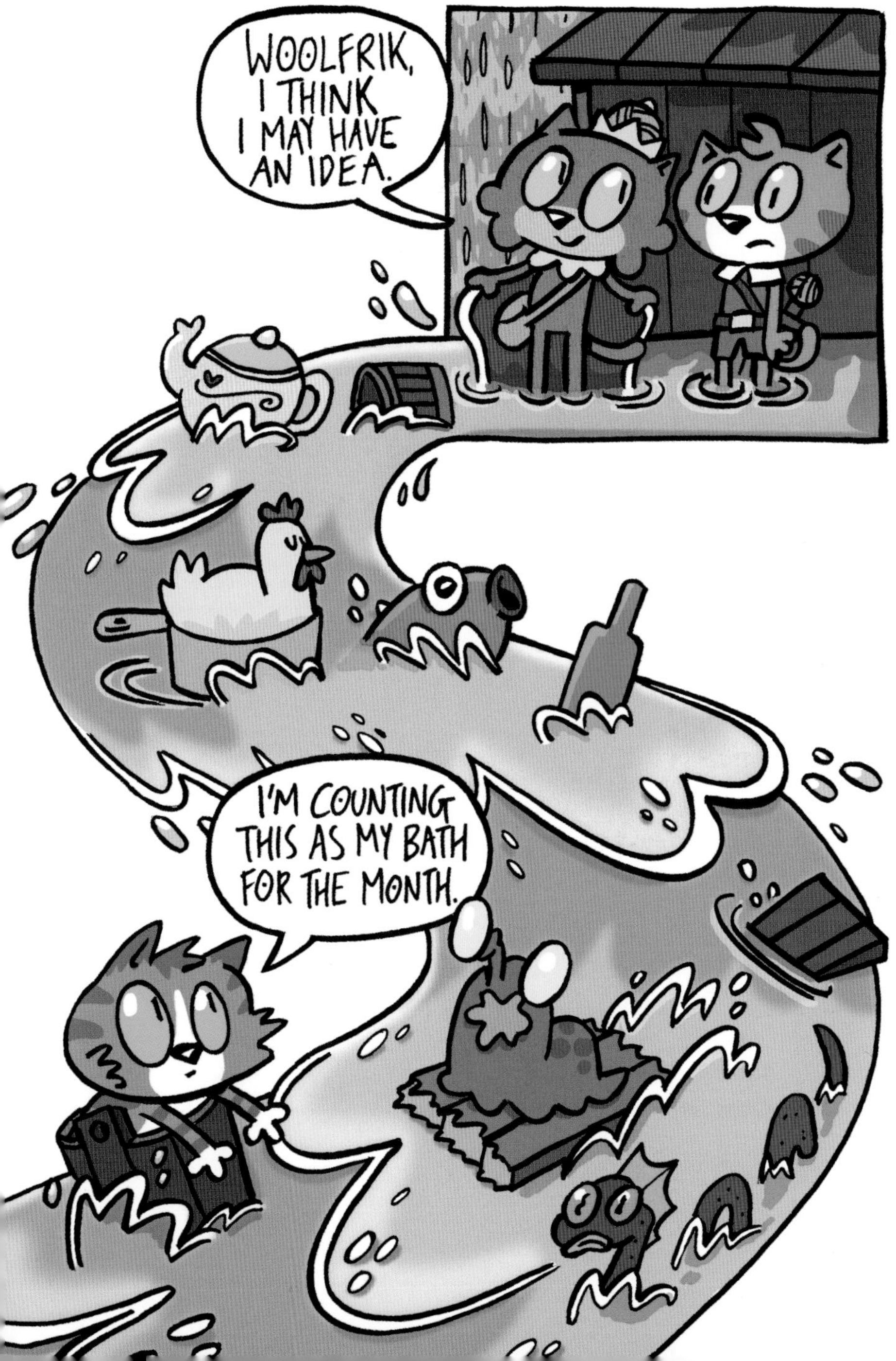
WOOLFRIK, I THINK I MAY HAVE AN IDEA.
I'M COUNTING THIS AS MY BATH FOR THE MONTH.

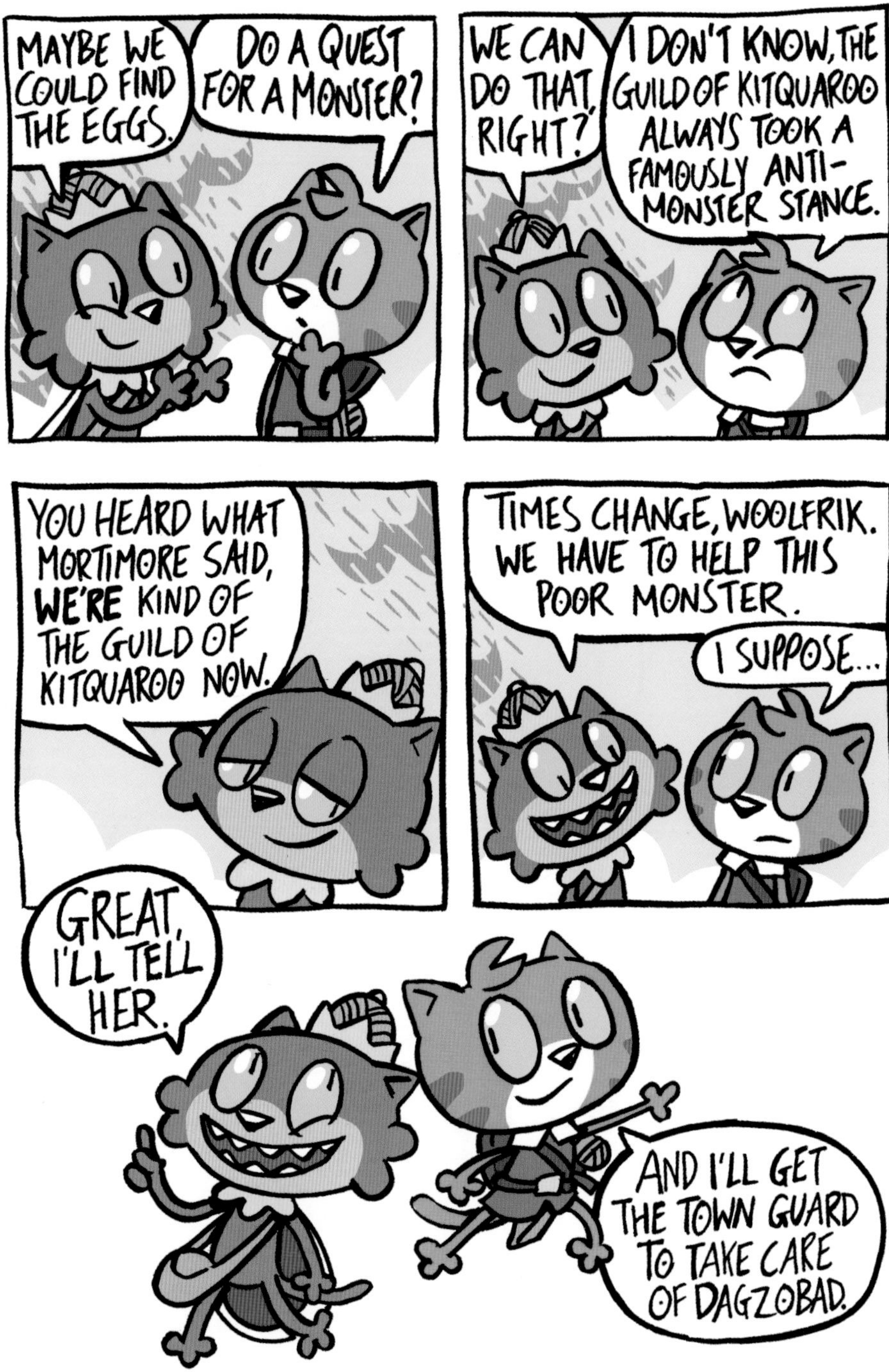
MAYBE WE COULD FIND THE EGGS.
DO A QUEST FOR A MONSTER?
WE CAN DO THAT, RIGHT?
I DON'T KNOW, THE GUILD OF KITQUAROO ALWAYS TOOK A FAMOUSLY ANTI-MONSTER STANCE.
YOU HEARD WHAT MORTIMORE SAID, **WE'RE** KIND OF THE GUILD OF KITQUAROO NOW.
TIMES CHANGE, WOOLFRIK. WE HAVE TO HELP THIS POOR MONSTER.
I SUPPOSE...
GREAT, I'LL TELL HER.
AND I'LL GET THE TOWN GUARD TO TAKE CARE OF DAGZOBAD.

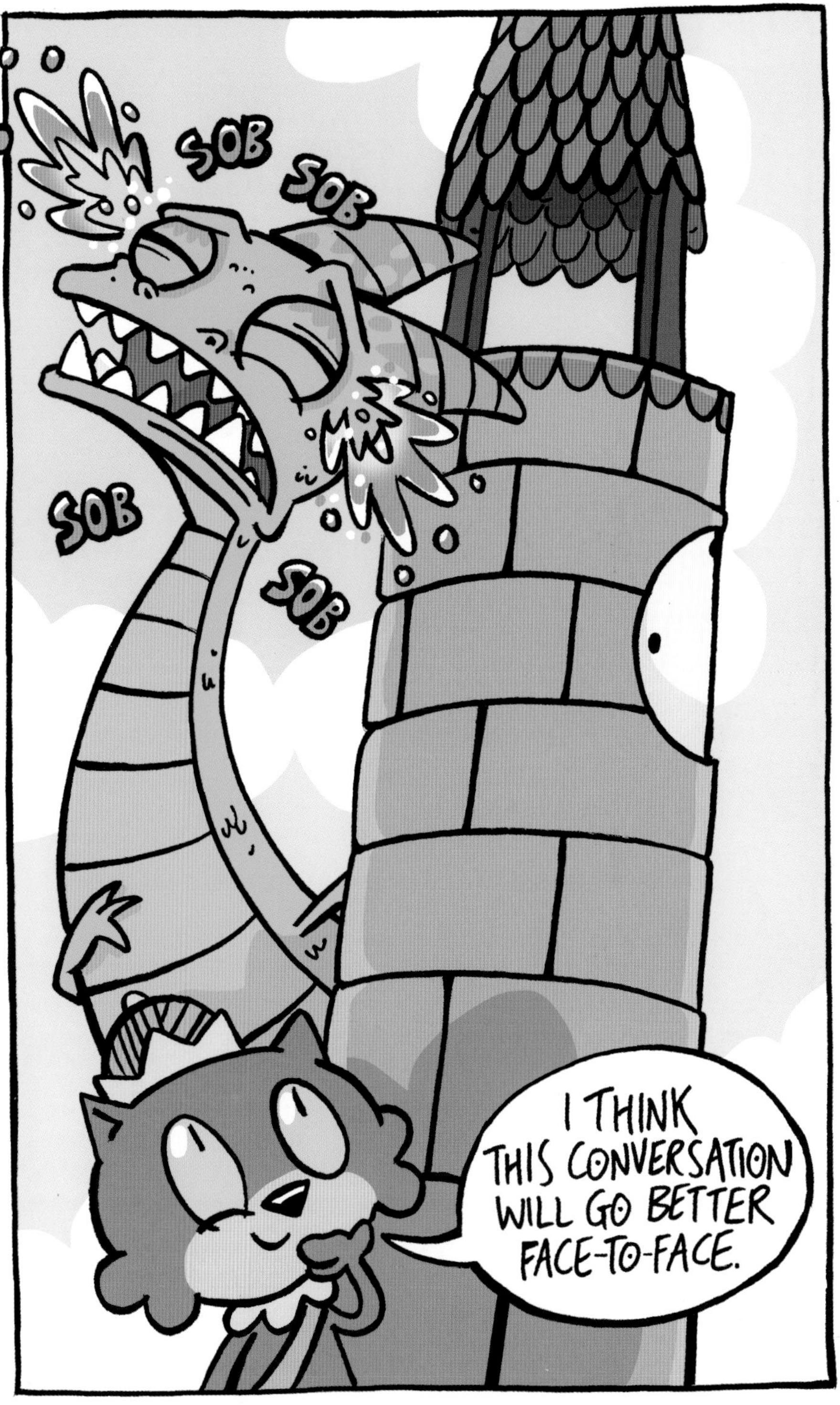
SOB
SOB
SOB
SOB
I THINK THIS CONVERSATION WILL GO BETTER FACE-TO-FACE.

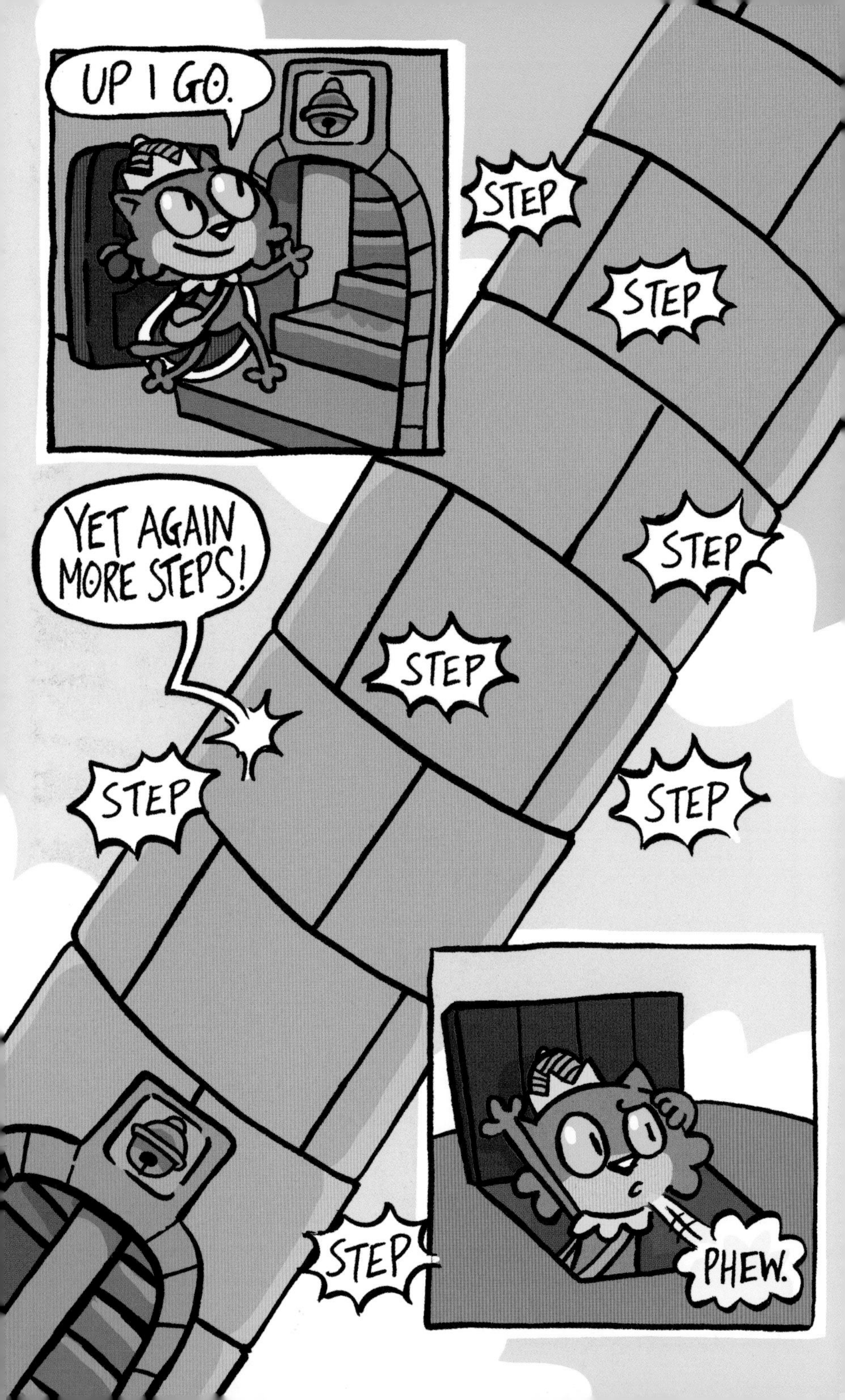
UP I GO.
STEP
STEP
YET AGAIN MORE STEPS!
STEP
STEP
STEP
STEP
STEP
PHEW.

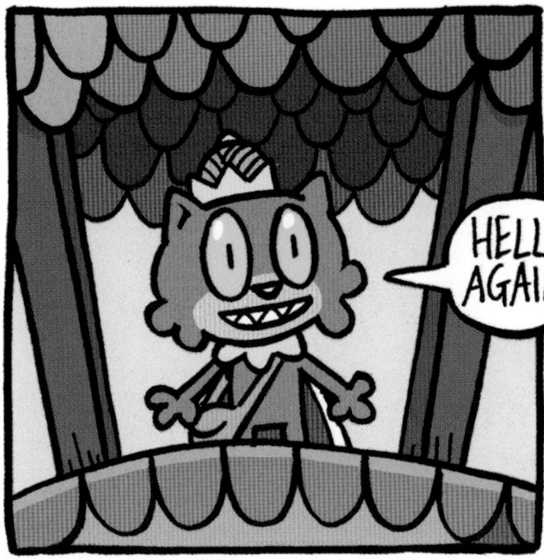
HELLO AGAIN.

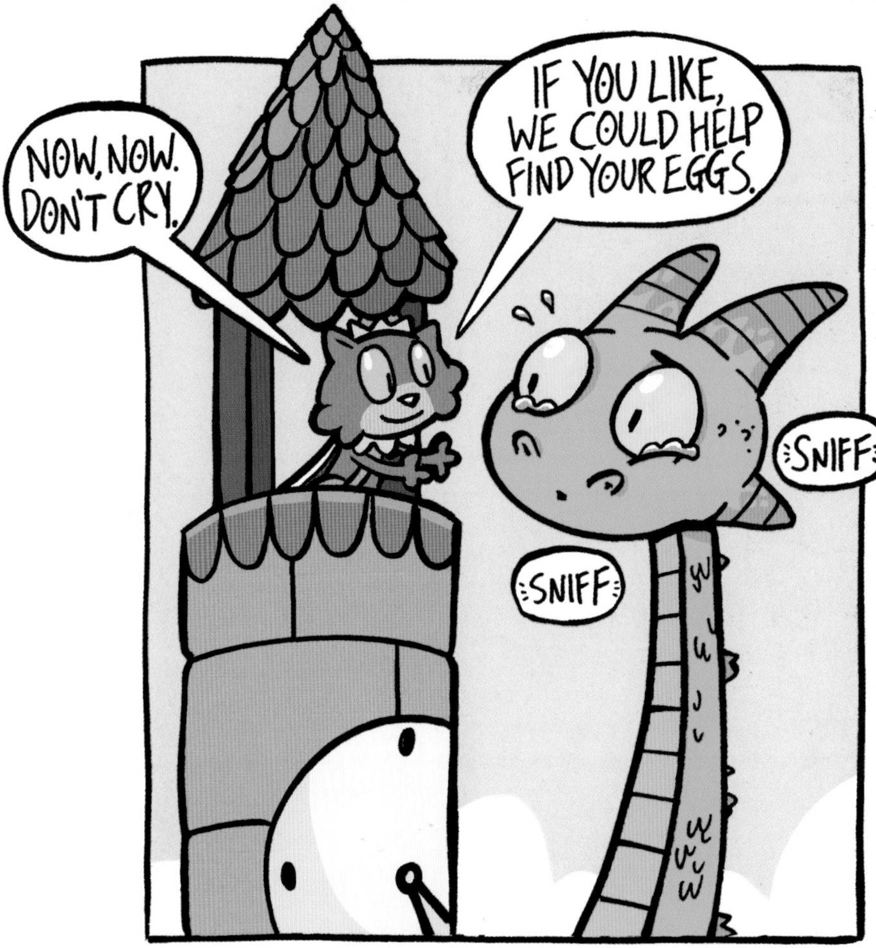
NOW, NOW. DON'T CRY.
IF YOU LIKE, WE COULD HELP FIND YOUR EGGS.
SNIFF
SNIFF

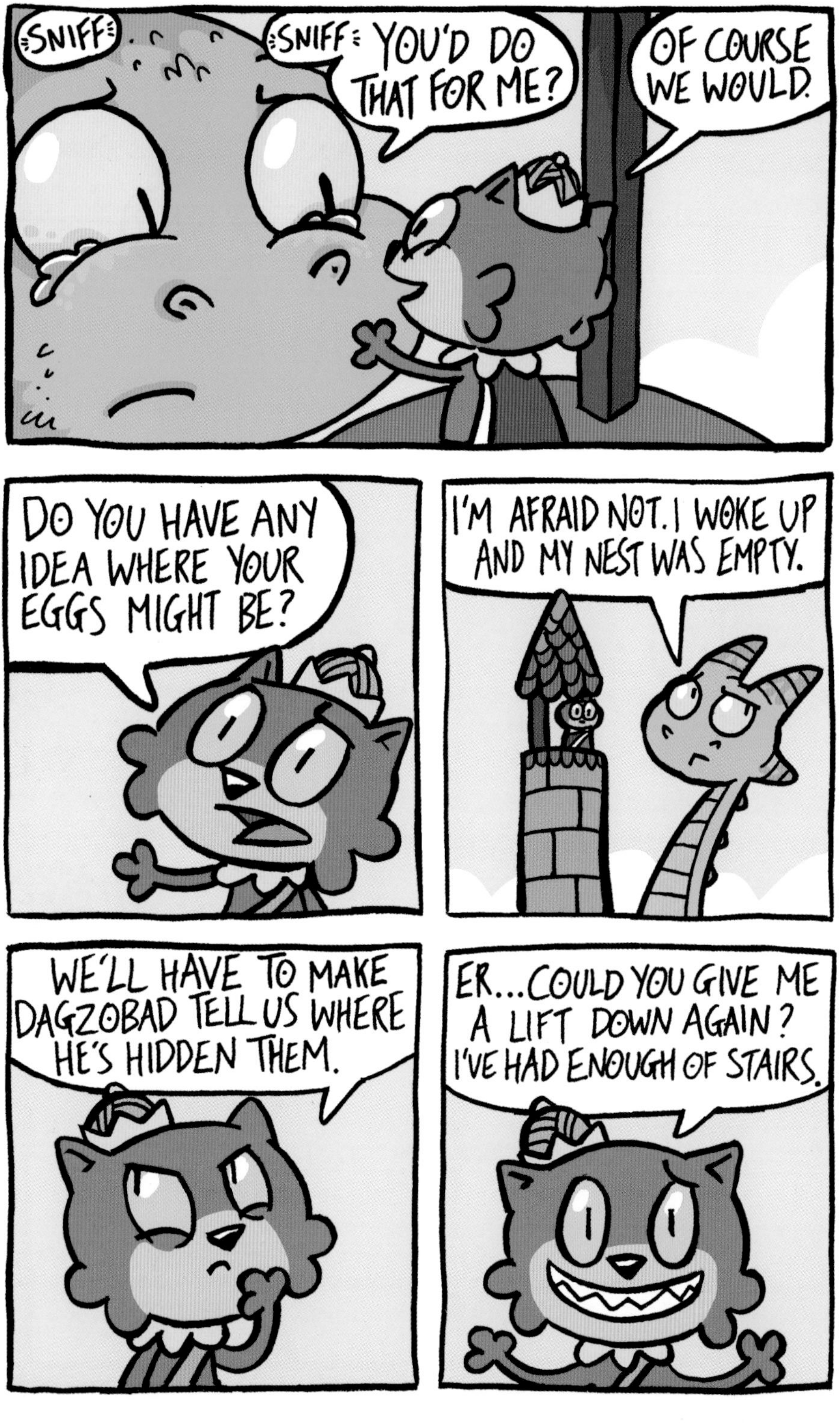
SNIFF
SNIFF YOU'D DO THAT FOR ME?
OF COURSE WE WOULD.
DO YOU HAVE ANY IDEA WHERE YOUR EGGS MIGHT BE?
I'M AFRAID NOT. I WOKE UP AND MY NEST WAS EMPTY.
WE'LL HAVE TO MAKE DAGZOBAD TELL US WHERE HE'S HIDDEN THEM.
ER...COULD YOU GIVE ME A LIFT DOWN AGAIN? I'VE HAD ENOUGH OF STAIRS.

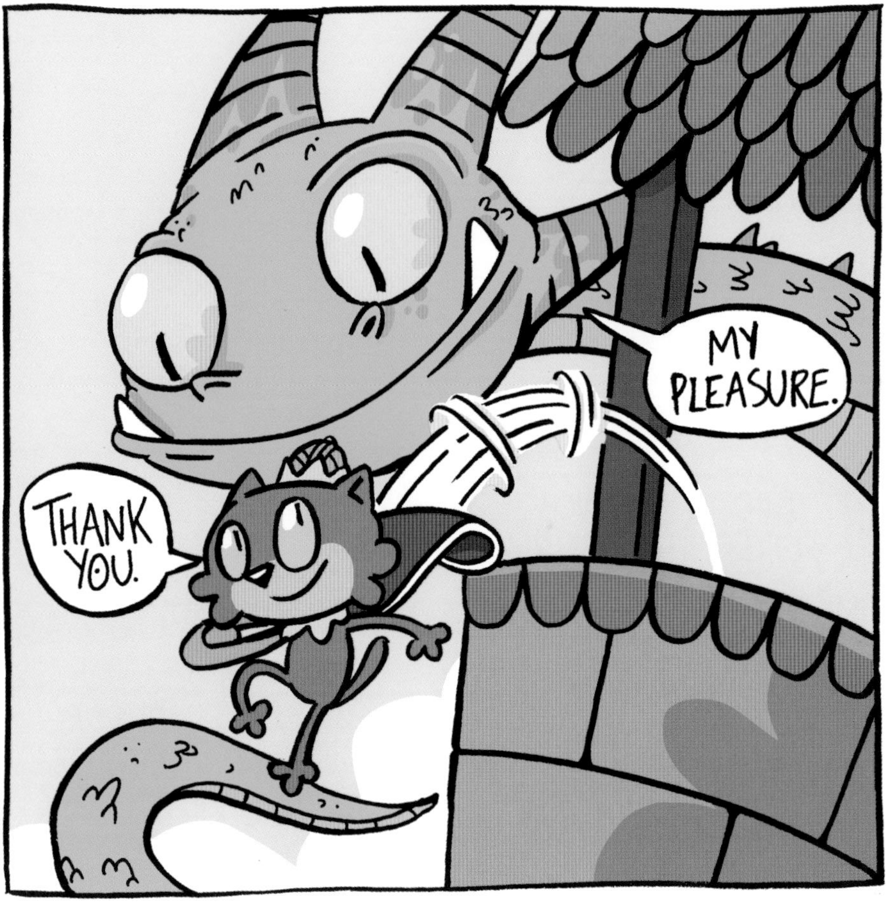
MY PLEASURE.
THANK YOU.

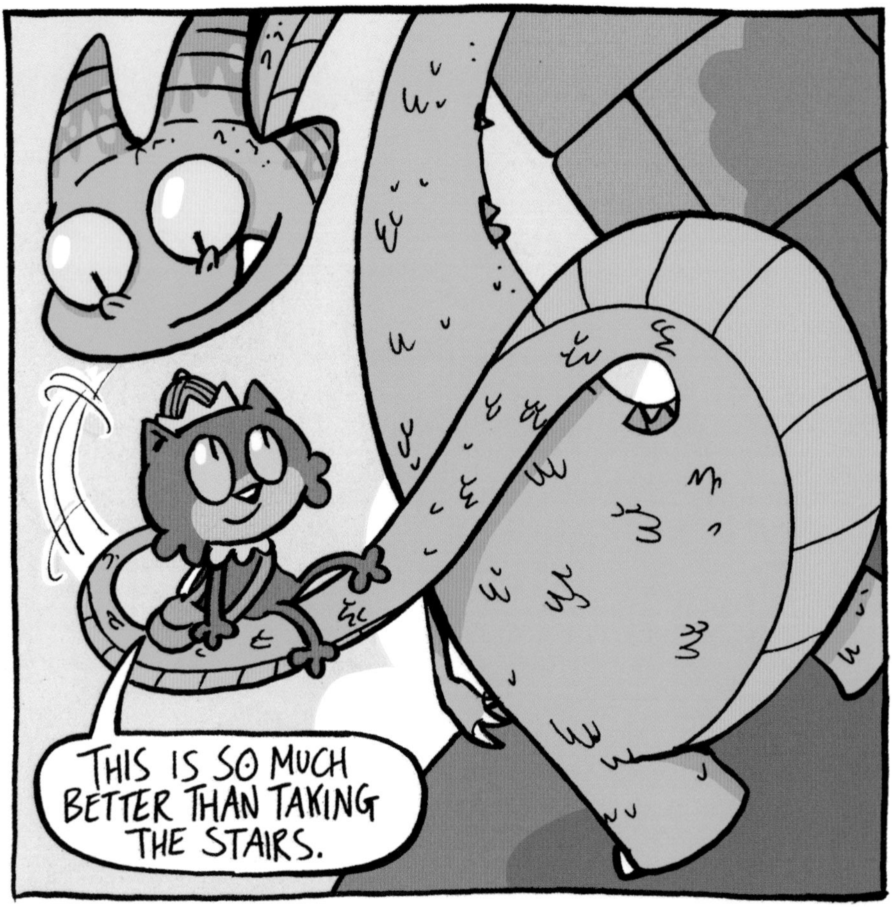
THIS IS SO MUCH BETTER THAN TAKING THE STAIRS.

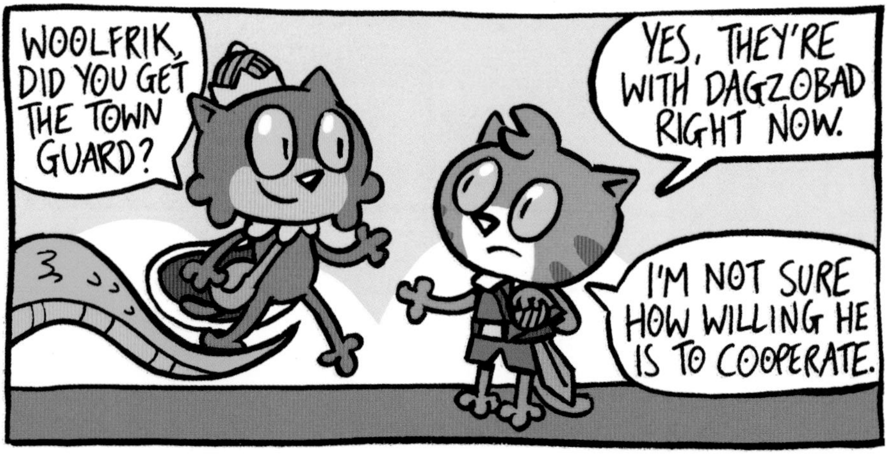
WOOLFRIK, DID YOU GET THE TOWN GUARD?
YES, THEY'RE WITH DAGZOBAD RIGHT NOW.
I'M NOT SURE HOW WILLING HE IS TO COOPERATE.

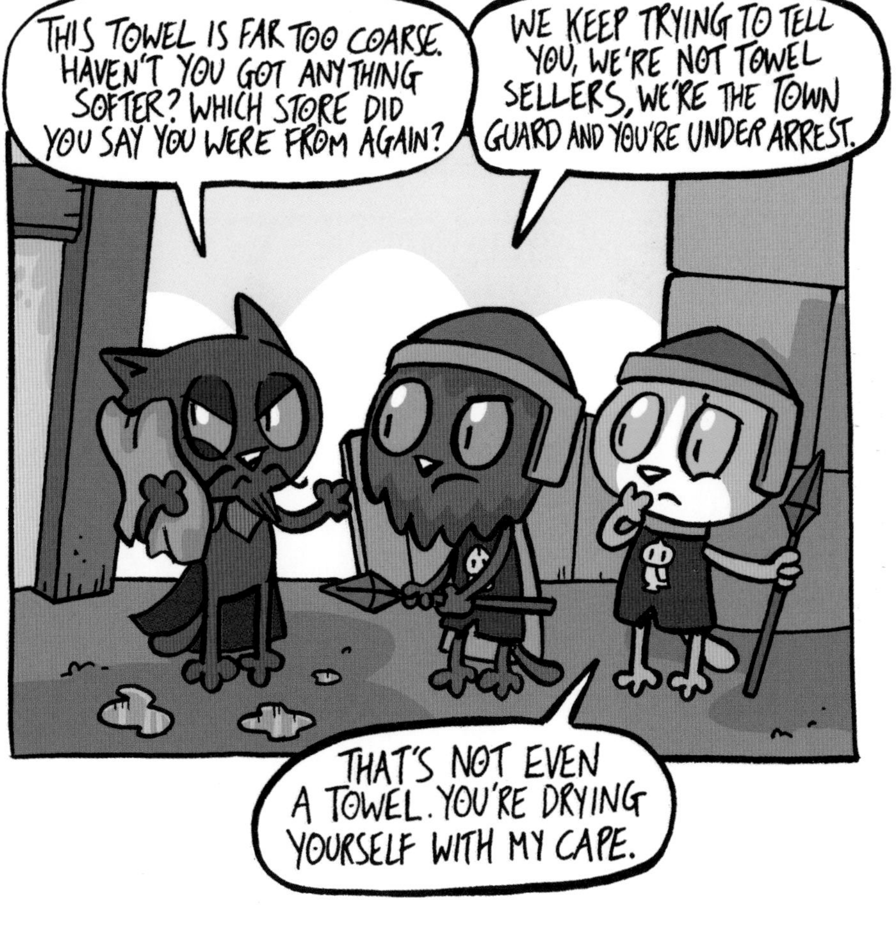
THIS TOWEL IS FAR TOO COARSE. HAVEN'T YOU GOT ANYTHING SOFTER? WHICH STORE DID YOU SAY YOU WERE FROM AGAIN?
WE KEEP TRYING TO TELL YOU, WE'RE NOT TOWEL SELLERS, WE'RE THE TOWN GUARD AND YOU'RE UNDER ARREST.
THAT'S NOT EVEN A TOWEL. YOU'RE DRYING YOURSELF WITH MY CAPE.

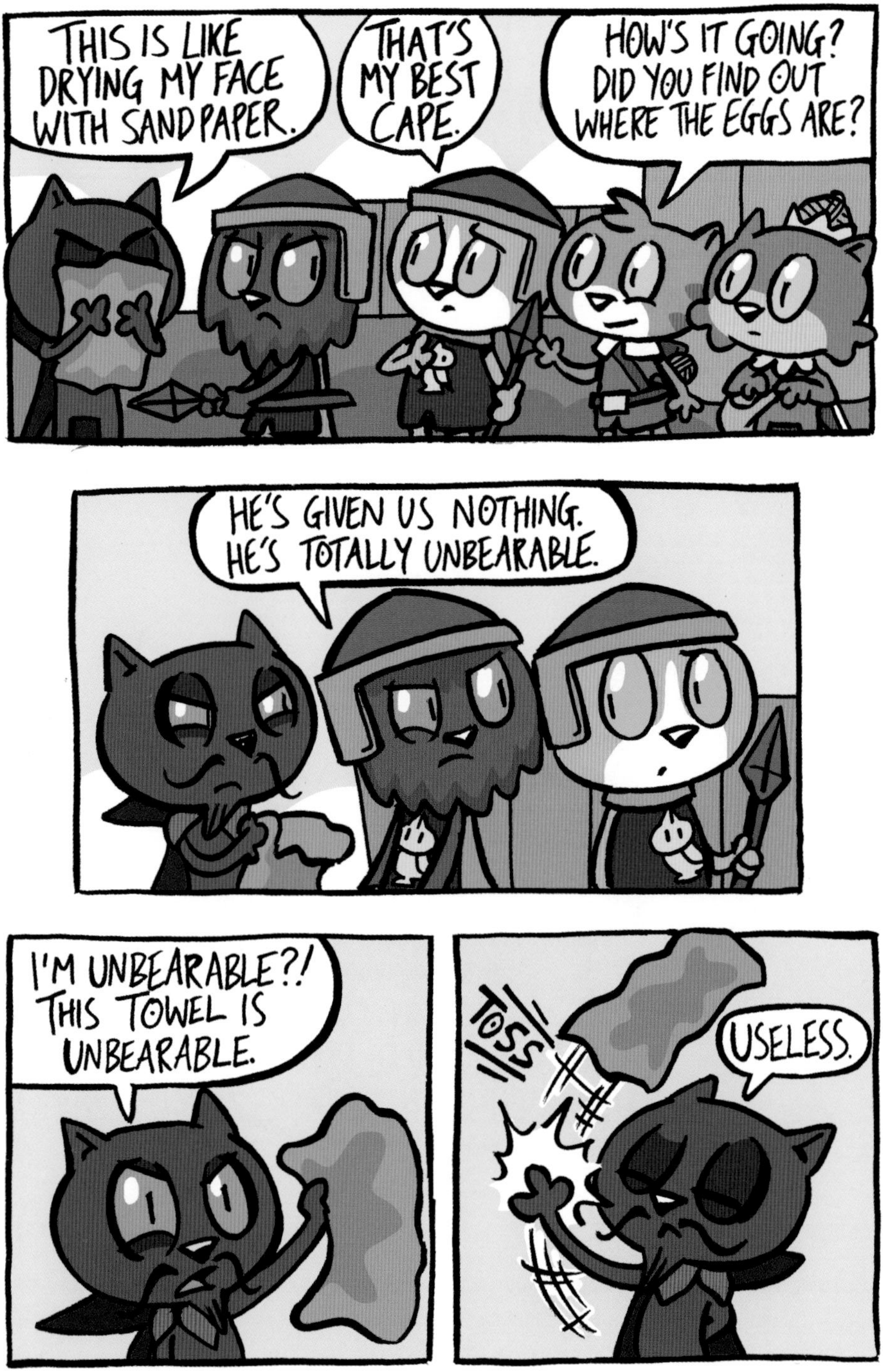
THIS IS LIKE DRYING MY FACE WITH SANDPAPER.
THAT'S MY BEST CAPE.
HOW'S IT GOING? DID YOU FIND OUT WHERE THE EGGS ARE?
HE'S GIVEN US NOTHING. HE'S TOTALLY UNBEARABLE.
I'M UNBEARABLE?! THIS TOWEL IS UNBEARABLE.
TOSS
USELESS.

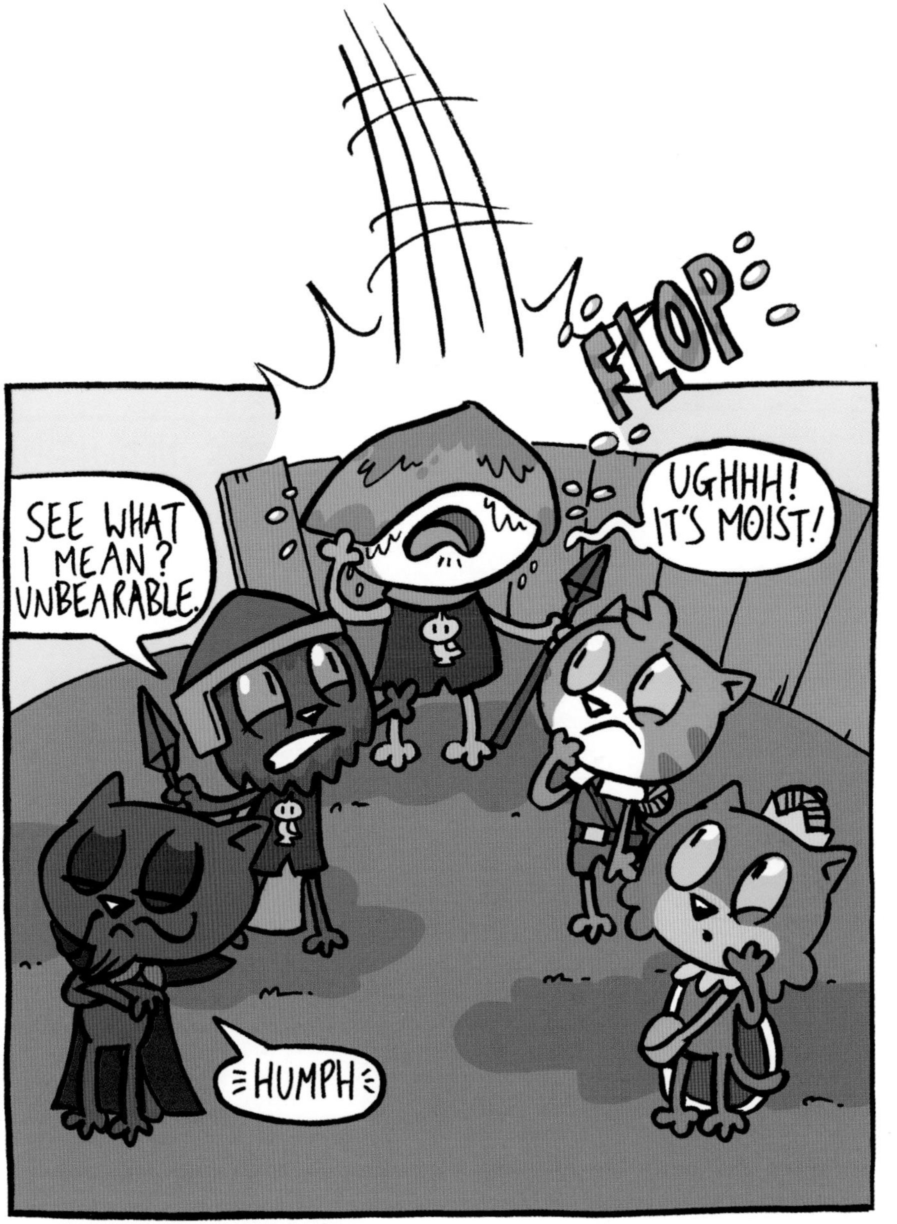
FLOP
SEE WHAT I MEAN? UNBEARABLE.
UGHHH! IT'S MOIST!
HUMPH

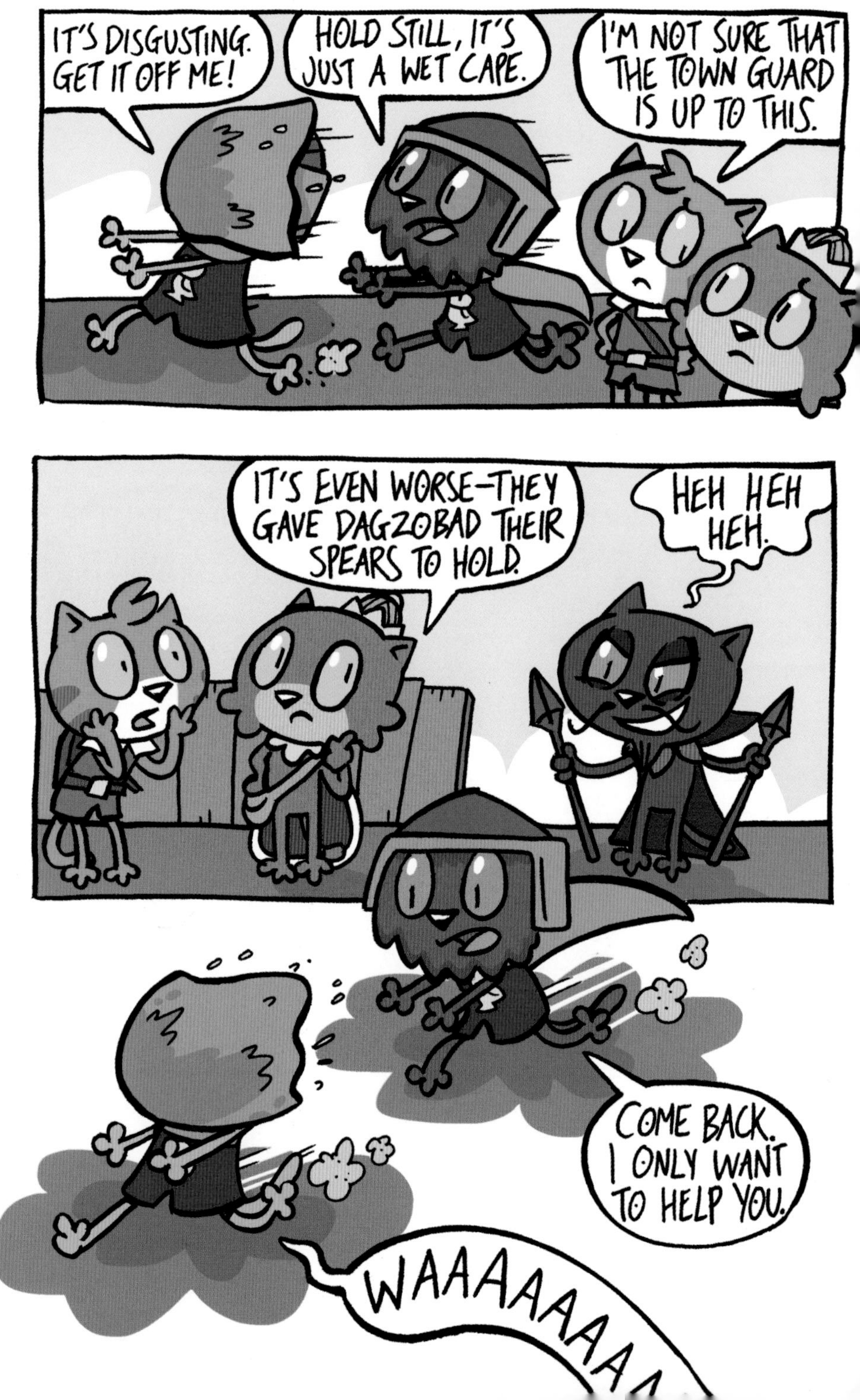
IT'S DISGUSTING. GET IT OFF ME!
HOLD STILL, IT'S JUST A WET CAPE.
I'M NOT SURE THAT THE TOWN GUARD IS UP TO THIS.
IT'S EVEN WORSE—THEY GAVE DAGZOBAD THEIR SPEARS TO HOLD.
HEH HEH HEH.
COME BACK. I ONLY WANT TO HELP YOU.
WAAAAAAA

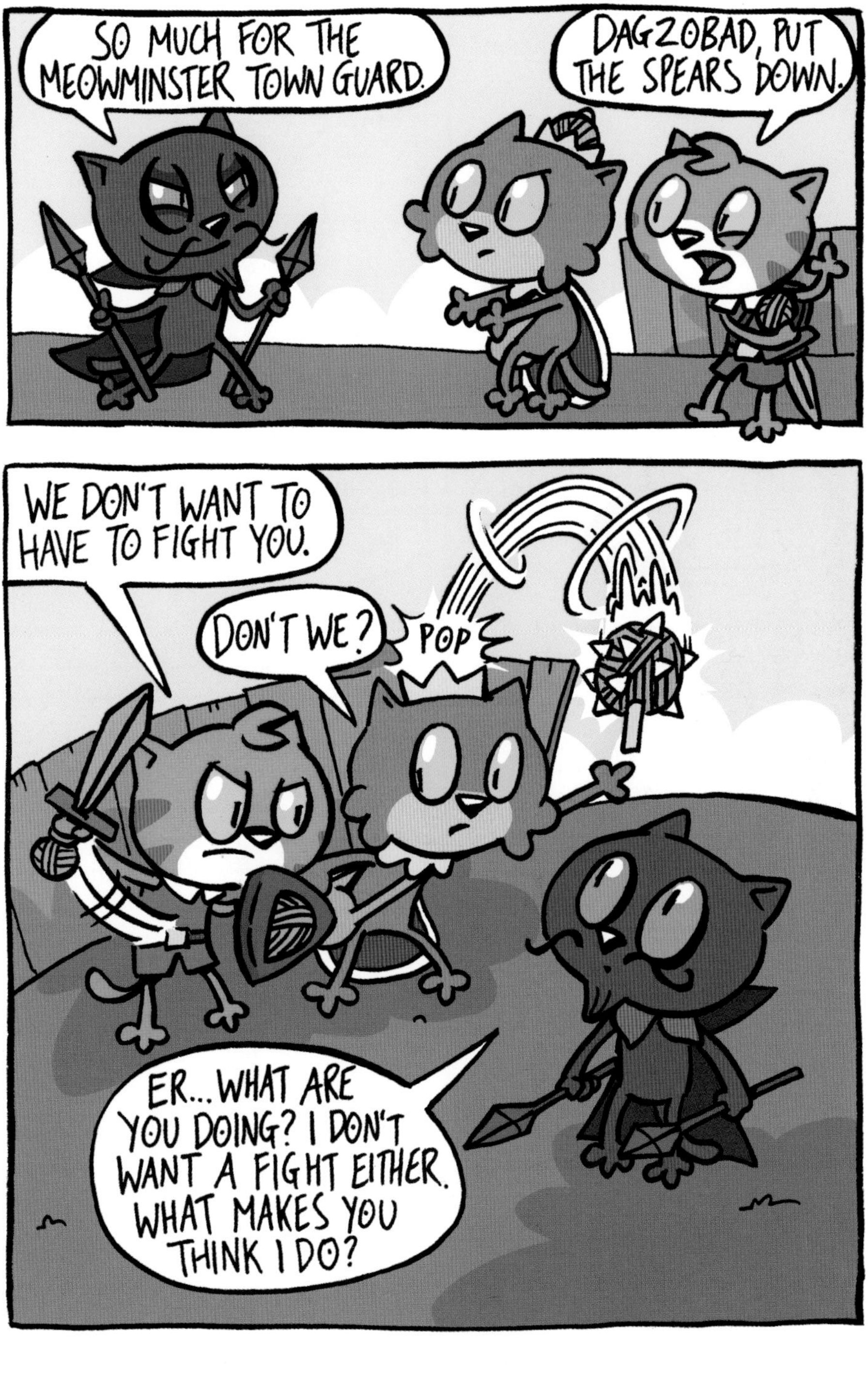
SO MUCH FOR THE MEOWMINSTER TOWN GUARD.
DAGZOBAD, PUT THE SPEARS DOWN.
WE DON'T WANT TO HAVE TO FIGHT YOU.
DON'T WE?
POP
ER... WHAT ARE YOU DOING? I DON'T WANT A FIGHT EITHER. WHAT MAKES YOU THINK I DO?

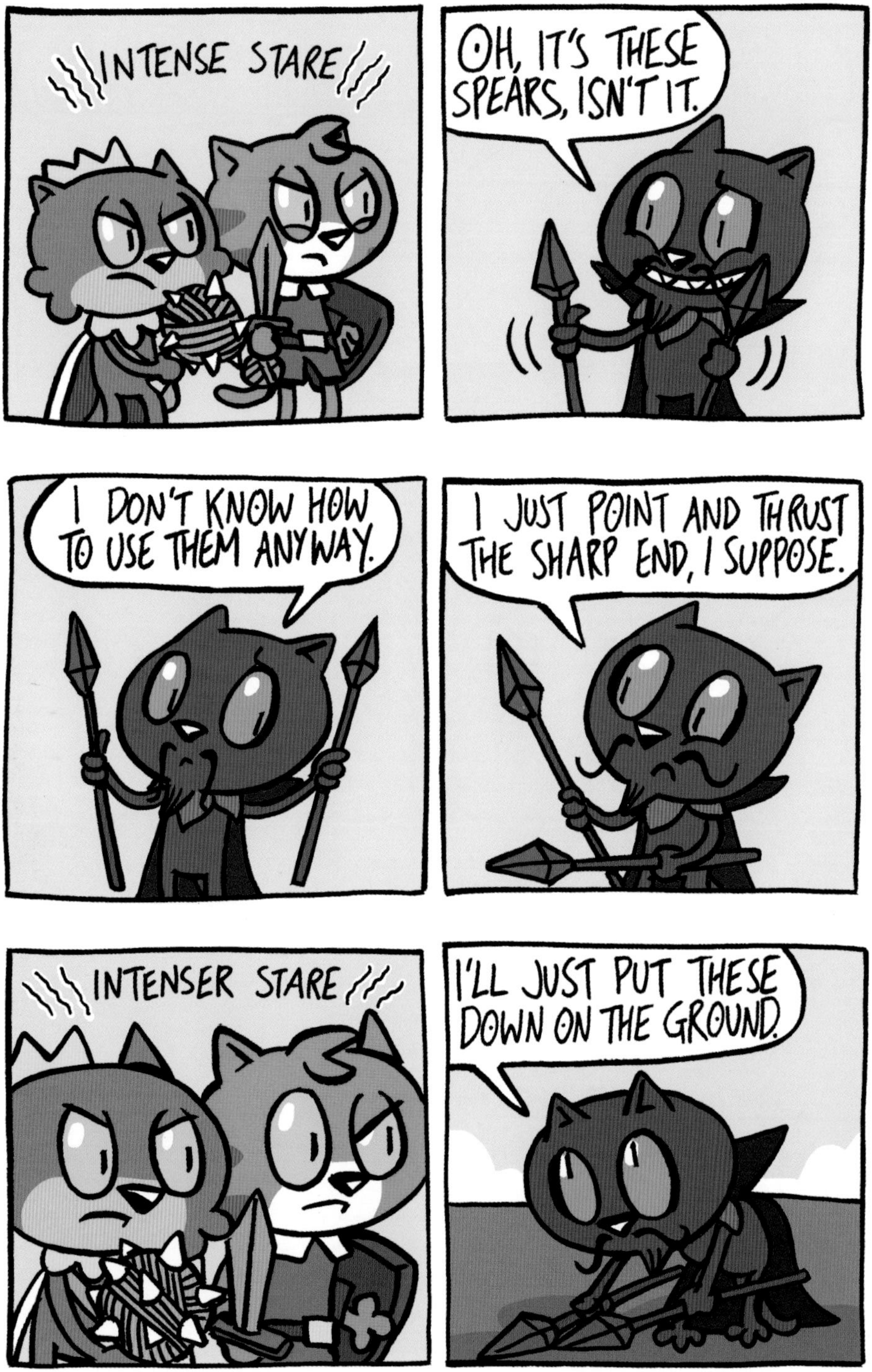
INTENSE STARE
OH, IT'S THESE SPEARS, ISN'T IT.
I DON'T KNOW HOW TO USE THEM ANYWAY.
I JUST POINT AND THRUST THE SHARP END, I SUPPOSE.
INTENSER STARE
I'LL JUST PUT THESE DOWN ON THE GROUND.

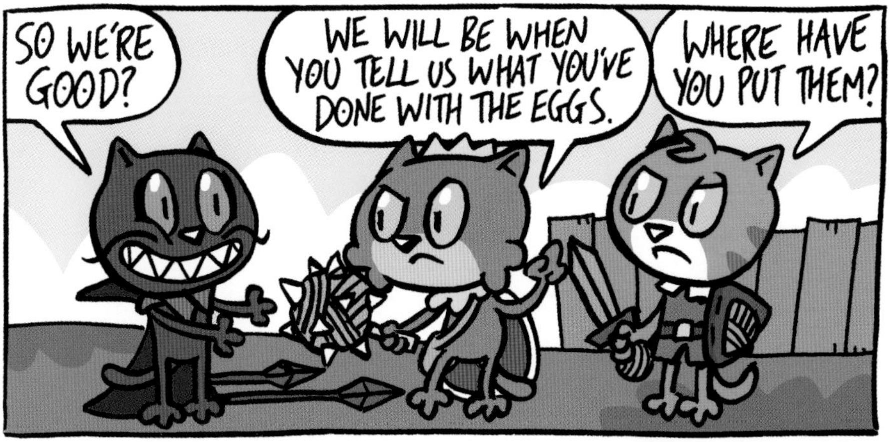
SO WE'RE GOOD?
WE WILL BE WHEN YOU TELL US WHAT YOU'VE DONE WITH THE EGGS.
WHERE HAVE YOU PUT THEM?

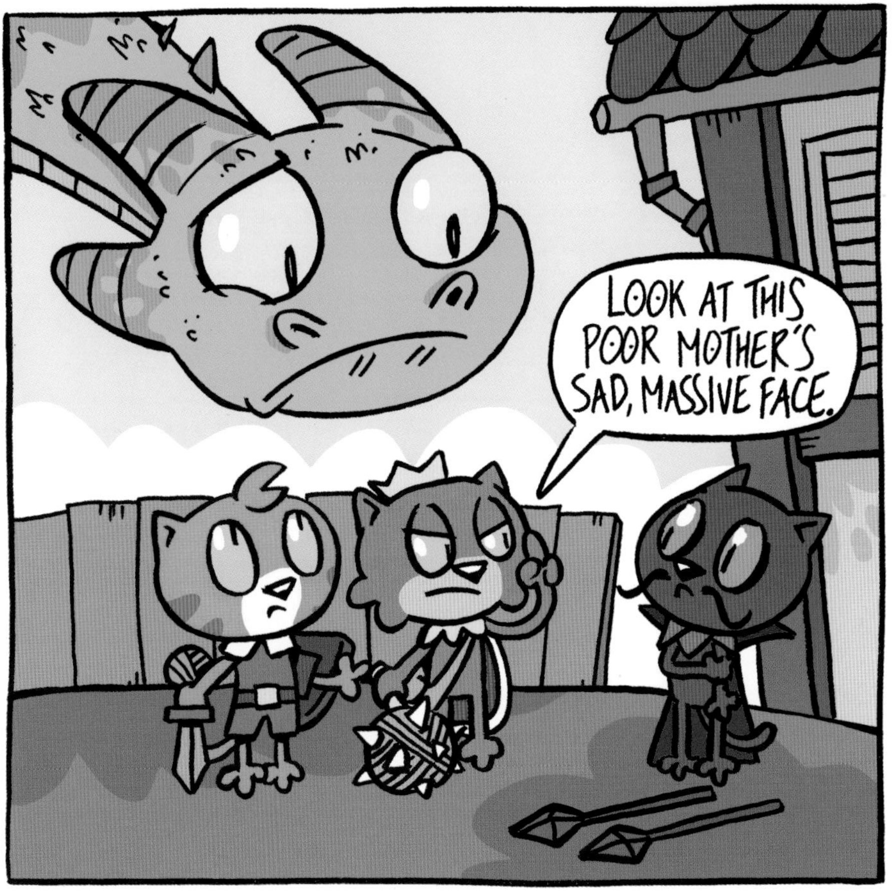
LOOK AT THIS POOR MOTHER'S SAD, MASSIVE FACE.

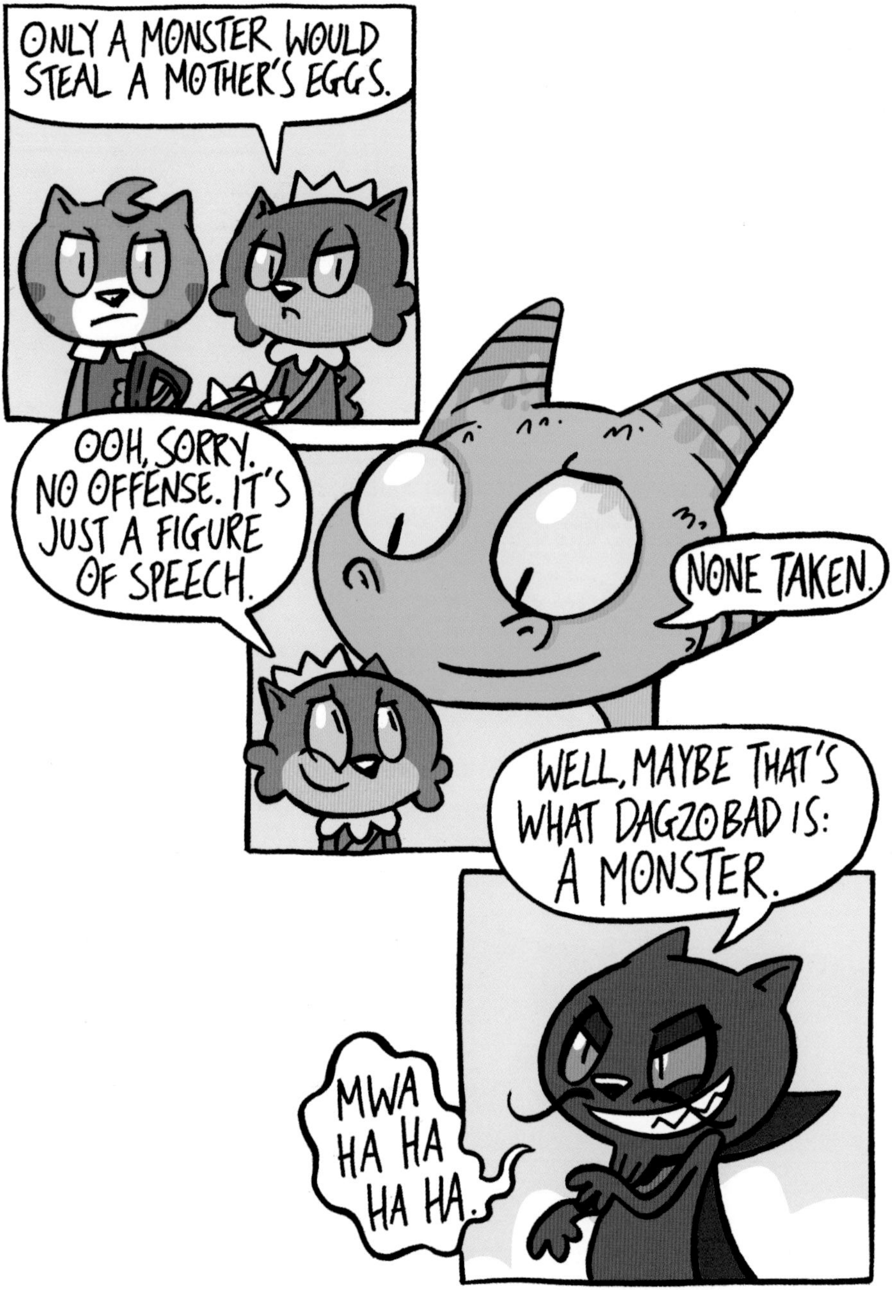
ONLY A MONSTER WOULD STEAL A MOTHER'S EGGS.
OOH, SORRY. NO OFFENSE. IT'S JUST A FIGURE OF SPEECH.
NONE TAKEN.
WELL, MAYBE THAT'S WHAT DAGZOBAD IS: A MONSTER.
MWA HA HA HA HA.

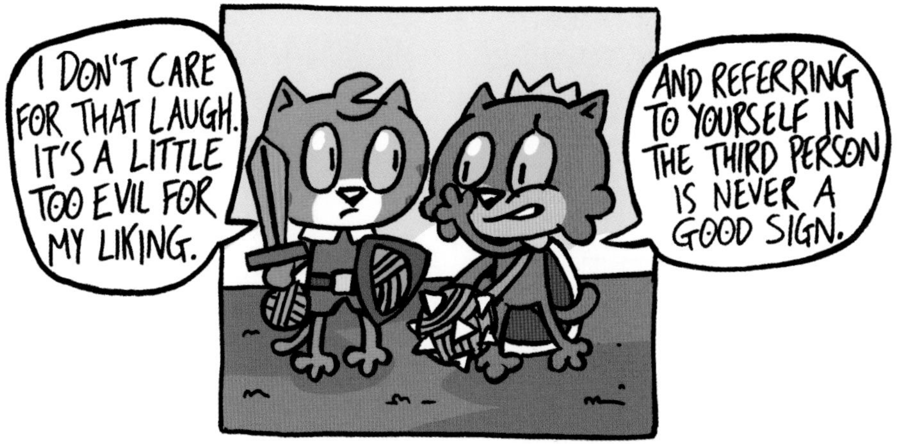
I DON'T CARE FOR THAT LAUGH. IT'S A LITTLE TOO EVIL FOR MY LIKING.
AND REFERRING TO YOURSELF IN THE THIRD PERSON IS NEVER A GOOD SIGN.

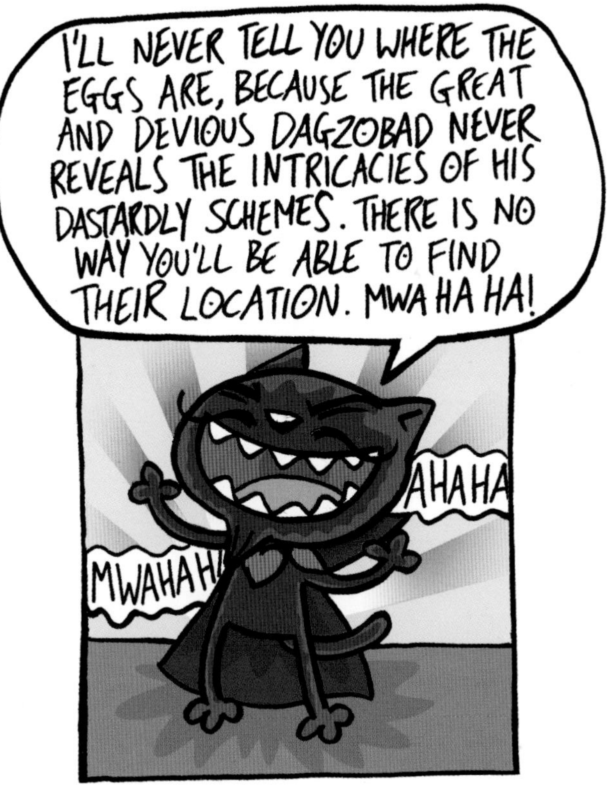
I'LL NEVER TELL YOU WHERE THE EGGS ARE, BECAUSE THE GREAT AND DEVIOUS DAGZOBAD NEVER REVEALS THE INTRICACIES OF HIS DASTARDLY SCHEMES. THERE IS NO WAY YOU'LL BE ABLE TO FIND THEIR LOCATION. MWA HA HA!
MWAHAH
AHAHA

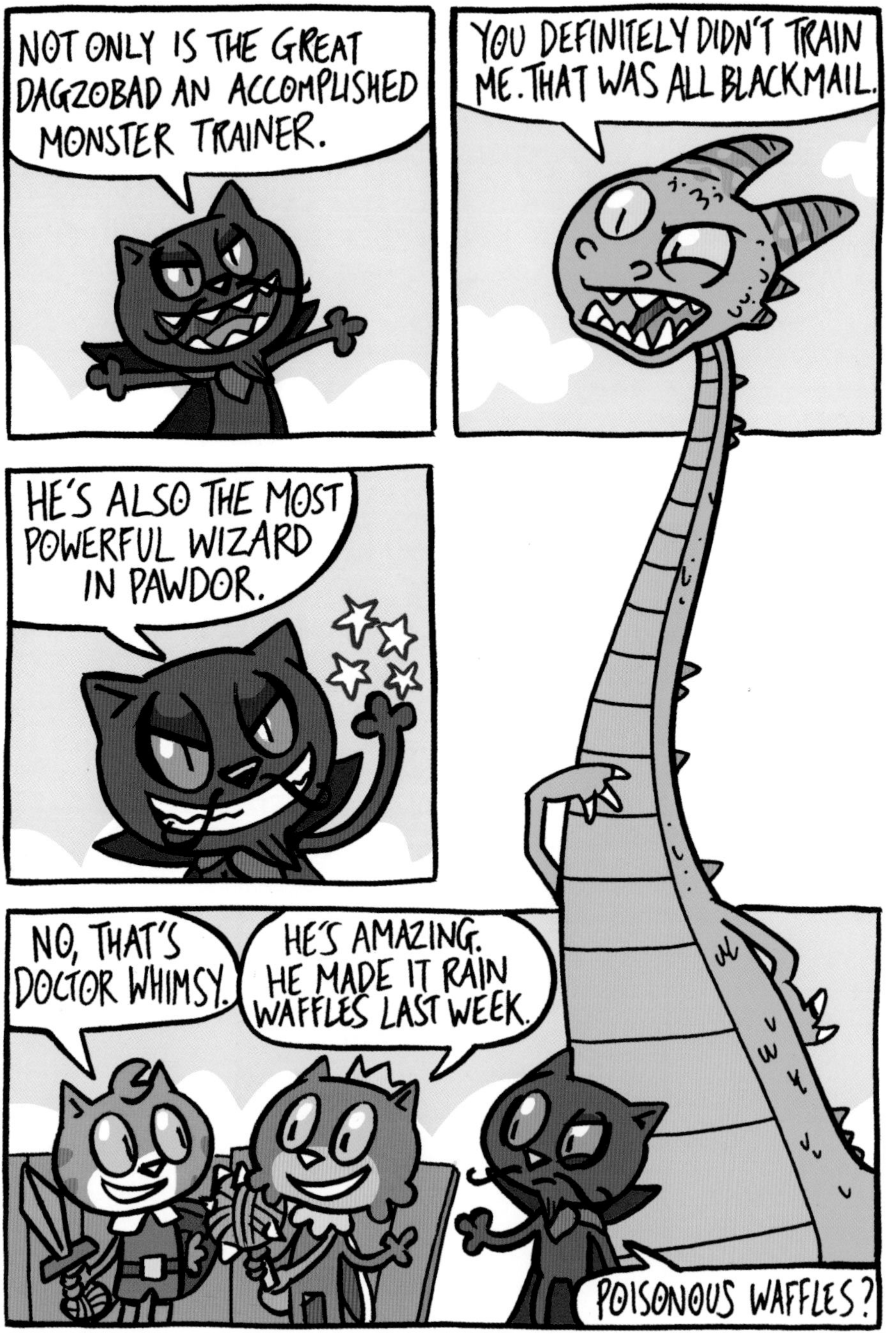
NOT ONLY IS THE GREAT DAGZOBAD AN ACCOMPLISHED MONSTER TRAINER.
YOU DEFINITELY DIDN'T TRAIN ME. THAT WAS ALL BLACKMAIL.
HE'S ALSO THE MOST POWERFUL WIZARD IN PAWDOR.
NO, THAT'S DOCTOR WHIMSY.
HE'S AMAZING. HE MADE IT RAIN WAFFLES LAST WEEK.
POISONOUS WAFFLES?

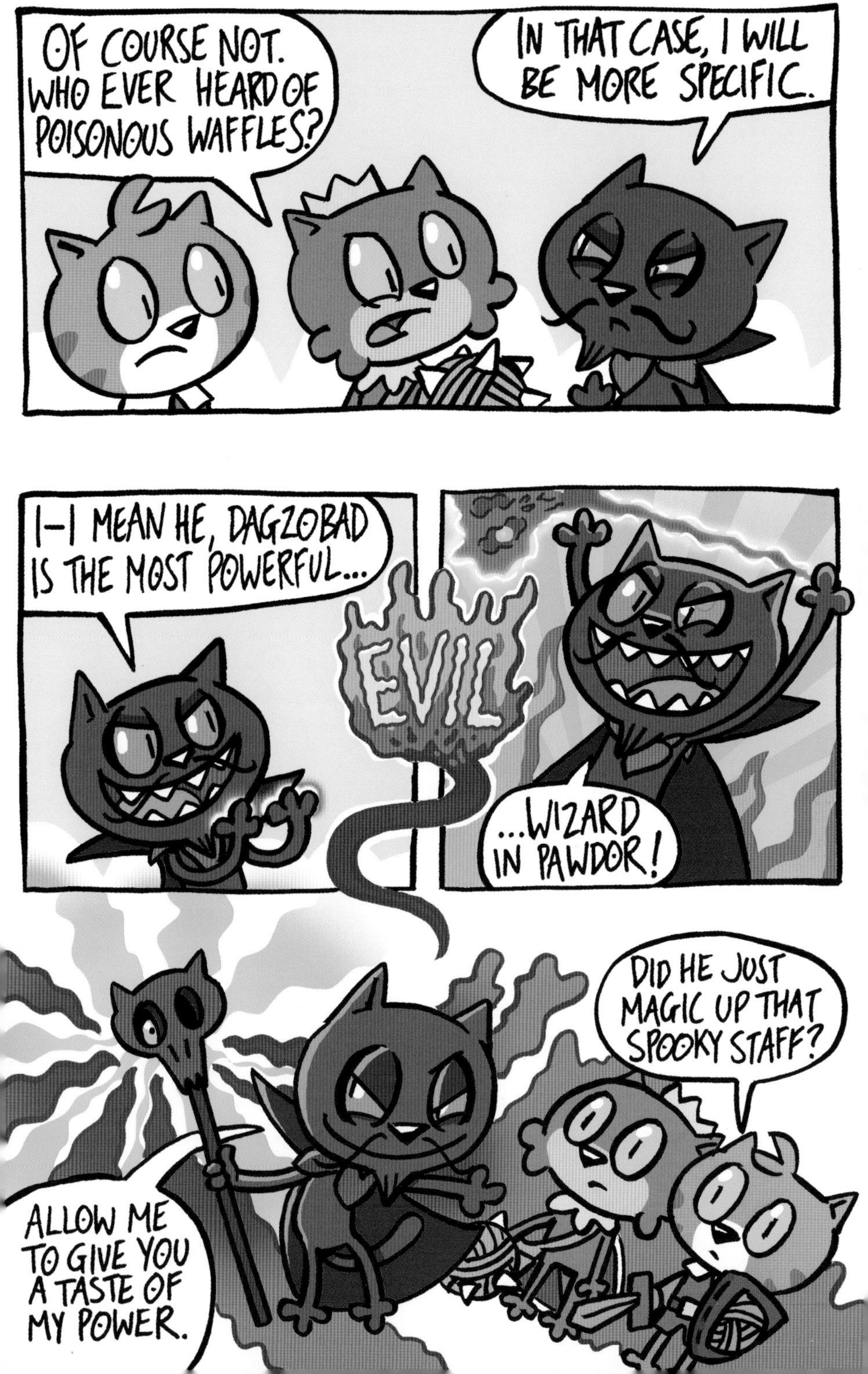
OF COURSE NOT. WHO EVER HEARD OF POISONOUS WAFFLES?
IN THAT CASE, I WILL BE MORE SPECIFIC.
I–I MEAN HE, DAGZOBAD IS THE MOST POWERFUL...
EVIL
...WIZARD IN PAWDOR!
DID HE JUST MAGIC UP THAT SPOOKY STAFF?
ALLOW ME TO GIVE YOU A TASTE OF MY POWER.

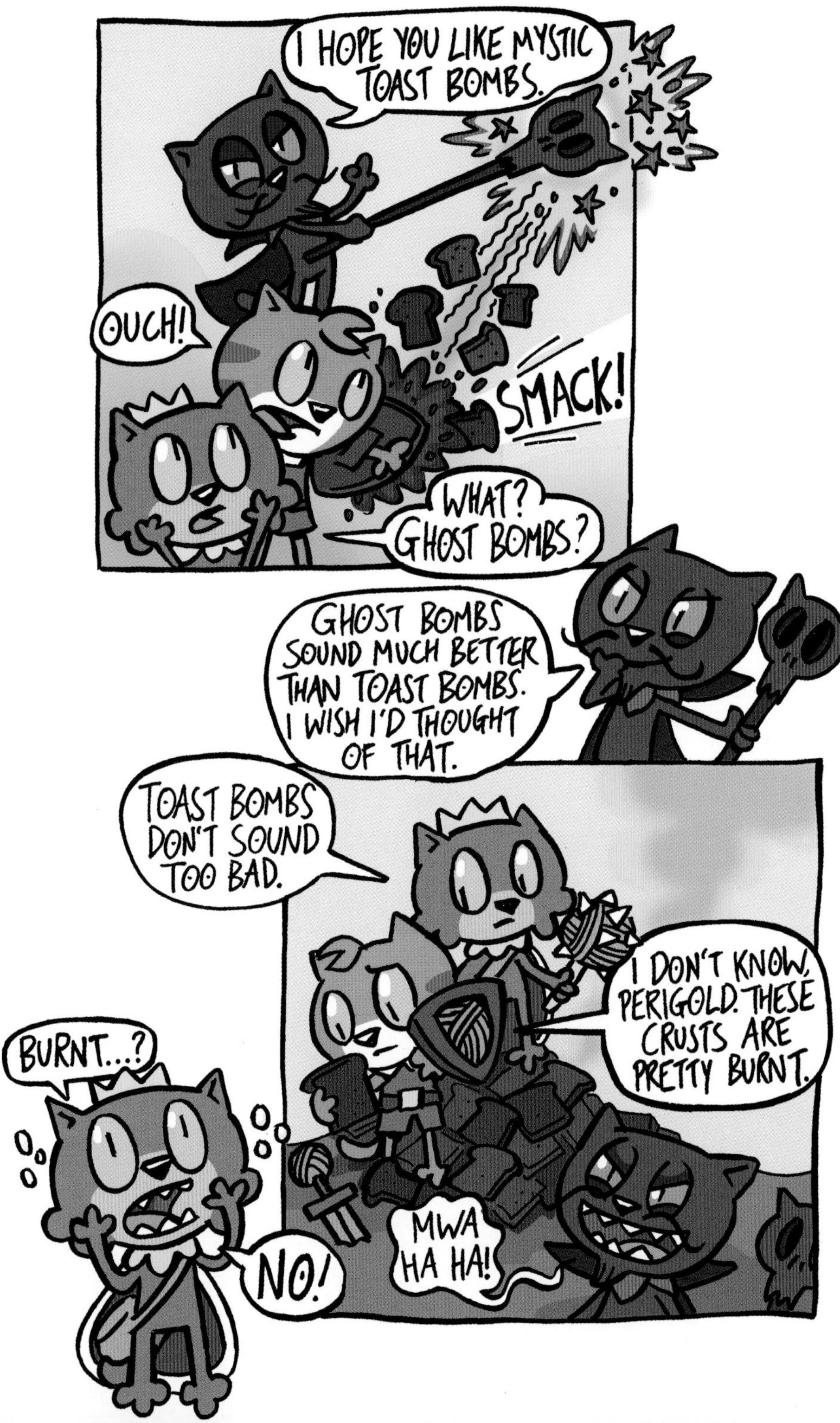
I HOPE YOU LIKE MYSTIC TOAST BOMBS.
OUCH!
SMACK!
WHAT? GHOST BOMBS?
GHOST BOMBS SOUND MUCH BETTER THAN TOAST BOMBS. I WISH I'D THOUGHT OF THAT.
TOAST BOMBS DON'T SOUND TOO BAD.
I DON'T KNOW, PERIGOLD. THESE CRUSTS ARE PRETTY BURNT.
BURNT...?
NO!
MWA HA HA!

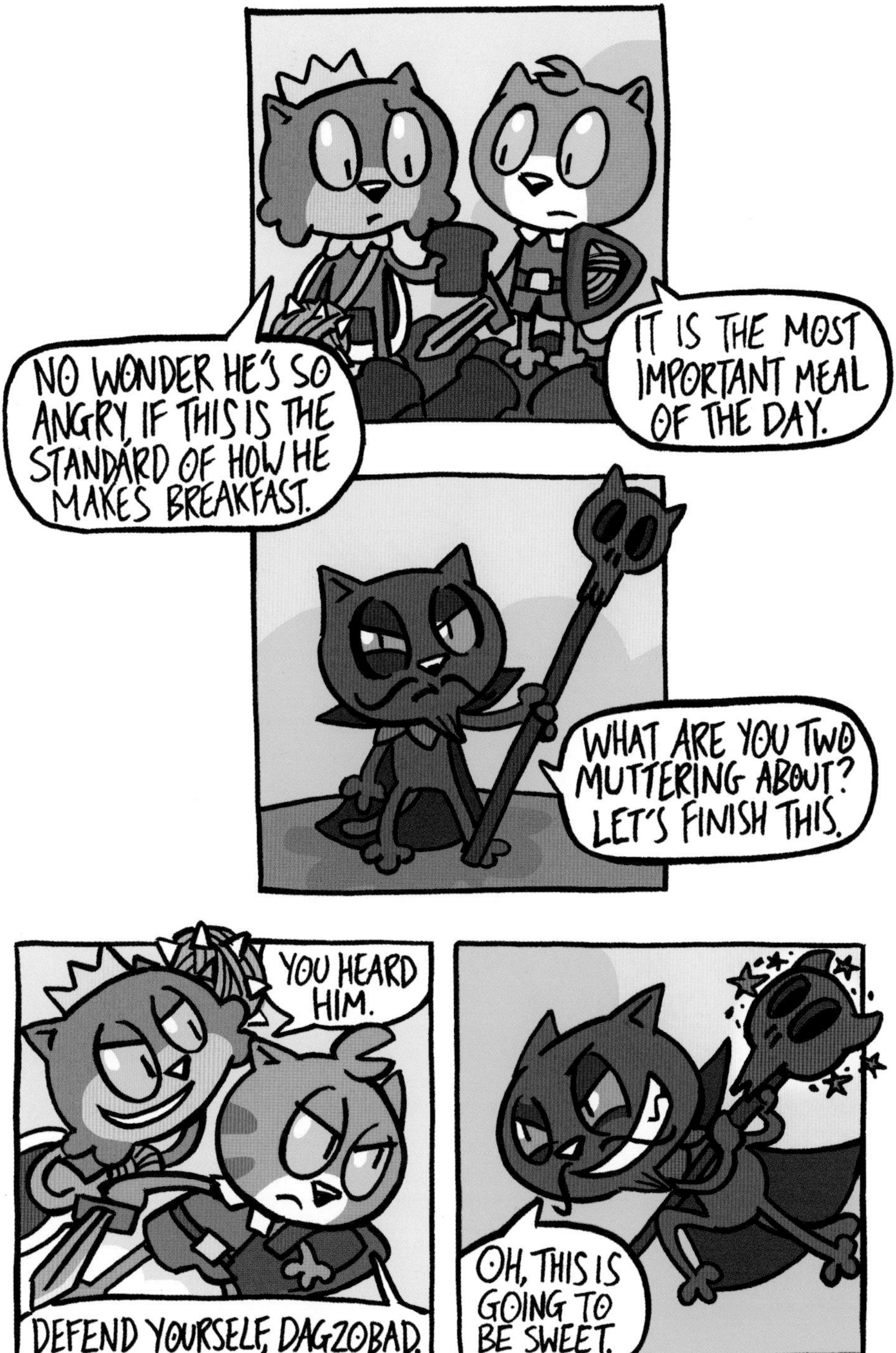
NO WONDER HE'S SO ANGRY IF THIS IS THE STANDARD OF HOW HE MAKES BREAKFAST.
IT IS THE MOST IMPORTANT MEAL OF THE DAY.
WHAT ARE YOU TWO MUTTERING ABOUT? LET'S FINISH THIS.
YOU HEARD HIM.
DEFEND YOURSELF, DAGZOBAD.
OH, THIS IS GOING TO BE SWEET.

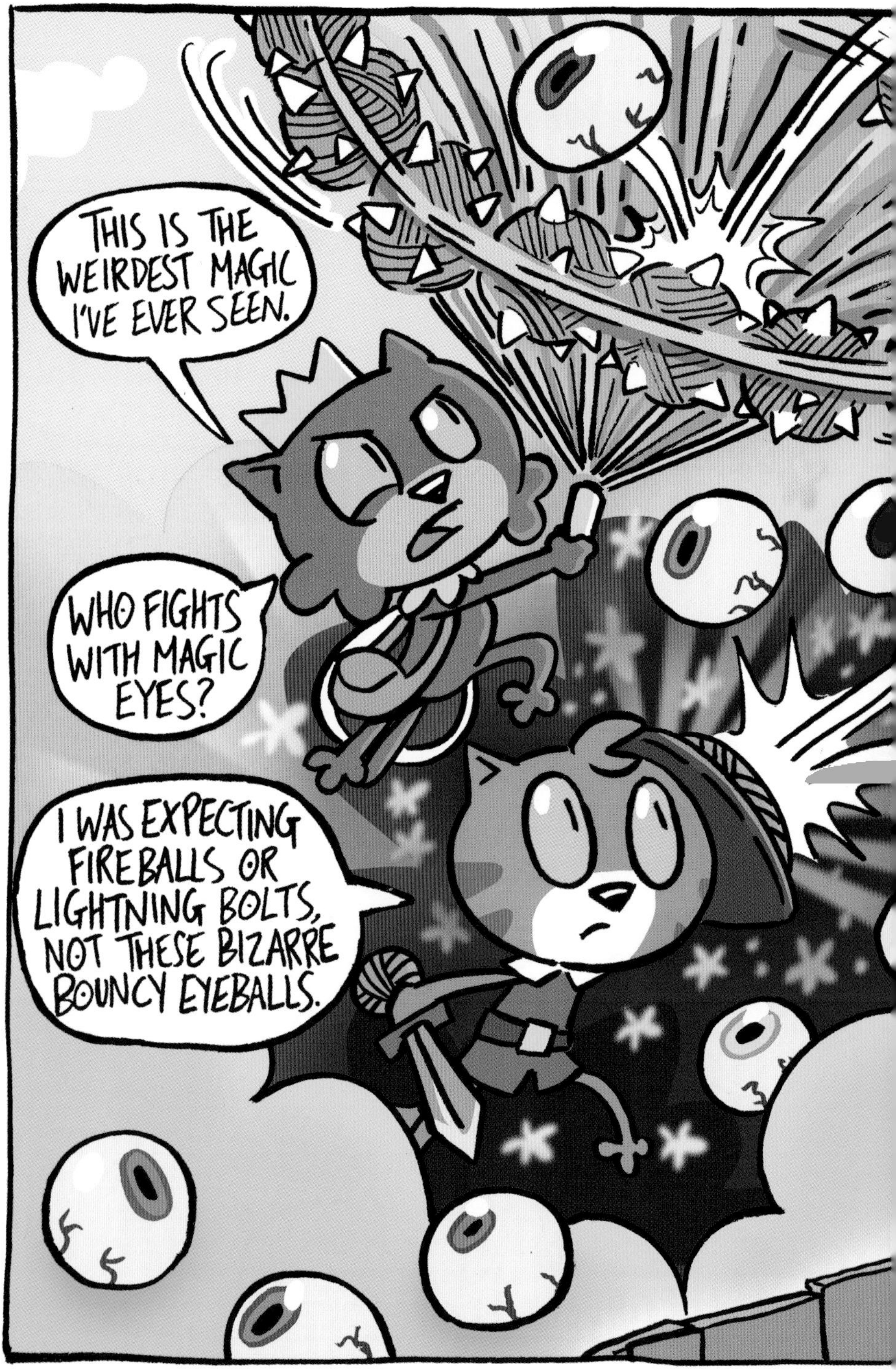
THIS IS THE WEIRDEST MAGIC I'VE EVER SEEN.
WHO FIGHTS WITH MAGIC EYES?
I WAS EXPECTING FIREBALLS OR LIGHTNING BOLTS, NOT THESE BIZARRE BOUNCY EYEBALLS.

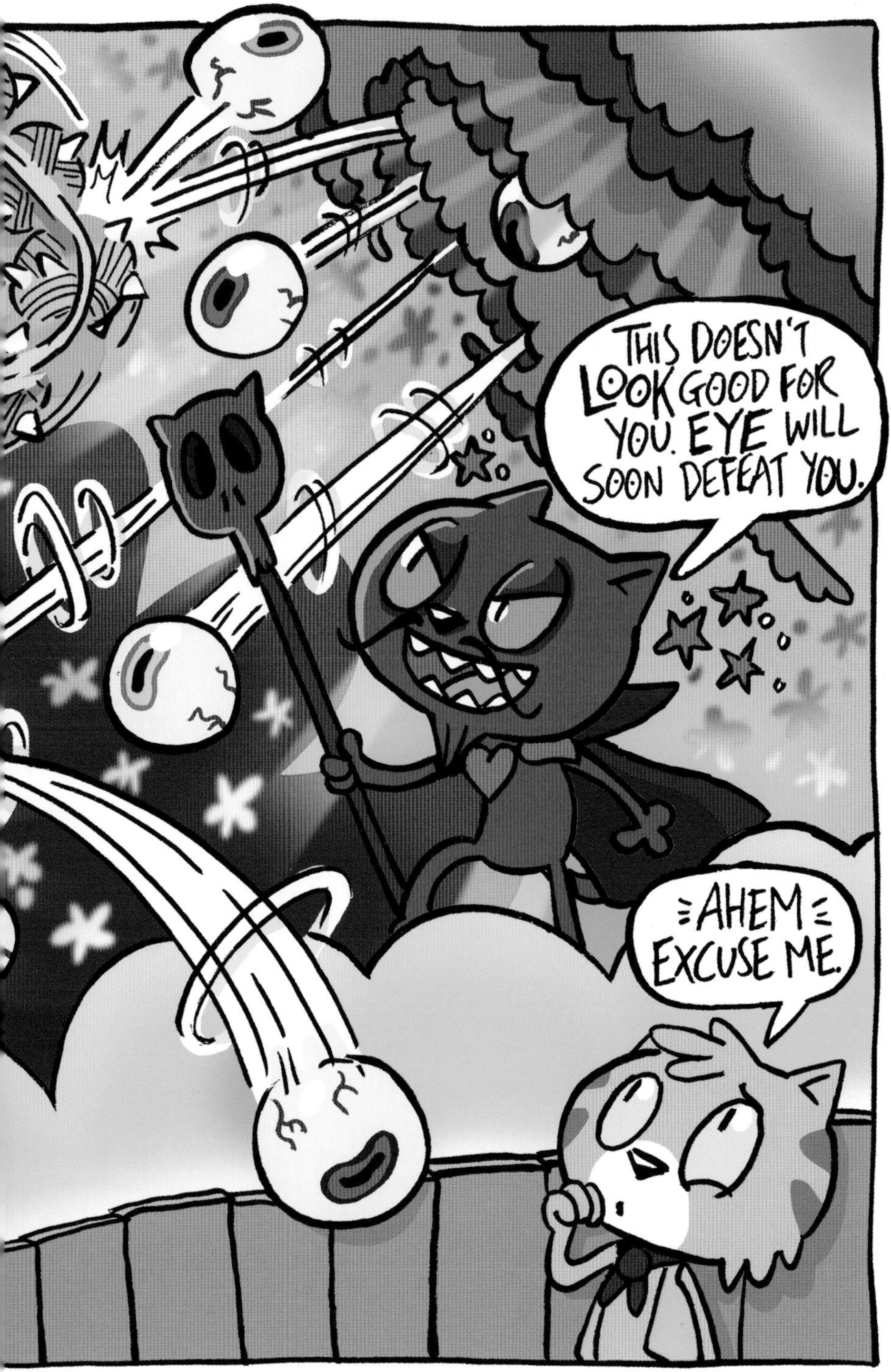

THIS DOESN'T LOOK GOOD FOR YOU. EYE WILL SOON DEFEAT YOU.
AHEM EXCUSE ME.

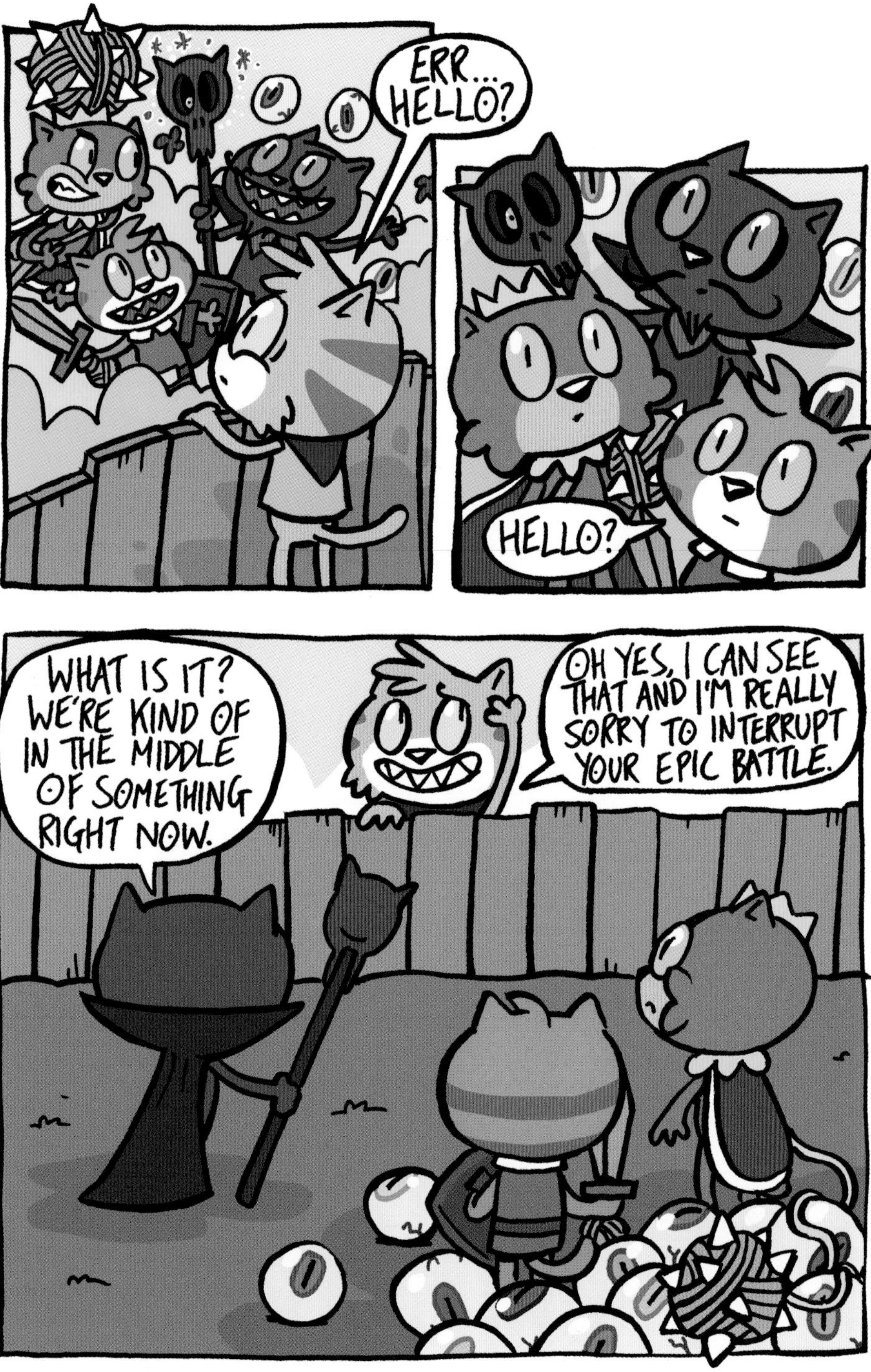
ERR... HELLO?
HELLO?
WHAT IS IT? WE'RE KIND OF IN THE MIDDLE OF SOMETHING RIGHT NOW.
OH YES, I CAN SEE THAT AND I'M REALLY SORRY TO INTERRUPT YOUR EPIC BATTLE.

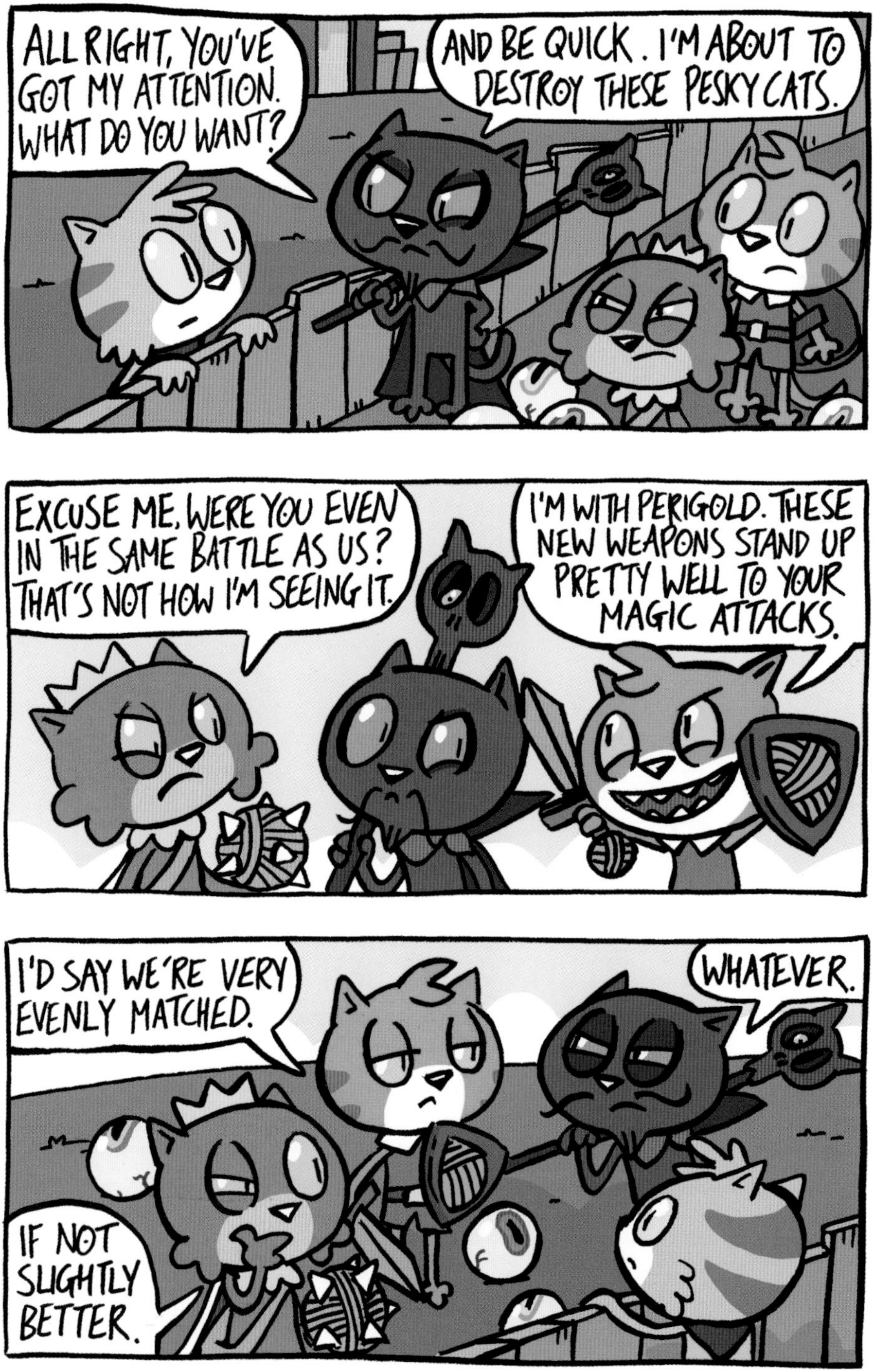
ALL RIGHT, YOU'VE GOT MY ATTENTION. WHAT DO YOU WANT?
AND BE QUICK. I'M ABOUT TO DESTROY THESE PESKY CATS.
EXCUSE ME, WERE YOU EVEN IN THE SAME BATTLE AS US? THAT'S NOT HOW I'M SEEING IT.
I'M WITH PERIGOLD. THESE NEW WEAPONS STAND UP PRETTY WELL TO YOUR MAGIC ATTACKS.
I'D SAY WE'RE VERY EVENLY MATCHED.
WHATEVER.
IF NOT SLIGHTLY BETTER.

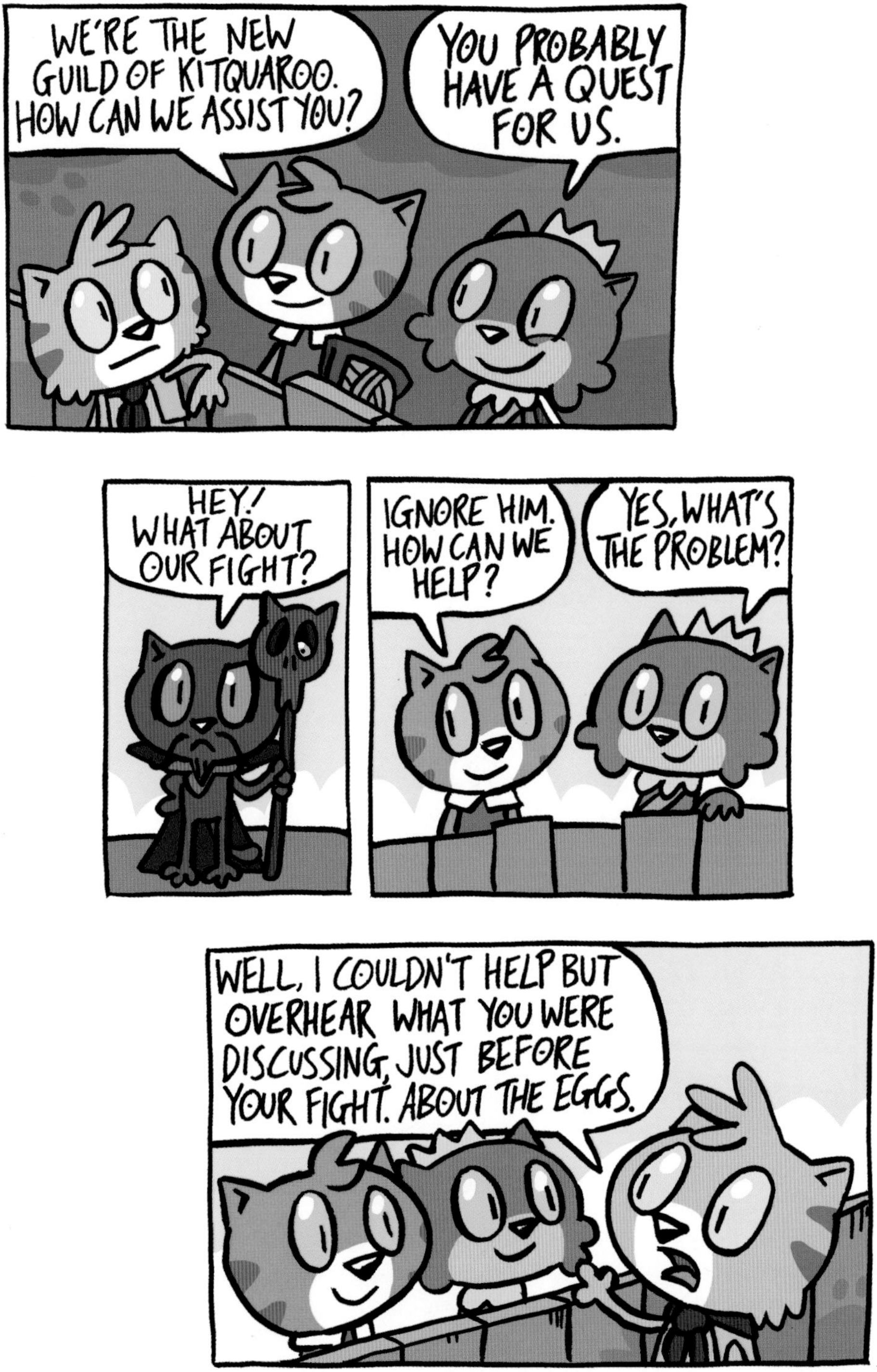
WE'RE THE NEW GUILD OF KITQUAROO. HOW CAN WE ASSIST YOU?
YOU PROBABLY HAVE A QUEST FOR US.
HEY! WHAT ABOUT OUR FIGHT?
IGNORE HIM. HOW CAN WE HELP?
YES, WHAT'S THE PROBLEM?
WELL, I COULDN'T HELP BUT OVERHEAR WHAT YOU WERE DISCUSSING, JUST BEFORE YOUR FIGHT. ABOUT THE EGGS.

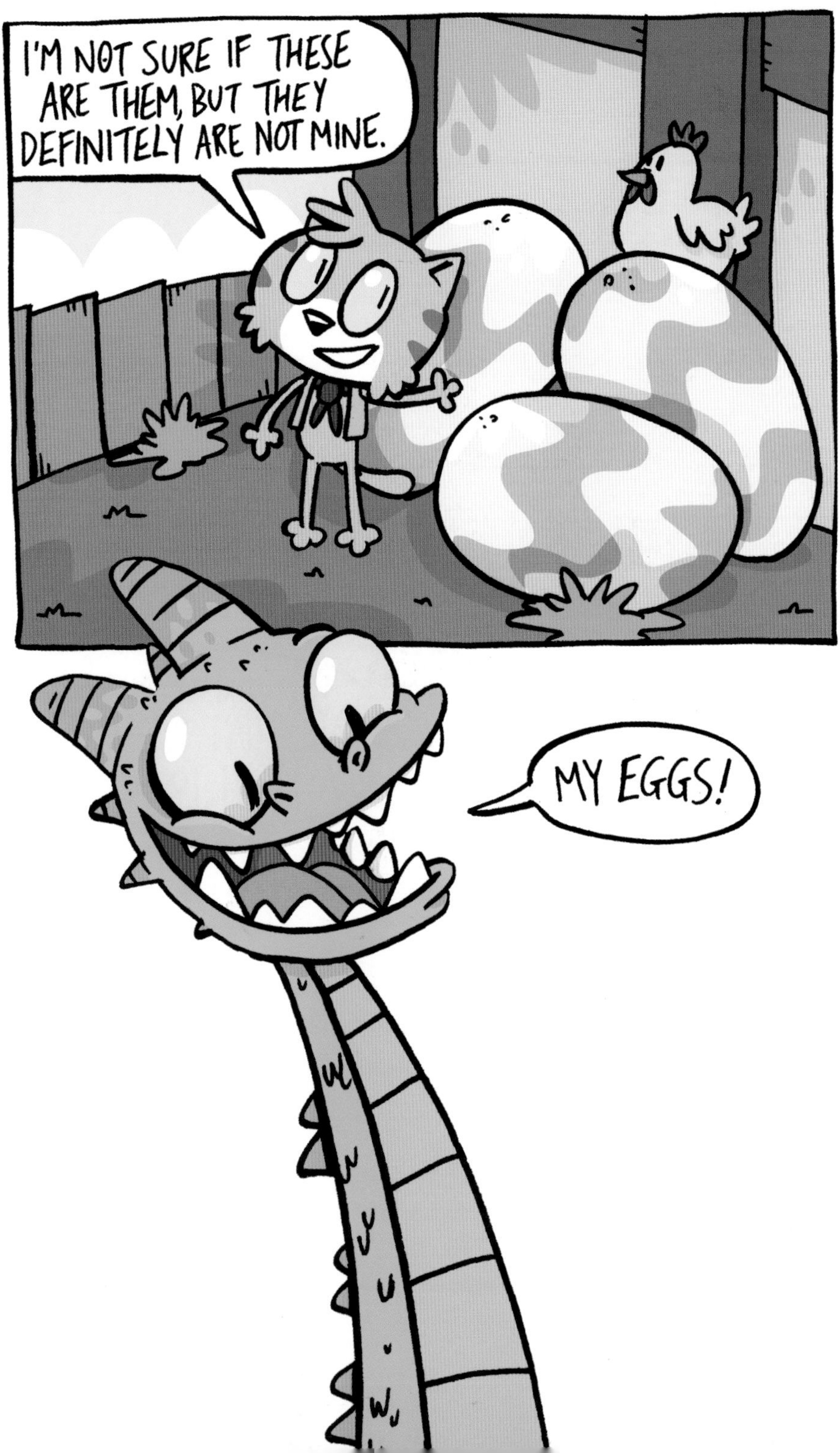
I'M NOT SURE IF THESE ARE THEM, BUT THEY DEFINITELY ARE NOT MINE.
MY EGGS!

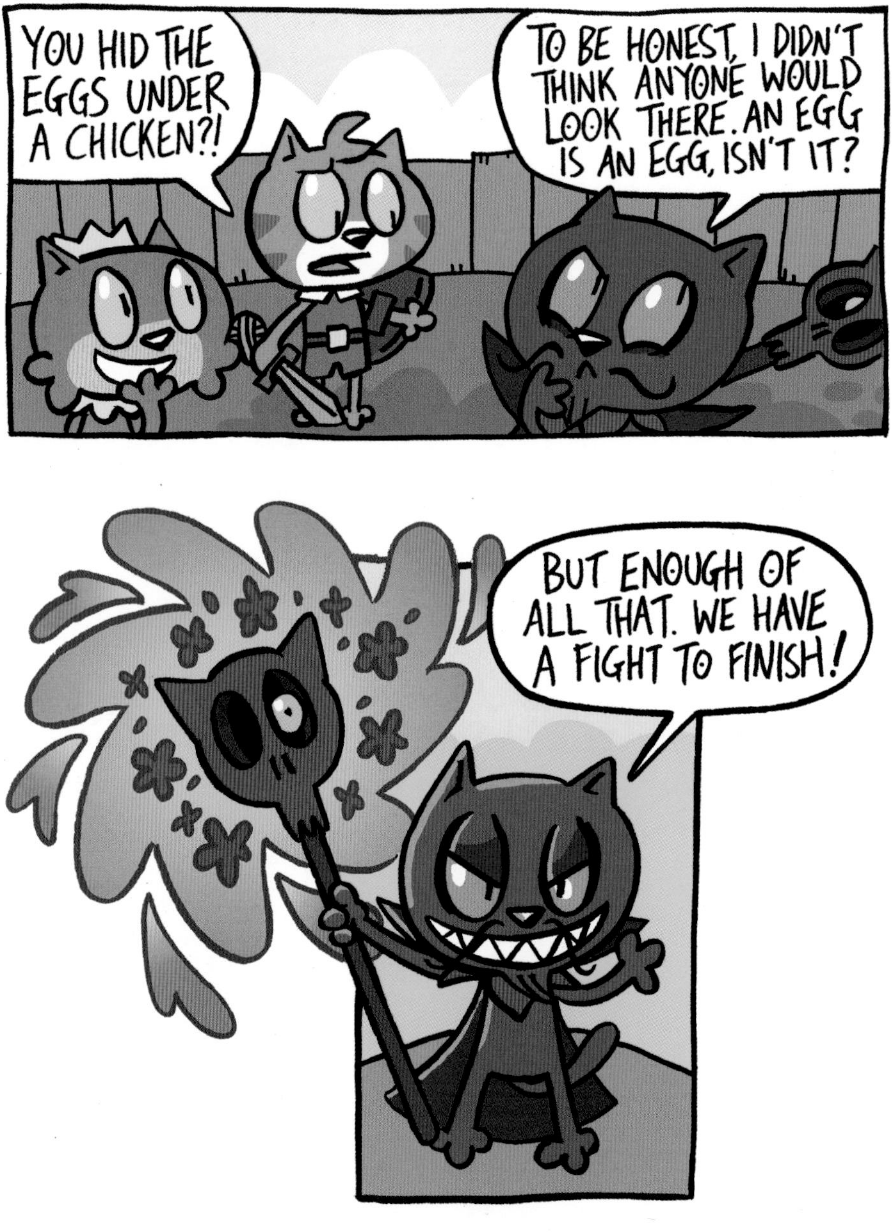
YOU HID THE EGGS UNDER A CHICKEN?!
TO BE HONEST, I DIDN'T THINK ANYONE WOULD LOOK THERE. AN EGG IS AN EGG, ISN'T IT?
BUT ENOUGH OF ALL THAT. WE HAVE A FIGHT TO FINISH!

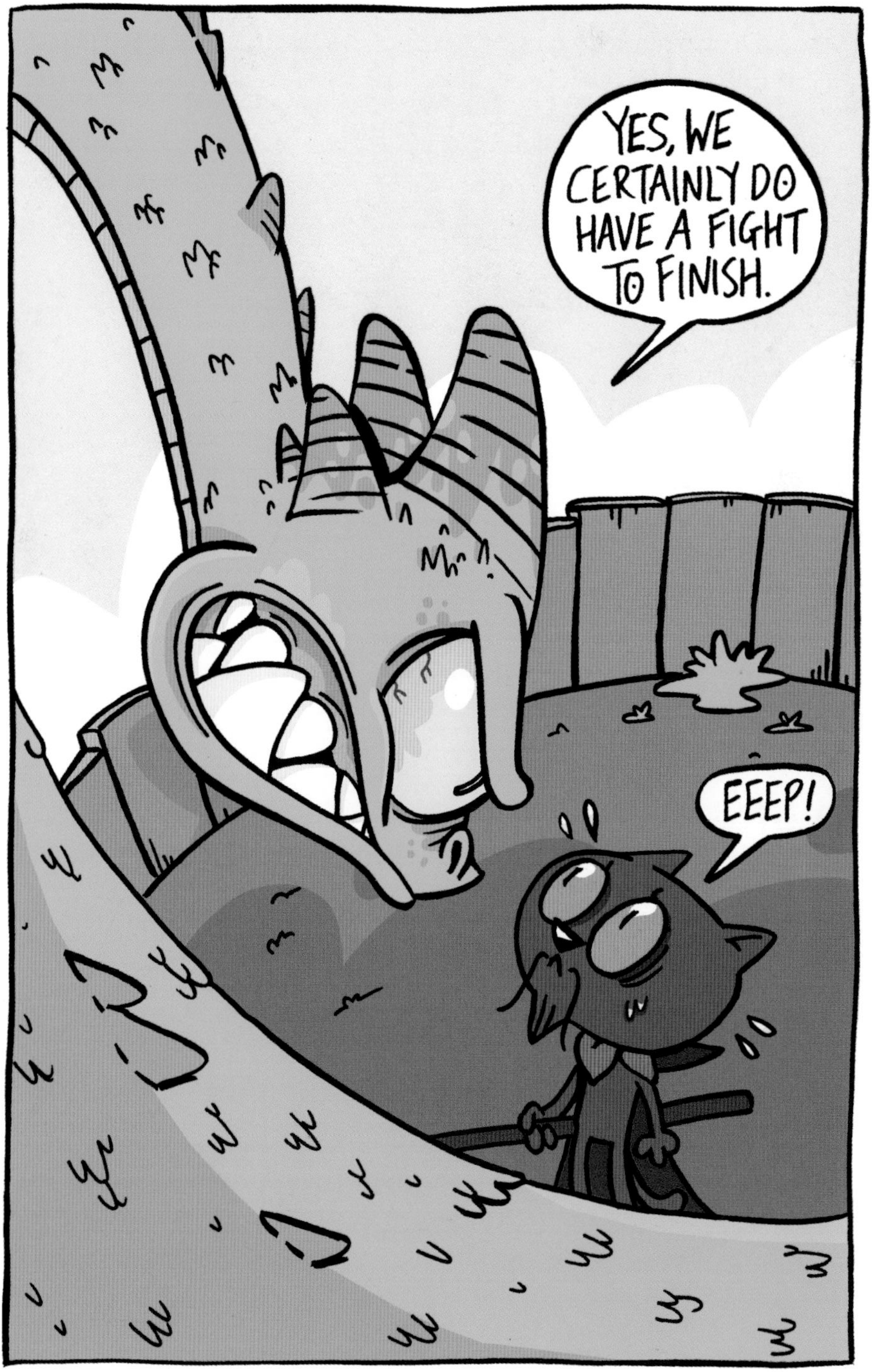
YES, WE CERTAINLY DO HAVE A FIGHT TO FINISH.
EEEP!

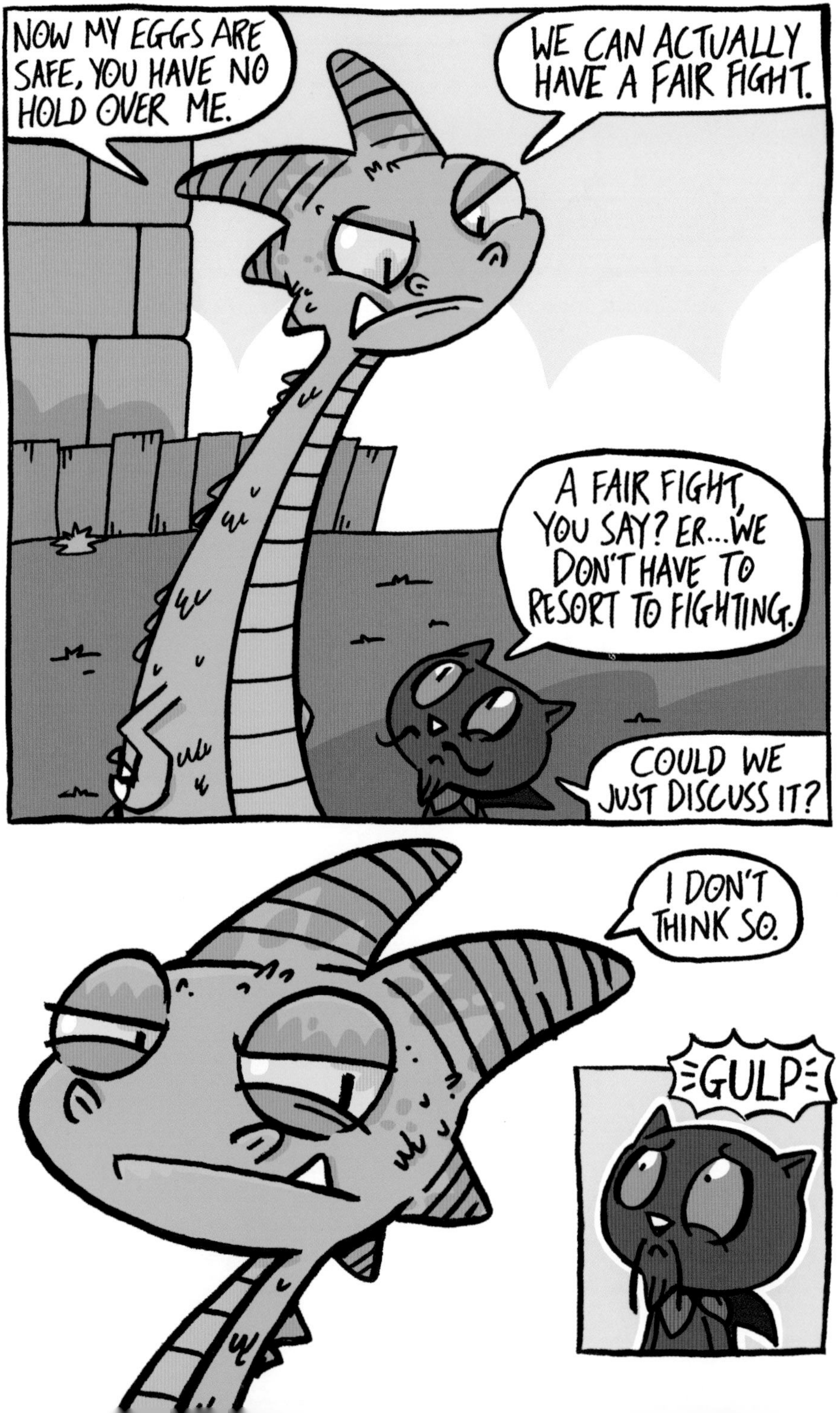
NOW MY EGGS ARE SAFE, YOU HAVE NO HOLD OVER ME.
WE CAN ACTUALLY HAVE A FAIR FIGHT.
A FAIR FIGHT, YOU SAY? ER...WE DON'T HAVE TO RESORT TO FIGHTING.
COULD WE JUST DISCUSS IT?
I DON'T THINK SO.
GULP

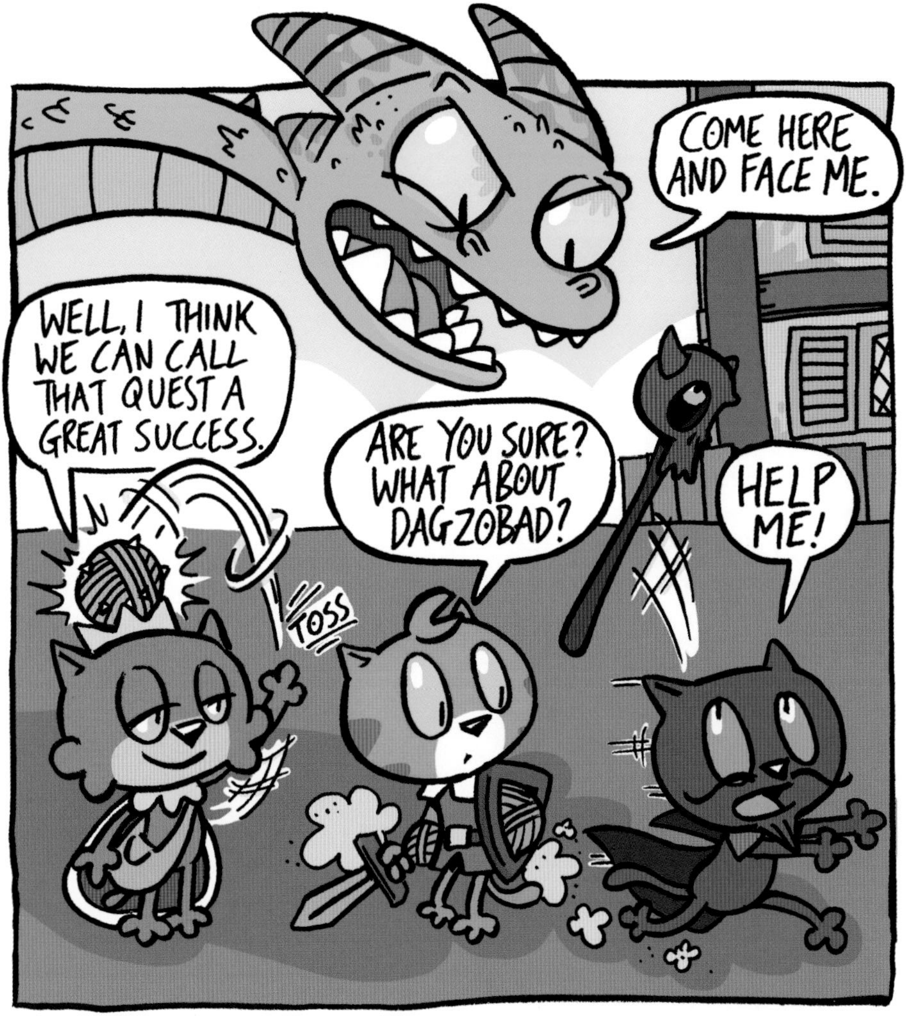
COME HERE AND FACE ME.
WELL, I THINK WE CAN CALL THAT QUEST A GREAT SUCCESS.
TOSS
ARE YOU SURE? WHAT ABOUT DAGZOBAD?
HELP ME!

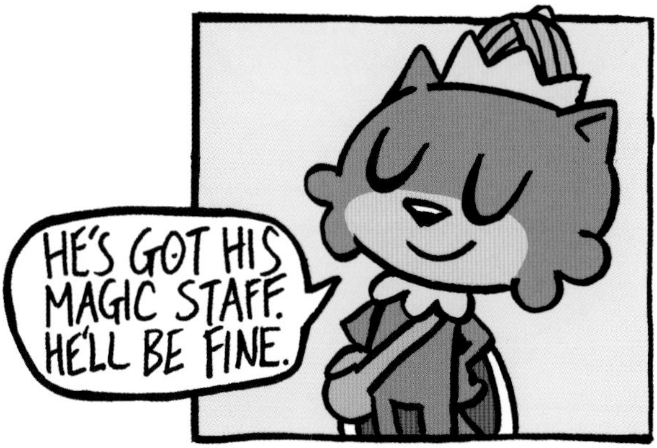
HE'S GOT HIS MAGIC STAFF. HE'LL BE FINE.

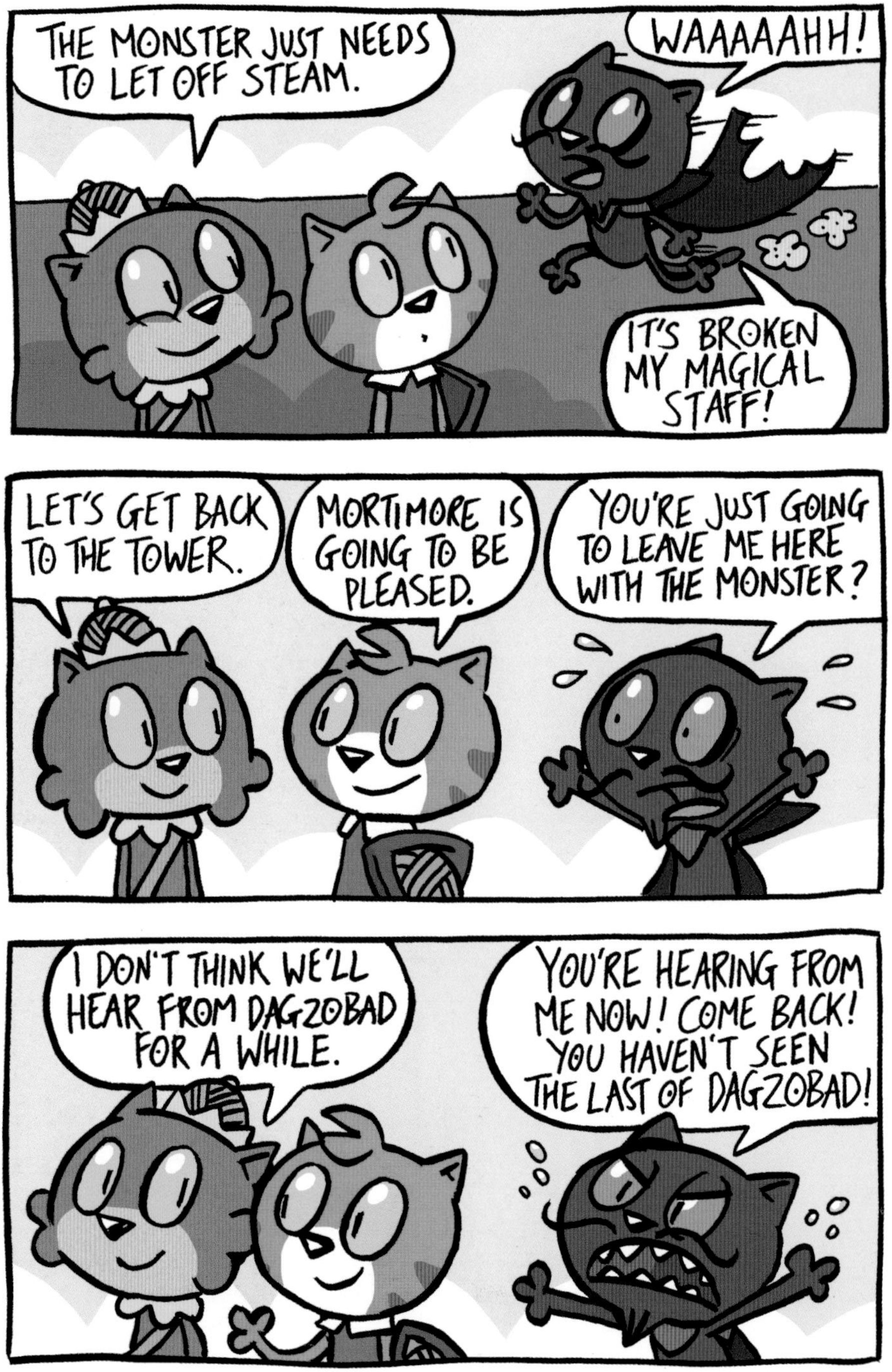
THE MONSTER JUST NEEDS TO LET OFF STEAM.
WAAAAAHH!
IT'S BROKEN MY MAGICAL STAFF!
LET'S GET BACK TO THE TOWER.
MORTIMORE IS GOING TO BE PLEASED.
YOU'RE JUST GOING TO LEAVE ME HERE WITH THE MONSTER?
I DON'T THINK WE'LL HEAR FROM DAGZOBAD FOR A WHILE.
YOU'RE HEARING FROM ME NOW! COME BACK! YOU HAVEN'T SEEN THE LAST OF DAGZOBAD!

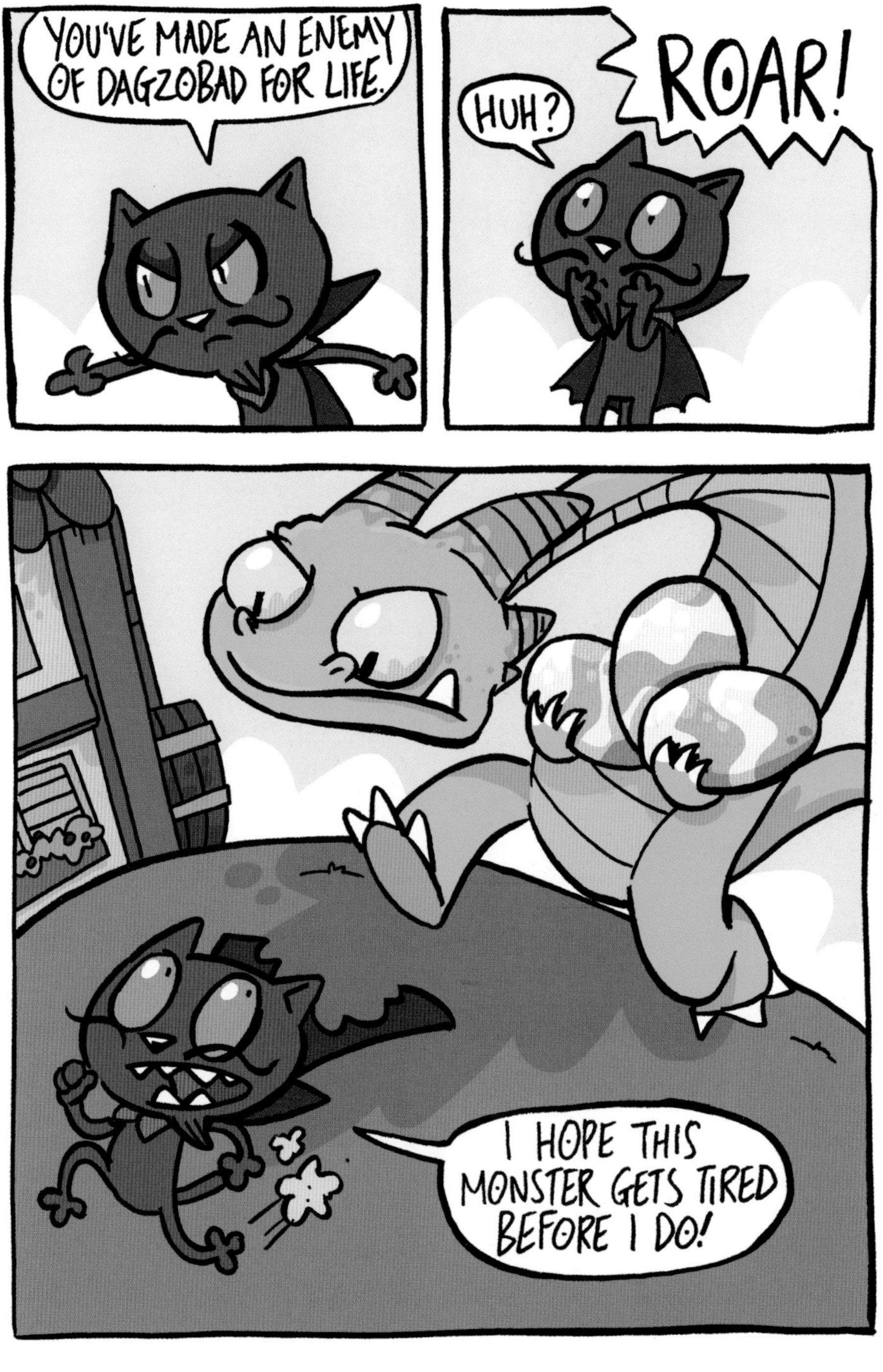
YOU'VE MADE AN ENEMY OF DAGZOBAD FOR LIFE.
HUH?
ROAR!
I HOPE THIS MONSTER GETS TIRED BEFORE I DO!

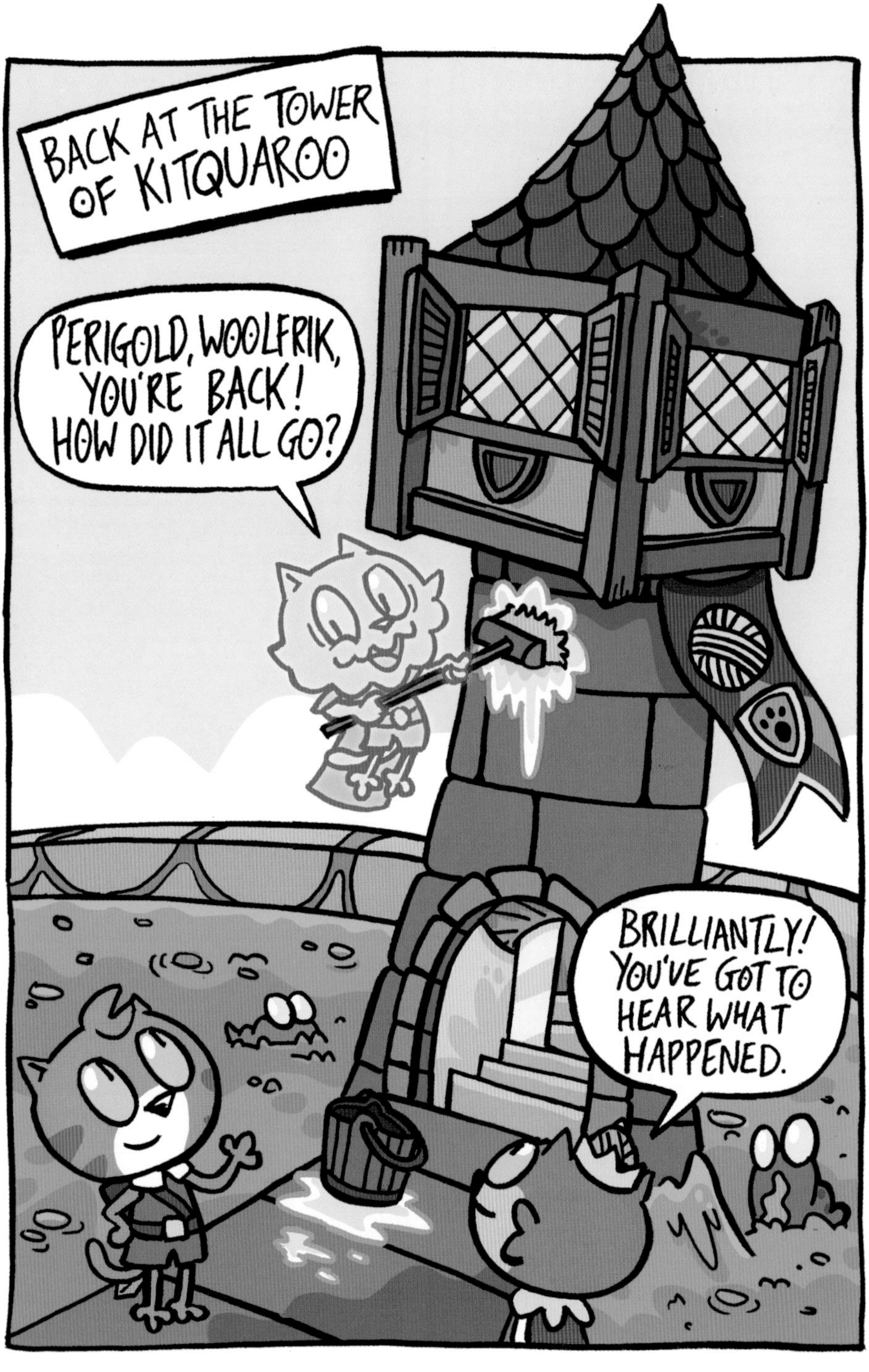
BACK AT THE TOWER OF KITQUAROO
PERIGOLD, WOOLFRIK, YOU'RE BACK! HOW DID IT ALL GO?
BRILLIANTLY! YOU'VE GOT TO HEAR WHAT HAPPENED.

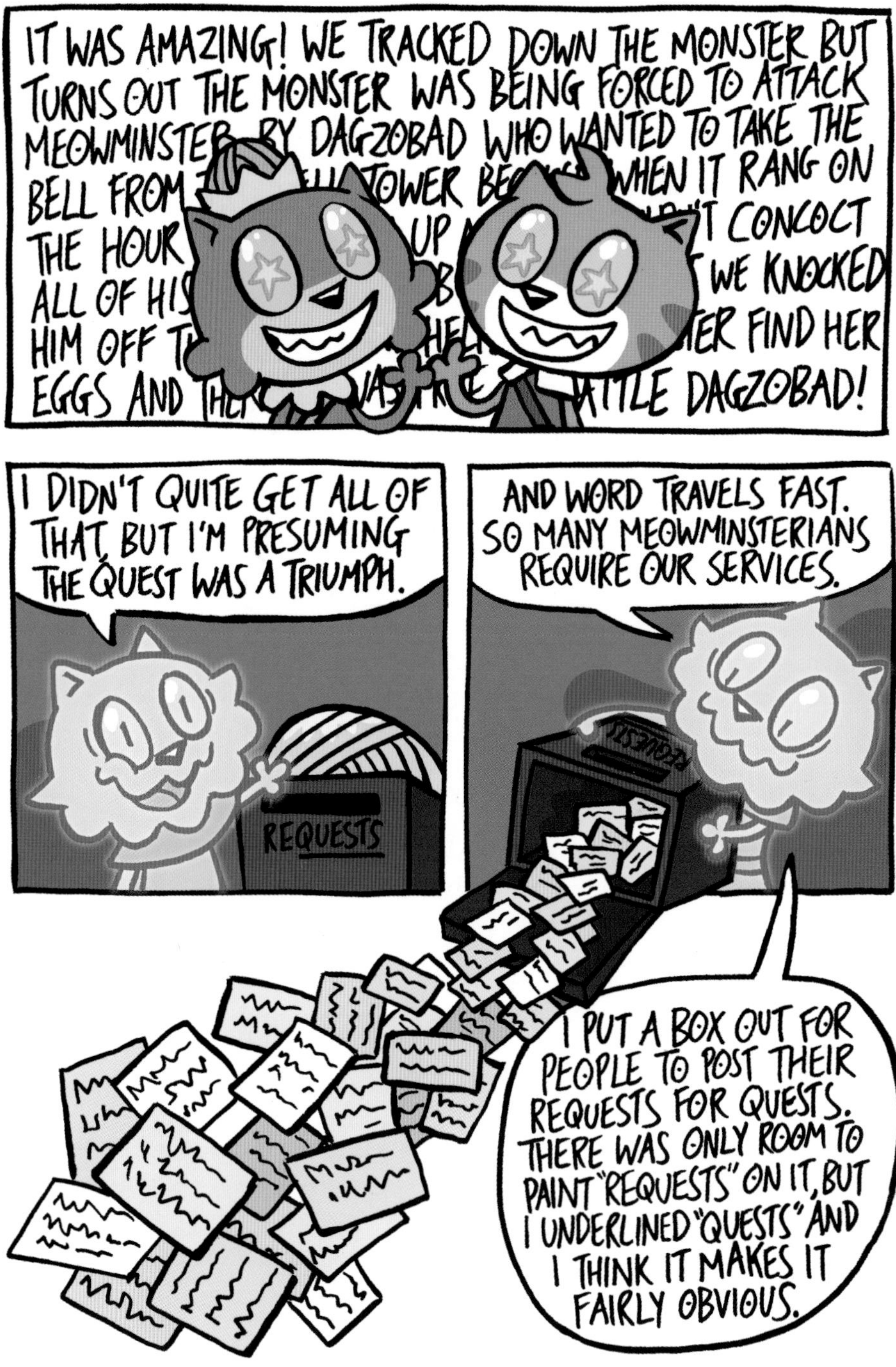
IT WAS AMAZING! WE TRACKED DOWN THE MONSTER BUT
TURNS OUT THE MONSTER WAS BEING FORCED TO ATTACK
MEOWMINSTER BY DAGZOBAD WHO WANTED TO TAKE THE
BELL FROM
TOWER
WHEN IT RANG ON
THE HOUR
UP
T CONCOCT
WE KNOCKED
HIM OFF
ER FIND HER
EGGS AND
TTLE DAGZOBAD!
I DIDN'T QUITE GET ALL OF THAT, BUT I'M PRESUMING THE QUEST WAS A TRIUMPH.
REQUESTS
AND WORD TRAVELS FAST. SO MANY MEOWMINSTERIANS REQUIRE OUR SERVICES.
I PUT A BOX OUT FOR PEOPLE TO POST THEIR REQUESTS FOR QUESTS. THERE WAS ONLY ROOM TO PAINT "REQUESTS" ON IT, BUT I UNDERLINED "QUESTS" AND I THINK IT MAKES IT FAIRLY OBVIOUS.

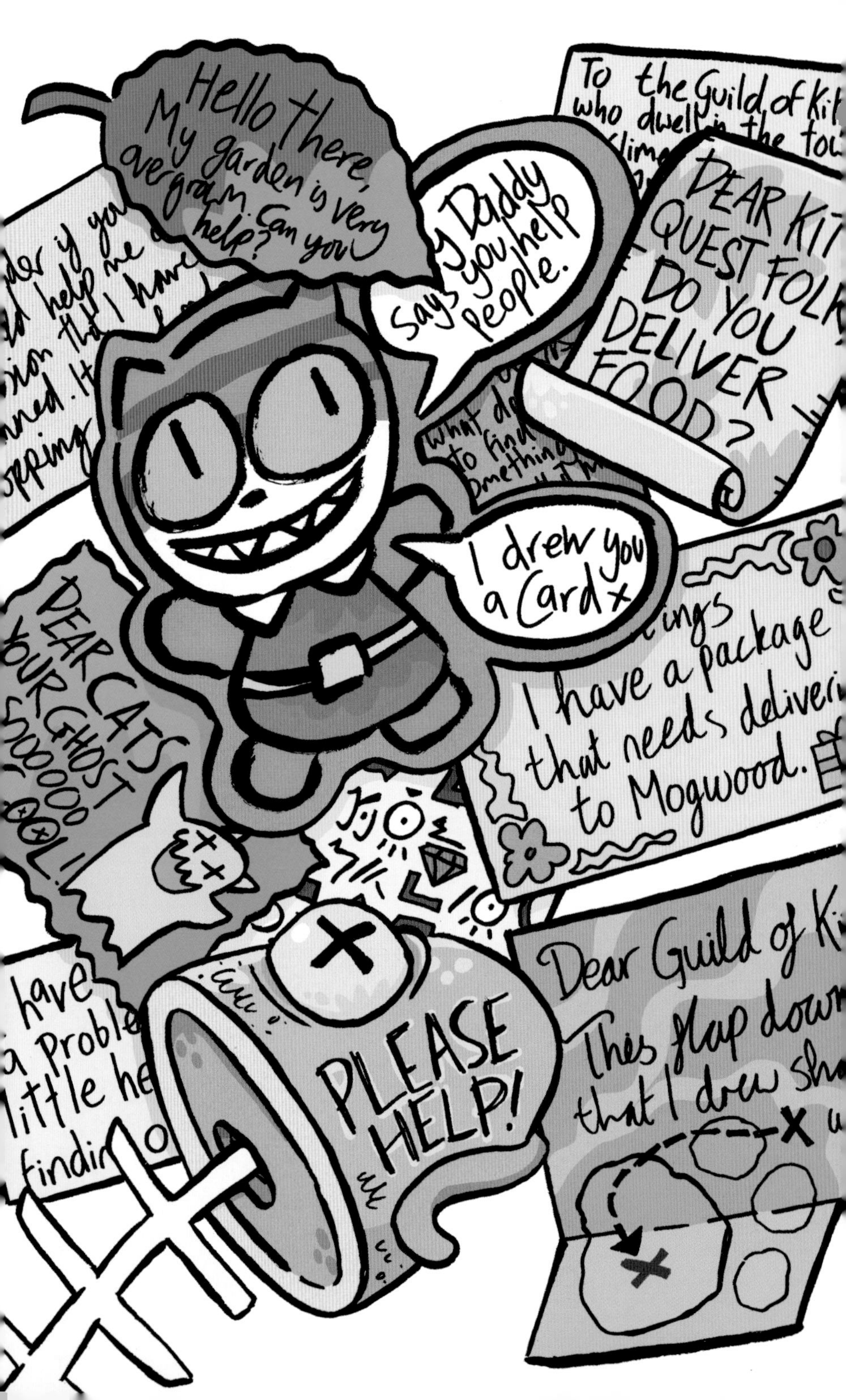

To the Guild of Kit
who dwell in the tow
Hello there, My garden is very overgrown. Can you help?
y Daddy says you help people.
DEAR KIT QUEST FOLK DO YOU DELIVER FOOD?
I drew you a Card x
ings I have a package that needs deliveri to Mogwood.
DEAR CATS YOUR GHOST
PLEASE HELP!
Dear Guild of Ki
This map down
that I drew sh

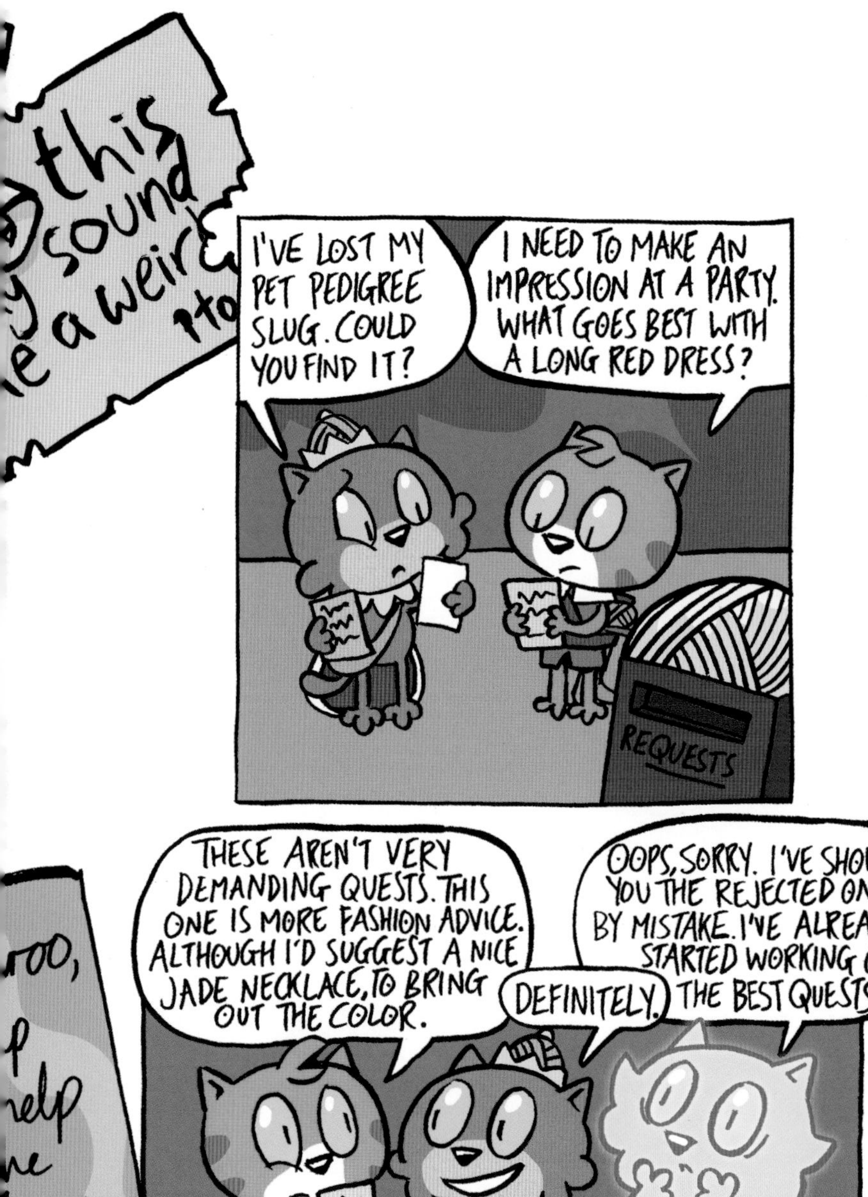
I'VE LOST MY PET PEDIGREE SLUG. COULD YOU FIND IT?
I NEED TO MAKE AN IMPRESSION AT A PARTY. WHAT GOES BEST WITH A LONG RED DRESS?
REQUESTS
THESE AREN'T VERY DEMANDING QUESTS. THIS ONE IS MORE FASHION ADVICE. ALTHOUGH I'D SUGGEST A NICE JADE NECKLACE, TO BRING OUT THE COLOR.
DEFINITELY.
OOPS, SORRY. I'VE SHOWN YOU THE REJECTED ONES BY MISTAKE. I'VE ALREADY STARTED WORKING ON THE BEST QUESTS.

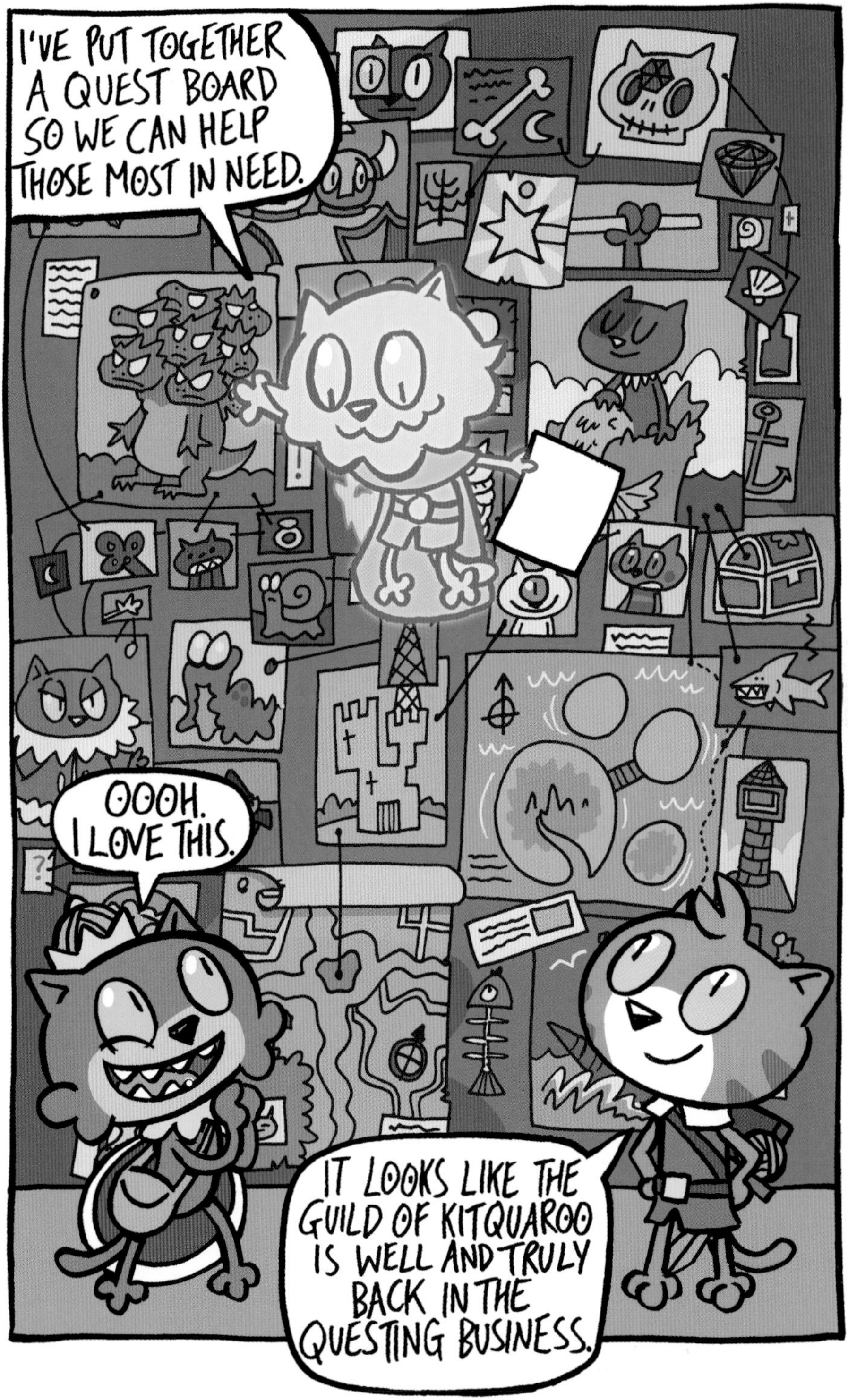
I'VE PUT TOGETHER A QUEST BOARD SO WE CAN HELP THOSE MOST IN NEED.
OOOH. I LOVE THIS.
IT LOOKS LIKE THE GUILD OF KITQUAROO IS WELL AND TRULY BACK IN THE QUESTING BUSINESS.

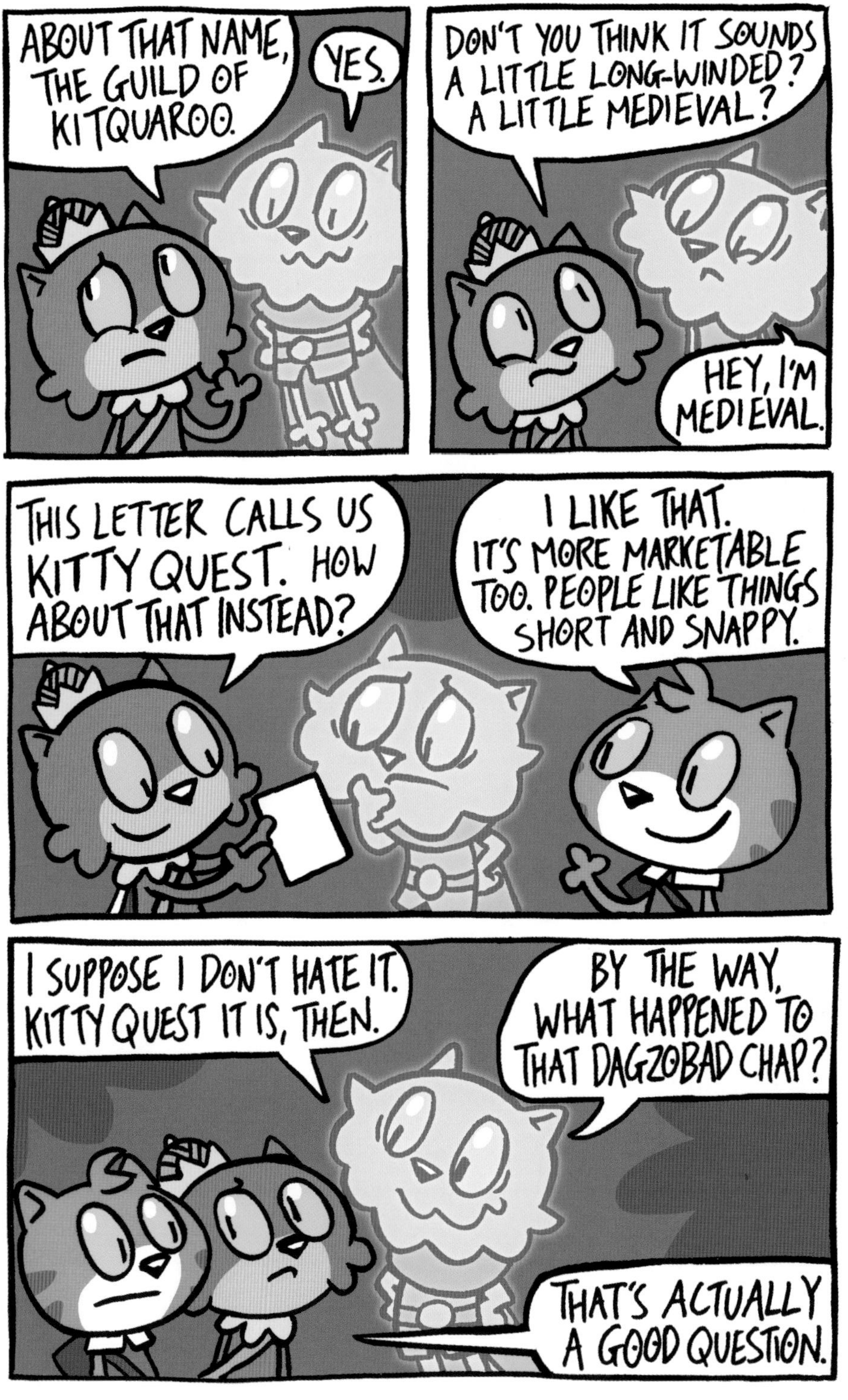
ABOUT THAT NAME, THE GUILD OF KITQUAROO.
YES.
DON'T YOU THINK IT SOUNDS A LITTLE LONG-WINDED? A LITTLE MEDIEVAL?
HEY, I'M MEDIEVAL.
THIS LETTER CALLS US KITTY QUEST. HOW ABOUT THAT INSTEAD?
I LIKE THAT. IT'S MORE MARKETABLE TOO. PEOPLE LIKE THINGS SHORT AND SNAPPY.
I SUPPOSE I DON'T HATE IT. KITTY QUEST IT IS, THEN.
BY THE WAY, WHAT HAPPENED TO THAT DAGZOBAD CHAP?
THAT'S ACTUALLY A GOOD QUESTION.

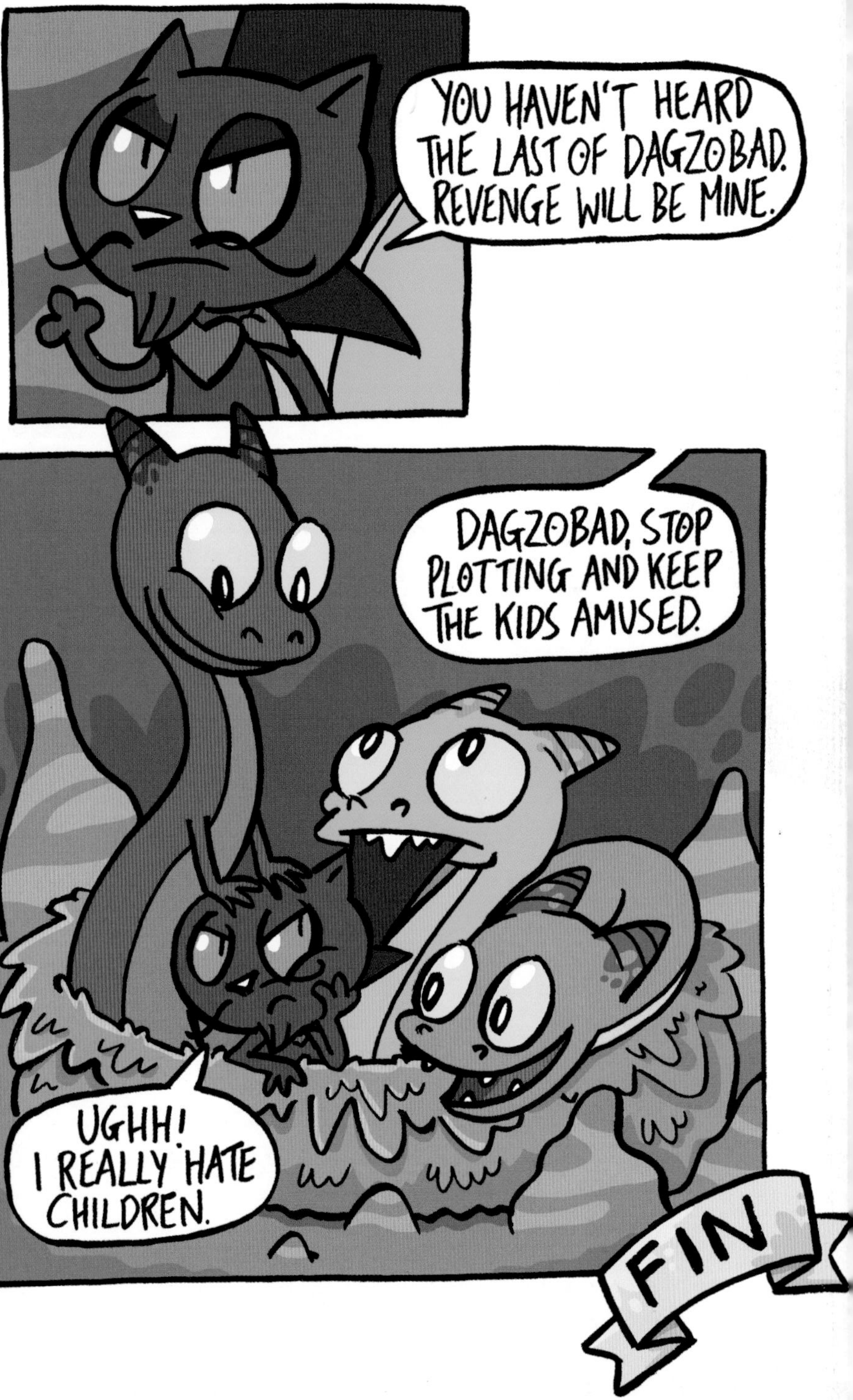
YOU HAVEN'T HEARD THE LAST OF DAGZOBAD. REVENGE WILL BE MINE.
DAGZOBAD, STOP PLOTTING AND KEEP THE KIDS AMUSED.
UGHH! I REALLY HATE CHILDREN.
FIN

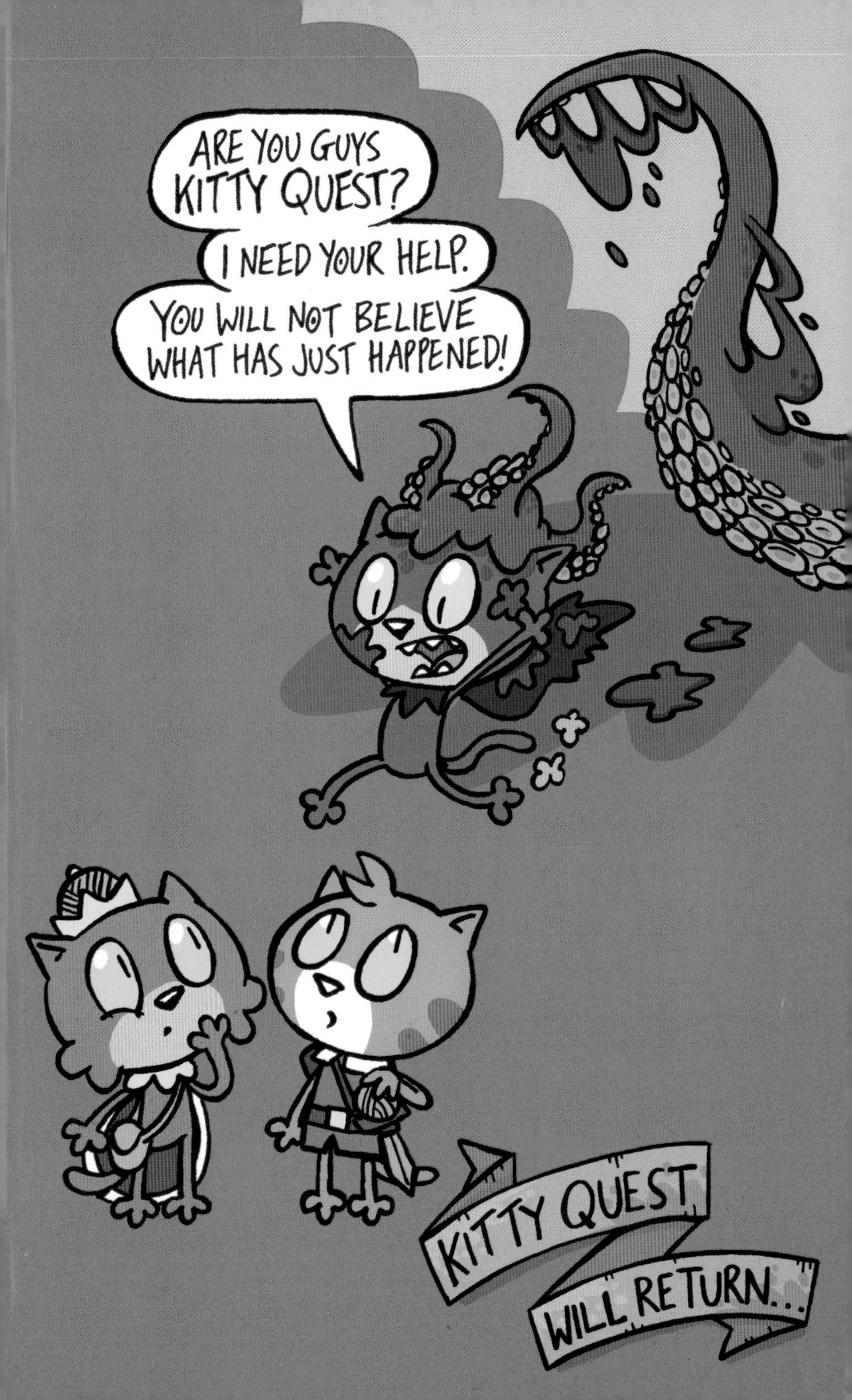
ARE YOU GUYS KITTY QUEST?
I NEED YOUR HELP.
YOU WILL NOT BELIEVE WHAT HAS JUST HAPPENED!
KITTY QUEST
WILL RETURN...

For Mum & Dad

RAZORBILL

An imprint of Penguin Random House LLC, New York

First published in the United States of America by Razorbill,
an imprint of Penguin Random House LLC, 2021

Visit us online at penguinrandomhouse.com.

LIBRARY OF CONGRESS CATALOGING-IN-PUBLICATION DATA

Names: Corbett, Phil, author, illustrator.
Title: Kitty quest / Phil Corbett.
Description: New York : Razorbill, an imprint of Penguin Random House LLC, 2021. |
Series: Kitty quest ; book 1 | Audience: Ages 8–12. | Summary: Guided by the last,
incorporeal member of an ancient guild of protectors, aspiring adventurers Perigold and
Woolfrik successfully subdue a rampaging monster and the bumbling wizard controlling it.
Identifiers: LCCN 2020049742 | ISBN 9780593205440 (hardcover) |
ISBN 9780593205464 (paperback) | ISBN 9780593205976 (ebook) |
ISBN 9780593205983 (ebook) | ISBN 9780593205457 (ebook)
Subjects: LCSH: Graphic novels. | CYAC: Cats—Fiction. | Monsters—Fiction. |
Wizards—Fiction. | Adventure and adventurers—Fiction. | Fantasy. | Graphic novels.
Classification: LCC PZ7.7.C6715 Ki 2021 | DDC 741.5/942—dc23
LC record available at https://lccn.loc.gov/2020049742

Manufactured in China

1 3 5 7 9 10 8 6 4 2

Design by Maria Fazio